KEEP ON LOVING YOU

ERIKA KELLY

KEEP ON LOVING YOU

Erika Kelly

ISBN-13: 9781677318711

Cover design and formatting by Serendipity Formatting

every page. If you love stories with heart, steam, and plenty of swoon, don't miss this one!" —USA Today Bestselling Author J.H. Croix

"With the Calamity Falls series, Kelly doesn't shy away from charming. She captivates with delectable characters that wrap themselves around a heart. From the first hello to the final goodbye, Rosalina and Brodie are a match made out of the unpredictable, but the sweetest kind of heaven. JUST THE WAY YOU ARE is the perfect example of why I am hooked on this series. SWOONWORTHY READ!" —Hopeless Romantic Book Reviews

IT WAS ALWAYS YOU

"This book was full of every emotion you could ever feel. Gigi and Cassian proved you can conquer anything with true love." —Cat's Guilty Pleasure

"I could not put this book down! Erika Kelly always delivers a great love story and never disappoints! I recommend this book for romance lovers looking to get lost in a great love story." —Reading in Pajamas

CAN'T HELP FALLING IN LOVE

"I love everything about this emotional and sexy, second chance story. Erika Kelly writes a story that makes me feel like I'm right there with the two main characters, Beckett and Coco. It is a slow burn, passionate story with lots of underlying tension. I not only enjoyed this story, but I found it impossible to put down." —Cocktails and Books

"I loved everything about this book. I loved all the characters, from Beckett, 'I don't believe in love,' to single mom, small business-owning, closed-off Coco, to a fairy-believing five-year-old who will steal your heart! I cannot gush enough about how spectacular I thought this book was." – Bookcase and Coffee

WHOLE LOTTA LOVE

"BRILLIANT! This book was incredible, I could not put this book down, that is how good Lu and Xander's story was. I fell in love with these two characters instantly." – Harlequin Junkie

"Whole Lotta Love was absolutely perfect! You will instantly love this couple and their journey to find happiness!" – Just Love Books

YOU'RE STILL THE ONE

"Griffin and Stella really are soulmates. They bring out the best of each other, and when they're together, everything is better. Their world is better with the love they feel for each other. And I think they made my world better a bit, too." – Jersey Girl's Bookshelf

"WOW! WOW! WOW! Welcome to all the feels! I ADORED Stella and Griffin's story. I was completely lost in this book and didn't want to put it down. I FELT everything, and I can't tell you how much I loved it." – Books According to Abby

minute of this book. It was an emotional journey from the first chapter to the last. This is Erika Kelly at her best, and this is a not-to-be-missed book!" —Sharon Slick Reads, Guilty Pleasures Book Reviews

"Erika Kelly damn near pulled my heart from my chest with Delilah and Will's story. It's so well-written that you feel everything. My heart got tugged so hard! I honestly cried at a few moments in the book. I fell all the way in love with "Wooby." It's hard not to, really." —Ree Cee's Books

THE VERY THOUGHT OF YOU

"Wow, THE VERY THOUGHT OF YOU was simply OUTSTANDING! This second chance, friends to lovers romance is enchanting and entertaining." —Spellbound Stories

"I just finished this story, and I want to start all over again. Or maybe at the start of series. To once again feel the events, the emotions, that brought these amazing characters together. To hear the banter and the arguments, the sorrow, the loss and the happiness that brought a family together and closer." —Nerdy, Dirty, and Flirty

JUST THE WAY YOU ARE

"An alpha cowboy and a smart, sassy princess collide in JUST THE WAY YOU ARE in Erika Kelly's latest, and it was fabulous! I was cheering for Brodie and Rosalina with

PRAISE FOR THE CALAMITY FALLS SERIES

KEEP ON LOVING YOU

"I adored this book! It is exactly what I love in a second-chance romance. The characters are so vibrant and real, I was rooting for them with every page." —*USA Today* Bestseller Devney Perry

"*KEEP ON LOVING YOU* is such a fun and sexy second-chance romance that I didn't want it to end. Their connection is a swoony blend of tender first love and sizzling heat, and Erika Kelly delivers a highly entertaining and sigh-worthy romance that shouldn't be missed."
—Mary Dube, USA Today

WE BELONG TOGETHER

"I loved every sweet, heart-wrenching, crazy, mixed-up

MINE FOR THE WEEK

Sign up for my newsletter to read the EXCLUSIVE novella for my readers only! You'll get two chapters a month of this super sexy, fun romance! #rockstarromance #teenidolturnedboyfriend Also, get PLANES, TRAINS, AND HEAD OVER HEELS for FREE! I hope you'll come hang out with me on Facebook, Twitter, Instagram, Goodreads, and Pinterest or in my private reader group.

This book is dedicated to my children.
I'm so proud of the men and women you've become.

ACKNOWLEDGMENTS

- To Superman, my everything. Thank you for always listening, always being there and, most of all, always loving me.
- To Olivia: it makes it so much more fun to share this journey with you.
- To KP: thank you for your kindness and expertise. You make the journey a thousand times better.
- To Sharon: your friendship and endless support mean the world to me.
- To Kristy DeBoer: you made this book so much better; thank you for your friendship.
- To Abbi Nyberg and Brock Butterfield: your help on this series is invaluable. Any mistakes are either creative license or my bad.
- To the romance writing community: I couldn't do this without the bloggers and reviewers like Obsessed with Romance, Krista's Dust Jacket, Guilty Pleasures Book Reviews, About That Story, Reading in Pajamas, Zoe Forward, Shirin's Book Blog and Reviews, Reads and Reviews, and Isha Coleman—to name just a

few; and my friends in writer groups like the Dreamweavers, The DND Authors, CTRWA, WRW, and CoLoNY.

HER SENSES FILLED WITH THE SCENT OF LAUNDRY detergent, Calliope Bell leaned against the washing machine as she read the comments from Traci Allen's Instagram page.

You rat bastard. There is no excuse. You hear me? None. I don't care if you miss the Pope's wedding, you don't abandon your girlfriend when she needs you. Fin Bowie, you suck!

Oh, my God, you left your girlfriend alone in a hospital in a foreign country??? How heartless can you be? You are the worst boyfriend, Fin Bowie!

He totally is. Fin Bowie's seriously the worst boyfriend ever. I can't even.

Ha! Fin Bowie = world's worst boyfriend!

#worldsworstboyfriend

Callie couldn't believe it. What had Fin *done*?

A bark of laughter jerked her attention out the mudroom window to the rehearsal dinner going on in her parent's backyard. The lowering sun glanced off silver bolo ties, gold bangles, and belt buckles. She should be out there with her brother and his bride, but these comments... so many women advancing on Fin with pitchforks in their hands.

As much as she wanted to revel in his just-rewards, she knew how horrifying this kind of attention would be to him. He wanted to be a known as a champion like his older brothers—not some social media celebrity.

Well, he'd brought it on himself. Since breaking up with her six years ago, he'd gone off the rails. At first, seeing him party with so many women had gutted her. Scooped out her heart and rendered her a puddle of goo. So, she'd blocked him. It had been the only way to get on with her life.

On some level, she'd understood. Until the breakup, he'd only ever been with her. Of course he'd go hog-wild with other women. He was a passionate, wild man.

Only this time he'd messed with the wrong woman.

Her thumb flicked the bottom of the screen, unleashing a whole new wave of comments.

Who leaves their girlfriend alone in a foreign country? Kick that dog to the curb, Traci. Sending you healing vibes. #worldsworstboyfriend

Something about this whole thing was off, though. As far as she could tell, Traci Allen, the famous snowboarder, had posted a screenshot of a text Fin had sent her. Callie scrolled back up to read it again.

Thanks for a great time. ☺ **Gotta jet. Talk soon**.

But Traci hadn't explained it. She'd just left an ambiguous comment.

When you're in the hospital and Fin Bowie sends you this.

Traci's whole life was documented on her Instagram page, so if she and Fin had been romantically involved, wouldn't there be pictures of him? Callie couldn't see a single one. And Traci had only mentioned his name once, when she'd talked about going on one of his backcountry trips.

So how had that one post turned Fin into the World's Worst Boyfriend?

Callie reread the initial responses. In the beginning, her fans had asked questions. When Traci hadn't responded, they'd begun to speculate. And those assumptions had turned into a story: Fin had dumped his girlfriend to catch a flight back to the States so he could go to his friend's wedding. Within a matter of hours, he'd begun trending.

And the hashtag was *everywhere*.

"Oh." Her mom tossed an armful of damp kitchen towels into the washing machine. "What're you doing in here?" She looked at the phone in Callie's hands. Hope enlivened her tired features. "The fellowship?"

A hot flush of shame had Callie pressing the phone to her stomach. Between finals and graduation, she hadn't been in touch with her family, so they didn't know her plans. "No, the interview isn't until August twenty-fifth."

"Oh." Her mom's expression turned curious. "So, is it about a job?"

"No." Because why else would she be holed up in the laundry room at her brother's rehearsal dinner when she was only in town for three days? "Actually, I've decided to just work part-time at the diner and the bar. Julian's parents invited me to hang out with them this summer so they can introduce me to the movers and shakers of the Manhattan art world. It would take me a decade to make the kind of connections they have."

"Makes sense." Pushing her long, gray-streaked hair off her face, her mom nodded to the phone. "So, what's got you so enthralled that you'd leave your handsome boyfriend alone with a bunch of strangers?"

The arrow hit right in the center of her conscience. Reflexively, she glanced out the window, searching for him. "Is he okay?" Since they'd only been dating six months, she hadn't brought him home yet. Julian didn't know a single person in Calamity Falls.

"Oh, come on. He's Prince Charming. Nothing but gracious and kind."

She wanted to be proud of her well-mannered

boyfriend, but there was something slightly off in her mom's tone.

Her mom made a *gimme* motion with her fingers, and Callie turned the phone around.

One glance, and her mom got it. "Ah. How many comments are we up to now?"

Callie couldn't have been more grateful for a mom who never judged her. "Ten thousand."

Her mom's eyes widened. "Wow." She rested her hip against the dryer and folded her arms across her stomach. "I don't know. I'm having a hard time believing Fin could abandon his girlfriend in a foreign hospital."

Callie gaped at her mother. "Are you kidding me?"

"Oh, stop it. It's not the same thing. He's not seventeen anymore, and you weren't hospitalized."

"Mom, he bailed on me three hours before we were supposed to leave for the airport." *To be with his brother.* Just like he'd abandoned Traci for Ryder's wedding. Fin and Callie's brother might not be related by blood, but the bond went as deep.

Amazing how six years later the crap she'd buried could rise like steam and give her hot flashes. *I thought I was done with this.*

Her mom adjusted the belt of her peach-colored dress. "Does it make you feel better knowing it wasn't you? It's just who he is?"

"No." Nothing would ever make her feel better about how Fin had ended their relationship. The shock of it still moved inside her body, a live thing trapped and scrabbling against the walls. "Because you're right. Something's not right about it. Other than posting the screen shot, Traci's been off social media. Her fans are making assumptions."

"Then why are you so interested in reading the comments?"

"Because it's happening to *Fin*. That's pretty crazy, right? That my ex has turned into a meme?"

"Well, he's a Bowie. They're celebrities."

"Yeah, in the world of extreme sports." While trophies and awards motivated—*validated*—his brothers, Fin was a true artist. He trained and hit the slopes to push himself, his body, and to breach the limits of his capabilities. Being known as a scoundrel would strike at the very core of his identity. "He doesn't want this kind of attention."

Her mom's gaze flicked outside, clearly anxious to get back out there. "Oh, I don't know. A man with his own website can't be too worried about attention."

Fin probably only ran it to prove to his brothers he wasn't just playing around out there. That he was as serious an athlete as they were.

Like she knew anything about him anymore. She hadn't talked to him in six years.

But she'd have to talk to him today, wouldn't she? The minute she left this room, he'd come for her like a heat-seeking missile. Her skin crackled with anticipation.

"Come on, let's go." Her mom started for the door but hesitated when Callie didn't follow.

"I'll be right behind you. I just..." *You what?* She wasn't ready. "I need to take a quick look at my emails."

Her mom watched her for a moment before letting out

a harsh breath. "He's the best man, Callie. You've had a lot of time to prepare for this."

"I'm not..." She didn't want her mom to see her as the drama queen teenager she'd once been. "Look, I haven't seen him in a long time. It's just...it's going to be uncomfortable."

"Isn't that why you brought your boyfriend with you?"

Normally, she loved that her mom pulled no punches. Tonight, though, a little pretending wouldn't hurt. "God, Mom." She stuttered out an uncomfortable laugh. "I wanted you guys to meet him." But her bluster collapsed under her mom's unrelenting stare. "I mean, obviously, on some level..." *Oh, just say it.* "Yes, okay? That's one of the reasons I brought him."

"There you go. Find your shield and stand behind him."

Oh, ouch. All at once she could see her mom's attitude was anything but casual. "Why are you angry at me? So, I need a few minutes to myself. It's not easy for me to be around him."

"Yes, Callie, I get that. We all get that. But it's been six years. And if you'd just talk to him, you wouldn't have to keep avoiding him." Her mom blew out a frustrated breath. "Don't you *want* to move on?"

The words stung. *Move on?* She'd done exactly that. With her undergrad and graduate degrees from NYU, she'd made her dream of living in New York City a reality. A few years from now, she'd—hopefully—become a museum curator.

She wanted to say, *Look at me.* There was none of the

old Callie left. How could her mom not see that? "Are you kidding me? I have completely moved on. I'm a few months away from working at the MoCA. I have the best boyfriend in the world." Who couldn't be more different from Fin. "He and his parents have been wonderful to me. I love my life." And, frankly, it hurt that her mom couldn't see it.

"Yes, you've done a bang-up job of reinventing yourself. Congratulations. But I don't know how you think you can start a new relationship when you haven't closed out of the last one. You've got the degrees and clothes and bank account of an adult, so now act like one. Go out there and talk to Fin. Face the terrible decisions you both made so you can move on."

Frustration and anger got her blood pumping. "I'm not an adult because I won't talk to my ex-boyfriend? *There's nothing to talk about.* He made his decision, and I made mine not to put up with his crap anymore." It wasn't like her mom could relate. She'd married her high school sweetheart. "Mom, he's never going to change. This meme proves that. He's always going to put his brothers before anyone else." *Before me.* "Moving on means accepting Fin for who he is and not trying to change him. *That's* closure."

"Then why are you hiding in the laundry room at your brother's rehearsal dinner?"

"Ellen?" The caterer leaned in. "We're about to pass out the champagne. You want to give the heads-up to anyone giving toasts?"

"Sure." Her mom nodded warmly, and then turned back to Callie. "Put your phone away and be here for your brother, okay?"

Callie ran her fingers over the heavy, jeweled bracelet Julian had given her for graduation. "Of course." Heart pounding, she followed her mom out the back door. As she crossed the scarred wooden deck, she dropped her phone into her clutch, accepting that her mom was right.

Callie had lost touch with her brother; she barely even knew his bride. She wanted to get to know her four-year-old nephew and spend time with her parents without the constant worry that Fin might show up. It was time to put the past to rest and just...be home.

Stepping off the deck, she thought of Julian's mother, the way she so fluidly and elegantly worked a room. *Yes. Be Mrs. Reyes.* She'd simply act like she was at an art gallery opening, and Fin was just someone in the room.

Well, someone she'd had sex with. A lot. In pretty raunchy ways. *Oh, Lord.*

Stop it.

Think about the meme. Because if Fin had bailed on Traci like that, then he hadn't changed. And that emboldened her. Because it meant he could never hurt her again.

She'd never give him the chance.

When she stepped onto the grass, she put her weight on her toes to keep her sharp heels from sinking into the dirt. She scanned the yard. The moment her gaze landed on Julian, the pressure on her chest lifted.

Urbane, polished, and charming, her boyfriend stood out among the other guests in their Western-wear and more casual attire. In his custom-made Brioni suit and crisp, white dress shirt, his hair slicked back off his handsome face, Julian looked like a model for a watch ad.

Callie made a bee-line for him. Weaving through round tables covered in white linens, she noticed the pink and lavender flower centerpieces with flickering candles were the only nod to décor. But with the Grand Tetons as a backdrop, what else did they need? The striking sight never grew old, especially now when twilight cast purple and peach shadows over the starkly rugged peaks.

With a smile in place, she glided past familiar faces. A jolt of anxiety zinged through her when she saw a wall of muscle blocking her boyfriend. Two of Fin's brothers reached for champagne flutes on a wicker tray. *Crap.* The heel of her five-inch stiletto sank into the grass, breaking her stride. A cold sting of embarrassment shot through her, but she quickly corrected. Perspiration sprang out on her forehead. She stopped herself from patting it away so she didn't mess up her foundation.

Fortunately, they'd moved on by the time she got there, revealing Julian's companion.

Megan. Ugh. Obviously, she'd known her friend would be at the wedding. She just would've preferred if their first reunion in years didn't take place in front of her boyfriend. No one understood her better, though, so she had to hope her friend got why she'd fallen out of touch. "Megan. It's so good to see you."

But when she leaned in for a hug, her friend's arms remained at her sides. "Hey." She didn't even smile.

Heat raced up Callie's neck, enflaming her cheeks. Trying to cover for her embarrassment, she placed a hand on Julian's biceps and channeled his mother. "I see you've met Megan."

"Yes, I have." Julian gave a gracious nod to her old friend. "We've been chatting about her yoga studio."

"Well, it was nice to meet you." But Megan's flat tone said otherwise, and she turned to go.

Underneath the shock of her friend's blatant rejection ran the horrifying awareness that Callie had earned it.

How in the world had she assumed Megan would understand what she'd gone through when Callie had never told her? "Megan, I—"

Her friend stopped and turned to her with a challenging expression.

Did she really want to have this conversation in front of Julian? Later tonight, she'd pull her aside and they could talk. But for now...For now, Callie needed to keep it together. "It's great to see you. So, you teach yoga? Where?"

When Megan didn't immediately respond, Julian said, "Here. In Calamity."

"That's great." But she couldn't hide her surprise. Megan had always wanted to be in theater.

"I keep trying to get Calliope to use my yogi, but she refuses," Julian said.

Having grown up with obscene wealth, Julian had no understanding of her financial situation. Not only couldn't Callie afford yoga classes, but she wasn't about to sponge off her boyfriend. *Crashing at his place is bad enough.*

"*Calliope?*" Megan seemed surprised to hear Julian use her full name. No one did that.

"Yes." Julian beamed a proud smile and wrapped an

arm around her, tucking her in against him. His expensive cologne overwhelmed the scents of sage and mountain air. "Calliope and I met in the graduate program at NYU." He gave her an adoring smile. "I fell in love with her the moment I saw her."

Gratitude flooded her. She loved his unwavering devotion. But she had to fix things with Megan, so she reached for her friend's forearm. "Hey, can we talk later? I'd love to catch up with you."

A server appeared, offering them a tray of flutes.

"Ah, perfect." Julian lifted two glasses and handed one to Megan and the other to Callie. He took a third one for himself before thanking the server. "I'm so pleased to meet Calliope's friends and family. How long have you two known each other?"

"We met in elementary school." Callie hadn't told him anything about her past, so now wasn't the time to reveal that she'd had no real friends until Megan. An introvert, she'd kept mostly to herself. Well, until she and Fin had gotten together—and then the whole world had split open. "She was my closest friend."

Megan's attention roamed the crowd, barely acknowledging her.

She'd try another tactic. "Do you remember that time we—"

"What's with the hair, wild thing?" The all-too familiar voice cracked through her like a thunderclap.

It might have been a while since she'd heard it, but her body responded like a rosebud starved for sunlight. Every cell bloomed and strained in his direction.

Her stomach lurched, and she did *not* want to turn around. She didn't want to look at him. With fight or flight kicking in, it took every bit of strength she had not to run like he'd just tossed a lit match at her feet and set her on fire.

"Hey, Fin," Megan said.

Brushing Callie's arm as he reached across the small circle they made, Fin met Megan in the middle for a hug. His scent—that hint of sage and clean clothes, the essence of *Fin*—swirled around her, filling her senses and sending her crashing back in time. She had a matter of seconds to pull herself together and treat him like an acquaintance. Julian didn't know about him, so she needed to just be *normal*, but turbulence scrambled her system, and her mind went blank.

And that pissed her off. She'd prepared for this moment. Hell, she'd rehearsed it. But living it, having him right *here*, she just...*dammit*. No matter how many nights she'd lain awake scripting this interaction, she couldn't control her body's reaction.

Come on. She gave herself an internal shake. *He's just a guy.*

But when he pulled back, he turned his full attention on her and...*Oh, my God.*

For the first time in years, she looked Fin Bowie, in all his six feet two inches of rock-hard muscle, in the eyes. A tremble started from deep within, rising in velocity until her composure shook like a tree in a violent storm. The last time she'd seen him, he'd been a boy. A gorgeous, untamed, mischievous boy who'd kept her on edge for most of her life. His wild, free spirit made him impossible to nail down.

But the boy she'd loved so fiercely had nothing on the man who stood before her. With his overgrown dark hair and bright blue eyes, he was a shock of rugged, raw power next to her lean, elegant boyfriend.

Of course he'd worn jeans to a rehearsal dinner, the white button down shirt the only nod to the dressy occasion. Not like Julian's pressed shirt, though. No, Fin's looked like he'd swiped it off a pile of discarded clothes on the floor on his way out of the shower. He'd shoved the sleeves up to his elbows, exposing tanned, muscular forearms.

Julian would have carefully folded the cuff until it fell just below the elbow. And he would've spent a minute adjusting it in front of a mirror.

Fin didn't own a mirror.

"Fin." The way he tilted his head in confusion made her think she sounded more stuck-up than pleasant. *Snap out of it right now.* But she couldn't—not when he looked at her as if he could see straight through her make-up and fancy clothes, right down to the trembling heart of her.

He reached for a lock of her hair and tugged it. "You iron it?"

Julian, always well-mannered, stepped back to include the new addition in the conversation. "Her hair?"

Fin tugged it again. "It's brown."

"That's her natural color." Julian's smile remained fixed despite the crinkle on his brow. He reached out his hand. "Julian Reyes."

"Fin Bowie." Fin shifted his beer bottle to his other hand so they could shake, and Callie caught the moment Fin noticed the slight sheen on Julian's manicured fingernails.

Too quickly, Fin let go and turned his attention back to her. He didn't move closer, but somehow she felt crowded by him. The entire backyard and all its guests faded away until it was just the two of them. She could smell the mountain air on his skin. He was sun-warmed meadows and bracing snow-covered summits. He was tangled sheets and calloused hands. Bone-melting kisses and thrilling gropes in public places.

He was abject heartbreak.

"Liked it platinum." Fin's deep, rough voice sounded like it might crack from the heavy emotion it carried.

"Platinum?" Julian spluttered. "When have you ever colored your hair?"

"Are you serious?" Megan laughed. "How long have you known her?"

"Two years." Julian gave Callie an assessing look.

She squeezed his hand. *Later.* "We should probably find our seats."

"She used to dye it a new color every semester." Megan had a gleam in her eyes. "That was her thing."

"I would've liked to have seen that," Julian said.

Gracious words, but she knew better. She'd have been invisible to Julian back then. He thought people who wore gauges and piercings and dyed their hair pink were compensating for a lack of authentic creativity. They showed the world how funky they were because they lacked the guts to actually create something.

"Come on." Callie pulled on his arm. "It's time for toasts." She shot Fin a look. *Thanks for starting this.*

But instead of his usual challenging response, he just looked baffled.

"Actually, I'd love to know what she was like back then," Julian said.

"She was a total tomboy," Megan said. "She got into more trouble than—"

"I don't know what a *tomboy* is," Fin said. "But if you're trying to say Callie could run faster and stomp landings and kick our asses up to Dead Man's summit, then, yeah, she was a badass." He turned fully to Julian. "You're from the east coast. You grow up making snowmen?"

"I might have made one." Julian offered a guarded smile.

"Yeah, well, my brothers and I didn't make snow *men.* We made snow targets. We'd build a row of snow mounds with holes in the middle. Big hole for the first one, smaller hole for each one down the line, until the last one had a hole the size of a small skillet. We've got pretty good aim, but this one?" He tipped his chin toward Callie. "She was the only one of us that got a snowball through the smallest one."

The tinkle of silver tapping glass cut the hum of conversation. Everyone turned to the head table where her brother stood. "Could you all please take your seats? We're about to start the toasts."

The crowd around them started moving, but Fin's

compelling gaze kept them rooted. "Tomboy?" He shrugged. "I only know that Callie was confident, strong. Fearless. Everything a woman should be."

Her heart clenched painfully that he'd come to her defense like that, but it only took a moment to see that he wasn't defending her at all. His gaze held no warmth.

He was just telling the truth. *That's how he sees me.*

Pressure weighed on her chest—loss, regret, frustration, and pain. So much pain.

Megan gave Fin a challenging look. "Oh, cut it out. You know exactly what I mean. It's not an insult. It's who she was. She didn't care about make-up or clothes. She didn't even brush her hair half the time."

A slow, delicious smile kicked up the corner of Fin's mouth. "Wild thing."

Jesus. Julian knew nothing about her past. He didn't need to hear her old nickname or see the way Fin looked at her—like they'd just stumbled out of a closet with their hair mussed and her panties balled up in his pocket.

"I'm going to find our seats." Callie got one step away when she heard Fin say, "Know how I became an extreme athlete?"

"I didn't know you were an athlete, but I'd like to hear the story," Julian said.

"*Fin.*" Callie gestured to the table where her brother stood waiting for the guests to settle. "Aren't you making a toast?"

"This won't take long." He turned back to Julian. "We were snowboarding. Me and my brothers and Callie. Right there." He lifted his beer bottle to the Tetons. "We wound up on this spine we'd never been on before, and we were all just flying. Time of our lives. Well, this one" —he pointed the bottle toward Callie—"flew off the edge of a cliff. Jesus, it was like..." His thumb rubbed his lower lip. "I thought I'd lost her. No way could anyone survive a fall like that. And it all happened so fast, it wasn't like we could do anything to save her. One minute we're tearing down the mountain, the next....she was gone. I wanted to jump off right after her, but Will, my brother, grabbed me." He gestured with both arms what a bear hug would look like from behind. "I stood there watching her sail—free falling—sure she was going to hit a rock and crumple into a broken heap. But you know what she did?"

She doubted anyone would notice the unease beneath Julian's fixed smile. He listened with rapt attention, yet the undercurrent of *what the hell* pulsed through him. He looked like he'd blinked and opened his eyes to find himself surrounded by Oompa Loompas.

But whose fault was that? She hadn't told him any of this.

"What?" Julian's tone was bright, interested.

"She landed it. She fuckin' landed it. Never seen anything like it."

Callie remembered the moment vividly. She *had* been in freefall. The world had gone silent, a blur of colors: white, bright blue, green. A strange stillness had settled over her, her entire being on heightened alert. The earth had come up fast, mostly rock, but a patch of glistening white called to her and she'd leaned in that direction. She hadn't prayed or screamed or anything. Just remained perfectly still and focused.

And when she'd landed on deep, powdery snow, her bones rattling, her teeth clacking, she'd felt a heady sense of elation.

But the best moment came later when she'd come to a stop, heart flopping in her chest like a live fish on a dock. She'd looked up to see the stunned faces of all four Bowie brothers. At that point, the older ones had already made a name for themselves in snowboarding and skiing competitions in the state. They were big, brawny, fearless athletes. All of them had stood there gobsmacked.

But it was Fin's expression—the awe, the pride—that stuck with her. She'd never doubted Fin's love. He'd always been hers. But in that moment, he'd given her something else: a profound sense of confidence.

"And on that note," Megan said. "I'm going to sit down." She took off through the crowd.

The moment she left, Julian said, "So, piecing things together here, you two dated?"

"Ah, I wouldn't call it *dating*." Fin's tone conjured tangled sheets and sweaty bodies, deep, sensuous kisses, and fists full of hair.

The shock of it had Julian's eyes going wide.

Oh, dammit all to hell. Heat spread through her limbs, and perspiration prickled under her arms. *What have you done?*

She was an idiot not to have filled him in on her past. But, honestly, while they'd known each other for two years, they'd only been dating six months. As friends, they'd talked about their classes, dinner plans, and gallery openings. So, when they'd started going out, they'd been long past those getting-to-know-you conversations.

Thinking back, though, she realized he'd never asked. He'd known she was from Wyoming, had briefly and occasionally chatted with her parents on FaceTime, but he'd never asked about her exes or old friends or anything. He'd never wondered what she'd been like before he'd met her.

After the party, she'd answer all his questions. "Fin and I dated in high school."

Julian gave a broad smile. "And, more importantly, you *snowboard*?"

A couple of times over the years, he'd invited her on ski trips with his family, but she'd always declined. Even if she could afford to ski in Aspen, she couldn't give up a week's pay to go on vacation. "Well, we live in the mountains. Everyone here does."

Okay, enough chitchat. She'd embarrassed Julian, and she had to make it right. Grabbing her boyfriend's hand, she forced a tight smile. "It was wonderful catching up with you." Before turning away, though, she caught the disappointment in Fin's eyes.

Wow, this was not going how she'd expected at all. She'd pictured giving Fin a cocky eat-your-heart-out smile when he saw how well she'd turned out. She'd never imagined he'd look at her like *that*. She led Julian to their table, unused to his body being so stiff and unyielding.

With a hand holding his suitcoat closed, he leaned across the table and shook hands with their tablemates.

Then, he held a chair out for her. Tucking in close, he said, "I would've appreciated a little warning."

"I know. I'm sorry."

"Callie, sweetheart." A stout woman approached with her arms open wide.

Callie popped back up and leaned into her aunt's embrace. "Hi, Aunt Muriel."

She smelled of cough drops and bacon from the canapés. "It's been too long. How's my favorite girl?"

Her uncle pried her loose and hugged her so hard her feet lifted off the grass. Her heel slipped out of her shoe, so when he set her back down she had to reach for Julian's arm to steady herself.

"I didn't recognize you." The elderly man clamped his big paws on her shoulders. "Your aunt said, Oh, there's our Callie, and I said, Where?" He gave a hearty laugh and then turned his attention to Julian. "Isn't she a stunner? She used to—"

Oh, God, no. No more stories. "Uncle John, Aunt Muriel, I'd like you to meet my boyfriend, Julian Reyes. Julian, this is my Aunt Muriel and Uncle John."

Her handsome, polished boyfriend gave her uncle a firm handshake. "Wonderful to meet you. I'm so pleased to finally meet Calliope's family."

"We're so proud of her," Aunt Muriel said. "*Two* college degrees. And just look at her. Sweetheart, you take my breath away. I can see that New York City's everything you wanted it to be." She pressed hand over her heart. "We've missed you so much. I'm sorry we didn't make it for your graduation."

"Oh, no, don't worry. It's not the same thing for graduate school."

"How's the job hunt, angel?" Her aunt looked concerned.

She'd mentioned the competitive job market when she'd come home over Christmas, but she'd failed to fill her family in when she'd settled on a plan, and that made her feel pretty lousy. "I'm starting with a fellowship, actually. In the art world, it's the best way to get the job I'm looking for. Julian and I have both applied to the Museum of Contemporary Art." With his parents on the board, the fellowship was a sure-thing. She gave Julian a conspiratorial look, but he kept his smile fixed on her relatives.

Whoa. She'd really hurt him.

"Did you apply to any fellowships out West?" her aunt asked.

Before she could answer her uncle jumped in. "Can't remember a time our Callie didn't talk about moving to New York City and being an artist."

Her aunt let out a *Ha!* "*I* can't remember a time she didn't race in twenty minutes late, her jeans filthy, her hair wind-blown, and out of breath from whatever mischief she'd just gotten into."

"Mischief, huh?" Resentment edged into Julian's tone.

"Oh, this girl." Her uncle smiled with pure delight. "She's always been a handful."

"She and those Bowies." Laughing, Aunt Muriel shook her head. "My goodness, they were rabble-rousers. But look at her now. I hardly recognize her." She smoothed a hand down Callie's stick-straight hair. "You look gorgeous, honey."

A tingle at the back of her neck had her glancing over to the head table. With his gaze on her, Fin lifted his champagne flute.

"We should take our seats." Aunt Muriel gave her a big smile. "We'll catch up later."

Fin didn't have to say a word for the guests to quiet down. All eyes on him, he pointed to a table on the far left. "Lloyd, I speak for the entire wedding party when I say thank you for grooming."

Laughter rippled across the lawn, and a man shouted, "Naomi gave him a cut and a shave this morning. I sent a picture into the Calamity Falls Press."

After the laughter died down, Fin's finger shifted to somewhere in the middle of the lawn. "Miss Sandy, I owe you one. If you hadn't sent me home from school that day in third grade, I might've wound up looking just like Lloyd. Or a Yeti. So, thank you."

Callie found it hard to join the laughter at that one. Fin's dad only had five rules for his boys, and the first was that they couldn't leave anyone behind. But his older brothers didn't want to be held back by their youngest sibling, so they'd sneak out in the morning or while he napped or did homework.

And it drove Fin *wild*. So, he'd set his alarm to wake up early and wait for the sound of their footsteps in the hallway. That meant most mornings in grade school he'd shown up in whatever filthy clothes he'd worn the day before. Until Miss Sandy had sent him home to get cleaned up, forcing their dad to do something about it.

"All right." Fin's tone quelled the chatter. "Let's get these toasts done so we can dig into the wonderful meal provided by the Bell family."

The guests clapped, and someone called, "Woo hoo." Her brother had his arm stretched along the back of his bride's chair. Everyone watched Fin, but when he didn't immediately speak, a strange tension gripped the crowd. Either he hadn't prepared anything, or he'd forgotten what he wanted to say because he looked down at his place setting and tugged on his scruff.

Until he looked abruptly at her, and awareness flashed across her skin.

Something in his expression told her he was about to blow her world wide open.

2

"In kindergarten, when I was five," Fin began. "I got put in time-out for not sitting still during the morning meeting. Ryder Bell left that hell called circle time, scuttled off to his cubby, and pulled his Game Boy and a little bag of Goldfish out of his backpack and brought them to me."

Oh, thank God. For a moment there, Callie had thought he'd address *her*.

Self-involved much?

"Of course, he ran right back to the circle and crossed his legs like the good little kiss-ass he is, but still."

"Hey." Ryder grinned.

"A friendship was born. When I was eight, I tried to flip my dirt bike and wound up breaking my wrist. Ryder came to my house every day after school and brought me food from the diner." He glanced at her parents, seated on the other side of her brother. "I *suppose* you could've slipped him some coin to do it, but I think maybe you just raised him right. And, by the way, Mr. Bell, your beef stew's still the bomb." He turned back to the audience. "When I was fifteen, I challenged Marc Krasnow to a duel."

A bark of laughter rang out. Marc shouted, "I remember that."

"Ryder said, Dude, this isn't the fifteen-hundreds. You don't have to defend my sister's honor. She can do that on her own." His gaze slid over to Callie. "And, of course, if you know her, you know she definitely didn't need me to kick someone's ass for her, let alone Marc Krasnow's."

"Hey, now," Marc said.

"In fact, she kicked it so hard he missed a week of school."

"In my defense," Marc said. "It wasn't exactly my *ass* she kicked."

Julian leaned close to her ear, his cologne wafting around her. "You beat someone up?"

Pressing her hands together so hard her rings dug into her skin, she ignored him, keeping her focus on Fin. Now was not the time to explain.

It's a wedding. Aren't people supposed to be telling stories about Ryder and Lynne?

"What did you do that kept him out of school for a week?" Even at a whisper, Julian's tone was harsh.

Callie closed her eyes against the image of kneeing Marc in the balls after finding out he'd told everybody she slept with all the Bowie brothers "on the regular."

She looked so forward to sharing these lovely memories with Julian, who ate his pizza with a fork and knife and sent his silk underwear out to be dry cleaned. *God help me.*

"From the time we met, Ryder's been a fifth brother." Fin's lips pressed together, and he stared unseeingly across the yard. "Until I was seventeen. When I screwed up." He looked miserable. "And he stopped talking to me."

A sickening wave of heat washed through her. He wouldn't go there. Not at a rehearsal dinner. *No, no, no.*

"I did a stupid thing." He scrubbed his jaw.

Dammit, Fin. Shut up.

"It took him a while to forgive me, but I'm glad he did, because Ryder's the best man I know. And it makes me damn happy to know he's found the best woman for him."

"And that's coming from the World's *Worst* Boyfriend," someone shouted.

A few people snickered, but Fin ignored it.

Now that surprised her. In the past, he'd have shut that guy down. He wouldn't let anyone get away with making fun of him.

"Given my track record," Fin said. "You'd think I'd be the last guy to give relationship advice, but actually I'm your man. Because the vows you make tomorrow are supposed to last a lifetime." He shifted, confidence burning through his discomfort. "And that's something I know a lot about, since I blew it with my girl." He swallowed, staring at Callie with his heart right there on display for anyone to see.

"What the hell's going on here?" Julian's breath gusted at her ear.

"I promise we'll talk later." She couldn't miss a word of this speech.

"And *that's* the worst thing I've ever done," Fin said tightly.

She couldn't take a full breath, and she went dizzy because, standing there before the people who knew him best, Fin exposed his pain. His heartache.

Fin didn't do that. He'd only ever lifted the veil for her. And to let his brothers, those intimidating champions he idolized, see his vulnerability...Fin *did not* do that.

He didn't give them ammunition to make fun of him.

"In the thirty-three hours it took me to get here from Austria, I had a lot of time to think about my speech. I wrote a good one, lots of jokes, something heartfelt at the end. But then I got here, and it hit me how easy it is to take it all for granted. To assume it'll last just because you got a ring on her finger." He shot a look to Ryder. "Don't do that. Don't take one minute with her for granted."

Ryder held his gaze with a solemn expression.

"So, instead of the speech I prepared, I'm gonna give you a list so you don't mess up like I did." He shoved a hand deep into his pocket. "Number one, be honest. About everything. You know how something happens and you think, Eh, I'll hold off on telling her that? Maybe you haven't made a decision yet or you don't want to upset her?" He held Ryder's gaze until his friend nodded in acknowledgement. "Tell her. Tell her what you're thinking. Don't shut her out, don't think she doesn't need to hear about it, and definitely don't think you can handle whatever it is on your own. That's not how relationships work. You get tighter when you work through things together. That's the glue, man. That's the damn glue."

Not a person in the yard shifted in his seat or whispered to the person next to him. And it struck her just then that he got it. He got what he'd done wrong all those years ago. It turned her blood fizzy and made her skin tingle.

It didn't change anything, but it *mattered*.

She swallowed past the knot in her throat. She would've given anything if the end of their relationship hadn't taught him that lesson.

"Number two, put each other first. Yeah, you got a job. You got bills. You got a kid. All that matters, not discounting it, but you've got to put her first. Trust me on that. Because once she's gone, I guarantee you're going to regret all the stupid crap you put before her. Don't do that."

"He's still in love with you." Julian sounded part incredulous, part strained.

She swung around. "No. He's *not...*" When his eyes flared, she realized how aggressive she sounded. She didn't care. He misunderstood. "He did a terrible thing, and he regrets how he ended it. But that's it. There's no love left."

"I don't know whether you're lying to me or to yourself." His features didn't reveal an ounce of his anger, as he shifted back in his chair.

She didn't want to make a scene, but she couldn't have him thinking there was anything left between her and Fin other than unresolved anger and resentment. "I don't care about him anymore. I haven't talked to him in six years."

But his attention had returned to Fin.

"Find something good and real to tell her every day. Tell her you love her. Tell her she's beautiful when she first wakes up. Tell her she's awesome when she graduates with a four-point-oh."

Fin had just reached in and cupped her heart with all the warmth and strength of his big hand. She'd had no idea he'd watched her all these years. That he'd lived with these regrets. She'd thought he'd been partying and having the time of his life.

"Don't hold back. Because, believe me, when you lose that privilege? Of talking to her anytime you want? It's going to gut you." Drawing in a breath that straightened his shoulders, he smiled to the crowd. "So, that's it. That's my speech. Learn from my lessons, and your marriage will go the distance." He lifted his champagne flute. "Let's raise a glass to Ryder, the best guy I know, and Lynne, the only woman good enough for him."

The guests clapped, while Ryder got up and embraced Fin. They slapped each other's backs, and Callie saw the emotion on her brother's face. Ryder was a good guy. He'd take Fin's lessons to heart.

After Fin and Ryder took their seats, the father of the bride pushed his chair back. All attention fixed on the head table in anticipation of the older man's toast. Thank God, because she needed a moment to let her emotions subside. She didn't need Julian to see her expression right then.

But right before Lynne's father lifted his flute, Julian stood up.

"Excuse me." He had the carriage of a prince, but her normally confident boyfriend looked wild-eyed. "I'm sorry to interrupt." He let out an awkward laugh. "I'd planned on doing this another time, but after that wonderfully inspirational speech, I'm going to seize the moment." His gaze swept the crowd. "Tonight, I'm a stranger to this group of friends and family, but I hope soon that won't be the case." He turned to Callie.

Blood barreled through her veins so fast she went light-headed.

Don't do this don't do this don't do this.

"Calliope Bell, I fell in love with you the moment I laid eyes on you."

Heat billowed through her. Through her panic she had an awareness of restlessness around her. People shifting in their seats, craning to get a better look. In her peripheral vision she saw her mom clapping both hands over her mouth.

But the world was narrowing, darkening, and she thought she might pass out.

"My admiration for you has grown stronger with each day we spend together. You are the calm in the craziness of my life, my north when my compass goes haywire, and the one person I know I can count on no matter what life throws my way."

Oddly, her only thought was, *Your life isn't crazy, and your compass has never once gone haywire.*

But all thoughts flew out of her head when he reached for her hand and pulled her out of the seat. Instinctively, she resisted, but the crease between his eyes deepened and he tugged more firmly. She got up on shaky legs. He drew closer and whispered, "Breathe." Holding her hand like they were at a coronation, he smiled. "Calliope, will you do me the honor of becoming my wife?"

Someone gasped. A few others said, "Aw." And her mom shouted, "Oh, my God."

An oppressive heat clung to her, like entering a hot house in the dead of summer. Her mind scrambled for purchase. Finding none, it just let go. And the world spun around her.

Needing to get her bearings, she leaned into him. She turned her face away from the audience and pressed her hot cheek against his cool, white dress shirt that smelled of dry cleaning chemicals.

His arms enveloped her. "I love you, Calliope. I really do."

The applause seemed deafening, and all she wanted to do was get away from the prying eyes. But she couldn't leave. It was her brother's rehearsal dinner, and the speeches had just begun.

The moment she started to pull away, Julian clasped her hand and raised it high in the air. Everyone clapped at what they thought was her engagement. *Holy shit.*

And then a whistle pierced the air. Fin made the time-out sign with his hands. "Hang on." When the crowd quieted, he said, "I didn't hear an answer."

Julian's prideful smile flattened. Everyone stared at her.

"Was that a yes, wild thing?" Fin said. "Because I didn't hear it."

Stunned, she had no idea what to do. Time felt suspended, reality torqued.

"Calliope? Sweetheart?" Julian squeezed her elbow a little too hard, his fingernails pinching her skin.

The sting woke her up, and she shot Fin a quelling look. *Stop it.*

But he didn't back down. "Could be my bad, but I didn't hear an answer. Is it a yes, then?"

A cold bead of perspiration trickled down her back. She couldn't take a full breath.

She looked up at Julian. "Can we talk in private?" She said it quietly but, of course, everyone heard her body language.

Julian drew in a short breath before turning to the crowd. "Please continue. Excuse me for interrupting the festivities." He gave a dignified nod to the crowd and then turned away from her. With his chair boxing him in against the table, he bent over to lift it and set it aside. Then, he stalked across the lawn, chin high, shoulders back.

Callie took off, but the stupid ice pick heels kept catching in the grass. She peeled the strap off each ankle and slid out of the delicate sandals. In bare feet, grass tickling her soles, she raced around the side of the house to catch up with her boyfriend.

He strode down the driveway, phone in his hand.

"Julian!" Grass gave way to gravel, and she had no choice but to shove her aching toes back into the sandals, allowing him to gain further ground away from her. "Would you please wait for me?"

He lifted the phone to his ear.

"Julian, dammit." *Awesome.* Not only was she sweating, but she'd just shrieked at her Upper East Side boyfriend.

At the end of the driveway, he pocketed his phone,

glancing first toward the Tetons and then toward the town of Jackson. Damp with perspiration and out of breath, she reached his side, her stomach cramped and aching.

He cut her a sideways glance. "I'm not ready to talk to you."

"Let me explain. I made a mess of this."

"Yes, you did. But right now, I need to process what just happened."

In New York, she didn't think twice when he used expressions like "process that." But in Calamity, it stood out like an elk with a glittery antler. *That's not where your mind should be.*

Okay, but she was totally discombobulated and didn't even know where to begin. "I hate that I embarrassed you, but I wasn't expecting a *proposal*." Seriously, all she'd wanted was to show everyone how well she'd turned out. Present her boyfriend, her sophisticated new look and graduate degree, and show them she wasn't that wild, reckless girl anymore.

Instead, she'd wound up hijacking her brother's rehearsal dinner. How had this happened?

"I wasn't expecting to issue one." Each word came out as hard and compact as a metal bead.

"Then why did you? It's my *brother's* night."

"I'm aware of that, Calliope." He gave her his back.

"Were you really going to propose?" The idea shook her. *Marriage?*

He glanced at her warily. "Why do you make it sound so distasteful?"

"I'm just surprised."

"We *live* together. Where did you think this relationship was going?"

"But we just finished school. We don't have jobs." *Stupid comment.* Julian didn't need to worry about something as plebian as a job. Even without his master's in Museum Studies, he'd land the best job possible thanks to his parents. In fact, the fellowship did nothing more than take the criticism of nepotism off the table. "*I* don't have a job."

"I thought we were doing this together." His tone softened. "Graduate school, starting out. I thought we'd be like my parents."

Alarms rang in her brain pan. Why did that sound all kinds of wrong?

It shouldn't. What could be better than the Reyes' lives? Elegant patrons of the arts, the college sweethearts basically ruled the Manhattan art scene. Of course she wanted that life.

If she married Julian, she'd have it.

So why did her body physically reject the idea? "I'm sorry for embarrassing you." *Sort of?* No, she *was* sorry about that. She just didn't understand the proposal in general. They weren't there yet.

And, frankly, it felt more territorial than some impulsive declaration of love.

The rightness of that theory cinched tightly.

Julian had been blindsided. In Manhattan, he and his family were at the top of the food chain. Here in Calamity, he was a fish out of water, and the killer whale—*Fin*—had publicly declared his ownership.

"It's not…I'm not *embarrassed*." He lifted both arms, palms to the sky, and then lowered them. "You think my primary emotion right now is embarrassment? Jesus, Calliope. *Wild thing*? Platinum hair? Beating up a guy when you were fifteen?" Eyes wide, his fingertips combed through his carefully arranged hair. "Who *is* that girl? How does my girlfriend, the woman I want to spend my life with, have anything to do with the girl"—he jabbed a finger toward the house—"they're talking about?"

"I was a kid, Julian. I've grown up since then." He didn't look convinced. "Are you the same person you were at seventeen?"

"*Yes*. I am." His outburst seemed to surprise himself, and he worked for composure, nostrils flaring as he inhaled deeply. "Let me be clear. I don't care that you had platinum hair. I don't care that your family's…" He paused, looking at his dust-covered black dress shoes. "Different from mine." His gaze snapped to hers. "Is that why you've kept all this from me? You thought I'd judge you?"

Outrage rose up and bitch-slapped whatever remorse she felt for turning down his public proposal. "Judge what, exactly? That I come from a Western town? That my family owns a diner, which just happens to be the most popular restaurant in the entire county? That my parents worked their hands to the bone to give us an amazing life? I can't imagine what you see here that you could find in any way less worthy than your life."

"I didn't mean it like that."

"It sure sounded like you did." She needed to make herself very clear. "I *love* my family. I'm proud of them."

"Then why didn't you tell me about them?"

"You didn't ask."

"Do *not* put this on me." He leaned into her. "What did you want me to ask, exactly? If you've ever had platinum hair? Beat up a kid so badly he missed school for a week? I'm sorry but, given your reserved nature, it didn't occur to me that you'd had a torrid love affair in your past."

"My..." *Reserved?* What was he saying? "Did you just tell me I'm not good in bed?"

"No, I didn't...*Dammit*." He tipped his head back. "How did this all go so wrong?"

Like *he* was an animal in bed? He'd certainly never grabbed her hips from behind, hiked up her skirt, and palmed her ass in the balcony of a movie theater. Or caressed her inner thigh under the table, driving her so wild she had to drag him into the ladies room to relieve the throbbing ache.

Her blood pulsed with excitement from the rush of vivid memories.

Dammit. Stop thinking about Fin. It was just so hard—after seeing him, hearing his heart-felt speech—to cross back into the present with Julian. She wanted to linger a little longer in the world Fin had conjured.

But her relationship—her future—was on the line. "It went wrong when you proposed to me at my brother's rehearsal dinner."

"Excuse me, but your ex-boyfriend, who is clearly not over you, just made a play for you in front of me. He acted like *I'm* not your boyfriend now."

Right. It *had* been territorial. "You proposed to make sure everyone knows who I belong to?"

"Of course not." His brow creased. "I don't know. I didn't expect any of this." He dug his hands into his pockets and kicked a rock into the street. It skittered and then stopped in the middle of the road. "You should've prepared me."

"I know that."

"Look, I asked you to move in with me because I wanted to live my life with you." His tone had grown more somber. "Did I plan on proposing tonight? No. But of course I planned on doing it. One day."

Wait, was he talking in past tense? Was he saying he no longer saw a future with her?

He tipped his head back. "You're never going to be mine, are you?"

Oh, my God. This is like a pile-up on a highway, one hit after another. "Slow down for a second. First of all, I'm not with Fin. I'll never be with him again."

"It's not about *Fin.* It's about you. It took me a year and a half to get you to go out with me. When you finally did, you still held me at arm's length. I'd hoped, when you agreed to move in, that you were finally ready to be all-in with me. But I was wrong. I guess when you invited me to your brother's wedding..." He shook his head, one side of his mouth pulling up in frustration. "I thought I was getting into the inner sanctum. But hearing those people talk about you made me realize I don't have you at all. So, yes, listening to your ex talk about you like...like you're his soulmate, I'm man enough to admit I made a grab." He shrugged, clearly pissed off. "I just wanted you once and for all to be *mine*."

"You realize this is the first time I'm hearing any of this? You never told me you thought I was holding back."

"I've been taking my time with you for two years, Calliope. Every step you took closer to me felt like a hard-won victory. Tonight, I see I've achieved far less than I'd thought."

"No, no, no. You can't put that on me. I didn't know you needed more." Would she have given it? After Fin, she'd been depleted emotionally. If Julian had asked for more, could she even say she'd had anything left in her reserve tank? "But now that I know, I'll try harder."

"You shouldn't have to try. After two years, you should trust me—love me—enough to share everything with me. I should be the one you talk to. Confide in. But I see that's not going to happen. You left your spirit here."

"No, I didn't. You've got it all wrong." *So explain it.* "Fin and I...it was all about the drama. Come on, it was a *high school* relationship. We fought, we..." *You what? Made up with crazy, wild sex?*

Calm down and fix the situation. "He was my first boyfriend, and it was a tempestuous relationship, and I don't want that anymore. If you want to know why I'm taking it more slowly with you, that's it. All that fire...it burns out. And, frankly, I never want to feel that again."

"Love? You never want to love like that? Because that's how I love you."

Oh, Julian, you don't have a single clue about that kind of love.

"I love you, Calliope." He reached for her, and every cell in her body rebelled against it. When she saw his horrified look at her rejection, she told herself it was because she didn't want to be possessed or consumed ever again.

Or maybe it was just the moment. Seeing Fin again —*his speech, God*—Julian's proposal. All she knew was she didn't feel the slightest bit romantic at the moment.

Julian took a step back. A prideful resolve settled over his features. "Do you love me? I've waited two years to hear the words, and I've never pressed you for them."

She wanted to remind him he was eighteen months ahead of her in this relationship, and that was something she couldn't fix.

When she didn't answer right away, his features tightened. "It's a simple question, Calliope. And it doesn't take time to figure out. You either love me or you don't."

How could she explain that her feelings had been muted since Fin? Julian could never understand the kind of combustible relationship that had you screaming at each other one second and tearing your clothes off the next. That had you staying up all night talking because you never ran out of things to say. That desperate need to stay connected. Gripping, holding, thrusting into each other so hard and still not getting as close as you needed, because human beings couldn't fuse even when their hearts and souls demanded it.

She and Julian had a good relationship. And she didn't want to lose it. "I love our relationship. I love our life together."

Hurt flashed in his eyes, and his jaw gaped open.

She scrambled to find better words. "Everything you heard tonight...I don't want to be that person anymore. I've worked hard to become the woman you fell for. This is who I am now. That's never going to change. Do you understand?"

He glanced down the straight, two-lane highway. Headlights crested the rise in the road. "Sure."

Anxiety gripped her. He could not get into that taxi. She wrapped a hand around his biceps. "I know this was an awful experience for you. I never imagined any of these stories would come up this weekend." At her brother's *wedding*. "I'm sorry I didn't tell you about my past. I hope you understand that I'm not trying to hide anything. I'm just focusing on my future. I *like* our future."

"But that's the thing." He twisted out of her hold. "You *are* hiding." He looked at her like she'd betrayed him. "Tonight, I realized I only know the pieces you choose to show me. The great student, the beautiful woman with a smile that slays me. I know the creative thinker who keeps her cool under pressure. The woman who picks up after herself in my apartment like a weekend guest and makes sure I take my vitamins."

"That's me. That's who I am now."

"I don't think so. The girl they were talking about in there? She hasn't gone anywhere. I'm guessing she's just nursing her wounds after a traumatic breakup." Headlights bounced on the bumpy road, and the car slowed. "Look, you asked for time, and that's exactly what I'm going to give you."

"I don't want time *apart*." He couldn't leave. She needed to keep him here. "I'll tell you everything you want to know. I don't have secrets, no matter what it might look like. Let's just go back inside so I can be there for my brother, and we'll talk when we get back to my parents' house."

The car slowed, and Julian raised a hand in acknowledgement. Then, he turned back to her, his mask of graciousness back in place. But she could see the sadness in his eyes. "Please go and enjoy your brother's special night. I'd like some time to myself. We'll talk in the morning."

"I'm not...." She glanced to the house. What the hell was she supposed to do? She couldn't leave, but she wasn't about to let her boyfriend take off with their relationship up in the air. "I'll go home with you."

"You can't miss your brothers' rehearsal dinner."

"You're more important. I'll—"

"I insist." He looked at her like she was some drunk chick in a bar desperate to hook up with him. "Goodnight, Calliope."

For two years he'd pursued her unflaggingly. She'd been the object of his attention.

Now, she watched him head toward the car, panic rising at his total detachment. "Julian."

He opened the door and lowered himself into the back seat.

As the car took off, he didn't even glance at her.

3

LEANING INTO THE TURN, FIN ACCELERATED. THE thrill of controlling his bike, of pushing the angle so far he could smell the asphalt, sparked his aggression. *Hell, yeah.*

A form in the middle of the road sent a shock of awareness through him, and he pulled back on the throttle. After a moment, the figure clarified into a body. A man.

His brother.

Fucking Will.

Pretending to be an aircraft marshal, Will pointed a finger at him and then motioned to the side of the road. *Forget that.* Fin needed to ride out this crazy energy. But just before blowing past, he glimpsed the lights of Calamity a half-mile away. After all he'd gone through to make it home in time for the wedding, he couldn't risk getting arrested the night before.

Edging onto the shoulder of the road, he planted his boots on the ground. "*What?*"

Will tipped his head in the direction of their ranch,

completely dark at this hour. "Saw your headlights on my way into town."

"Yeah. Out for a ride."

"Good night for one." He came closer. "Brodie's got us a table at Sweet Baby Jane's."

With a curt nod, Fin said, "I'll catch up with you later."

"That proposal?" Will gave a slow shake of his head. "Came out of nowhere."

Fin cranked the handle, making the engine roar. He needed to ride. Shake it off.

"That had to be tough to watch," Will said. "You okay?"

The way his brother looked at him, eyes filled with concern, made Fin kill the ignition.

"No."

"Yeah. I get that. But..." Even though he gave a casual shrug, Will watched him carefully. "She's changed, though, right? She's not the girl you grew up with. Looks like she's moved on."

In other words, *You should, too.* Fin's fingers flexed on the rubber grips. He'd run over Will before talking to him about Callie. His brothers didn't get it. Never would. "Sure, man. Now let me finish my ride, and I'll meet up with you guys in an hour." His gaze cut away, toward the dark, imposing peaks of his mountain range. The snow glowed in the moonlight.

That woman tonight—that wasn't Callie. She'd leveled that cool gaze on him like he was just someone she'd passed in the hallway from time to time. *What the hell happened to her?*

Christ, her boyfriend had *proposed* to her. Fin couldn't stand it. Just couldn't fucking stand it.

"Thing is, Brodie's only in town for two days," Will said. "So how about we grab a beer and you can tell us about Austria?"

He didn't want to be around anyone. Maybe he'd head up the trail and ride the rim of Dead Man's cliff. Only that kind of rush could chase the darkness out of his head.

"Hey." Will gave the handlebars a shake. "When was the last time we had three brothers in town at the same time?"

"I'm riding." He bit off each word.

"At night. On a dirt bike." Will grinned. "And I saw the sparks when your kickstand hit the pavement."

Fin smiled. "That was cool, right?"

His older brother nodded. "Yeah, man. It was. Now, come on. Let's not leave Brodie alone with all the pretty tourists. It isn't fair to the other guys."

Fin swung a leg off his bike. Their dad didn't have a lot of rules for his sons, but not "pissing in their own pool" was one of them. Made sense. In a small town like Calamity, their dad had wanted them to be on good terms with everyone.

Since his brothers weren't all that interested in romantic relationships, they'd figured that meant steering clear of dating townies. But women loved Brodie—and not just for his looks and brawn, but because of his attitude. He just didn't give a damn. Always preoccupied with some project or another, he didn't ogle or flirt. Women seemed to want to be the one to win him.

Fin walked his bike to Will's truck. Together, they lifted it and shoved it onto the bed.

Will clapped him on the shoulder. "Glad you're back, man." Their boots crunched on asphalt as they headed for the cab. Just as Will opened his door, he said, "And, listen, don't let it get to you, okay? It's just a meme. Something new will pop up tomorrow."

Meme? Fin had no idea what he was talking about.

An old Western tourist town at the foot of the Tetons, Calamity was hopping in June, so they parked in the back lot of the yoga studio.

The last thing Fin wanted to do was sit in a crowded, airless bar, but he did want to spend time with Brodie before he headed back to Utah, so he followed Will down the narrow alley towards Main Street.

He just...he couldn't get that guy out of his head. Callie's boyfriend—fiancé?—wore a bracelet. That shine on his fingernails meant he got *manicures*. What the hell was she doing with a high-maintenance guy?

Except she'd looked just like him, hadn't she? In that sleek black dress and pearls and those black spikey heels... since when did Callie blow her hair dry and wear *pearls*?

His phone buzzed, and he saw a text from Nolan, one of his snowboarding buddies.

Took your advice, tweaked the take-off, and it worked. Still slow, though. Don't know what's going on.

Fin didn't need to think about it. **Get a notebook. Write down everything you eat for 2 weeks.** Most athletes got tired of keeping up the degree of fitness required to compete at an elite level, so in the off-season they eased back. Fin would bet anything Nolan was drinking too much and loading up on carbs. Keeping a log would help him figure that out.

His friend wrote back right away. **I eat good, man. You make sure of it**.

Nobody wanted to give up booze, sugar, and bread, he got that. But then they shouldn't complain about their performance.

He texted back. **You can keep being frustrated and slow or, for 2 weeks, you can write down everything you eat and drink**.

Nolan responded right away. **Fuck off**.

Fin smiled. **Your choice**.

Once they hit Main Street, they entered the flow of pedestrian traffic. The air smelled of barbecue from Skeeter's Bar and Grill. Three long streets filled with businesses that sold everything from taxidermy animals and Old West antiques to clothing and food faced the town green.

Families sat on benches eating ice cream cones, skater boys zig-zagged through the crowd on the sidewalk, and couples peered into store windows looking at art, Western wear, and giant mounted grizzly bear and moose heads.

But the only thing he could see was Callie's expression when she'd come back after chasing her boyfriend. She'd been upset throughout dinner, and Man-Bracelet hadn't been with her. Something had gone down between them.

Was she getting married or not? She'd always wanted to go to NYU, so he was glad she'd done it. But marrying someone? Living there permanently?

She'd be out of his life for good.

He couldn't wrap his head around it. She was supposed to forgive him at some point.

Anxiety barreled through him. He had too much energy and no outlet. The idea of her not coming home...of never forgiving him...*Jesus.*

He couldn't accept it. He wouldn't. From the time they were little kids they'd had a connection. His brothers used to make fun of him for his "crush," but even back then he'd known it wasn't as simple as that. It was a bond. It was... they were just two parts of a whole. He blew out a breath.

Everything felt wrong. His world had tipped sideways, and he couldn't get his bearings.

When they reached the bar, Will held the door open, but he might as well have been trying to shove him off the edge of a cliff. Because Fin wasn't going. He needed to talk to Callie. *Right now.*

Three months after she'd left for college, she'd blocked him on her phone and social media. Each time he'd flown to New York City to talk to her, she'd iced him. And on the rare occasion she came to town, she was like a ghost.

But she was here now, and it was time they had a damn conversation. Just as he spun around to leave, his brother said, "Brodie heads back on Sunday. One beer?"

Fin drew in a breath. *Fine.* One beer with his brothers.

Then, he'd go see Callie.

He stepped inside to the blast of heat, country music, and buzz of conversation.

Familiar faces gave him chin nods and smiles.

An old friend came up and shook his head. "You can't do anything at a normal level, can you?"

Fin had no idea what the guy was talking about and, right then, he didn't give a damn, so he just gave him a fist bump and moved on. He tipped his chin to people he knew as he moved through the crowded room.

Until it struck him that people weren't actually smiling. They were *laughing* at him.

"Way to make a name for yourself, bro," someone shouted from across the room.

"Fin Bowie, takin' it global," someone else said.

What were they talking about? His gut twisted when he remembered his toast. Yeah, he'd put himself out there, but he'd meant every damn word. Except...these guys hadn't been at the rehearsal dinner, so had someone talked about it? Had it become some joke in town?

His chest tightened, but he shook it right off. Not only had he given Ryder good advice, he'd sent a message to Callie, so they could all go fuck themselves. He powered through the mob.

A guy from his old college ski team stood up from a table. "Only you could piss off a woman bad enough for it to go viral, dude." He held up his phone. "Check it out. It's up to thirty thousand comments."

"Comments?"

Confusion pulled on the guy's features. "The meme.

You don't know about it?"

Will stepped between them. "Come on. Brodie got us a table in the back."

What did a meme have to do with him?

It had to be the proposal. Relief slammed him. Someone had probably recorded it with a phone. That shit would definitely spread. A guy proposing in the middle of toasts at someone's rehearsal dinner? And then running off like a bitch when his girlfriend didn't answer? If Fin hadn't been involved, he'd be laughing, too.

Man-Bracelet didn't know Callie at all if he thought proposing to her in front of an audience would work. For all her guts and confidence, she was an introvert. She liked quiet, one-on-one conversations. She needed intimacy.

But, of course, Man-Bracelet didn't know her. That woman at the rehearsal dinner in the fancy dress and pearls? With that uppity voice? That wasn't Callie. That was Callie playing the role of Calliope.

As they passed a table, a big dude shouted, "Yo, World's Worst Boyfriend!"

World's Worst Boyfriend? A quick scan of faces revealed everyone was in on the joke.

"Sit down, and I'll explain it." Will steered him to the booth, where Brodie sat with a bunch of his high school friends. When he gave them an expression that said, *You mind?* they all started clearing out.

"Don't do anything yet," Brodie told the guys. "Give me some time to think about it, and let's meet on Monday, okay? I'll have some ideas by then."

With murmurs of agreement, the friends said quick

goodbyes.

Fin slid into the booth. "Hey."

"Hey, man." Brodie gave him a warm smile.

"So, what's going on?" Fin asked. "What's with the Worst Boyfriend thing?"

His two oldest brothers shared a look before Will pulled out his phone, tapped the screen, and then held it out to him. "That last text you sent Traci, when you left her in the ER? She posted it on Instagram."

Oh, shit. Had he said something stupid? He couldn't remember.

He read the screen.

Thanks for a great time. ☺ Gotta jet. Talk soon.

That seemed pretty basic. "Okay?" Just as he peeled his gaze away it snagged on the comment section. "What the hell?"

Fin Bowie, you suck.

What is the matter with you? How could you do that to your girlfriend?

"Traci's not my girlfriend." He pulled the phone out of Will's hand and read more of them.

I've seen some shitty things in my life, but leaving your girlfriend to have surgery alone in a foreign country?

Fuck you, Fin Bowie. Fuck you.

He looked up at his brothers. "I didn't leave her alone." He scrolled the page looking for Traci's handle. What had she said to make people think that?

But he didn't see it anywhere. "I don't get it. Do they think we were on some kind of romantic vacation together? There were six of us in two tents. Five guys and Traci. We were snowed in for a week." Fin made his living making movies of him snowboarding on uncharted terrain. It was extremely rare to have an accident, but on this trip Traci had fallen into a crevasse and damaged her knee.

Will tapped his fingertips on the scarred wood tabletop. "Looks like her fans came to their own conclusions."

"Why doesn't she correct them?"

Brodie gave him an annoyed look. "She's in *surgery*."

Right. Of course. "Then she'll explain it when she's out."

"Yeah," Brodie said. "That'll be her first priority."

Rereading the text, he could see how callous it sounded. "I was joking. She was a mile away from base camp, long past any real danger, when it happened. It was shit luck. What could I say to that? I knew she'd be scared out of her mind. I was being sarcastic." He hadn't thought for a second anyone but Traci would see it. "Why does anyone care about some text I sent?"

Brodie tipped back his beer bottle and drained it. "Because she's a famous snowboarder whose career might've just ended."

Both Fin and Will watched their brother. They knew

what lived behind Brodie's impassive expression. Three months before the Olympics, Brodie had reinjured his knee, forcing him to retire. The whole world had been watching the eighteen-year-old skiing phenom, so it had been a hell of an adjustment when his career had ended.

Brodie had never planned on college or getting a job, so his whole world—his identity—had transformed overnight. Now, he designed the courses his brothers competed on.

So, yeah, dealing with social media wasn't on Traci's agenda right then. He got that.

A group of guys approached the table. "Damn, Fin. Why you gotta do everything to the extreme? You're not just a shitty boyfriend like the rest of us. Hell, no. You're the world's worst."

Will glanced up at them. "Can you give us a minute?"

With nods, they turned and disappeared into the crowd.

"You know I didn't do this, right?" Fin looked between his brothers. "I've never been with Traci."

Brodie snorted out a laugh. "Yeah. Believe me, we know."

All right, enough of this shit. "Hey, listen. I've got some news." He hadn't wanted to mention it. Not until it was a sure-thing, but he didn't want his brothers thinking about him as the World's Worst anything. "Looks like I'm on the short-list for *National Adventurer's* 'Athlete of the Year.'" His manager had a contact at the magazine who'd confirmed Fin's name was listed along with a rock climber from Nepal, a cave diver from Poland, and two others. *Fuck yeah.*

"No shit?" Brodie sounded impressed.

Pride surged through him. "Nominees haven't been announced, so don't say anything. But Bram's gonna get some footage up as soon as he can." He shrugged as if scoring the cover didn't matter to him.

"Ah, you'll get it," Will said. "They'll want a pretty boy on the cover."

Frustration rose hard in him, but he tamped it down. He'd long ago learned the more upset he got, the more they ribbed him.

"But just to seal the deal, let's get some shots of you without a shirt," Brodie said.

His brothers broke out laughing.

He grinned. "Fuck off. It's a big deal. If I make it, I'll be the youngest athlete in the magazine's history."

"Hey." Will turned his attention to Brodie. "What were you saying to Chris and those guys about meeting them on Monday? Thought you had to get back to work?"

"They're talking about moving," Brodie said. "San Diego, Seattle, some place where there's more opportunity. It sucks, right? With all our resources—national parks, lakes, the whole Wild West shit—we should have enough jobs in this town. So, I was just kicking around some ideas with them, and I think I got one. It's big, and it would make use of the ghost town."

A flash of white-blonde hair caught Fin's attention, and he half-rose out of his seat before he remembered Callie didn't look like that anymore.

The second to last time he'd seen her—August, six years ago—she'd worn jean cut-offs, a red polka dot bikini top, and hot pink patent leather Dr. Marten boots. They'd taken their dirt bikes up the Bowie Pass to Skinner's Falls.

She'd kicked off her shorts, raced to the edge of the cliff, and hurled herself off. He'd jumped right after her, landing in water that even in August was ice cold.

The moment he'd popped up and shook the hair out of his eyes, she'd latched onto him, legs, arms, and mouth. Kissing him like the wild, uninhibited girl she'd been.

His heart seized with a mix of happiness and soul-deep loss.

He had to get out of there. He nudged his brother.

"Hang on." Will turned his attention back to Brodie. "What's the idea? You want to turn it into a tourist attraction?"

"Yeah, man." Brodie seemed excited. "Why not?"

"Because it's historic." Will didn't like change. Discipline required routine, and there wasn't a man alive who had his brother's level of discipline. "You want people crawling all over the original buildings of Calamity? You want graffiti on the jail house? The saloon?"

"I want to restore all the old buildings. Let's bring the saloon back to life, man. Turn it into a restaurant—"

"You're turning a historic town into a theme park so your friends can have jobs?" Will asked.

"Not just my friends. The whole town will benefit. We'll have a hotel, a restaurant...Wild West re-enactors with daily shoot-outs." Brodie smiled. "This is good. Think I'll stay in town a few weeks, see if I can get it off the ground."

The memory of Man-Bracelet proposing to Callie hit

Fin's solar plexus, and shock radiated through his central nervous system. He couldn't sit through another second of their conversation. "Let me out." He gave Will a shove.

His brother slid out of the booth, and Fin took off. He checked the time on his phone. Not even ten. Not too late to show up at the Bell house.

"Dude." A friend made a grab for him as he strode past.

Fin kept going, but the guy followed. "Traci Allen's hot, man, but looks like you messed with the wrong woman."

"I didn't mess with her. She's just a friend."

Will pushed between them. His brothers were big, fit guys, but Will was the biggest. Pure muscle, he stood a good two inches over Fin's six-two frame. With the combination of size and intensity, people gave his brother wide berth. Fin's friend backed off.

By the time he'd made it to the door Fin had heard *World's Worst Boyfriend* half a dozen times. He'd have to shut it down. *Later*.

Bursting out the door, he sucked in the cool mountain air. He took off at a jog for Will's truck.

"Hey." Brodie grabbed his shoulder, hauling him back. "Where you going?"

"Got something to do."

Will came up on his other side. "Well, hang on. We'll head home with you."

"Not going home." He didn't need their crap, so he swung around in the opposite direction. He'd walk to Callie's.

"Dude, what're you doing?" From his expression, though, Brodie had already figured it out.

So, he just copped to it. "Going to Callie's."

"You sure you want to do that?" Will asked.

Ignoring them, Fin stepped off the curb. He couldn't talk to her at the wedding tomorrow, and she'd likely leave the morning after, so his only chance was now. He dashed across the street, hopping the curb on the other side and heading around the town green. In the gazebo, a jazz band played. Families, couples, and groups of friends sat on lawn chairs, some with picnic baskets. A man threw a Frisbee for his dog, and a mother and daughter argued under a tree.

Brodie kept up with him. "You realize she's with her boyfriend, right? Who might be her fiancé by now."

Fin swerved around a cluster of teens blocking the sidewalk.

"Hang on a sec." Will grabbed his arm. "Just listen."

Rage boiled over. "I did that, remember? You and Dad and Coach. I listened to all of you. And look what it got me."

"It got you a life," Will said. "A pretty cool one."

"Look, man, you know I respect you, and in any other situation I would hear you out. But when it comes to me and Callie? You don't know shit. All your advice—that it was just some high school crush, that I'll forget about her? That I should go and have some fun? Well, guess what? I didn't forget her, and I'm not having fun. You want to know why?" He stepped into Will's space. "Because I *loved* her. And I lost the only woman I'm ever going to love because of you guys." He turned away and kept walking. "So, no offense, but I'm done listening to you."

Will kept up with him. "Okay, so you show up at her

door, and she's standing there with her boyfriend. Then what?"

"Then we have it out. Like we should have done years ago."

"In front of her fiancé?"

"She's not marrying him." And right then the dark shroud lifted, because he knew without a doubt Callie would never marry Man-Bracelet.

"You're right," Brodie said. "The Callie you grew up with would never marry that guy. But she's changed. You gotta see that, man. Unless you want to move to New York and wear a suit and work in a cubicle, you have to face it. You guys have grown apart."

Hitting a stoplight, Fin shoved his hands in his pockets, the June air chilly on his bare arms. He tipped his head back to take in a sky full of blazing stars. "You shouldn't have interfered. I don't know what your problem was with her anyway."

"Never had a problem with her," Will said. "Callie's great. It was about you. You were too young to be so into her."

"You were going to move to *New York*." Brodie gave him a look that said, *What kind of life would that've been for you?*

After Brodie tore his ACL in a skiing accident when he was nine, their mom moved the three youngest sons—Brodie, Gray, and Fin—to New York. She'd said she'd wanted the best care for Brodie, but everyone knew she hated Calamity.

If she'd thought she couldn't manage them in the

mountains, though, she'd had an even harder time in Manhattan. They hadn't lasted a year before she'd shipped them back home to their dad.

But Fin had only been six. He didn't have the bad memories of city life his brothers had.

Nor had he cared. He'd just wanted to be with Callie.

"I'll tell you the truth, man." Will leaned in, shutting out the people around them. "You scare the shit out of me. Since she left, it's like you've got a death wish. You're lost without her, and I wish you'd just let her go and get your life on track."

Rage pumped through him. "This *is* my track. I'm good enough at what I do that *National Adventurer* wants me on their cover." Why was he standing there talking about the same old shit? Each minute that passed drew Callie closer to leaving town again.

Fin struck off across the intersection, but Will kept right up with him. "Would you just think about it first before you go over there and make a scene? It's ten at night. Are you going to storm into her bedroom while she's with her boyfriend?"

Right in the middle of the street, Fin lost it. That image —*Jesus*—of Callie in bed with another guy. *No.* "I don't care what you have to say, okay? I let you keep me from her last time. It's not going to happen this time."

The red glow from the traffic light tinted their skin, as Brodie quietly held his gaze. "No one kept you from her. You made the decision to go with Dad and Will on your own."

He knew that, and it drove him crazy. To this day, he'd

wake up in the middle of the night jolted by the force of his colossally stupid decision. The twist of regret made him want to crawl out of his skin. There was no escape from the decision he'd made.

A car honked, and the trio continued to the other side of the street.

To be clear, Fin didn't regret his decision. He'd made the right one, but he should have handled it differently. *And that's what I need to tell her.* "I think we all know how much I let you influence me, but yeah, okay. I own what I did. It was the world's shittiest thing—"

Laughter exploded beside him, and some guy grabbed his arm and raised it. "You hear that? Fin Bowie just admitted he's the World's Shittiest Boyfriend."

People crowded around them. "Is that him?" someone said.

"Are you serious? That's the actual World's Worst Boyfriend?"

"That's hilarious."

Fin swung around, hands curled into fists. He felt the press of his brothers, the tension in their bodies. "Jesus Christ, I didn't do anything."

Lights from camera phones went off.

"Cool it," Brodie said in a low voice.

Christ, if everyone knew about the meme that meant Callie did, too. The idea of her seeing thousands of women calling him exactly what she must've thought about him ratcheted up his anger.

He didn't give a rat's ass what strangers thought of him, but Callie? He needed to explain—*fuck*, he had to get to her. But the crowd boxed him in at the same moment someone came up from behind and shoved a paper Burger King crown on his head.

"Here he is," the guy shouted. "The World's Worst Boyfriend."

"Quick, get a picture."

Slapping the hat off, Fin charged through the crowd, his shoulder knocking into someone. He did *not* need this shit right now, but then, out of nowhere, the guy he'd bumped into said, "Fucker," right before coldcocking him. Fin's neck snapped back, the pain exploding in his cheek.

What the hell? With bodies pushing and shoving around him, Fin swung, his fist connecting with a meaty gut, and then it became a blur of punches and grunts. His brothers pushed into the mêlée, shoving the strangers aside. Just as they reached Fin, bike cops arrived at the scene. A moment later a cruiser's siren tapped out three beats.

The crowd parted, as rubber-soled shoes scurried around them. One of the guys picked himself up off the ground and pointed at Fin. "Dude knocked me down."

Strong hands got hold of Fin's biceps, and his arms were jerked behind his back.

"Hang on," Will said. "He didn't start this."

Cold metal cuffs snapped around his wrists. As the cops led him to the cruiser, Fin caught the concerned looks on his brothers' faces.

Dammit. Ryder's wedding was tomorrow.

4

Fin started picking fights with me over every little thing. And then he started losing weight, getting rid of that flabby-ass beer belly. I figured he was freaking out over the wedding. I tried to be supportive and understanding, gave him lots of extra lovin' (wink wink). But then, the night of the rehearsal dinner, he didn't show. No one knew where he was. Not his brothers, his parents, or his friends. Finally, I got a text from him late that night— really late, like maybe 2 or 3 in the morning. CALLING OFF THE WEDDING. I mean seriously WTF? We got into it, and he finally told me the girl he'd liked in high school had started following him on social media a few months earlier. She'd "inspired him" to lose weight, made him feel like a "man." Yeah, so, Fin Bowie dumped me hours before our wedding so he could finally get with his high school crush. #worldsworstboyfriend.

Callie looked up from her phone, only then becoming aware of the early morning chill and the ache in her neck from staring down at her lap. She hadn't been able to sleep last night, so she'd come outside to watch the sunrise from the deck. Instead, she'd gotten lost in Fin's meme.

At some point the comments had turned from reaming Fin out for abandoning Traci into a forum for sharing stories of heartbreak—with the scorned people substituting Fin's name for the actual significant other.

She'd read hundreds of them, and the pain out there, the heartache...it was killing her.

The screen door rattled on its runner, shattering the morning quiet.

"Hey, Callie-bean." Her dad stood with a mug of steaming coffee in his hand, one bare foot on the deck, the other in the kitchen. "He left, huh?"

Tears threatened, but she blinked them away. Julian had packed his bags and stayed at an airport hotel last night. He'd actually dumped her. "Yep." Frustrated with herself, she clicked out of Traci's Instagram page and opened the text Julian had sent an hour ago. She held it out to her dad.

If you give me your address in Calamity, I'll send your belongings first thing Monday morning.

None of this made sense. How had he gone from pursuing her relentlessly for two years to dumping her at the first sign of trouble?

Her dad, standing there with his messy salt and pepper hair, his threadbare Van Halen T-shirt and cargo shorts, handed the phone back. "Ride with me."

Her body felt sluggish, but she couldn't afford to fall apart. Her life had just turned upside down and obsessing over Fin's meme would accomplish nothing. "Give me a second to change."

Steam rose from his mug, and he swallowed. "You're home now, sweetheart. You can go just as you are."

She glanced at her leggings and purple NYU baseball-style T-shirt. Even as an undergrad, she'd never left the apartment looking so unkempt. In the depths of her depression over her breakup with Fin, her roommate, Delilah, had told her if she walked around looking like a slob, she'd act like one. That, instead, she should dress like she was ready to kick ass and take names, so she'd eventually adopt that attitude. Her friend had been right.

But today she could relax. It was Calamity. No one would notice her clothes.

Pulling the car keys off the hook by the back door, her dad headed into the garage. It smelled of gasoline and fresh-cut grass from the ride-on mower. Callie stepped over a car vacuum to get to the other side of her dad's old truck.

An accumulation of twenty years of active family life cluttered the space. Four dirt bikes dangled off a rack from the ceiling. Tennis rackets, sleds, rakes, and shovels hung off hooks on the walls. She got a pinch in her heart when she thought of all the family outings her parents had planned but missed because of the demands of the diner.

Callie got into the passenger seat and latched the seat belt.

"Can you text your brother?" Her dad turned the key in the ignition. "Let him know we're on our way?"

"Sure." As she typed, she asked, "Is Theo going to be the ring bearer?"

"Nope. He's a shy one." Her dad slung a hand across the bench seat and twisted around as he backed out. He gave her a sweet smile. "Like you used to be." At the end of the driveway, he turned onto the highway. As soon as she sent the text, she clicked on the Instagram icon and went to Traci's page.

Holy crap. She saw dozens of new comments. *This is crazy.*

I met Fin online and fell for him hard and fast. We'd been dating about a month when he suddenly ghosted me. I was so pissed. It made no sense. He'd come on strong, treated me like his queen. Talked about this amazing future we were gonna have. Our wedding, our kids, our house, even the kind of dog we'd get. I shoulda known it was too good to be true but come on. He said everything I wanted to hear. And then—poof—he vanishes into thin air. A few weeks later my sister starts gushing about some dude she met online. Her soulmate. Love of her life. I didn't pay much attention cuz I was still freaking out over Fin ghosting me like that. But pretty soon I started paying attention cuz I'm noticing this dude's telling her the same shit Fin had told me. So, I show up at the club she said she was going to and don't you know it was Fin fucking Bowie grinding on my sister's ass on the dance floor? Let's just say the bouncers had to pry my fingernails out of his face. #worldsworstboyfriend.

"You got a plan?" Her dad's gentle voice broke through the quiet.

Right. Julian. "Not a clue. I guess I'm waiting for him to change his mind." He was upset, sure, she understood that. But he'd calm down. Nothing else made sense.

An uneasy feeling crept through her as they sped past the bison preserve. "I really hurt him, Dad. I've known him for two years, and I never mentioned Calamity."

"Is Calamity code for Fin?"

A smile broke the tension across her features. It had been too long since she'd spent time around her parents. "Yes."

His brow crinkled. "Your boyfriend's an ass."

"Julian? No, he's not. He's a great guy."

"A great guy doesn't propose to you just because he's threatened by your ex. Only a jackass would do that."

"Dad." But her tone lacked any real conviction. As much as she wanted to defend Julian, she couldn't. Because he *had* done that. "Okay, but I dropped him into the situation unprepared. It wasn't fair." Her dad still didn't look convinced. "But he's a good man. And he treats me..." *Politely. Sweetly.* "He treats me like a princess."

"Well, no wonder you said no to his proposal."

"What?" Who wouldn't want to be treated like a princess?

"Not really your style, is it? Having to be on your best behavior all the time? Acting like you're better than everyone else. You're more the kind of girl who gets her hands dirty."

His words called up delicious memories. Plunging her hands into pastry dough in the diner's kitchen, in dirt working alongside her mom in the garden. In paint when she'd thrown herself into her canvases.

She'd forgotten that part of herself. How strange was that? To have forgotten the sensual pleasure she'd gotten from touching things? She hadn't gotten dirty in years. "My life in New York is so different." That wasn't a bad thing, but the contrast did surprise her.

"You went there to be an artist."

"Oh, I made peace with that years ago. It took me all of one semester to figure out I'm not suited for the life of a starving artist." Mostly, to realize she didn't have the kind of talent it took to make it in the big leagues.

"You hardly gave it a chance."

"I lost the fire." Her teachers kept asking her to dig deeper, but she just hadn't had the energy. "But, honestly, it was more than that. I didn't want to be a poor, struggling artist in New York City. It's one thing to do my art from the comfort of my parent's basement, when all expenses are covered. It's a whole other thing to live in a sketchy part of town, work multiple jobs, and then have to decide each day between food and paint."

"So, what does this mean for you, now that he's ended things?"

She wanted to say, He'll come around. But he was sending her *belongings* to Calamity.

Which meant...*holy shit*...she had nowhere to live. Reality was slowly sinking in.

Two months ago, her roommate had gotten a job offer in Minneapolis, leaving Callie with an apartment she couldn't afford. So, when Julian had suggested crashing with him, she'd agreed. *Now what?* "I have nowhere to go."

"What about Delilah?"

Her first dorm mate and closest friend in the city lived a fancy life. "She gave her cousin her apartment for the summer while she studies at the Cordon Bleu in Paris."

"Guess it's a good thing your mom didn't let me turn your room into a brewery."

Wait, Calamity? The idea of being banished to Wyoming for the summer rocketed through her like a speed ball. "I'm not staying *here*, Dad." Her pulse kicked into overdrive. She had two jobs...her life was in New York. Julian knew that. He wouldn't do this to her.

Then again, the apology she kept waiting for wasn't coming. *Not if he's asking for my forwarding address.*

This is really happening.

She had to talk to him, get him to change his mind. But her body rebelled against the idea. He'd not only broken up with her, but he'd kicked her out of his apartment when he knew she had nowhere else to go. What kind of person did that?

She had to think of someone who'd let her crash on their couch until the fellowship started. Oh, and she had to get her full-time hours back. "I can't just not show up to work." Dammit, the whole point of spending time with the Reyes' was to make sure she got the fellowship.

Wait...was the *fellowship* in jeopardy?

No. Not a chance. She was the perfect candidate, and she'd nail the interview.

Except...she could just imagine the board members glancing at her resume and wondering about the three-month gap.

"Let's see...you graduated in May...what have you done since then?"

"Well, I lived in my parents' basement and waited tables at their diner in Wyoming."

Yeah, that's not gonna work. She *had* to get back to the city. "I'm still leaving tomorrow morning."

"You need a little green to get you through the next month?"

Affection streamed through her, and she rubbed his shoulder. "I love you, Dad." But there wasn't a chance in hell she'd take his money. He worked too hard for it.

"I love you, too, Callie-bell. And you can always stay in town for a bit, save up some cash before you go back to the city."

Saving up money would help so much, but she couldn't be out of the art world that long.

The other candidates were most likely doing interesting work this summer.

Her dad slowed, making a turn onto a dirt lane. "Besides, it'll give you a chance to hang out with your nephew."

The truck bounced on the rutted road. When a small house came into view, her dad cut the ignition.

"Ryder lives here?" Last she'd known, her brother had lived in the apartment over the diner. It made it easier for him to leave Theo with her parents when he worked.

He looked at her strangely. "Since the beginning of the year. Once Lynne agreed to move out here, they bought a house together."

Her brother and Lynne had done things backward. She'd gotten pregnant when they'd just started dating, and neither believed in marriage for the sake of a baby. Since she lived in Idaho Falls, two hours away, they'd continued getting to know each other long-distance, while sharing parenting duties. Fortunately, they'd gotten their happy ending.

Her dad got out of the truck. "Come on. Let's get our boy so Ryder and Lynne can get ready for the wedding."

Sun glinted off the metal flashing of the ranch-style house, and the sage-scented air brushed across her skin like a cool silk scarf. God, she'd forgotten how clean the air smelled out here.

The front door opened, and Ryder stepped out in gym shorts and a navy blue and gold Montana State University T-shirt. "Hey, Dad. Callie."

On the battered porch, her dad pulled his son in for a hug. "You don't look much like a groom."

"Give me five minutes, a toothbrush, and a monkey suit."

"That oughtta do the trick." Her dad smiled and headed into the house.

Callie walked into her brother's arms, breathing in his fresh, soapy scent. When his hold around her tightened, it hit her hard and fast how much she'd missed him. Given their eleven-month age difference, their parents had started them in school at the same time. That, plus their parents' crazy work hours, had made them close.

She pulled back to look at him, noting the fine lines around her eyes and the deep tan from working outdoors for so many years. "You done good, big brother." Clasping his hand, she gave it a squeeze.

But when she tried to release it, he held on. "Hey, you remember when you wanted to take that art class in Idaho Falls?"

An uneasy feeling shifted through her. She nodded. Why would he bring that up now?

"You didn't have any way to get there, and you were going to have to miss out on it?"

But, of course, she knew why. She knew exactly where he was going.

"We all knew what that class meant to you, some famous artist teaching it. So, Fin spent all the money he'd saved to get himself a beater truck to buy you a car."

That sweet memory bore down on her so hard it hurt to breathe. It was the kindest thing anyone had ever done for her. Fin hadn't asked if she wanted his help buying a car. He'd known she'd never take his savings. He'd just gone ahead and bought it for her. "I remember."

Her brother smiled. "Good. I know he hurt you, but I want to make sure you remember the good things he's done, too."

In his toast, Fin had mentioned Ryder cutting him out of his life. She hadn't known about that. "Is that why you forgave him?"

Her brother nodded. "He's got his faults, like all of us, but he's a good guy, Callie. Now, let's get my boy settled so I can get ready for my wedding and honeymoon."

She loved her brother so much. When he got back from his honeymoon...well, she'd be gone by then. But she'd make more of an effort to call him and get to know his family.

When she followed him inside, she took in the sparse furnishings. A simple brown couch faced a big screen television, and a plain desk took up a corner of the room. Her dad scooped Theo, clad in pajamas, off the couch and brought him over to a chair that held a pile of clothes. As her dad pulled the top over her nephew's head and replaced it with a T-shirt, the two talked quietly.

"Hey, Theo." She gave him a wave, but he just buried his face in his grandpa's neck. Her dad's big hand cupped the back of the little boy's head. "Look how much he's grown."

"You haven't seen him since Christmas."

A hot dart of remorse shot through her. Though her brother's tone held no anger or resentment, she deserved it. He'd moved into a new home, his son had grown from a toddler into a little boy...and Callie'd missed all of it.

Ryder pulled a plastic Spiderman backpack out of a closet next to the front door and handed it to her. "Here's his stuff."

"Okay." She slung the strap over her forearm. "So, you nervous? Got cold feet?"

"No, I'm looking forward to being a real family." He glanced toward their dad and Theo. "When do you go back?"

"Tomorrow morning."

Her answer seemed to disappoint him. "I just..." He rubbed his clean-shaven jaw. "I'm not sure they can handle Theo while we're away."

Handle him? "I thought his sitter was staying with him?"

"Well, yeah, but we just hired her. He's not that comfortable with her yet, so everyone's pitching in to help out. Mom and Dad try to spend as much time with him as they can, but with the summer rush at the diner and Dad's heart attack, I think it might be too much."

Fear flew in and dive-bombed her. *"Heart attack?* What are you talking about?"

He cocked his head. "Dad had a heart attack a few months ago. Didn't they tell you?"

"No, they didn't tell me." She could hardly take a breath. Her dad had had a heart attack? "What...what happened?"

"He thought it was indigestion, but Mom wasn't taking any chances, so she gave him aspirin and took him to the hospital."

"Is he all right?" *Oh, my God.*

"Sure, but, I mean, it's his *heart.*"

Callie felt like she was standing on one of those Plexiglass platforms a hundred floors above the city. Her heart pounded thickly, and fear closed like a fist around her throat.

"They hired extra help in the kitchen, and he's exercising for the first time in his life. Mom's watching him like a hawk."

"Is he going to be all right?"

"Well, a heart attack's never a good thing, but I talked to the doctor. He said the good news is that it was mild, but the bad news is that he had a heart attack. There's something wrong with his heart, and they have to monitor it."

On his knees, her dad held out a pair of flip flops for Theo. The little boy rested his hands on her dad's broad shoulders, putting first one foot in and then the other. As her dad tugged up the little boy's sagging shorts, his shaggy hair—still more pepper than salt at age forty-eight—shook in the light streaming in from the windows.

Her *dad*. She'd been such a selfish girl, hadn't she? Racing through the house to change her clothes, grab a shower, and a bite to eat. Hurrying past him as he tinkered on his snow blower, pulled weeds in the garden, or snoozed in the recliner with a book open on his flat belly. When had she offered to help? Hang out with him? He'd never complained. He'd never demanded her time or attention. He'd just given them a set list of chores each week and expected them to meet their responsibilities.

Her dad was the best man she knew.

She couldn't believe they hadn't told her about a *heart attack*. "No one told me."

He shrugged. "I guess they didn't want to worry you."

She closed her eyes, wanting to shut down all the noise in her head, but instead of blackness she got an image of her dad lying in a hospital bed hooked up to an IV. Fear jolted through her.

Her dad could've died. "I'll stay."

"What?" Ryder's attention snapped back to her.

She hardly knew her brother anymore, and she didn't know her nephew at all. No one had bothered to tell her about her dad's heart attack. She'd made a terrible mistake. One she couldn't take back. "I'll help out with Theo while you're on your honeymoon."

"Yeah? That'd be great. There's a lot of people watching him besides Mom and Dad. Lynne's parents, Fin—"

He must've caught her flinch, because his features hardened. "He's Theo's godfather, and he's great with him. He's better with Theo than anybody."

"Of course. I'm happy to help out however I can." What did she expect? Fin was inextricably linked to her life in Calamity. "How often does Fin come by?"

"Come on, Callie." His tone edged toward exasperation.

"What?"

"I'm going on a honeymoon and hoping Theo does okay with the people I'm leaving him with. I don't need to worry about you and Fin."

"No, you don't have to worry about anything. I'm totally going to help out with him while you're away. It's just better if Fin and I don't come at the same time. No one needs to be around the Fin and Callie Show, so I'll just work it out with the sitter."

"Jesus, Callie. It was six years ago. He was a high school boyfriend. Grow up."

Hot shame rose from deep within. She stood there speechless.

"And, honestly, if you're going to have issues with Fin, then forget it. If you're not all-in with Theo, then you're no help at all."

Fin had been joking when he'd offered Ryder the bunkhouse for the wedding reception. His friend didn't have much money and wouldn't accept any financial help, so Fin had suggested the Bowie man-cave, filled with every game table imaginable.

It was huge, with a massive kitchen and a custom dining table built to feed forty hands at one sitting. The era of ranching had ended with his grandfather's death since neither of his sons had an interest in cattle operations, so the place had gone unoccupied until Fin and his brothers had decided to turn it into a gigantic game room. They'd blown out walls, turning dorm-style bedrooms into master suites. The lake wasn't far, so after a swim, they'd have bonfires out back. In high school, this place had seen a ton of action.

They'd never hosted a formal event, though, Fin hired a wedding planner to transform the place. They'd wound up adding French doors off the kitchen so the guests could walk out onto the newly installed stone patio.

Now, with the reception in full swing, Fin liked the way it had all turned out. The Bells had set out a buffet on the long dining table and, outside, guests danced to a DJ's tunes. He scanned the familiar faces—just about everyone in his life that mattered was right here. Except Gray, the brother closest in age to him.

And his dad. This was the first major event without him—and the loss slashed across his heart.

Callie appeared in the doorway, sunshine glinting off her glossy, dark hair, and Fin's body snapped to attention. Flanked by her parents, they headed to the outdoor bar. In a pale pink, shimmery cocktail dress—way fancier than what any other guest wore— she looked beautiful. But she didn't look like Callie. More like the Photoshop version.

Whatever hope he'd held that they'd find their way back to each other had crashed and burned the moment she'd entered the church with her parents that morning. She'd barely spared him a glance. He'd realized his worst fear—her indifference.

"You're being creepy." Megan grabbed his hand and jerked him onto the patio. "Dance with me."

"I don't want to dance." He wanted to shove his hands in Callie's hair and mess it up. He wanted to yank that fat string of pearls and watch the little pellets roll across the gray stone.

"Trust me, it's better than trying to mind meld with your ex-girlfriend." Megan dropped his hand on her shoulder. "Have you talked to her? She's bo-ring. I had to walk away when she was telling my aunt and uncle about some artist she did her senior thesis on. Yawn. You want to get Uncle Jim and Aunt Jo's attention? Tell them how you took down an elk from five hundred yards. Tell them about the new scope you just bought. But don't tell them about the job you're getting at the Museum of Fuck My Life."

He found himself on the verge of defending Callie, until he saw the glitter of humor in Megan's eyes. "Yeah, who needs that shit?"

Right then Callie glanced over, her features going rigid at the sight of him with her old friend.

Did she actually think he and Megan were a couple? *Doesn't feel so good, does it?* But whatever satisfaction he got from the flare of jealousy quickly subsided. No matter how much she'd pissed him off, he'd never want to hurt her. He'd hired Megan to give private yoga lessons to him and his brothers. They'd bonded over the way Callie had carelessly discarded them, but it had never been more than friendship.

"I can't believe you still look at her like that."

"Don't know why. It's not like I've ever loved anyone else."

"Fin." Her exasperated tone didn't match her wistful expression. "You realize you're every woman's fantasy, right? You're as alpha as they come—and yet you're the most unabashedly romantic guy I've ever known." She cut a look over to Callie. "She's a fool. You both are."

Right then Callie braced a hand on the edge of the bar and lifted her foot. As she reached back to adjust the strap of her high-heeled sandal, the fabric of her dress clung to her round breasts and ass. When she laughed at something her dad said, he caught a glimmer of his wild thing.

Fierce regret grabbed hold of his lungs and squeezed. He'd give anything to go back and change that one stupid decision.

As tenaciously as he held onto his anger towards her for cutting him out of her life instead of talking to him, he knew it was all on him. *I did this.* And it churned through him with unrelenting force.

Laughter fading into a sweet smile, she tipped her head back to reveal the graceful column of her neck. He'd kissed that neck. Run his hands over the swell of that smooth calf and gripped the back of her thigh. He'd touched every inch of her body.

And he was done standing there making cow eyes at her.

Instead of talking to her last night, he'd spent three hours in jail waiting while his brothers bailed him out. Wedding or not, it was time for them to talk. "I gotta go." He kissed Megan's cheek and made his way across the patio.

Her dad clocked him as he approached their small group.

"Hey, Mr. Bell. Congratulations."

"Fin." Her dad gave him a warm smile and firm handshake.

"Mrs. Bell." When he leaned in to kiss her cheek, he got a whiff of a subtle, floral perfume. He smiled because, normally, she smelled like a mix of scents from the diner.

"Fin." Her mom pulled away and rubbed a hand on his biceps. "You're doing an awesome job as Best Man."

"Thank you." He reached for Callie's hand. "Dance with me."

She snatched it away. "Maybe later."

"I don't think so, wild thing. You've avoided me long enough."

"It's my brother's wedding. Whatever you have to say can wait."

"Yeah, I'm done waiting, so if you want an audience, I'll say what I have to say right here."

Her eyes narrowed. "Can we not do this in front of my parents?"

He flashed a big grin. "That's what I'm trying to say." Grabbing her wrist, he held on as she tried to pull away.

"What're you doing?"

"Dancing with you." He glanced at her parents over his shoulder. "Excuse us."

Anger flashed in Callie's eyes, making heat detonate in his core. *Yes.* She was still in there, his Callie, and he wanted to hold onto her as long as he could. He towed her toward the center of the patio.

Not releasing her wrist, he raised it to his chest, while his other arm banded around her waist. He couldn't have cared less that everyone else was line dancing.

And, man, she smelled good. Not like his wild thing, who'd always carried the scent of paint and wildflowers, but elegant. A hint of fancy perfume, expensive shampoo, and that whiff of pure Callie that always stirred him down deep.

She remained stiff in his arms. "Why are you doing this?"

"Come on, Callie. It's just a dance." He paused. "In front of everyone we've ever known."

Her lips pressed together and pink spread across her cheeks. "You suck."

Her silky hair brushed his biceps, and goosebumps sprang up along his arms. "Nah. Just trying to talk to you before you slip away again tomorrow morning."

She released a long-suffering sigh. "I'm not leaving."

He stopped swaying. "You're staying in town?"

She nodded.

Holy shit. "For how long?"

She gazed right into his eyes, and the connection zapped him so violently it nearly flipped his heart over. "I'll stay while Ryder's on his honeymoon. He said he needs help with Theo."

Two weeks. He could do a lot in two weeks. *Like fix what I broke.* "Nice of you to help your brother out." Right then, holding her in his arms, their faces close enough to see the lone pale freckle under her left eye, his body went haywire. He had her right here—her lush breasts pressed against him, those feminine hands warming his skin, and the hazel eyes he'd thought he'd get to look into every morning for the rest of his life.

But she wasn't his. And his cock didn't know what to do about it.

Not that she noticed. Her attention was on Ryder, who seemed to be sending his younger sister a warning. "What's going on with you two?"

81

"I told him I'd help out with Theo."

Fin waited, but she didn't offer more. "Okay." Still, nothing. "He'd like that."

"He does."

"Callie?" He gave her a gentle squeeze.

She blew out a very annoyed breath. "I politely suggested I'd prefer to come around when you're not there."

Fin burst out laughing. This new Callie was actually kind of adorable. Because as hard as she tried to look annoyed, her eyes gave away remorse at putting her brother in an uncomfortable situation. "I'm guessing that didn't go over well."

She looked caught between hurt and indignant. "He told me to grow up."

"Did he offer to help pull the stick out of your ass, too?"

"Would you cut it out?"

Yeah, okay. He didn't want to push her away. "I'm just giving you a hard time. You're beautiful, wild thing. And if this is the life you want, then I'm happy for you."

Her eyes turned glassy.

Oh, damn. This woman. "Is this about Ryder? You want me to talk to him?" Reddened eyes, scrunched features...it didn't look like she was going to keep it together much longer. "Hey." Reaching for her hand, he led her off the patio and around the side of the long, rectangular building. When he tried to lift her chin, she resisted. "Talk to me. What's going on?"

"I just...everything."

"Start anywhere. Just let it all out."

"My dad had a *heart attack*."

"Yeah, he did. But it was mild."

She looked devastated. In the old days, he'd have his hands on her, grounding her while she let her emotions fly.

"He could've died."

"No. It was a warning, and he listened to it. He's changed his ways. A lot. He was eating crap at the diner, working twelve-hour days. Now we've got him on a—"

Her chin snapped up. "We?"

"Yeah. I worked out a diet for him, got him doing exercise."

"He's not training for the Olympics. He doesn't need your kind of diet."

Every time his wild thing shone through, a smile flashed through his body. "You this saucy with your fiancé?"

"I don't want my dad eating five metric tons of meat a day like you guys."

"You realize I adjust our diets and schedules according to the season, right? I know nutrition. And your dad actually likes the new plan. Instead of wolfing down a plate of whatever he's cooking, he's thinking about what goes into his mouth. And he's exercising. It's all good. It turned out to be the best thing that ever happened to him."

"A heart attack?"

"A wake-up call." He guided her onto a bench he and his brothers had crudely carved out of a fallen log.

"I can't believe you know more about my dad than I do." She shot him the evil eye.

He laughed. "I know about it because I'm here, wild thing."

He could tell she wanted to be angry at him, but instead her shoulders slumped. "They should've told me."

"If you'd kept in touch with them, they would have." Wind rustled across the sage meadow, lifting the hair off her shoulder. He reached to smooth it but stopped himself. He didn't get that privilege anymore.

She looked stricken. "I know that, okay? That's why I'm staying in town this summer."

"I thought you were staying for two weeks?"

"I changed my plans."

"Just now?" He couldn't keep from smiling.

She gave a terse nod. "It'll be my last chance to spend any real time here."

"Is your boyfriend staying, too?"

She looked away. "No."

Hope kicked hard in his chest. She'd be home all summer—*hell, yeah*. But was she with Man-Bracelet or not? "You sure you want to leave a good-lookin' guy like that on his own in New York City?"

"Don't worry your pretty little head about me and Julian."

He didn't miss how she called him by his name. Not boyfriend or fiancé. He reached for her hand, thumbing the ring finger. "You accept his proposal?"

She pulled her hand away. "Why did you call him out like that? It was a crappy thing to do."

"Worse than hijacking the toasts at a rehearsal dinner to piss on your girlfriend?"

She cringed but covered it quickly. "A gentleman wouldn't have called him out on it."

"No one's ever accused me of being a gentleman. And I make no apologies for who I am."

"Believe me, I'll well aware." She got up from the bench. "I'm going back inside."

But he wasn't ready to let her go. "You forget I know you, and I'd bet the ranch you're not marrying that guy."

"It's none of your business." That sweet ass sashayed away from him.

He had a shot at bridging the gap between them and, instead of talking to her, he'd provoked her.

Part of him thought, She's not Callie anymore. *Let her go.* But he'd seen her laugh with her parents at the bar, and it had thrown him back in time to when they'd been sixteen, hanging out on her bed after school. In jean shorts and a T-shirt, her dark hair streaked with purple, she'd belted out a Kings of Leon song.

She'd murdered the lyrics, but she'd insisted she had them right. When he'd pulled them up on his phone and showed them to her, she'd gone into a fit of hysterics.

That was his wild thing. Full of life and no inhibitions. They said whatever they wanted to each other, and if either one didn't like it, they fought it out.

"Wild thing." He had to fight. *Had* to.

She stopped and turned toward him with a wary expression.

"You remember when you danced to that Limp Bizkit song in the cafeteria, and everyone went nuts? Lloyd got all worked up because you got the lyrics wrong. He told me they played the song at the prom—"

Her body went rigid. "Do you mean the prom I didn't go to because you bailed at the last minute for your brother's snowboarding competition? Yeah, I remember everything, Fin. And, sorry, but Memory Lane's just not as scenic for me as it obviously is for you. Goodnight."

5

Fin was the love of my life. We dated all through college and then for ten years after that, but he would never give me a commitment. I knew he saw other people. I was okay with that. He didn't lie to me. I told myself I wanted him to get it out of his system, so that when he was ready to settle down, he'd have no regrets. Only, when he was ready, he did it with Sandra. Not me. I came home from work one day and started to make dinner. It was our anniversary. I was making him his favorite. Homemade macaroni and cheese and cheesecake. When he walked in, he looked really happy. I'd never seen him look that happy. And I thought, This is it. He loves me. He's ready. But when he came into the kitchen his smile faded. He asked why I was making cheesecake. Didn't I get his message? No, I hadn't. I'd gone straight from work to the grocery store, and then immediately started cooking. He tried to take the spatula out of my hand and said, Don't do this. I'm moving out. He didn't apologize or anything.

He just packed a bag and left. He moved on, and I've stayed in that kitchen holding the spatula for the past seven years. #worldsworstboyfriend.

CALLIE CLOSED HER EYES, FEELING A SICK TWIST IN her gut as if the story had happened to her.

Why did these stories wreck her?

With a quick glance to her brother's house, she wondered how long she'd been sitting in her dad's truck. She'd only meant to read one or two but, once again, she'd gotten sucked into Traci's Instagram page.

The image of that woman standing in her kitchen with a spatula? *God.* Her boyfriend should've talked to her, told her he'd fallen out of love. He didn't have to string her along like that. His selfishness had slammed that woman's heart shut like a bear trap.

All right, let it go. It was Monday morning, her brother had left on his honeymoon yesterday, and she had a whole summer ahead of her to get to know her nephew. *That's what matters.*

But...that spatula. She couldn't get the image out of her head.

What symbolized her relationship with Fin?

Easy. His boarding pass. Because the whole time she'd been making plans to go to NYU with him, he'd been on another path altogether. He just hadn't told her. So, in her blissful ignorance, she'd gone ahead and rented an apartment for them, set up a joint bank account, and booked their one-way flights. She'd even printed out his boarding pass.

He hadn't taken the initiative on any of it. If she'd been paying attention, she would've noticed that important detail. She would've been prepared.

When Fin had shown up at her house that morning to tell her he wasn't going with her, her world had shut down. And like that woman with the spatula, Callie was still holding that damn boarding pass. She took it everywhere she went. She'd had it tucked in her back pocket every moment she'd been with Julian.

A chill skittered down her spine. It was why she'd chosen him. Julian had pursued her relentlessly. He could've had any other woman in the graduate program— hell, in the city. But his interest in her had never waned.

She'd dated him because he was safe. His compulsion to be with her meant he'd never bail on her.

She let out a slow breath. Julian had done the right thing breaking up with her. Yes, it left her life in utter turmoil, but she'd been with him for the wrong reasons.

More than anything, she didn't want to be that woman with the spatula. She wanted to be free.

She had to get over Fin. The betrayal.

How, though? How do you heal?

She didn't have a clue. Lifting her phone, she swiped the screen. *Just one more.*

I hate what Fin Bowie did to me. I hate that I'm such a stupid cliché. My sister, also my roommate at the time, had been acting strange. We'd always been close, so when she got distant, I didn't like it. On my lunch hour one day I decided it was time to have it out, so I drove home to talk to her. I walked in the door and saw Fin Bowie's ass as he was banging my sister on the dining room table. I haven't talked to either of them since. I hate Fin. Hate him. But my sister broke my heart. #worldsworstboyfriend.

People sucked. *Okay, enough of this.* As she got out of her car, she checked the driveway. A lone car sat under a tree. A Camry. Definitely not Fin's.

She wanted to bash her head against the steering wheel. *You did it again.* Avoiding her ex had become a kneejerk reaction. *Suck it up, Princess.* It was time to get used to being around him.

As she maneuvered across the graveled driveway in her sandals, she heard a woman's voice. By the cadence, it sounded like she was reading a story. She climbed the porch steps and peered through the screen. "Hey, guys. It's Aunt Callie."

"Come on in," the woman called.

She pushed the creaky door open and dropped her tote on the floor by the closet. She found her nephew on the couch beside the sitter, a book perched on both their thighs. "Hey, Theo."

The boy's cheeks flushed, and his gaze quickly darted away.

"Hi. Sherry, right? I'm Callie."

The older woman got off the couch and extended a hand. "Wonderful to meet you. Wow, you look so much like your brother." She cast a bright smile at Theo. "Doesn't she look just like your daddy?"

Legs jutting straight out in front of him, Theo's feet started moving like a metronome. As a kid, she'd been shy around new people, too. She'd let him get used to her. "Can I sit with you while you read?"

"Sure." Sherry plopped back down, and Theo handed over the book.

He had a sippy cup between his pale legs and a red plastic bowl of Cheerios beside him. One hand rested on his thigh, the other on the stuffed white dog beside him.

As Sherry continued with the story about a boy and his carrot, Callie took in the yellow linoleum floor and dark wood cabinets of the kitchen. A window by the desk in the living room looked out onto a small backyard with a swing set. Maybe she could take Theo outside for a bit?

When the story finished, Sherry closed the book. "Another one?"

He shook his head. Being sandwiched between two women he barely knew seemed to make him uncomfortable, so Callie shifted to the coffee table. "Have you been to Ballard's Pond?" He gave a teeny nod. "Maybe we could get some boats from Bazoo's Mercantile and float them. Would you like to do that?"

"Oh, that sounds fun," Sherry said.

"And then we could get an ice cream cone when we're done. I don't know if Bliss is still around, but I must've eaten a thousand cones from that ice cream parlor. Would you like to do that? I could totally go for a hot fudge sundae."

When Theo just hunched a shoulder, Sherry said, "His godfather's coming over, so maybe we should wait for him.

Theo loves him some Uncle Fin." The woman got up. "I think I'll get started on lunch." She flicked a finger between Callie and Theo and mouthed, *I'll give you some time alone.*

She shouldn't feel so intimidated but, really, what did she know about entertaining four-year-olds? What had she liked at that age?

Right then her mind sent up a sharp, clear image of herself as a little girl. Sitting cross-legged on the floor in the corner of someone's house, her backpack filled with art supplies—colored pencils, sketch pad, scented erasers—beside her.

She'd forgotten about that, the way she'd sit by herself and draw.

Before Ryder came along, her hippie parents had lived in their VW bus and traveled around the country. But once they had a child, they'd settled down in Calamity. Money had been scarce as they'd progressed from a food truck to a diner, so childcare had always been an issue. Sometimes she and Ryder hung out at a booth in the restaurant, the table cluttered in crayons and coloring books. More often, though, they'd be shipped to someone's house—usually someone with other children.

Callie didn't know it at the time, of course, but she'd been an introvert. She'd play for a while, but she'd always reach a point where she just needed to be alone. And she'd turned to art.

Was Theo just shy? Or was he an introvert, too? She didn't know anything about him, so she wasn't quite sure what to do to make him comfortable around her.

She pulled her phone out of her bag and typed a text to her dad.

Any tips for what I should do with Theo?

He responded right away. **I bake cookies with him. Your mom reads him stories. Fin takes him on adventures. Hang out with him until you find your way to be with him**.

She liked that a lot. *Find your way to be with him*. She thought back to her colored pencils and sketch pad and an idea struck. "Do you have any Play-Doh?"

Warily, he shook his head. "I don't think so."

"How 'bout we make some?" She got up and reached for his hand.

He didn't take it, but he did ease off the couch and follow her into the kitchen.

"If I promise to clean my mess, do you mind if I dirty up the kitchen?" she asked Sherry, who was reaching into the freezer.

"Not at all." The sitter dropped a box of chicken nuggets onto the counter. "Theo's a great helper."

Callie found the flour and oil easily enough. "Do you think they have cream of tartar?" Unless they baked, she doubted they would.

"No idea," Sherry said. "My best work comes out of a microwave."

Over the stove, Callie found a spice cabinet. She scanned the labels of the red-capped tubs. Cream of tartar. *Bingo*. Did that mean Ryder made their dad's famous biscuits? Pretty sad that she didn't know.

Callie got to work. She didn't see any food coloring, but that was all right. It might not be the prettiest playdough Theo had ever seen, but once he squeezed it between his chubby little fingers he wouldn't care about color.

Once the water boiled, she poured it into the flour mixture and stirred until it became a sticky dough. It was still hot, but she wanted to get Theo playing with it, so she kept kneading, giving her hands a break from the heat every now and then. "What do you think? Does this look fun?"

"What is it?" he said in his sweet, little boy voice.

"It's like clay. We get to make fun shapes with it. Come on, I'll show you." She brought the cutting board and warm dough out to the living room and set it on the coffee table. On her knees, she got busy pinching off small pieces—some for her and some for Theo. With the little boy watching, she rolled them into snakes, using her fingernail to make eyes on either side of the bulbous heads. Then, she started forming people. Pressing them flat on the board, she put a hat on one of them and a skirt on another.

"What do you want to make?" She wondered if the lack of direction made him uneasy. Which gave her an idea. "Do you have cookie cutters?"

"Yes." Theo shimmied off the couch, his little feet dropping to the floor, and he scampered into the kitchen. He came back with a big basket of them. She smiled, remembering that her dad baked with him.

"Oh, this'll be fun." With the heel of her hand, she pressed the dough flat and cut out shapes of gingerbread figures and pine trees. As Theo watched intently, he edged closer. And then he poked a finger in the dough. She continued cutting out shapes of leaves and flowers, but mostly she got a kick out of the way he squeezed it between his fingers.

"I like candy canes." She pulled out the shape and then slid the basket closer to him.

Tentatively, he reached inside, taking a moment to examine each one. He settled on a Halloween cat, it's back arched. Smashing the dough with his palm, he pressed the cutter down hard.

"Next time I'll bring food coloring so we can have different colors to work with. We can add red to make the stripes on the candy cane and black for the cat." She pulled out a tree-shaped cutter. "We've got a Christmas tree, so we'll make some green dough, too." She pulled out a pumpkin. "And purple for the pumpkin. Right? Pumpkins are purple?"

"Pumpkins aren't purple." When the shy little boy cracked a smile, Callie's heart swelled. And then he got on his knees on the couch so he could press down on the cookie cutter. She smiled when he stuck his tongue out of his mouth as he concentrated on peeling the shape carefully off the board.

The door creaked open, and light flooded the room. "Hey, little man."

Shock splintered her happiness. She hadn't heard an engine or his boots on the porch, so she wasn't prepared for Fin's arrival.

Theo jerked like he'd been electrocuted. "Uncle Fin." He scrambled to his feet and took off. Fin crouched, readying himself for impact, as Theo hurled himself again his godfather's body.

God, how many times had she done the same thing? So excited to see him after he'd come home from a family trip? Hell, after not seeing him for the two periods since lunch hour?

She remembered the elation at seeing her sexy, badass boyfriend, the look in his eyes that said, *Get over here and let me get my hands all over you.*

She remembered what it felt like to be wrapped in those powerful arms, the outdoors scent of him so masculine and decidedly Fin.

How many times had she burrowed into his neck and clung to him? She'd never felt more at home—more herself —than when she was with him.

With their matching grins, man and boy bumped fists. And then Fin got up, surveying the mess they'd made on the coffee table. "What'cha got there, little dude? Can I play?"

That voice she'd heard in her ear a thousand times, in the classroom, under the covers, and in the backseat of his car, made her heart flutter out of control.

She'd done an excellent job of vilifying Fin over the years. Every time he sprang to mind, she'd pull up the times he'd bailed on her because of his brothers. She'd missed both junior and senior proms because of their events.

But right then, seeing him on his knees beside Theo, as they leaned over a cutting board, rolling out dough and forming it into shapes, the crust broke, and joy came seeping up through the cracks.

Her brother was right. Fin had done more good things than bad. It was just that she'd relied on the bad ones to fan the flames of her hurt and anger. To keep her from getting near him.

Because she was still susceptible.

"Your Aunt Callie's pretty cool to make you clay."

Watching Fin be so wonderful with that little boy weakened the barrier, releasing a tidal wave of emotion. All the memories she'd stored away came crashing over her—and it hurt to know that most of them were sweet, happy...beautiful.

She'd loved Fin Bowie with all her heart, and he'd loved her, too. He'd been a good boyfriend. A really good one.

For the first time she understood it was okay to remember the good times. It was okay as long as she reminded herself she'd never again give him her heart. Her trust. Because there was one thing about him that would never change. As the youngest of four competitive brothers, as the one they'd always left behind and mercilessly teased, he'd always be chasing them.

Yes, Fin had loved her. She'd never doubted that, but he needed their respect above anything else. She'd always known that, so how was it fair to hate him for it in the end?

It was past time to forgive him. To let it go. "Tomorrow we're adding food coloring to the dough."

He twisted around to her. "Yeah? I'm definitely gonna be here for that."

Oh. Her blood turned fizzy just from a smile. That mess of thick, dark hair that always looked like he'd just pulled in on his Harley, the scruff framing a sensuous mouth, and the air of absolute confidence…yeah, no wonder she'd kept her distance. His potent masculinity hit her sweet spot.

He turned back around to the dough. "You talk to your dad this morning?"

Why would he bring up the honeymoon? It would only upset the little boy to remember his parents were out of town.

Theo nodded, looking uncertain.

"You want to see where they are right now?"

"Yes." The little boy sat back on his haunches, so much vulnerability in those big, brown eyes.

Oh. That was really sweet. And sensitive.

"You got a phone with you?" he asked Callie.

"I do." She handed it over.

"Come here, buddy." He reached out, and Theo wrapped his little arms around Fin's neck. With a hand under his bottom, Fin stood up and carried the little boy to the kitchen table. He sat down, settling Theo on his thighs. "Okay, let's pull up a map."

He swiped the screen, and a crease formed between his eyes. He shot her a look, and mortification crashed over when she remembered she'd left it open to Traci's Instagram page.

Heat flashed up her neck, burning to the tips of her ears. "Sorry." *Wait, sorry for what?* His meme had captured the attention of the entire world. "Well, it *is* a pretty big deal. Hometown boy turned international sensation."

"It's nothing." His tone shut down the conversation.

She'd never liked being shut down. "Not according to tens of thousands of women."

"You don't actually think I've dated those women, do you?"

She raised a brow, *Haven't you?* But, of course, she knew he hadn't dated *all* of them.

"I've had one girlfriend in my life. Don't believe what you read."

"Well, that's pretty much the issue right there." She thought of all the stories she'd read, and it really all boiled down to a lack of communication. "Maybe the relationship meant nothing to you, but it obviously meant something to Traci. She wouldn't have thought it was serious if you hadn't led her to believe it was."

He held her gaze. "I never dated Traci."

Theo swiveled around, angling himself so he could put both hands on Fin's jaw. "Show me Mommy and Daddy."

"Yeah, buddy. I'm on it." Fin clicked out of Instagram and opened a map application.

While it loaded, she said, "My point is that it might have been nothing more than a hookup to you, but to her it was more."

"Callie?" His tone meant business. "I never touched Traci Allen. The whole thing is bull—crap."

Theo nudged him. "Daddy."

Fin typed in directions from Calamity Falls, Wyoming to Catalina Island. "We're here." He traced the thick blue line to Los Angeles. "Yesterday your mom and dad got on an airplane and flew here. Then, they took a taxi to a town called San Pedro. From there, they took a ferry." He skimmed the distance between the coast and the island. "To here. This is called Santa Catalina Island. Do you want to see pictures of it?"

Theo shook his head, color spreading across his features.

With Theo's back to him, Fin couldn't have seen the little boy's reaction, so she had no idea how he knew to set the phone down and hug him tighter. "They're gone for fourteen days. It's been one already, so that went pretty fast, right?"

With wide eyes, Theo looked up at Fin with pure trust.

Her heart squeezed because she didn't have that kind of relationship with her nephew.

"Come here, buddy." Fin lifted the boy, turning him on his lap. Theo straddled his thighs and smashed his face into Fin's chest, holding on as tightly as if they were about to sky dive in tandem.

Fin closed his eyes, one big hand engulfing the back of Theo's head.

She knew exactly what that felt like, the comfort of being held in those big, strong arms.

And she missed it. "I'll give you two some time alone." She grabbed her phone and headed out the door.

6

FIN BREATHED IN THE SCENTS OF KID SHAMPOO AND Cheerios.

He didn't do it a lot, but every now and then Theo clung to him like a barnacle, and it shredded Fin's heart.

In his peripheral vision, he saw Callie gather her purse and car keys and move quietly across the room. The door creaked closed.

Dammit. He didn't know what had happened—or why —but for a second there her attitude had definitely warmed. He wanted more of it. He wanted her to stay.

Theo let out a deep shuddery breath, his body relaxing against Fin's, and Fin shut out everything else. "I got you, my little man. I got you."

When those little fingers gently patted Fin's shoulders, he about lost it. The boy giving *him* comfort? Yeah, this kid was something else. Sweet, smart...and full of compassion.

Bare feet padded across linoleum, and Sherry bustled

into the room with a big smile. "Okay, Theo, lunch is ready."

The boy slowly pulled back, blinking those big, baleful eyes at him.

It had to be scary to have your parents gone for two weeks. Fin would do whatever he could to make it easier on him.

Sherry headed back into the kitchen. "You staying for lunch, Fin? We've got my world-famous chicken fingers."

"Nope." Though lunch with his boy sounded a whole lot better than standing before a judge. "How about I come back later this afternoon and we do some fishing? Sound good, little man?"

"Can we get ice cream?"

"You bet." His phone buzzed in his pocket, and he pulled it out to find a text from Will.

Don't forget your court appearance.

"Yeah, yeah." He pocketed the phone. "Your uncle Will's being bossy again. I gotta go, kid."

Theo scrambled off his lap and climbed onto the chair next to him, the one with the booster seat.

"I'll be back in a few hours, yeah?"

Theo nodded.

Fin smiled and walked out the door. As he trampled down the porch steps, he shoved his sunglasses on and got a whiff of a feminine scent.

Callie leaned against the hood of her dad's truck, phone in hand.

"Everything all right?" he asked.

Looking polished and elegant, she gave him a cool

smile. "Of course. Just responding to some texts." She yanked the door open. "See you."

Her tone sprayed him like highway grit, and it made him want to dirty up her fancy shirt. *That* would wipe away that placid expression. "You in a rush to get somewhere?"

"Actually, yes, I am."

"Yeah? You got a job?"

"No."

"So then what's the rush? Gotta straighten your hair? It's looking a little..." He made a motion at the side of his head just to rile her. "Messy right here."

She drew in a breath, a clear attempt to compose herself.

But he'd gotten to her. He saw it in the clamp of her jaw. He grinned. "That oughtta eat up a whole hour. What else you got going on? Gotta polish your pearls?"

"Actually, it only takes twenty minutes to blow dry my hair, but your interest in my time management skills is noted." She flashed him a fake smile. "Well, this has been fun. I'll just be on my way now."

He was getting pretty damn sick of *Calliope*. "On your way where, exactly? I know you're not working in the diner, and the Museum of Taxidermy's not hiring right now, so what's the plan? You gonna hole up in your parent's house all summer and use your rich boyfriend's credit card to do some online shopping? Obviously, nothing for you to buy here in Wyoming."

Slamming the door so hard the truck shook, she whirled around to face him. "Do you know what I've been doing while you've been gallivanting around the globe pissing off unsuspecting women? Working my ass off. And, other than school loans, I've never taken anybody's money, you jackass. I've been working two of those menial jobs you apparently think *I* think I'm too good for, while putting myself through school."

There she is. He didn't like upsetting her, but he didn't get why she had to be all hoity-toity to be part of the New York City art world. Callie was awesome. Any museum would be lucky to get her as its curator.

"And the only thing I got from my rich boyfriend besides a place to live for the past month was his relationship to the board members at the MoCA, which I've lost now that he's broken up with me. So, if I'm a little preoccupied, it's because I just spent two years and money I don't have a hope in hell of paying back for a graduate degree that might turn out to be a gigantic waste. I have things on my mind, Fin, and they don't have anything to do with *you*."

Damn, she was hot when she got all fired up like this.

Never, not once in his life, in all his travels, among all the people he'd met, had he ever felt this kind of attraction to any other woman. Only Callie called to him at the deepest, most primal level. He wanted his hands on her warm skin, fingers scraping all that silky hair off her face. He wanted to shut that sexy mouth with a kiss he knew—he fucking *knew*—would pop her bindings and unleash the wild woman she was so damned determined to keep on lock-down.

She raised her arms in a gesture of, *What?* "Stop staring

at me like that. I'm not some stuck-up city girl who forgot her roots. I bought these clothes for the internships I did at museums and art galleries. Which I worked in addition to my jobs and schoolwork. So, stop trying to make me out to be some snob just to make yourself feel better about dumping me."

Anger whipped up so fast he found himself two inches in front of her without knowing how he got there. "I didn't dump you. I would *never* have dumped you."

"What do you call it when you show up at my house three hours before our flight to announce you're not going to New York with me? I don't know what you've been telling yourself all this time, but just so we're on the same page, it's called breaking up."

"We were supposed to stay together no matter—"

With both hands, she thumped his chest so hard he had to take a step back to brace himself. "I am *not* having this conversation. You want to know why I haven't talked to you? Because of *this*. I'm not going to listen to your twisted version of why you had to bail on me the day we were supposed to go to college together. There is no justification for that. The *only* thing on my mind right now is getting my life back on track."

"And you're doing that here? In Calamity?"

"I don't..." She growled. "You don't get it."

Of course he didn't get it. She wouldn't talk to him.

She tipped her head back and blew out a huff of frustration. "Nobody becomes a curator out of graduate school. You have to spend at least ten years as an archivist or in research, and since Julian's parents pretty much assured me I'd get the fellowship, I didn't bother applying for a job, but now I don't know where I stand with them, and my student loans became due the day I graduated a month ago, and Julian kicked me out of his apartment, which means I couldn't show up to work for either of my two jobs today." She narrowed her gaze on him. "So quit looking at me like I'm some pampered princess who can't decide whether to summer on Martha's Vineyard or the Hamptons."

"All of that sucks but, damn, I'm glad to see you. I wondered what'd happened to my wild thing."

She charged him. "*You* happened to her, you asshole. This woman with a stick up her ass is a product of you. This is what happens when you change your mind at the last minute and jump on a jet with your family instead of going with your girlfriend to college like you'd planned. Who *does* that? Only privileged assholes with billionaire fathers can take off on a private jet to Mount Everest."

Why don't you give me a chance to explain?

But she was right. He couldn't justify what he'd done. He'd known the moment he'd agreed to go on the trip that he'd messed up. Every mile that had ticked on his truck's odometer that terrible morning had tightened the chokehold around his throat. By the time he'd reached her house, his limbs had felt leaden.

And yet some instinct—survival?—had pushed him to her front door, past her confused father, and down the stairs to Callie's basement bedroom.

But he didn't want to provoke her anymore. He just wanted to talk to her. "Alaska."

"What?"

"We started in Alaska. They'd been planning the trip for months."

She looked wild-eyed. Betrayed. "Months?" She turned away from him, hands covering her mouth. "Your dad had been planning it for months, and you never bothered to tell me?"

"No. My dad and Coach planned it for Will, but they wanted me to take a gap year and go with them."

But she clearly hadn't heard. "You are unbelievable. Why would you play me like that?"

"I didn't play you. I never planned on going."

"Oh, my God, you let me go on and on about apartments and classes. I researched all the places where you could snowboard. I even talked to the president of the Ski Club, and you never had any intention of coming with me." Her eyes glistened. "Why would you do that? Why didn't you say anything? I knew you shouldn't go to New York. I wouldn't have broken up with you. I would've understood."

Fuck, he loved her honesty. That was one thing about her that hadn't changed.

She stood there in her slim black pants and those stupid fucking pearls, her heart bleeding out her eyes, and he *had* to get through to her. He had one shot to find the right words.

"I didn't tell you because I had no interest in going with them. It was Will's graduation present. Coach thought big mountain skiing would be the best training for him. They only invited me so I wouldn't go to NYU with you. But I never considered it. Not for a second. I didn't tell you because I knew you'd give my dad a piece of your mind, and I'm telling you right now it wouldn't have gone down well. My dad would not have been kind."

Underneath the crease of confusion around her eyes, he saw hurt. "What does that mean? I thought your dad liked me."

"He did, but he thought you were pushing me to go to NYU, and that it'd be the biggest mistake of my life."

He'd expected her to get right back in his face, offended at his dad's unjust assumption. Instead, she looked guilty. "I —" Her jaw snapped shut. She looked away. Guilt settled into a sad resignation. "He was right."

His protective instincts for her surged, and he shook his head. "You didn't. It was my choice."

"No." Her voice had gone flat. "Every time I brought up MSU, I was only saying it so you'd reassure me that you *weren't* going to choose it. Even though I knew how horrible it would have been for you, I still wanted you to come with me. Your dad was right."

"I *wanted* to go with you."

"No, you wanted to *be* with me. You never wanted to go to New York."

He couldn't argue. He didn't belong in a big city.

"But if you'd just told me what was going on it wouldn't have hurt so badly. I'd have been prepared for it." Her tone changed, grew more forceful. "You had a full ride from MSU for skiing. *Of course* you should have taken it. Fin, I wouldn't have broken up with you. We would've seen each other at every break."

"Yeah, I think we both know how that would've worked out. You just told me what your life's like, working two jobs, internships, and a full load of classes. You'd have built a whole other life."

"I loved you. New York might've been my dream, but you were my world."

He reached for her hand, and the thrill of touching her sent an electrical current up his arm. *It's still there. Everything between us...it's so fucking alive.* "Don't you get it? *You* were my dream. I wasn't letting go of you. Not for anything."

Hurt gripped her features, and a tear spilled onto her cheek. "But you did let me go. And so here we are."

"I didn't think you'd *break up* with me. I knew you'd be pissed. I figured you'd yell at me, maybe ignore me for a few weeks, but I never thought you'd fucking *block* me. Why would you do that? I screwed up. I know that. But I loved you. I wanted to be with you. Do you know what life is like without you? It *sucks*. We were together every day for most of our lives. You were everything to me. And then you just cut me off."

Her eyes narrowed. "But it wasn't too hard, though, right? Because, from what I've seen on social media and the news, you've been having plenty of fun over the last six years."

Not this crap again. "Are you talking about the damn meme? Traci's not my girlfriend. I haven't dated anybody since we broke up. My life's about training, planning my trips, and traveling. That's it. I haven't dated anyone."

"Here's what I know. While I was curled up in the fetal

position all alone in New York City, you were traveling the globe, hooking up with women at every stop along the way."

"Hooking up? I was with my dad, Coach, and Will. Jesus, Callie, you'd just shut me out of your life. Why would you think I was *laughing*?"

"I *saw* you. That's why I blocked you. Because your hookups tagged you in all their selfies. You want honesty? Then give it back. We have nothing to lose at this point. Just own what you did since I saw the pictures."

"You blocked me because you thought I was fucking around?" Whatever reasons he'd come up with, he'd never considered *that*. Cutting him off for something he'd never done? *Fuck that.* "You knew me, Callie. You fucking knew me. What, you thought overnight I'd just turn into a horndog? You're the only woman I've ever wanted. You knew that."

"Come *on*. You'd only ever *been* with one woman. Of course you wanted to have some fun."

How the hell had she ever gotten that impression? "You were enough, Callie. Jesus, you were enough for me. I have *never* wanted anyone else." *And I never fucking will.*

Color splashed across her cheeks, and he could tell she wavered, so right before she fell onto the side of mistrust, he got a hold of her. Cupping her cheeks, he held her gaze, letting her know with everything in him that she lived in his bones, his blood, in his heart and in his soul.

He waited for her to *get* it, that he'd never wanted anyone else. He held his breath as emotions battled across her beautiful face. *It's us, Callie. It's always been us, and it always will be.*

But, still, she stood there, lips pressed together, eyes uncertain.

She was killing him. *Trust me, goddammit.*

When her hands closed around his wrists and her features softened, his knees went weak with the flood of relief. Her lips parted, and the tip of her tongue peeked out to moisten them.

He felt that lick deep in his gut. Lust stirred, and his cock hardened.

She let out a shaky breath, eyes filled with resignation. "We blew it."

Yeah, they'd blown it, but they could recover. They *would* recover. Did she get that?

But she just lowered her hands and looked away. Opening the door, she hoisted herself onto the truck's seat. "I'll see you later, Fin."

He stood there, watching his heart take off down the driveway.

When she'd loved him, her stubbornness had been a good thing because it meant she'd never give up on him. Now, though, it meant she'd never forgive him.

He watched until the dust settled, and her truck turned onto 191.

He watched the empty driveway until his heart, covered in the sludge of loss, regret, and guilt, started beating with the rhythm of determination.

Because it wasn't over. Not by a longshot.

In fact, it was just beginning.

I'd loved Fin all my life. When he went to war, I wrote him with constant dedication, eager for him to know he was loved. I'd include a leaf from his front yard, an article cut from our hometown paper, anything to give him a piece of home. A reminder. He never wrote, and he never came back. Four years later I ran into him in Orbach's department store. Shopping with my former dear friend. They wore matching wedding bands.

Callie dropped her forehead to the steering wheel, her heart aching for a woman she'd never met. She had to stop torturing herself with these stories.

Tossing her phone into her black leather tote, she got out of her dad's truck and trudged up the walkway. When she saw the moving boxes stacked on the porch, she lost her rhythm and nearly stumbled.

He'd done it. Julian had actually kicked her out of his apartment, knowing it would leave her homeless. No matter his threat, she hadn't believed he'd actually go through with it. He'd had a week to cool down since the rehearsal dinner and realize how much he missed and loved her.

But he hadn't.

How does this make sense? He'd been the best boyfriend, always bringing her flowers, getting her orchestra seats for Broadway shows, ordering her favorite microwave popcorn in bulk so she never ran out. He checked in with her after finals and presentations to see how she'd done. He'd paid attention to everything.

She shouldered the door open, dropping her keys in the bowl and her tote onto the floor, before turning back around to haul the boxes in.

Whatever she'd done wrong, it wasn't bad enough to leave her *stranded*. He knew she had nowhere else to go in the city. He didn't care about the two jobs she'd had to quit, leaving her employers in a bind and her reputation damaged.

As she hefted a box and brought it to the dining room table, it struck her that her entire life in New York City fit into two boxes. She didn't know what that said about her, and she wasn't in the mood to contemplate it. The whole situation pissed her off.

Once she'd carried the second box inside, she grabbed a knife from the kitchen and slit it open. Was this some kind of *punishment* for having loved someone before him?

Well, screw him. He could've given her a chance to explain why she hadn't told him about Fin. But, no, Julian wanted things to be perfect. He didn't want deep or messy. He just wanted things to run smoothly.

She whipped her phone out of her purse and hit his speed dial.

He answered right away. "Calliope?"

And for the first time she could admit she hated the way he said her name. He wanted her to be a Caroline or Katherine or Elizabeth. But she was *Calliope*, and no upper crust tone could make it sound any different than what it was: a musical instrument from a Bruce Springsteen song. "I've got a question for you."

"Okay." He sounded wary.

"How did you go from loving me enough to marry me to clearing my things out of your loft?"

She could hear the rush of the city in the background. A cab honking, someone shouting. The roar of traffic. "I see the boxes arrived safely."

"You realize I have nowhere to live, right?"

"I sent them to your home."

"You know, I don't know whether this is because my family's so firmly middle class and you realized I don't fit into your world or because I didn't tell you about my high school boyfriend, but the idea that you'd dump me—leaving me homeless, jobless, my entire future upended—is disgusting." Digging into the box, she pulled out a freezer bag filled with her conditioner, shampoo, and lotion. *How very tidy of him.* "To discard someone you supposedly love...what kind of relationship is that?"

"Not a very good one. Not when only one of us is committed to making it work."

"We were *living* together. How much more committed did you need me to be?" She rubbed her forehead. "I'm sorry I didn't say yes to your proposal but come on. I just graduated. I don't have a job yet. I'm not ready to get married. You could've given me time."

"Time is exactly what I'm worried about. What happens when the pendulum swings back? When Calliope becomes Callie again or settles somewhere in between? I'm not willing to risk my heart on someone who doesn't know who she is."

"That's ridiculous. In Calamity, I was a girl. In Manhattan, I'm a woman trying to make her way in the art world."

"A woman with a past she's not acknowledging. Calliope, I saw you—"

"Stop calling me that. You can't make me into one of your prep school heiress friends. And all of this noise boils down to one thing. You think I might go back to Fin. And I'm telling you that's not going to happen."

"I saw the way you looked at him." He sounded exasperated, like reprimanding a dog that kept nosing his crotch. "The way you looked at each other. And I'm sorry, but the fact that you reinvented yourself so completely that your family and friends didn't recognize you? Well, it's a sign."

"A *sign?*" Reaching deeper into the box, she grabbed her winter boots and dumped them on the floor.

"Yes. A sign that you need to resolve your issues before you become involved in a new relationship."

"Let me see if I've got this right. You loved me enough to marry me, to spend your life with me, to raise your children and grow old with me, but not enough to learn about my past and stick by me while I work through whatever *childhood issues* I might have."

"That's not at all what this is about."

She was about to ask what it *was* about when she pulled out the pale pink cardigan with pearl buttons he'd given her a week after they'd started dating. In that moment, everything clicked. "I'm not your mother." Setting it down, she touched the bracelet he'd given her for graduation—a family heirloom. The pearls, the cardigan, the outings with his parents...slowly, but surely, he'd been incorporating her into his world. Turning her into the kind of woman he—and his parents—would be proud to introduce to their friends.

And isn't that exactly what they'd planned on doing with her this summer? They'd wanted her to quit her jobs so she could accompany them to Martha's Vineyard and the Hamptons. They were, in essence, grooming her to fit into their world.

Between school, work, and worrying about her future, marriage hadn't entered her mind. She'd just enjoyed the attention from his mom. Sophisticated, worldly, and well-respected, Jacqueline Reyes was the quintessential New York City patron of the arts.

"I'll never be her." Although, hadn't she aspired to be exactly that?

"I know that."

She thought of her hippie mom, usually harried, tendrils of her salt and pepper hair floating around her face, always warm, generous, and kind. So very different from Mrs. Reyes who never went out without perfect makeup and hair and looking anything other than polished in her designer outfits. Nobody *hung out* at the Reyes' house. No, if she had company, it was a catered event.

The woman never got her hands dirty.

"And I don't want to be."

. . .

When the door opened and her dad walked in from the garage, Callie got up.

She'd been watching him carefully, looking for signs of heart disease, but he hadn't been unusually sweaty or tired. He hadn't seemed in pain.

Frankly, he'd looked invigorated.

Thanks to Fin?

Smelling like a brewery, he walked past her to the refrigerator. Bottles clinked together as he set them on the shelf.

"Have you been drinking?"

"Nope. I've been working on your inheritance."

"You're going to drink yourself to death and leave me with a whopping insurance policy?"

"No, Callie-bell." He shut the refrigerator and arched his back, twisting from side to side. "I'm making beer. I believe you fancy folks call it *artisanal* beer."

"You're running a microbrewery in your garage?"

He grinned, and it warmed her to see him relaxed and happy. "I tried to run it in the basement, but your mom wouldn't let me. Good thing, huh?"

"I've known you my whole life, and you've never had a single hobby. This is great, Dad."

"Yep. I've got a winter brew made with rye that's dark, spicy, and crisp. And an English pale ale." He said it with a British accent. "That's full-bodied with a strong, assertive hop flavor."

She got a kick out of how much he seemed to be enjoying this. "Wow, Dad. Just...wow."

The screen door slapped closed. "Hey, sweetheart."

Her mom bustled in, arms loaded with take-away containers. "I brought some food if you're hungry."

Callie relieved her of the top two boxes. "Mom, it's almost midnight. I've eaten."

"I'll just keep it in the fridge. You can eat when you're hungry."

"Believe it or not, I've actually learned how to cook." She smiled at their confused expressions. Growing up with a chef for a father and an endless supply of diner food, she'd never bothered learning. And then, of course, she'd gotten a job waiting tables as soon as she got to New York, so she'd never gone hungry a day in her life.

"Cook what?" her mom said.

"I can make a crostini with fig jam, brie, and prosciutto."

Her dad grimaced. Her mom's brows shot up.

"Not to mention a mean blackened shrimp, avocado, and cucumber bite."

One side of her dad's mouth quirked. "Been attending cocktail parties, have we?"

Callie smiled. "Why, yes. Julian and his crowd are so very posh. I also make a cheesecake to die for." The Reyes' chef had taught her that last one. "It'll rock your world."

"Now that I'd like to try," her dad said.

"Sure, sweetheart." Her mom rubbed a slow circle over her dad's heart. "As long as you use low fat cottage cheese, gelatin, and lemon zest, we'd love to try it."

The reminder of his heart condition put a damper on her mood. "I would say that sounds disgusting, but I love my dad, so I'll do it. I've got some skills now." To a girl who'd grown up with picnics, bonfires, and cookouts, the dinner parties Julian's friends hosted had seemed strange at first. Young people wearing cocktail dresses and eating hors d'oeuvres? The people she'd grown up with hung out at bars or went hiking or waterskiing together. Only the people of Mr. Bowie's billionaire world threw dressy dinner parties.

But Julian had bought her a series of cooking lessons —*Ah*. He really had been turning her into his mom. She'd enjoyed the lessons, so she hadn't thought anything of it.

Why hadn't he just gone for someone from his own crowd? Why had he bothered with her?

Whatever. Screw Julian. She had way more important things on her mind. "So, listen, Julian's boxes came, and I guess that was my wake-up call, because I spent the whole day wracking my brain trying to come up with a plan for my summer, and I think I've got one. I will absolutely help out with whatever you need me to do here or in the diner, but I've got an idea that'll get me the fellowship."

"We're all set, sweetheart." Her mom turned on the faucet and washed her hands.

She knew that. Her parents hired high season help in January—and there was never a shortage of students looking for summer hours.

"Tell us the plan," her dad said.

"I'm curating an exhibition. Here, in Calamity."

Her mom reached for a dish towel, her lower back resting against the sink. "You want to open a museum here?"

"More like a pop-up exhibition. Just for the summer.

But I need a venue, and I thought I could use the apartment over the diner. I can't afford to pay rent, but I need to be in town, where I'll get foot traffic. The apartment's not ideal because it's small and there's a big staircase—"

Her mom shook her head, pushing off the sink and heading toward her with a gleam in her eyes. "Forget the apartment. You can use the old Town Hall."

"I have no money for rent."

"Listen to me. For two years now, they've been arguing at every town meeting about how to make use of that damn empty building. They never get anywhere because no one can agree. I finally got the bright idea to move the Farmer's Market into it during winter months. The Association pays a dollar a year for the whole bottom floor."

Hope flared. "Are you serious?" When she'd come up with the idea, she'd figured it'd be a long-shot. How could she pull off an exhibition in seven weeks? But with a venue, this could really happen. She'd keep it simple, bare bones. It was the subject matter that would draw people. She didn't need fancy displays.

"Tell me about it." Her mom seemed excited. "What do you have in mind?"

"You know how I'm obsessed with reading the comments on Fin's meme?"

Her sweet, honest parents couldn't hide the flash of pity, but they both nodded and let her continue.

"Well, it's not just me. Traci's Instagram post has over a million likes and thousands of comments. The hashtag on Twitter isn't dying down. I don't know what it is, but people *need* to tell their stories. It just seems like people who've been hurt and betrayed don't get over it. It wounds them in a way that doesn't heal."

Her parents looked at her with concern.

"But sharing their stories seems to help. Maybe it's seeing they're not alone, that there's a huge community of people who can relate." She grabbed one of her dad's beer bottles just to have something to do with her hands, because she was about to get real. "I have to face the fact that I never dealt with my breakup. I punched it down to a manageable size and then stuffed it away. And..." She glanced up at them. "I'm pretty sure it's why I chose Julian."

It was a little disconcerting to see their looks of understanding. Apparently, they'd figured it out after knowing Julian all of twenty-four hours.

Well, she'd woken up now. Maybe it was coming home and finally facing the man she'd loved with all her heart—discovering that just being near him flushed out all the fiery feelings she'd thought she'd gotten rid of—or maybe it was reading the stories and being forced to face what she'd avoided all these years. Probably a combination of a lot of things, but all she knew was she wanted to become a whole person again.

Her mom reached out and squeezed Callie's arm. "I'm glad to hear this. You have no idea."

"I think...after Fin...I lost some of my spirit." She said it quietly, worried they'd think badly of her. "And I want it back." But it didn't matter what they—or anyone—thought. What mattered was fixing the problem. "And I think, from reading those comments, that a lot of people want their spirits back. So, I'm going to make The Exhibition of Broken Hearts."

Two sets of eyebrows popped up. Her mom smiled. "I *love* it."

"Not sure how that's a museum," her dad said.

"Don't think of it like a traditional art museum. A pop-up is a temporary event. Basically, it takes over an empty store or building. My interview's not until August twenty-fifth, so that gives me seven weeks to get it up and running. If I could operate it for a full month, I'd be happy."

"Help me out here," her dad said. "What kind of artwork will you display?"

"If I can get the old Town Hall"—she shot her mom a look, *That would be amazing*—"I'll display the stories people are posting online. I'd love to do it electronically—because this is about the power of social media, right? One single text message created a massive community." Another idea hit. "It would be great to record some of them. I want these stories to surround the visitors, box them in...force them to pay attention." And right then her idea crystallized. "That's why this meme is healing people. Everyone just wants her story to be heard and acknowledged. The people who hurt them didn't care. They just did what they wanted and moved on, leaving their former lover with no way to...purge the pain." *Yes. That's exactly what I want to show.*

"What about a projector?" her mom said. "Or something that will scroll the comments. You know what I mean?"

"I love that idea, Mom. It's summer, so maybe the

high school would let me borrow some equipment. That's so good. Thank you." She popped out of her chair to give her mom a hug. "You guys are the best." Emotion rose so high it spilled over. She breathed in her mom's familiar scent—the floral shampoo she'd always used, the hints of diner food—and her heart clutched. "I've really missed you."

Her mom rubbed her back. "We've missed you, too, and we love you so much, sweetheart."

Callie couldn't remember the last time she'd relaxed around her parents. Flitting in and out of town and hiding from Fin had taken a lot of effort.

"Now, is this just so you have something to put on your resume?" her dad said. "Or are you hoping to actually draw people in?"

She pulled away from her mom. "I mean, yes, it's for my resume, but I definitely want people to see it. It matters to me. I want them to get something out of it."

"Then you might want to write something up for the local newspaper," her dad said.

"Great idea, honey," her mom said. "And if you really want them to pay attention, put in a call to action. Invite people to share their stories."

Callie thought of the spatula, and sparks went off in her chest. "I'll ask them to donate a symbol of the broken relationship. One thing that sums it up." That would be so powerful.

"I am *loving* this," her mom said.

She looked to her parents. "You really think I have something here?"

"Oh, Callie-bear, you do." Her mom looked at her with so much pride. "You really do. This is brilliant."

"You sure people are going to want to share their sad stories?" Her dad didn't look all that convinced. "I think maybe it's missing an angle. A hook."

She realized her parents didn't quite get it. They hadn't put two and two together. "This is the Exhibition of Broken Hearts, and it stems from the meme, right?" She smiled because it was just so damn perfect. "The central installation's going to be The World's Worst Boyfriend. Who just happens to live right here in Calamity Falls."

7

"THIS IS BULLSHIT." THE DAY AFTER MEETING WITH the judge, Fin climbed the steps to Town Hall. Shifting the cell phone to his other ear, he swung the door open and got hit with a blast of air conditioning.

"Yeah, it is." Wind created static, garbling Will's voice. "But Steve said the judge had his mind made up before you even walked into his courtroom. He's had it out for us for a while."

Their family lawyer hadn't been able to get Finn out of his community service sentence. *Six weeks?* All of July and the first two weeks of August threw off his training schedule for the entire summer. And for what? Some asshole had punched *him*. Fin had only defended himself.

You're twenty-three years old, Mr. Bowie. When you do you think you'll deploy something other than your body to get through life?

As he strode across the lobby, he looked for a directory. "It's eight hours a day. I don't have time for this shit."

"Steve said you shouldn't have brought up your workout routine. Apparently, the judge thinks we're full of ourselves. Whatever. We'll plan our training around the schedule they give you."

Fin found the glass-encased directory. *Town Manager 2A.* "I'm here. I gotta go."

"You coming home straight after? Brodie and I are at the lake."

"Yeah, I'll be there." Having three brothers home at the same time was rare, so it pissed him off to be stuck with community service instead of hanging out with them.

Disconnecting from the call, Fin headed up the stairs. The new building smelled like fresh paint and didn't have any of the character of the original Town Hall, housed in the historic section of town.

He walked into the office and right up to the counter. Three employees worked at their desks. "Can I help you?" a middle-aged man asked.

"Good morning, Fin." Mrs. Mallory, who used to drive the ice cream truck around town, got up, sending the guy a look that said, *I got this.* Holding out her hand for his court documents, she scanned it. Her gaze flicked up. "Six weeks?" As in, *what the hell did you do this time?* "He's expecting you. Go on in." She handed them over.

Damn, he wished he could take back that night. Should've kept riding his bike. He knew what he needed better than his brothers. "Thanks." He walked into an office crowded with papers, plaques, and files. "Mr. Solheim."

The Town Manager's chair creaked as he got up and

extended a hand. He took in Fin's athletic shorts and damp T-shirt. "Fin. Good to see you."

To keep up his training, he'd run into town, but in that moment he realized how disrespectful it looked to show up in the middle of a work-out. It wasn't Mr. Solheim's fault Fin had to be there.

He handed over the documents, and the manager took a moment to read them. Behind him, the filing cabinet held a bunch of framed family photographs, a beer stein, and a stuffed animal with a red bow around its neck, *Best Daddy* embroidered on its belly.

"All right." Mr. Solheim sat down and, with three hip-pumps, pushed his chair closer to the desk. "I'll be honest with you, there's not a whole lot for you. We're fully staffed in the high season."

Cool. The less he had to do the better. Since the hashtag continued to grow, thanks to recent coverage on network news, he and Bram had thought about making another film—maybe taking a few weeks in Alaska to get the focus back on Fin, the athlete, and off the World's Worst Boyfriend. But community service had shot that idea in the head.

"The good news..." Mr. Solheim leaned across his cluttered desk to pull a sheet of paper out of a plastic tray. "Is that we've found a use for the old Town Hall building, and I need to put someone on that."

"Doing what, exactly?"

"Basic janitorial work. You can get the building ready for use and make a punch list of electrical or plumbing problems."

Being alone in that uninhabited building meant he could run the stairs and do pull ups from the banisters. Lunch break, he could walk next door to Megan's yoga studio and take a class. Yeah, this would work. "Sounds good. Doesn't sound like it'll take six weeks, though."

"No, that'll just be the first few days. After that, you'll be helping out with the event." Mr. Solheim put on his glasses and peered at the paper. "There's some kind of exhibition going on this summer. I'll bet Callie could use a hand getting that up and running."

A hit of pleasure sped through him at the mention of her name. From the moment he'd stood before the judge and received his sentence, he'd been pissed.

But, just then, things started to look up. "Are you telling me my punishment's working with Callie Bell?"

The man nodded.

He grinned. "When do I start?"

The next morning Fin rode his BMX bike into town for his first day of community service. It gave him extra training and time alone with his thoughts.

He couldn't take the trip to Alaska, but he needed to do something to shift the attention away from the meme. Maybe put up footage of him riding his bike on the Devil's Rim? He got a lot of views from his tricks.

At least the story wasn't about him anymore—although he had no idea why his name was the stand-in for every bastard who'd ever betrayed a woman.

Dirt kicked up and brush whipped his jeans. With

every mile closer to Callie, he pedaled harder. He couldn't wait to get to her.

Racing down the winding roads of his family's ranch, he hit the back end of town. Two blocks ahead on Main Street, he could see early morning activity. Families headed for the diner, their vans loaded with camping gear. A crew of bikers gathered at the green, taking off their helmets.

A lively, old-fashioned Western town, tourists used Calamity as a base for their Teton and Yellowstone explorations. The population swelled from twenty-thousand year-rounders to over a million tourists during the summer and ski seasons.

He rode right up to the sun-splashed boardwalk in front of the old Town Hall. These historic buildings at the far end of town, built in the early nineteen-hundreds, still had the original advertisements painted on the sides, along with raised boardwalks.

With a punch from the heel of his running shoe, the kickstand hit the ground, and he swung his leg off the bike. His phone had buzzed a few times on the ride, so he pulled it out to check his messages. Aaron had left a voicemail. Without even listening, he called him back.

His manager answered on the first ring. "Fin."

"Yeah, man, what's up?"

"How important's the cover to you?"

Very "I don't know. Why?" He was nominated *this* year. He might not get it again. *Look at Traci. She might be out for good.*

"Because I've got some bad news."

Tension clutched his spine. He'd already told his

brothers he'd been nominated. He wanted to prove that he wasn't just some adrenaline-junkie show-boater. The cover mattered.

"That connection I've got in the *National Adventurer* office? He heard the editor saying they're not putting a 'social media celebrity' on their cover."

"Good." The word snapped like a twig. "Because I'm not."

"Well, unfortunately, right now you are. The Worst Boyfriend thing was bad enough, but when your arrest hit the entertainment sites, it turned the whole thing into a shitstorm. They're serious about their reputation and think putting you on the cover will dilute their brand. They only want 'extreme adventure athletes who go where no one else has gone.'"

That's what I do. A mix of anger and fear twisted in his gut. "Okay." So, a meme he had zero control over would kill his shot at the cover? *That's not right.*

He wished like hell he'd waited to tell his brothers about the nomination. Now they'd never let him hear the end of it.

World's Worst Boyfriend.

Jesus, Christ. How the hell had this happened?

Fin stepped into the shaded alley between the old Town Hall and Megan's yoga studio. "Anything we can do?"

"You can ask Traci to get on her Instagram account and correct everyone's impression of what went down on that trip. You hear from her yet?"

"Radio silence." Since her accident ten days ago, she'd been transferred to a hospital in Colorado near her family.

"Okay, so get in touch with her."

He made it sound so easy. "She's recovering from surgery. Her career could be over. I'm not bothering her with this crap."

"She started it. Why the hell did she put up that text anyway?"

"No idea." Damn, why had he gone for humor? He should've been sincere. *Worried about you. Will call when I land.* That would've gone down a hell of a lot better. "I thought I knew her sense of humor."

"How about this? I'll talk to her manager and see if he can jump on her accounts and fix it."

"Sounds good. I thought it would've died down by now."

"Yeah, but it just keeps getting bigger. Listen, if it were me, I'd have put an end to it a week ago. My best advice... call Traci. She's good people. If she knew this was happening to you, she'd shut it down. And if you don't want to call her, at least get a message to her people. She'll kill it. I know she will."

He knew her well enough to know if she was all right, she'd be talking to her concerned fans. She had to be in pain and freaking out. "Not gonna bug her about some stupid meme."

"Even if it costs you 'Adventurer of the Year?'"

The words sat like a wet blanket on his shoulders. Fin shifted, wondering how else to kill it.

"You know the endorsements you'll get from that?" Aaron asked.

A ton. And with that money he could take more trips. Even build out his family's training facility, just the way he'd like.

"You know what else I think you'll get from it?" Aaron asked.

Fin waited, a hand braced on the wall, his thumb rubbing the rough, aged wood.

"A contract."

A blast of excitement shot through him. *Braverman.*

"Braverman hasn't signed anybody new in the last two years. You make this cover, and I'd stake my career on him reaching out to you. Think about it, Fin. You'll get free rein to choose your own locations with his top crew and the force of his marketing and publicity teams. *That's* why this cover matters."

One of the first skiers to break away from the competition circuit in the 1960s, Walter Braverman had pretty much invented freeform skiing. Like Fin, restrictive rules and groomed courses bored him. He and his buddies used to film each other to critique and improve their techniques, and he eventually turned his hobby into a business. Now, he ran the biggest, most respected production company for big mountain skiing and snowboarding films. He only signed a few athletes at a time and only the very best in their field.

A contract with Braverman was the brass ring in snowboarding.

"I can't see your face, but I know what it looks like." Aaron paused. "You gonna call Traci now?"

He and his brothers didn't touch their dad's money. They benefited from it, obviously, by living on a three hundred thousand acre legacy ranch with enough staff that they didn't have to manage daily operations, but they supported themselves off the wages they earned from their livelihoods.

Fin funneled his income into his backcountry trips. His website with millions of subscribers ensured he had sponsors, but he traveled to remote locations with a crew of six. Travel, insurance, supplies... it all added up.

A contract would change his life. Money, better exposure, and the highest quality production team. It would blow his brothers' minds.

But the image of Traci in a hospital bed replaced the one of their proud expressions. "Now's not the time to talk to her. Go ahead and call her manager. In the meantime, I'll get some sick footage of me on my bike. Or maybe my brothers and I can take the heli to the Widow's Spine—"

"You're not getting it. They've already chosen you. Everything you've done the last six years got their attention. It's the *meme* that's getting in your way. Putting up film of you on your bike isn't going to change anything. You have to kill the meme."

He wanted to punch the wall. Get back on his bike and ride out the rampant frustration. *Fuck community service.* The only reason he'd report for duty was to see Callie. "Just...start with the manager. Find out how Traci is. If she's doing okay, I'll give her a call. If not..."

"If not, we'll come up with something else."

"Thanks, man." Fin disconnected and shoved the phone into his back pocket. He tipped his head back, taking in the slice of blue sky between the buildings. Who did he know who could get a message to her? They had a lot of friends in common.

No. He couldn't do it. Not when Traci was lying in a hospital bed, her career on the line.

"*Fuck.*"

"You use that mouth to kiss your two hundred and thirty thousand ex-girlfriends?" Megan smiled at him as she turned the key in the lock of her studio.

He gave her a chin nod to let her know he appreciated her support. Her humor meant she didn't buy into the meme's crap about him. As he crossed the boardwalk, music rattled the walls of the old Town Hall. *Callie.* The tide of negativity turned, and anticipation rushed in.

Pulling the door open, Fin was hit by a wall of guitars and a gravelly voice.

Van Halen. The familiarity of it shot him way the hell back in time to when she'd rock out to Sonic Youth and Guns N' Roses. Sometimes he'd watch from the basement doorway as she painted with music blasting. He panned the room, expecting to see her head-banging with an air guitar.

Rows of square columns, three deep, bisected the large, rectangular first floor. Rough wooden beams lined the low ceiling, and the stucco walls had yellowed with age. In the center of the room sat a sturdy oak table covered in brightly colored pieces of paper. Scissors, glue, double-sided tape, and stacks of clear Plexiglass frames lay scattered across it.

He noticed a tall ladder, and feminine legs encased in black leggings standing at the top. *Callie.* He headed towards it. A shower of colored paper dangling from clear fishing line hid the rest of her body. Once he'd gotten a grip on the frame, he punched the button on her laptop, killing the music. She swung around so quickly, she had to crouch and grab the ladder to keep her balance.

Her eyes went wide in fear. Until she saw him. "What're you doing here?"

"You shouldn't work alone on a ladder this size. You either need a taller one or someone to stabilize it."

"Says the man who races down the spine of a mountain on a *board.*" She nodded toward the laptop. "Turn it back on."

"Not until I get you a better ladder."

"I think I can handle it." She rolled her eyes. "What do you want, Fin?"

When he realized she had no idea he'd been assigned to her, he grinned. "I'm here to help you."

"I'm good. Thanks." She gestured to the door. *Run along.*

He pulled his phone out. "Nah, man. I got your SOS loud and clear." He hit the first song on his playlist. "I'm here to rescue you from the seventies with some Arcade Fire. For the next six weeks, I'm your court-ordered DJ."

"But what if one of your brothers calls? I think I'll stick with my laptop. It's more reliable."

He shut down the app and shoved his phone back in his pocket. "You might want to get some new material. Those lines are pretty old." Though they carried more weight than he'd admit to her.

"Fin, I don't have time to fight with you."

"Yeah? Well, luckily for me, I've got loads of time." He gave her a cheerful smile. "Specifically, eight hours a day for the next six weeks."

She stilled, eyes narrowing.

He grinned. "This is going to be fun."

"What're you're talking about?"

"Judge Pilson assigned me to you."

It took a moment, but awareness dawned. "You *just* got back from a trip, and you're in trouble already?" When the clarity struck, her eyes went wide. "Wait, he gave you community service with *me*?"

"You're the only one in town who needs my help."

Strangely, she didn't look annoyed or angry. She looked worried. "That's...not a good idea."

Because of her ex? Jealousy twisted through him. "Why, did you get back with Man-Bracelet?" Not a chance would Fin work here if that asshole planned on showing up. He'd rather sit behind a desk for eight hours a day in an airless room than watch his girlfriend with another guy.

My girlfriend? Where the hell had that come from?

"No, that's never going to happen. But you're not going to..." She let out a huff of frustration. "This is an art installation. About broken hearts." She shifted on the ladder. "It's not your thing."

You're my thing. "I'm not here to draw pictures. I'm here to help you get your museum up and running." He clapped his hands together. "Let's do this. Tell me what we're doing and when we're opening." He knew she had an interview in New York at the end of August, so that didn't give her much time to pull this place together.

"It's an *exhibition*, and I need it to open as soon as possible." She looked conflicted.

"Then you need help."

"Of course. But it can't be you."

Awareness struck like the jerk of blinds, and light flooded in. Because *he'd* broken *her* heart. And she just wasn't going to let it go. "Like I said, I'm not here to be creative. I'm here to help you get the building cleaned up and the art on the walls. Now, I can either stand here and hold the ladder or you can tell me what you're doing and let me help."

"I only have a few more to hang, so let me just finish this batch. Since you insist on hanging around, maybe you can jog in place or do some lunges or something." Hesitantly, she turned back to her project.

She attached a rope of transparent fishing line to the ceiling with a screw-in hook. An origami-style bright yellow piece of paper dangled off the other end, held onto the line with a tiny silver paperclip.

He noticed a pile of similar papers on the table, so he grabbed one.

We'd dated four and a half years, lived together for one and a half. I had an eight-year-old kid from another relationship. Fin was basically a father to my son.

Fin? A chill swept through him. He kept reading.

For my son's birthday, I took him to Harry Potter World. Fin couldn't come. He said he had work. My son and I came home from a great weekend only to find our house cleared out of Fin's things. No note, nothing. I called everyone I knew, his friends, his parents. No one took my call. Fin had just disappeared. On me. On my son. A few months later, I ran into his sister at the mall. She marched right up to me and said, My brother's an ass. You should know he met someone at work and is living with her. You should also know your son is better off without a coward like Fin for a role model.

Tossing that one aside, he picked through more papers. Each one had his name. What *the hell* did the comments from Traci's Instagram page have to do with her museum?

It's about broken hearts. It's not your thing.

He looked around the room, noticing a few items mounted in Plexiglass frames on the far wall. A shiny black high heel, a box of blueberry PopTarts, and a smashed cell phone.

What was going on? He opened his mouth to ask when he noticed a long, rectangular LED message screen. "Callie?"

"What?" She snapped right back at him.

But he didn't give two fucks about her attitude. "Hold onto the ladder."

She followed his gaze, worry tightening her features.

Which only pissed him off more. He crouched under the table and plugged in the cord.

"Wait. Fin."

He didn't want to hear anything she had to say. Red lights blinked several times before words appeared.

Thanks for a great time. ☺ Gotta jet. Talk soon.

Like a toy train circling a track, his text message scrolled continuously across the screen.

Anger fired him up like a blowtorch. He couldn't believe she'd stab him in the back like this. "Your museum's about the damn meme."

She let out a shaky breath, but any concern she might have had settled into determination. "No, it's about broken hearts. This one, the central installation...yes, it's about the meme. But it's important."

"You know what's even more important? That you don't fuck up my life."

"*I'm* not doing anything. The meme's already out there, and I had nothing to do with it. Besides, it stopped being about you a long time ago. Look, I don't know why this happened, but your text tapped into something big and important." Climbing down the ladder, her little black ballet flats clacking on the steel plates, she flipped the LCD switch off, killing the display. He noticed the tightness in her shoulders which told him, no matter how sure her tone, she had doubts. "This exhibition's going to help people heal."

"Cool. Do it. Do everything you'd planned on doing." His finger stabbed at the LED box. "Except that. You don't need the meme to talk about broken hearts."

"Yes, I do. It's a cultural phenomenon. A single text message triggered a tidal wave of reaction around the globe.

It's big, and it's important. And I'm sorry, Fin, but The World's Worst Boyfriend's going to be the central installation." That regal voice, calm, haughty, sent his pulse skyrocketing.

He held her gaze. "Find something else."

"I can't. It *is* the story. Look, I swear it's not about you anymore. I have no idea *how* it ballooned, but it's somehow giving a voice to people who've been living with a terrible pain they can't get over."

"They can pay a therapist for the same result."

"You're not getting it. Talking to their friends or sisters or therapists hasn't worked. I think this meme is working because it's helping them see that they're not alone. That—"

"That asshole boyfriends are common? Call it what you want, but this is nothing more than a mob mentality. You've got a bunch of angry people gunning for the assholes who hurt them."

"That's not what it's about at all. Read the comments. It's people sharing their stories and finding a community of support. It's *healing* them."

She obviously wasn't going to budge, and he wasn't going to argue. "You don't have my permission to use the meme."

"I don't need your permission. Look, it's gone viral for a reason, and the fact that it's still going strong tells you it's touched a nerve. That means something important, and I'm going to explore it in this exhibition. I swear, this is not about Fin Bowie."

"Every fucking comment has my name."

"But it's not *you*. Everyone knows that. It's a placeholder that stands for the source of pain."

"That's great in theory, Callie, but it's affecting me. We had to shut off comments on my website. I had to deactivate my social media accounts. I need this thing to die down, and what you're talking about—showcasing it in my hometown? You're dumping gas on a burning building."

"The building's already burning, and the whole world's watching. I'm just one person out of millions talking it about in a tiny little town in the Tetons. Nothing is going to come of my little pop-up exhibition."

As much as he wanted to throttle her, he understood her point. Her museum meant nothing in the scheme of things.

"I don't mean to upset you." Underneath her tone of conciliation, he heard a slab of resolve.

And that pissed him off. "You sure about that?"

"Oh, come on. You can't seriously think this is some kind of retribution?"

"Don't bullshit me. On some level, you know it's exactly that."

"This is what I do, Fin. I'm a modern art museum curator. It's my job to explore the cultural ethos."

Okay, he'd had enough. "You can fuck right off with your cultural ethos bullshit. I don't need this kind of crap in my hometown."

"Then guess what? If you don't like when shit blows up in your face, quit crapping on the people you're supposed to love."

"Are you talking about you or Traci right now? You've got them both so twisted up I can't tell."

"I'm not doing this to get back at you but, of course, it has something to do with you. The whole reason I'm fascinated by these stories is because of what happened to me. I don't think you understand. What you did…Fin, it was the hardest thing I've ever gone through."

"I know that." His voice bounced off the low ceiling and slammed right back into him. "You think I don't know that? But, Jesus, I was a seventeen-year-old kid. I'm a man now, and I wouldn't make that same mistake today. I'm sorry, Callie. I'm so fucking sorry, but…" How did he get through to her? "You have to let it go."

"I'm trying. Do you think I want to feel all this…this anger?" She turned away from him, and he watched her features settle into something new. It took her a moment to speak again. "It isn't anger. It hasn't been that for a long time." She sounded defeated. "It's hurt. I'm so incredibly hurt by what you did. I want to let it go. More than anything I want to…flush it all out of me. But I can't. I just can't."

Tears glistened in her eyes, and he couldn't stand it. He took a step toward her, but she held up a hand to warn him off.

"This meme…the comments…I can't explain it. I guess it helps to know it's not just me who can't let this kind of hurt go. That there are literally hundreds of thousands of people who've been damaged in the same way."

He'd *damaged* her, the woman he'd loved more than anything or anyone. He had no words, only a blistering wound of remorse. He couldn't stand the distance—the inability to make her feel better—so he reached out and touched her fingertips. This time, she didn't jerk away.

They stood so close he could feel her body heat. The pain in her eyes gave way to something else...something hopeful, and his pulse kicked up. Desire burned in his core, and he thought maybe this was the moment he could make things right between them.

Yes, he was angry with her—for not forgiving him, for using the meme for her own gain—but at the same time he just fucking yearned for her. He could see Callie peering at him through Calliope's eyes, and he needed...he needed her so much his body couldn't take it.

But when he leaned closer, catching a whiff of her sweet, feminine scent, her expression turned guarded. So, he forced himself to take a step back. She didn't want him like that.

Drawing in a breath, she reclaimed her composure. "The point is that, without an outlet, a...*resolution* for the pain, it just lives inside you." She snatched a few sheets of paper off the table and shook them at him. "These stories free people from the heartache they've been living with."

You don't need the meme. You just need to give me a chance to fix it. "I hate how I handled it, Callie. I think about it all the time. I would do anything to go back and change how I handled the situation."

"I believe you, I do. But you *can't* change what happened and putting together this exhibition might give me the closure I need." As she turned toward the table, taking in the heap of colored paper, the doubt hardened into resolve. "Look, I don't want to make things worse for you, but I have a very tight timeline here and I have to get back to work. So, if you'd like to grab that taller ladder, that'd be great. Otherwise..." Her chin lifted to the door behind him.

Was she *dismissing* him? *Oh, hell, no.* "Because the judge ordered me to, I'll help you with your museum"—he waited for her response to his word choice and got a nice hit of satisfaction when her nostrils flared and her shoulders tensed—"but you're getting rid of anything to do with me." Not waiting for her response, he swept past her to find the janitor's office.

"This *exhibition*..."

Her hard, professional tone stopped him cold.

"...is my ticket to the fellowship. And it's the popularity of the World's Worst Boyfriend that's going to get it for me. So, if you're going to have a problem with it, you might want to choose another assignment. Because this *is* going to happen."

8

"Did you see Solheim?" Brodie set the sizzling platter down on the kitchen table.

Before Fin could answer, his phone pinged. "Hang on." He pulled it out of his pocket to find a text. "It's Nolan."

Something's still off. Look at this clip and tell me what you think.

Fin wrote him right back. **You keep the log?**

No. I already eat what you tell me to. That's not the problem. Look at the footage and see what I'm doing wrong.

"What's up?" Brodie asked. "He still not doing what you told him to?"

Fin shook his head while he typed. **Next time I look at your film, it'll be after you've kept a log**. He shoved his phone back in his pocket, ignoring the three pings in a row that told him Nolan didn't like his response.

Laughing, Brodie spread his napkin across his lap. "Don't know why he doesn't just listen to you by now."

"It's off-season. He doesn't want to be bothered keeping track of what he eats and drinks." Fin speared a steak and dropped it onto his plate. It took him a second to realize the platter only had two steaks for the three of them.

Will trampled down the stairs. Once in the kitchen, his oldest brother went straight for the cabinet, pulled out a glass, and filled it with tap water. "I'm starving." With his bare foot, he dragged the chair away from the table and dropped into it. His brow furrowed when he saw the platter thick with blood and peppercorns.

But no meat.

Will glanced between his two brothers. "Where's mine?"

When they burst out laughing, Will shoved back his chair and pulled open the oven to find his dinner. Shaking his head, he brought it to the table and reached for his knife and fork.

Their dad had had a strange way of teaching his sons about the world. He'd grill four steaks for the five of them, which meant the last one to the table didn't get fed. As a little kid, Fin made sure to be first every time. He wouldn't be left out of anything. But as they got older, the boys had come up with their own solution. They'd silently cut off a third of their steak and give it to the brother who'd shown up last.

Mack Bowie had been a hard man, but his lessons had paid off. They'd made his sons tight and fiercely loyal to each other.

"I miss Dad." Fin's voice broke the silence.

"Yeah." Will sounded resigned.

Brodie stopped chewing.

Their dad had died a year ago, and they'd yet to talk about anything other than funeral arrangements, estate details, and how hard it had impacted their Uncle Lachlan, who spent way less time on the ranch these days.

Will stabbed a couple spinach leaves with his fork. "Hey, how come I have grass and he gets *that*." He pointed to Brodie's salad, which was nothing like theirs.

Guess we're still not talking about Dad. Fin had loved his father fiercely, and he missed him every single day.

He glanced at Brodie's plate, noticing the beets, pear, goat cheese and...candied pecans? "Where'd you get that?"

"Marcella made it for me." Brodie drew his plate to the edge of the table, one beefy arm curled around it to ward off Will's fork.

With his steak knife, Fin pointed to the pecans. "That's candy. And the beets and pears are nothing but sugar."

"Yeah, it has actual flavor," Brodie said. "And I like it, so fuck off."

"He's right." Will nudged his salad plate away with the back of his hand. "Mine tastes like ass."

Fin made a show of forking as many spinach leaves as he could and shoving them into his mouth. He and Marcella had come up with a simple dressing of balsamic vinegar infused with herbs, some salt, pepper, and granulated garlic. It tasted good. "This is real food." Still chewing, he pointed to Brodie's. "That's dessert."

"It's got fruit, vegetables, nuts..." Brodie said. "Everything to make this growing boy strong."

"*That* comes from a goat's tit." Will pointed to the goat cheese and shuddered.

"Besides, there's nothing wrong with a little sugar every now and then." Brodie's chair scraped back. He started toward the pantry but swung around to take his salad plate with him. Pulling a tin of butter cookies off the shelf, he brought it to the table and pried off the lid. Inside was a treasure trove of movie-size candy boxes. M&Ms, Milk Duds, licorice bites, Reese's Peanut Butter Cups and Junior Mints. Tearing open each box, he dumped a pile of crap all over his salad.

Will grinned and plucked a few pieces off.

"Mm, tasty," Brodie said around a mouthful of candy.

Still laughing, Will popped them into his mouth. Immediately, he reached for his napkin and spit it out. "How old is this shit?"

Brodie unleashed the smile he'd been fighting. "No idea. It's dad's stash." He pushed his plate away.

"Dad hid candy?" Fin set his fork down.

"He didn't need to eat like us." Will shrugged.

That was news. "He ate exactly like we do."

"Yeah, around us," Brodie said. "But he wasn't in training, so he kept little stashes around the house."

Of all of them, Fin thought he'd known their dad the best. He'd actually *talked* to him. About stuff other than travel plans and competitions. Still, it had been impossible to get into his dad's head. He'd lived by his own code.

Their dad had wanted nothing to do with a cattle

ranch, so he'd left for college at Stanford, married his college sweetheart, and started a Venture Capital career in Sonoma Valley. After his wife's second pregnancy, he came home to raise his sons in the mountains. An extremely competitive man, he'd given his boys the freedom he believed would turn them into strong, successful men. He taught lessons through actions.

"Hey, so what happened with Solheim?" Will dipped a forkful of green beans in the steak juice. "Did he give you another assignment?"

After his conversation with Callie, Fin had headed over to the Town Manager. But he hadn't even entered the building before he realized he wouldn't let an opportunity to be with her pass him by.

When would he get another chance? "I didn't bother going in. He already told me he doesn't have anything else for me."

"So, what're you going to do?" Brodie said. "She doesn't have to use the meme to pull off a museum about people who got dumped."

"There's nothing *to* do," Will said. "She's not inventing anything. She's piggy-backing on something that's already out there. And, if you ask me, she's smart to do it."

What the hell? "It'll cost me the cover."

"No, the meme did that," Will said. "She's using it to her advantage."

"I still don't want it in my hometown," Fin said.

"And how's it going to die down if she makes a museum out of it?" Brodie asked.

Will dumped a pile of baked sweet potato slices onto

his plate. "First of all, everyone in town already knows about it. And secondly, this is *Calamity*. Hanging a box of PopTarts on the wall here isn't going to have any impact on the global popularity of the meme." He grabbed a slice and shoved it in his mouth.

Brodie gave Fin a pointed look. "Why don't you make a public statement? Quit waiting for Traci to break her silence and tell your side of the story. Aaron can book you interviews."

"That's the last thing you should do." Will drank some water and wiped his mouth with his napkin. "Look, this thing stopped being about you a long time ago. You jump on social media and start waving your arms, and you'll turn the spotlight right back on you."

What Will said made sense, but it killed him to think that everyone he knew would walk through that damn museum and see him as some kind of shitty boyfriend.

But mostly what grated was having Callie behind it. Because he'd wanted to be the best damn boyfriend to her. And he'd failed. "Easy for you to say. It doesn't affect you."

"It's your *life*," Will said. "Of course it affects me."

A fierce sense of affection burst in his chest. He loved his brothers.

"Since it's not something you can control," Will said. "You should just ignore it and get on with your life. And you know the best response? Help Callie put this museum together. *That's* how much it's not about you."

"That's bullshit," Brodie said. "Get Solheim to find something else for you to do. You don't have to put up with that."

Fin balled up his napkin. *Fuck it*. He'd just tell the truth, no matter how they might take it. "I want to work with her."

His brothers stilled, shooting looks to each other that telepathed, Mayday, mayday, mayday!

Brodie sat back in his chair looking genuinely baffled. "You're not thinking of getting back together with her, are you?"

He did *not* want to have this conversation, but he wasn't going to bullshit them. "I never broke up with her." And he meant that in every way possible. He suspected his brothers knew that.

"Aw, Christ," Brodie said. "It's been six years. And she's got a new guy."

"They're not together anymore," he said.

"Is she still going back to New York?" Will asked quietly.

"Of course. Let's just drop it, okay? I don't want to talk about it." He sank his fork tines into a couple of green beans, but he'd lost his appetite.

"You know we're just worried about you, right?" Will said. "Look, I was there. I saw how hard that breakup was on you. Those first few months...I'd never seen you like that. You were always the happiest out of all of us, and then...she broke you."

Fin shot him a look. "*I* broke us. I did it."

His brothers went wide-eyed. He knew as much as they wanted to help him, relationships were completely outside their wheelhouse.

Which is why their advice doesn't matter.

Will cleared his throat. "Yeah, okay, so there you go. You've carried the guilt for a long time." His effort to get therapeutic with him would've been comical if Fin didn't know where his brother was trying to lead him. "And hanging out with her now...it's good. You're making things right. That's a good thing. But maybe it's not about getting back together." He looked to Brodie for help, but when he offered nothing, Will exhaled. "I mean, is Callie even thinking along those lines?"

Jesus, they didn't get it at all. His heart didn't stop beating for her just because she might not be *thinking along those lines*.

"You remember what Dad used to say?" Brodie perked up, like he'd come up with the perfect words to get through to him. "He told us our twenties were for screwing around, getting shit out of our systems. Remember?"

Of course he remembered. He remembered every line his family had ever pulled to trivialize his feelings for his girl.

"He didn't want us to hit forty and go, *This is it? This is all I've got to look forward to the rest of my life?*" Brodie seemed satisfied, like he'd really nailed it.

And, surprisingly, he had. Fin tossed his napkin on the table. "Good talk, man. That really drives it home." It did. It took all his anxiety and forged it into resolve. "Because nothing would make me happier than being with Callie every day for the rest of my life."

His brothers looked like he'd just announced his decision to try out for the American ballet.

"Okay, hang on," Brodie said. "I think you're getting confused. Callie's a great girl. You like her. We all like her. But this is just about fixing the shit you broke. It doesn't have to be anything more than that."

"I want it to be more than that."

"But does she?" Will asked. "And unless you plan on moving to New York, I'm not sure what kind of future you have with her."

"You can point out all the obstacles, but it won't change anything. My feelings for her won't change."

"Wait, wait." Brodie was all revved up now. "You've just got to look at it in a different way. Think about it like this. You got all these feelings, right?" He pushed his plate away. "All you have to do is turn them off. Imagine a light switch or...or an ignition. You get these feelings, and you turn them off. It's not gonna work out with Callie. Not now, not ever. So..." He made a sharp flicking motion with his hand. "Turn it off.

"You guys are clueless." Fin pushed his chair back. "You actually think you can decide whether or not you fall in love with someone. Well, I've got news for you. It doesn't work like that." He got up. "You think you can choose the timing or whether or not someone's your type, but I promise you this, the moment you meet *her*, it's going to slam you so hard you're not going to know what hit you." He'd laugh his ass off if it ever happened to them. "You think you can walk away, that one girl is just like another, but you're dead wrong. Because that girl—*your* girl?" He shifted his gaze from Will to Brodie. "You're hardwired for her. *I'm* hardwired for Callie, and there's not a damn thing I can do about it."

He strode out of the room, knowing exactly where he needed to be.

———

Her parents came in from the garage, reeking of hops.

"Look, you guys." Callie pushed back from her laptop to show them the screen.

"Hang on." Her dad headed into the kitchen. "Let me wash up."

Her mom leaned in, gathering Callie's hair into a ponytail. "Oh. It's published already?"

Callie couldn't believe it, either. The day after her dad had suggested it, she'd sent her piece about the Exhibition of Broken Hearts to media outlets in Wyoming, Idaho, and Montana. In it, she'd included a call to action, requesting one hundred-word story submissions, along with a donation that symbolized the broken relationship.

Tonight, she'd gotten an email from the *Idaho Statesman* with a link, letting her know it had been published. She'd come up with the idea for the exhibition a week ago, and it already had traction.

Her mom pressed her cheek against Callie's, her long, wavy hair smelling like beer mixed with her herbal shampoo. "I'm so proud of you."

Her dad came out of the kitchen, his hands wrapped up in a dish towel. "What'cha got, pumpkin?" But a knock had him bypassing her to answer the door.

"Who'd come by this late?" her mom asked.

Anticipation buzzed Callie's nerves. Everyone knew her parents ran the diner and came home absolutely destroyed with exhaustion, so it seemed most likely that someone had come to see *her*. And there was only *one* someone who'd do that. Especially after the way they'd left things at the old Town Hall that morning.

Low male voices reached from the foyer, and electricity spiked through her body. *Fin.* She'd recognize his deep, rumbly voice anywhere.

If he came in, he'd see her supplies all over the kitchen table. The index cards, Plexiglass frames and label covers, rolls of fishing line, glue, and the staple gun. Guilt got a good, solid grip on her and squeezed. "Mom, do you think what I'm doing is unfair to Fin?"

Her mom dropped into the adjacent chair and picked up a length of nylon, wrapping it around her index finger. "Did you know Bazoo's is selling World's Worst Boyfriend T-shirts and mugs?"

Callie shook her head. She'd hardly left her building.

"Adam's Ale is, too. And Bliss has an ice cream called hashtagWorldsWorstBoyfriend. The ingredients are cacao nibs, sour gummy worms, and 'heartbreak,' so, no, I don't think what you're doing is unfair." She dropped the fishing line and reached for Callie's hand. "Everyone's trying to make money off the fact that the World's Worst Boyfriend lives here. You're actually doing it to help people."

"I'm doing it to get a job."

"Okay, but underneath that, this exhibition is a way for

you to heal along with everyone else. Isn't that what you said?"

"Yes, absolutely. And, Mom, all I did was mention it to a few people who stopped by to see what I was doing with the old building, and already donations have started coming in." *This is going to be big.* She just knew it.

"Wait here." By her dad's tone she could tell he was already on the move. "I'll see if Callie wants to talk to you."

Warmth spread through her. She loved that her dad always looked out for her. Closing her laptop, she pushed back from the kitchen table. When her dad appeared in the doorway with a question in his eyes, she nodded. "I'll be right back."

Callie hurried across the living room, and the sight of Fin Bowie standing in her foyer hit like opening the door to a surprise party. That disheveled hair and facial scruff, his big, muscular body and moody expression...it just made her heart flip over.

His black leather jacket hung open, exposing a white V-neck T-shirt. Faded jeans encased powerful thighs, the frayed hem bunching over black leather boots.

"Hey." Did she have to sound so out of breath? Her heart pounded like she'd just been chased through the woods at night by a bear.

And it didn't help that his gaze took a slow roll up her body, from her red-painted toenails to her bare legs—her upper thighs covered in ruffled cotton sleep shorts—to the pink long-sleeved T-shirt covering her chest. When he finally reached her eyes, his nostrils flared, and his expression turned carnal. A zing of awareness shot through her.

And then he smiled. And when Fin Bowie smiled it was like the finale of a fireworks display. "What's up?" She hated the slight tremor in her voice. Worse, she hated the fuse he lit inside her.

"Let's take a ride."

The girl she'd once been would've raced right out the door, bare feet and all. Which is why the woman she'd become knew not to go anywhere with him. "It's late, and I have to get up early. I have a lot to do in very little time."

"We're going to be working together for the next six weeks, so we should probably clear some things up. Why don't you put on some clothes and meet me in the truck?"

See, the problem was that she *wanted* to spend time with him. It took all she had not to hurl herself down to the basement, grab a sweatshirt, jam her feet into sneakers, and fly out the door. Fortunately, she had one last ounce of restraint left in her. "We can just talk on the porch." She gestured for him to turn back around and lead the way out the door.

But he didn't budge. "I want us alone. Just you and me."

Her parents murmured in the kitchen. *Right.* "Fine. Give me a second." She made it sound like she was so put-out, but she found herself hustling to her room, yanking a pair of jeans out of her suitcase, pulling a fleece jacket she hadn't worn since high school off the hanging rack, and shoving her feet into an old pair of white Vans.

As she headed back up the basement stairs, heart fluttering in her throat, she called to her parents. "Be back soon."

"You're twenty-three," her dad called. "You don't have to check in."

Her mom laughed quietly.

Hearing them *chuckle* slowed her down. She'd just told herself not to be that reckless teenager, and here she was flying out the door to be with him. Breathless, heart racing, willing to drop anything. *Forget* everything.

She tried to reclaim her composure, but she simply couldn't do it and, as she headed to the door, the bridge of time collapsed, plunging her into freefall.

Images flew at her, immersing her in a tumult of sharp, vivid emotions.

The thrill of Fin unhinging the basement door she'd locked after he'd told her he couldn't go to their junior prom because of his brother's skiing competition. So much anger—no, *outrage*—expressed in a furious fight that had ended in desperate, raw sex.

The naughty pleasure of riding him in his truck, her fingers clutching the back of his seat, her hips slamming down and grinding. That wild imperative to get closer, deeper, to *meld* with him.

The boundless joy as they'd leapt off the cliff together, hands joined, her smile stretching so wide it hurt. Plummeting into ice cold water. And the indescribable happiness when they'd popped up and reached for each other—her legs wrapped around his waist, his arms cinching her tightly. She'd never felt anything like it since.

And the pure relief of slamming into the wall of Fin's chest in the hallway after she'd found out Piglet, her little runt of a mutt, had been struck and killed by a minivan. The deep satisfaction, when she'd collapsed into his arms, of knowing her soul had a harbor, and it was Fin Bowie.

He'd been there for her more times than not, but the times he'd let her down stuck in her joints like burrs, reminding her with sharp twinges every time she so much as rolled over in bed.

Blocking out the good memories had been easy...until she'd come home. Here, they were everywhere. She breathed them in at night in her childhood bed, and she ate them for breakfast at the kitchen table.

Fortunately, when she closed the front door behind her, the cool mountain air rushed over her skin and snapped her back to the moment. The hints of sage from the surrounding meadow and smoke from the town's nightly bonfire woke up her senses.

It was okay to remember. Important, actually, because she'd never resolved anything. She'd just thrown herself into work, gone into survival mode. Finals, projects, hurrying to the diner, the bar, racing to get errands done in stolen moments.

She never would've stopped, would she? If Julian hadn't dumped her, forcing her to live at home for the summer, she'd still be running from her past.

So, sure, she'd take this ride with Fin, confront the memories, and then she could finally let them go. Let *him* go.

She'd finally be free.

Country music floated out of Fin's idling truck. From the driver's seat, he watched her come down the stairs. She had to smile because Julian always held doors open for her, always had a hand at her lower back to guide her into a room or a waiting car. Even though it made her bristle, she'd allowed it because she'd figured it was his way of showing he cared. In reality, though, it just felt condescending. And, frankly, he'd been trained to do it. He didn't do it because he thought she might topple over or wander off without his guidance.

When Fin leaned over to push open her door, the interior light lent a golden glow to his skin. His scruff accentuated his sexy lips. She grabbed the handle and hoisted herself inside. Just his nearness sent a spray of goosebumps popping out across her arms.

After buckling herself in, she drew her fleece tighter around her. Fin immediately shrugged off his jacket and held it open for her.

"That's okay." She wasn't cold, but she wasn't about to explain her body's reaction to him. "Maybe just turn on the heat."

"It's July, wild thing. Not turning on the heat." He shook his jacket. "Here."

She had enough issues to fight him about; putting on his jacket wasn't one of them. But, damn, did being in this truck with him bring back dangerous memories. How many times had they pulled off the road in the middle of the night, both of them scrambling over the seat to topple into the back, tearing off clothes, reaching for warm, naked skin...

She closed her eyes against the onslaught of sensation. *Stop it.*

Just... stop.

Once Fin hit the unlit highway, they drove in a silence gripped with tension. She toyed with the zipper on his jacket, waiting for him to start talking.

But he didn't say anything, and she wanted to get the conversation over with. "So, what's up?"

His fingers flexed on the steering wheel.

Okay, fine. I'll just say it. "I'm not changing my exhibition."

His attention fixed on the road, he gave no reaction.

The Bowies always got their way. Not just because of their money or their intimidating physiques, but because they believed—*staunchly*—that they were right. They had obscene amounts of confidence, thanks to a lifetime of mastering their bodies in the most dangerous situations.

But this time, *this* Bowie, wouldn't win. "It's a really good project, Fin, and it's the only thing that'll get me the fellowship."

Headlights from a car in the opposing lane flashed inside the cab, lighting up his intense expression. If he wanted to fight her on this, he could just save his breath.

"Look, I'm in Calamity for the summer, and I need to do something important. And this project...did you read the article on the World's Worst Boyfriend in the *Huffington Post*? This horse is so far out of the barn, there's—"

"Do you love him?"

He might as well have tossed a hot cup of coffee at her. "What?"

"Man-Bracelet? You love him?"

That's what he wants to talk about? "I'm not talking to you about Julian."

"A man doesn't propose if he isn't damn sure he's gonna get a yes."

"We already figured out he felt threatened by you."

"I'm talking about *you*. Do you love him?"

Abruptly, the truck turned off the highway and onto a rutted dirt road that cut through a sage-covered meadow. "*Fin*. I'm not going to Boner's Ledge."

He accelerated, making the road bumpier. "Not going there to bone." He had to shout over the roar of the engine and creaking axles. "Answer the question."

Clots of dirt and pebbles pinged against the metal.

God, he was exasperating. "No, okay? I don't." She didn't want to talk about it, mostly because she didn't understand how she could have missed something so elemental. Julian had been driving them toward marriage, while she'd been focused solely on gaining traction in the workforce.

From the start, they'd never been on the same page.

"But you lived with him."

"Yes, because..." The more he probed, the sicker she felt, because how obvious had it been? Julian had pursued her for two years. He'd incorporated her into his life, his family. When he'd asked her to move in, he hadn't said, *Crash with me.*

Move in with me. He'd said it with that gentle, confident smile. He'd been steering the relationship all along, and she hadn't noticed.

Yeah, because she'd been busy. She had major issues on her mind. Marriage? *You've got to be kidding me.* "My roommate took a job out of state, and I couldn't afford the rent on my own." It sounded like she'd used Julian, but that hadn't been her intention. "Between finals and graduation, not having a full-time job—and then losing my roommate..." She'd been focused on herself. "I jumped when he offered to let me move in." She had to own her self-involvement. "I got a break from paying rent, an opportunity to hang around the movers and shakers in the art world and...I took it."

But she'd never meant to hurt Julian. She certainly hadn't meant to take advantage of his feelings for her. "From my perspective, I was moving in with him until I found a new roommate."

"And from his perspective he was heading toward marriage?"

"I guess."

When the truck hit the incline at the base of the mountain, Fin shifted gears and floored it. She braced a hand on the dashboard.

"You *guess*?"

"I'm sorry, when exactly did you get your law degree, counselor?" Why did he care about any of this? "What's with the questions?"

"Jesus, Callie. You got close enough to someone to *marry* him."

"It's been six years. What did you think would happen?"

"I thought you'd come back." His impassioned voice filled the cab with furious energy.

The words hit her skin like sparks from a bonfire. Panic had her batting them away, because she didn't know what to do with them. On the one hand it was unbearably sweet and touched her in a way that made her want to weep. But on the other hand...

He pulled off the road onto Boner's Ledge and jerked the truck into Park. When he cut the engine, the sudden silence buzzed in her ears. He didn't wait for her to get out of the truck, just swung around the front and struck off.

I thought you'd come back.

On the other hand...he could go to hell. She shouldered the door open and followed him to the edge of the cliff that offered a panoramic view of the valley. Pockets of light revealed the scattered towns, the largest clusters from Jackson and Calamity. "Come back to what exactly? More chances for you to blow off *my* plans so you could travel with your brothers? No, thank you. I get that the *prom* hardly compared to big, important Bowie events, but it mattered to me."

"I know it mattered. Of course it did."

"No, Fin. It didn't. I don't care what you say, your actions told the truth. You bailed on me."

"I'd planned on going to the prom. I'd rented a tux. But Coach couldn't be two places at once, and Will needed my help at that last competition of the season. Those points put him at the top spot."

"Do you even get that you just proved my point? Will's competition was more important than our senior prom."

She waited for it to sink in. And when he winced, she knew it had.

"I know you loved me. And you were a good boyfriend in many ways, but how many times did you drop me to go running when your brothers called? I'm done with that, Fin."

"I was seventeen. You can't hold those choices against me now. You think I haven't learned my lesson? Trust me, I fucking learned."

The truth welled up so hard and fast it spilled over before she had a chance to check it. "You *can't* learn. It's not even your fault. It's just too ingrained in you to keep up with them. Fin, you slept on the trail when they started rappelling out Will's window to avoid you."

"I was a little kid."

"That's what I'm saying. *That's* how ingrained in you it is. What you want more than anything is your brothers' respect." She got right up in his face. "More than you want me."

"That's not...true." His voice broke on the last word, and he twisted away from her, staring out at the valley. "*Dammit.*"

"I'm not blaming you. I'm not even angry, because I understand. I really do. But the thing is, I'm not some high school girl hoping like hell her boyfriend doesn't blow off prom. I've got a real life now. I'm starting a career. I won't ever go back to the days when your plans trump mine. Do you understand that?"

He scraped a hand through his hair. "Yeah. Sure." He

drew in a deep breath. "I just...I never thought you'd move on. I didn't think it was possible."

"You thought I was pitching a six-year tantrum?"

He smiled, but it held a note of embarrassment. "I guess so." But the smile fell away. "I mean, no. I knew you were living your dream." He toed a pine cone closer and then kicked it off the ledge. "I just thought you'd come home afterwards."

His guarded expression made her heart ache. God, what a complicated mess. Part of her wanted to hate him, part of her recognized the man he'd become, and another bigger, messier, and stickier part still loved him.

How could she not? He was handsome, sexy, smart... loyal, brave...he was everything a man should be. He just... he couldn't be completely hers.

Gazing out across the valley, he let out a bitter laugh. "I don't get how you can *move in* with some other guy. How you can settle for anything less than what we had."

That snapped her out of it. "Because I don't want what we had. I never want that kind of crazy relationship ever again. I want..."

"Yeah, I know. You want Man-Bracelet."

"That's not what I was going to say. Just give me a minute to get my thoughts together."

"No." He whipped around. "I don't want to talk to Calliope right now. The woman who has to think about her words before she says them. I don't want you to 'process' your feelings. I want you to let them rip. Remember, Callie? How you'd figure out your shit just from ranting at me? So rant. Just be fucking real."

"This *is* me being real, but you don't want to accept it. You want me to be wild and fun and free, but I'm not those things anymore. I'm twenty-three, and I have bills to pay and a career to build. I have grown-up problems, and I don't want to have a relationship where all we do is fight and—"

"Fuck."

A rumble of desire churned in her core. *Unwelcome* desire. "Make up. I don't want that kind of..."

"Passion?"

"If that's your definition of passion, then no, I don't want it. Look, we're built differently. I know I was pretty wild around you, but that's not my real nature. I'm a quiet person. But you just...bamboozled me. It's what you do. You make everyone feel like the most special person in the world."

"If you felt like the most special woman in the world, it's because you *are*. You're my heart, Callie. And I can promise you this, I've never had this kind of 'passion' with any other woman because I've never felt for anyone the way I felt for you. *You* were the center of my universe."

"You don't get it. You never will, so let's stop talking about it." She rubbed her arms, even though she wore fleece under his leather jacket. "We should get going."

She started for the truck, but she didn't get more than a few feet when he stalked towards her. "You were your *best* self around me. You let down your guard and got to be everything you truly are. You know how I know? Because it's when you don't feel safe that you're quiet. And that passion you don't want? That's who you are. And just because you decided to shut it off doesn't mean it's gone."

"What we had isn't…" How did she explain? "It isn't a mature love."

"You mean it isn't safe."

"You make it sound like that's a bad thing. I could count on Julian. You don't know how much I appreciated that."

"Yeah, I see that. He's a real dependable guy."

He got her there. "Well, I thought I could."

"Guess what, Callie? Love isn't safe. It's messed up and crazy, and it hurts like hell. But why would you want anything less than what we had? Jesus, what we had—it was more than love. It was…*Goddammit.* Why do I have to explain this to you? I'm empty without you, and no other woman, no friend or brother—*no one* can take your place. You're part of me. And I'm sorry, but I'm not buying that you've moved on. We screwed up, and we got lost, but I will be damned if I accept that you'd rather have some boring, bland relationship than me." He reached for her, pulling her hard against him, gaze focused on her mouth.

Slowly, he leaned in, overwhelming her with his masculine scent. He pressed a soft, gentle kiss that sent an alarming rush of desire through her body. A lick of his tongue across her lips had her mouth opening to him, welcoming him, and then it happened.

Fin kissed her. Kissed her the way he always had—hungry, desperate, a barely contained expression of carnal need.

He kept his hands to himself, their mouths the only point of connection. His kiss tasted sweet like love, hot like passion, like everything beautiful in the world grew out of *this*, the tender intimacy of two souls finally, finally rejoining.

The moment she reached for him, restless for the press of his hard body against hers, he tore his mouth away. "You wanna settle for less than *that*?"

9

THE ALARM WENT OFF, NEARLY GIVING FIN A HEART attack. He'd barely slept last night. Every time he'd start to drift off, he'd remember her mouth, the luscious stroke of her tongue, leaving his body vibrating.

Swiping the screen to silence his phone, he rolled out of bed. In the darkness, he made his way to the bathroom, tripping over his running shoe. *Dammit.*

He needed to train today, not help Callie put his meme on display for the entire town to see. The town that already saw him as a hellion. The punk son of a billionaire. He grabbed his shorts, jammed his feet into his running shoes, and headed downstairs.

Both his brothers stood by the front door, illuminated by the single lamp on the table in the foyer. "What're you guys doing up so early?"

Will shrugged. "I like training with you. Keeps me on track."

Pride punched him hard, and he bit back a smile. "Cool. Let's do this."

Brodie opened the door to darkness, and the three of them crossed the wide porch and trampled down the steps. Fin took the lead. It never got old knowing his brother—a freeskiing champion—needed his help.

Too bad Gray's not here. He'd been on his way home for Ryder's wedding when a tsunami hit off the coast of Japan. He and his posse had changed their travel plans to catch the swells in Hawaii. Hopefully, he'd be home before Brodie left so all four brothers could be together.

"Where'd you go last night?" Brodie said.

He didn't want to talk about it. They'd never understand.

"You good?" Will asked. "With letting Callie go ahead with her museum?"

"Like you said, the more noise I make, the more attention I draw to myself."

"Right. Cool." Will picked up the pace as they rounded the bend in the driveway.

As soon as the meme faded away, the magazine might reconsider him for the cover. Just thinking about it stirred up hope. He wished he didn't care that much.

At the end of the driveway, his brothers pulled back. "What's up?" Since their ranch backed onto National Forest, turning three hundred thousand acres into an endless playground for them, they usually worked out on the property. "There's a trail behind the elk preserve that has great rises. I've been using it for interval training."

Dawn broke over the horizon, sending a wash of pale

yellow light across the land and highlighting a huge tri-fold poster board set up on two metal folding chairs beside the mailbox.

Crudely drawn arrows pointed toward their property, as if it were a stop on the map of celebrities' homes. An enlarged photograph of Fin shirtless, wearing sunglasses and a cocky smile, took up the center board. Images of women ugly-crying were glued all around him. In bold, black Sharpie someone had written: *Stop here to see the World's Worst Boyfriend!*

His brothers' laughter filled the early morning quiet.

A shock of hurt nearly took out his knees. "Fuckers." He gave Brodie—the nearest asshole—a shove. But another glance at the sign had him cracking a smile. So, they wanted to play? *It's on.* "Mount Motherfucker it is." He took off in the opposite direction, toward the trail that shot up the mountain at a sixty-degree angle.

"Hey," Will called. "You said we were doing interval training."

The five-year age difference meant Fin could kick his brother's ass with stamina and endurance. He looked forward to watching Brodie, who didn't work out nearly as much as the others thanks to a desk job in Utah, puke at the summit.

"Dammit, Fin," Brodie shouted.

Fin sprinted ahead, Callie's comment running on a continuous loop in his mind.

What you want more than anything is your brothers' respect. More than you want me

Whatever. He couldn't control Callie's feelings. He

couldn't get his asshole brothers to see him as anything more than an adrenaline-junkie with a death wish.

The only thing he could control was his own damn life. When he got to town, he'd talk to some of Traci's friends. Get someone to jump on social media and explain they'd never dated. Then, he'd get Brodie to film him training—maybe doing flips on the trampoline. It was bullshit, but if it got the focus off the meme and back on his athleticism, he'd do that crap all day long.

Fin showed up to work sweating. Already an hour late, he didn't want to stop for a shower at Megan's yoga studio. He'd check in with Callie first, see what she needed.

He opened the door to a hive of activity. Damn, she worked fast. Had she only started this project a little over a week ago? Displays filled two of the walls and hung from the ceiling in an explosion of color. A kid crouched under the library table in the center of the room with a multiple-outlet surge protector.

Callie stood at the far wall, talking with a grizzled older man. When she glanced towards the door, her gaze snagged on Fin. Taking in his soaked T-shirt and athletic shorts, her good mood faltered.

As he approached them, Fin recognized their high school's A/V teacher. "Mr. Martin."

"Fin Bowie." He grasped his hand and gave a hearty shake. "I thought I told you to keep out of trouble."

"I'm trying, sir."

"Not nearly hard enough, apparently." His white teeth peeked out of a thick, heavy beard.

"Mr. Martin's helping me with the electronics." She gestured to the boy under the table. "And his summer school students, too."

"Nice." The cool air rapidly dried his skin. He needed water. "Let me grab some water, and you can put me to work."

As he walked away, he heard Mr. Martin say, "I think we're all set. We'll be back tomorrow with the supplies, and we'll get things up and running."

Fin hit the drinking fountain against the far wall and sucked in the ice cold water.

A clatter of rubber soles on the wood floor accompanied Callie as she walked the teacher and his students to the door. "Thank you so much." She gave the old man a hug. "You've just made my exhibition a lot more interesting."

"Happy to help out" The older man gave Fin a wave before heading out with his students.

Once they were alone, Fin scanned the large room. "What can I do?"

She watched him for a moment, obviously disappointed.

"Sorry I'm late. When I got home after my run, I found a house full of contractors and architectural plans. Did I tell you about Brodie's idea to turn the ghost town into a tourist attraction? It's actually pretty good. He's going to make it a living history museum." She'd like that. "He's going to restore the buildings and turn them into a working saloon, hotel, and mercantile. It'll be cool. The workers will dress in costume, and we'll have shoot-outs scheduled every couple of hours. It'll bring a bunch of jobs to town."

She held up her hand. "I don't want to hear about your brother's plans. You're on my time right now, okay?" Her look said, *Don't you get it*? "It's not about taking a picture so I can show the board members I created an exhibition. It has to be successful. It has to draw visitors. And if I have to expend a single ounce of energy wondering if you're going to show up, then just go and choose another project to meet your court-ordered hours."

Clarity struck him right in the solar plexus.

All these years, they'd been talking at each other. In his mind and heart, he knew he loved Callie. He'd taken for granted she'd be in his life forever. So, when she complained about him putting his brothers first, he thought he'd hurt her feelings. That she thought she was in some kind of competition with them.

But Callie was independent. If she wasn't working at the diner, she was studying or doing her art. She hadn't needed him to check in with her all the time. She was good on her own. No, the real issue was that he showed up late to everything. His whole family did. Because their competitions came first. Before classes, proms, anniversaries—anything.

He hadn't seen it until this moment. Callie owned his heart, plain and simple. But she didn't own his time. His family did. They lived by their own code, their own rules, and those came before anything or anyone outside of them. Raised without a mother, by two staunchly independent—

and some would say eccentric—men, they were mountain men through and through.

Callie'd never had a problem with his loyalty to his brothers. She'd had a problem with his *dependability*. If he said he'd go to the prom with her, he needed to go to the damn prom. Period.

For the first time, he got it. "I won't be late again."

He watched her anger melt into confusion. One beat, two, and then she said, "Thank you." Though, she still sounded skeptical.

"You've got me for six weeks, minus a day. Clock's ticking, wild thing. Tell me your plans and let me know how I can help."

She looked down at her shiny black flats. "Okay. Mr. Martin had some great ideas for the central installation. He's going to bring in some big screen TVs, on loan to us from the A/V department, and we're going to run the comments across them in a continuous feed from laptops." She gestured to the walls. "I'm mounting the smaller donations on the walls, but I'll need to figure out a way to display the larger ones."

"The basement's got a lot more of these library tables," Fin said. "We can set them up around the room." The huge rectangular space could accommodate at least ten of them and still allow patrons to wander around with ease.

"The donations keep pouring in, and I can't display all of them, so I'll need help cataloguing them. For now, I'm going to store them upstairs." She turned to take in the room, her brow creased with concern. "Mostly, it just looks drab, so I'd like to make it more exciting. More interactive."

She gestured to a space behind the hanging origami papers. "I was thinking about making a tree. Something with a sturdy trunk and lots of bare branches, so visitors could hang their own stories." She turned back to him. "I don't know. That's all I've got so far. I want to keep it simple, but it definitely needs a little more pizzazz."

"Lighting would make the place look less drab."

She gave a wistful smile. "That would be great, but I don't have the time or resources to make that happen."

I do. He smiled, really fucking glad he had something to offer her. Checking his watch, he realized the timing couldn't be better. "Come with me."

The closer to Main Street they got, the denser the tourist population. Callie didn't have time to follow him around. The days when his life took precedence over hers were long gone. "*Fin.*"

Shooting a glance over his shoulder, he didn't break his stride. "Almost there." His mirrored aviators made him look like a dashing fighter pilot, and the damp T-shirt and athletic shorts showed off his powerful physique. When he lifted an arm to wipe the sweat off his brow his biceps bunched, and she could almost feel the smooth, hard muscle on the palms of her hands.

He stopped and waited for her to catch up. When she got there, he said, "This is for you, wild thing. Trust me?"

She gazed up at this man she'd once loved with all her heart. Who'd given her a community and the sense of belonging she'd missed in her childhood. His love had freed her, enabled her to live out loud, releasing her laughter, her anger, her fears, and more love than she'd known she'd had the capacity to feel.

He'd made a mistake. A bad one, but still. A mistake.

Of course, she trusted him. A surge of regret crested hard and fast, leaving a bitter taste in her mouth. "I'm sorry, Fin. I shouldn't have cut you out like I did."

He didn't answer at first. The hot sun beat down on them, and perspiration beaded over his lip. He scanned her features for a moment, and then gave a tight nod. "We're good."

Considering the damage she'd done, he shouldn't have forgiven her so easily. But the fact that he did made her understand that *this*—his unconditional love—had allowed her to truly be herself. And she only knew that because for the last six years she'd been on her best behavior in class, at work, on internships...with Julian and his parents. Always upbeat and polite, even when she felt exhausted and bitchy. Like Mrs. Reyes, she never left her apartment without dressing well and applying make-up.

Because Julian's love had been conditional.

"You all right?" Fin tugged her arm.

She'd messed up. Taken her heartbreak to level *Extra*. And it had caused her to hurt so many people. "You're a good guy, Fin." He hadn't deserved her total black-out. "I should've..." Guilt whipped through her, as strong as a gust of wind on the summit. After spending this time with him and remembering all the good she'd blocked out, she couldn't live with it anymore.

Tears blurred her vision, and she touched her fingertips to his abdomen. "I'm so sorry about your dad." Shame bore down on her. How could she have let hurt feelings stand in the way of being there for him after his father had passed away? God, she'd been so selfish. "I should've gone to his funeral."

Just like the assumptions people had made about his text to Traci, she'd come to her own conclusions after seeing countless pictures on social media of Fin partying. So many women had tagged him, acting like they were having the time of their lives, and she'd believed them.

But he was right. She did know him. He wouldn't have gotten over her that easily—he'd have been hurting as much as she had. And when he'd needed her the most, she'd looked away.

The press of his hand over hers only amplified her guilt. His willingness to forgive her—*no, dammit, accept her*, faults and all—shamed her. She didn't deserve it.

He tipped her chin. "Hey." His thumb swiped away the tears.

But they just kept spilling. "I should've put my feelings aside and come home." It wouldn't have been some sign that she'd let him off the hook. It would've been basic human compassion. "I can't imagine what you went through. How scary it must have been to lose your dad. He was such a huge presence in your lives."

Mack Bowie was larger than life. He laughed the loudest, told the most riveting stories, and loved his sons with enough force to move mountains.

Fin's features pulled into a grimace, and his arm fell to his side. "Yeah. We miss him every day."

She noticed the *We*, his way of distancing himself from the pain. "I'm so sorry."

"We notice it, you know? Every time I walk into the house, I brace myself. Ready to hear his booming voice on the phone or shouting to Marcella, *You got my boots? Can't find my damn boots.*"

She gave a bittersweet smile. "I heard he died on Mount Owen."

"Yeah. Avalanche."

The image of that big, powerful man skiing down a mountain while twenty football fields of snow crashed over him sent waves of horror through her. *What a terrible way to die.*

"My brothers and I stood up there with a flask of his 1926 Macallan and toasted him." He gave a wistful twist of his head. "He died way too soon, but that's exactly how he would've wanted to go."

"I should've come home for the funeral." She brought her hands to her cheeks and swept away the dampness. "I've been such a brat." She looked up at him. "I'm sorry."

He cupped her chin, his thumb gently caressing. "I've missed you." He brought her hand to his chest. "Swear to God, it's like someone shot a hole right through my heart."

She pushed through the impulse to withdraw and instead let her fingers fist in his T-shirt. This close, she could see the wedge-shaped scar on the apple of his cheek and the achingly familiar look of adoration in his bright blue eyes. The messages sent up from his heart burned a path up her arm, across her shoulders, and then cascaded down through her body. "I missed you, too." And if she hadn't shoved them all in a closet, this load of emotion wouldn't be crashing over her a block away from the center of town.

He bridged the distance between them by pressing a kiss to the corner of her mouth. At her exhalation of surprise, his eyes narrowed, and his intent became clear. This time he didn't hesitate to part her lips and kiss her. Heat sparked in her core and spread like flash fire. Nobody kissed like Fin Bowie. Nobody. He had the softest, warmest, sweetest mouth.

Until he licked inside and sweet turned carnal. He didn't even wait for her response, just clasped her hips and pulled her up against him. Light flashed inside her body like an electrical storm. He tightened his hold, cupped her jaw, and angled her head to take her just how he wanted.

Oh, dear God, she *loved* the way Fin wanted her. Like always, she went weightless, sinking, spiraling, losing herself in his possession. And just before the last bit of her slipped under the wave of desire, awareness snapped in her brain. She shoved her hands between them and ended the kiss.

When the dazed expression broke, he let her go, exhaling in raw frustration.

"I like..." Her body trembled. *Pull yourself together*. "I like that we're...that we're talking again and...reconnecting —but not like this, okay? I don't...*this* isn't going to happen." *It can't*. Flustered, she forced herself to step away from the body magnetically connected to hers. "I'm leaving for New York in six weeks. I *live* there."

His shoulders pushed back, and he lowered his sunglasses. "Come on." He turned away from her. "We don't want to miss them."

"Miss who?" She had to hurry to catch up with him, her mouth still tingling, desire still whirling like streamers inside her. "Where are we going?"

When he hit Main Street, he turned right, a man on a mission. At her parents' diner, he held the door open, the cow bells clanging.

Country music walloped them as they stepped inside. The jukebox played Brooks and Dunn's "Boot Scootin Boogie," and the wait staff did a line dance in the center of the black and white checked floor. Toddlers stood up in red booths, old folks clapped with huge smiles, and people sang along.

From behind the counter, her mom stood on her toes, waving wildly, gesturing for Callie to join in. Even though she couldn't keep the smile off her face, Callie shook her head. She wasn't part of the staff anymore.

Fin nudged her, and when she stood firmly, he gave her a mischievous smile, wrapped an arm around her waist, and dragged her into the line. Some of the staff, the ones who'd been with her parents most of her life, shouted and clapped.

"Callie!"

"Bring it, girl!"

What the hell, right? So, she joined in. She threw herself into it, just like the old days, swinging her hips and flipping her hair. Fin watched like she was the sexiest thing he'd ever seen, and that just made her go harder. She belted out the lyrics along with everyone else, and it felt so damn good.

When the song ended, she held a hand over heart, out of breath and exhilarated. The staff rushed to get back to work, the patrons turned back to their meals, and her mom gave her a thumbs-up.

Callie turned to find Fin right there, and she had to catch herself by grabbing hold of his arms. That look in his eyes—she'd seen it so many times—like he wanted to drag her off somewhere alone and hike her up against the wall—sent a tumult of emotion through her.

"Callie..." His jaw clamped tightly, making the muscle pop. "You know what's sexier than watching you laugh and shake your ass like that, all wild and free?"

Her fingers curled into his arm. "What?"

"Not a goddamn thing. Now get that sexy ass to table twenty-three before I grab it and give it a good, hard squeeze."

Her eyes went wide, and lust spread through her in a hot rush.

"Don't think I won't do it."

Forcing her feet to move, she headed to the far side of the room, where table twenty-three sat under the picture window that overlooked the snow-capped Tetons. Someone had shoved four tables together, and a group of senior citizens engaged in lively discussion.

Callie waved to some of the familiar faces. The group of around thirty retired people had a standing date in the diner every morning at eleven, and they showed up whenever they could.

Fin's breath hit her ear. "We're in luck. Some of the ones we need are here."

Turning to face him put her mouth an inch from his. Heat bloomed in her body, and she had to look away. "What exactly do I need?"

Fin moved ahead of her, approaching the table with a big grin. "Hey, there, Babs. You're looking particularly glowy this morning." After kissing the woman's cheek, he reached out and shook an older gentleman's hand. "Stan." He wrapped an arm across Callie's shoulders and drew her closer. "For those of you who don't already know her, this is Callie Bell. Her parents own the diner."

"She's quite the dancer," one of the guys said.

"It's lovely to see you, sweetheart," one of the women said.

"She's got a cool project she's working on and needs some help putting it together," Fin said. "And who better to help her out than a bunch of old folks with too much time on their hands?"

"Don't listen to this guy." A lean, white-haired man got up to bring an empty chair over from a nearby table. "I founded my company thirty-five years ago. Brought it up from my kitchen table to a world-wide conglomeration, and I just retired two months ago. You won't hear me complaining about having too much time on my hands for a change." He reached out a hand. "Stan Poplar. Have a seat, Ms. Bell, and tell us your troubles."

"It's great to meet you, Stan." She grasped his hand

before sitting down. "I don't...I wouldn't say I have *troubles*."

"Sure she does." Fin gripped the back of her chair. "She's putting together a museum and needs help getting it up and going."

"Okay, first of all it's a pop-up *exhibition*. Not a museum. But, yes, I could use some help. I need to open it as soon as possible." Though she had no idea what role the Cooters could play.

Fin pulled up a chair and sat beside her. He reached for her knee, but when she reflexively tensed, he quickly removed it. "You in?" he asked the Cooters.

"Can you give us a little more information?" A petite woman with sun-weathered skin leaned forward. "I'm Barbara, by the way. The 'glowy' one."

"Nice to meet you, Barbara." She shook the woman's hand. "Yes, absolutely. So, it's the Exhibition of Broken Hearts, and we'll be displaying stories of people who've been betrayed by their lovers."

"Why would anyone want to read about someone else's broken heart?" Stan asked.

Barbara balled up her paper napkin and tossed it at him. It landed several feet short, on top of someone's half-eaten slice of apple pie. "Because it's the human condition, you knucklehead."

"Yes, exactly," Callie said. "But there's more to it. There's a meme going around called The World's Worst Boyfriend. It all started with a simple text message a woman posted on her social media account. Without context, her followers made up a whole story about her boyfriend's betrayal. It turns out that not only didn't the woman have a boyfriend, but she never posted a follow-up comment to explain anything. But that one text created a community of scorned people sharing their own stories. It's a fascinating cultural phenomenon."

"Well, everyone's had their heart broken," Barbara said.

"Yes," Callie said. "And the meme's somehow created a kind of support group. You know how they have them for grief? Divorce? Well, this is a cyber one for people with broken hearts. So, this exhibition's going to explore both ideas and tie them together: the power of social media to create global communities, and the ability of those communities to effect healing by sharing personal experiences on a public platform. I think..." Callie glanced down at her entwined fingers. "For some reason, betrayal's a particularly lingering pain. And your friends and family are only going to listen to you for so long. Which leaves you alone with it. It seems like taking your turn at this social media podium helps purge it from your body." Embarrassed, she looked up with a smile. "Or something like that."

"I get it." All eyes turned to the striking, elegant woman at the end of the table. "There's something cathartic about knowing you're not alone in a heartbreak of that magnitude."

Energy surged through her. "Yes. I've been obsessively reading the comments, and I was so frustrated with myself. Why couldn't I stop? They had nothing to do with me. My boyfriend broke my heart, but he didn't do the terrible things I was reading about. But it didn't matter. Every story sucked me in. This pain, it's universal, and there's just no outlet for it. I don't know how to explain it other than to say that for the first time I found myself in a chain of people with broken hearts. It was like holding hands, you know? It made me acknowledge my own hurt in a way I never had before."

"I think it's a wonderful idea," Barbara said.

"Well, if you're here to get me to talk about my broken heart, you can forget it," Stan said.

"She doesn't want to hear your sad stories, old man," Fin said. "She needs your help."

Stan nodded. "What can I do?"

"I don't really know." Callie hesitated, worried about imposing until she realized Fin wouldn't have brought her here if he didn't think they'd want to participate. "Right now, I just have basic displays hanging on the walls. I'm going to have some TV screens, but mostly it's just bland. I need to kick it up a notch."

"She needs to plug it in."

Fin's voice was like flint to her heart. Just the sound of it sparked heat, excitement...and...something else. Something indescribable. She couldn't help reaching out to him, placing her hand on top of his where it rested on his thigh. Immediately, he turned his over and entwined their fingers.

Home.

That snap of connection? It felt like coming home.

"Will it be interactive?" Barbara asked.

"I'd like it to be. I'd like to create a tree so visitors can write down their personal stories and hang them off the branches. On the other side of the room, I'm dedicating a wall to give people a chance to ask the one question they desperately need answered by the person who broke their heart. If I could just find a way to make it more—"

"What would yours be?" the elegant woman at the end of the table asked. "The one question?"

She didn't hesitate, because the answer sprang off the tip of her tongue as if laying in wait for this opportunity. "If you loved me, how could you treat me like that?"

Fin gave her hand a hard squeeze.

"Mine would be, Did she make you happier?" A woman tossed her bag on the table and then dropped into a chair. She smelled strongly of cloves. Everyone stared at her. "What?"

"I didn't know you had a heart to break, Judy," one of the men said.

Judy, heavyset with a white bob, chuckled. "Bastard took it with him when he left me for another gal."

"How old were you?" Callie asked.

"Forty-four. He left me twenty-two years ago."

"Do you ever see him?" She probably shouldn't have asked, but Judy had been pretty free in sharing.

The others looked away, so Callie knew she'd hit a sore point.

Judy barked out a laugh. "He's the former mayor, so yep. I got to see him all the time."

Callie's heart ached just hearing about it. "I'm sorry. I can't even imagine what that must have felt like."

For one moment Judy's snarky persona faded, and pure unadulterated hurt took its place. And then, in a blink, it disappeared. "So, what's the plan? You need a crew to get you going?"

"I'd be happy to be a docent," the elegant woman said. "And, once we spread the word among our friends, you'll have a dozen more for your exhibition."

"She's going to need more than a bunch of old ladies standing around." Stan tapped the table with his knuckles. "You need workers." He pointed to the man across from him. "Barry's a retired electrician. I ran Poplar Media, a communications firm. And Judy here, she owns the biggest construction company in the state. How about we run over there after lunch and take a look at the place, see what we can do to perk things up?"

"I'd love that." She squeezed Fin's hand.

"The only way you're gonna get me running is if Clint Eastwood's walking down the street," Judy said.

Everyone cracked up.

"Sound good?" Stan asked.

"Sounds amazing." Automatically, she turned to Fin to share her enthusiasm, but his expression had turned stony.

For a moment there, she'd gotten so carried away she'd forgotten the cost to him. And, damn, if that didn't cut right through her happiness.

He'd brought her here to help with the very thing that was destroying his reputation.

10

WHAT THE ACTUAL FUCK?

Fin sat on the edge of the coffee table, watching Traci Allen lie on national television.

"We've been together on and off over the years, but it was never serious. Given our careers, it couldn't be. I've always understood that about him, that his career comes first. That's just who Fin is. Everyone knows that."

He found her word choice interesting. *Been together* didn't mean dating.

The camera angle switched to *Entertainment Update's* host. "But he abandoned you in a strange hospital in a foreign country. That's..." The reporter shook his head in disbelief. "How did that make you feel?"

Fin shot to his feet. "Tell him the truth."

"It was scary." Traci let out a shaky breath. "Scariest thing I've ever gone through."

Yeah, the *accident* was. But that had nothing to do with *Fin*.

Tell them.

With his closely cropped blonde hair and artfully groomed beard, the reporter leaned forward as if Traci were about to tell him the secret to pulling off a frontside 180. "But this time it was different, right? You'd blown out your knee—on a trip you took for *him*. I mean, Fin Bowie takes these risks all the time. But you're a champion. You can't take risks like that. You've got the Olympics to think about."

You're a champion. And Fin was what? A dilettante? He scrubbed his face with both hands. *Okay, not the point.*

He waited for Traci's answer. *Tell them you asked to come.*

"I wanted to go. That's on me."

Thank you. He waited for her to fill in the rest of the story, but she just kept looking at her hands like she wanted to say something but wasn't sure if she should. To anyone else watching, she probably looked like a woman who'd had her heart torn out by her boyfriend.

He tipped his head back in frustration. "I'm not her boyfriend."

Callie rushed into the room. "Shh." They'd just gotten Theo to bed.

"You really are a champion, aren't you?" the reporter asked.

Traci's head snapped up, obviously not sure what he meant.

"You wake up alone in a foreign country, in pain, your career on the line, wondering where your boyfriend is, only to find out he's at a wedding. And here you sit, calm as can be, forgiving him." The reporter shrugged. "That's a true champion."

Traci shifted, clearly uncomfortable. "Look, Fin's not a bad guy."

"That's right," Fin said. "I'm not."

"Not a bad guy?" The reporter practically snorted. "You tore your ACL *and* your MCL. Your career might be over." He looked disgusted. "And the man who's supposed to love you and take care of you is just...outta there. It's beyond callous. Even on a first date, I wouldn't leave a woman alone in a situation like that."

"Yeah, but you've got to know Fin," Traci said. "He's... driven. And he had a wedding to get to. He was the best man. He wasn't going to miss it for anything."

Fin couldn't believe this shit. "I'd have missed it if my four other teammates hadn't promised to stay until your coach and family showed up."

"I think you're being far more understanding than most of us would be," the reporter said. "I have to wonder, though, as you sat all alone in that hospital, not speaking the language, not knowing if you were facing a career-ending injury...what did it feel like to read that text? You see it's from your boyfriend. You must have expected kind words. Concern. A plan of action, right? Like, I'm contacting your parents or, I'm working on transferring you to a hospital in the States. *Something* that would help you. Instead you get..." The guy put on his glasses and read from a blue index card. "*Thanks for a great time?*" The camera zoomed in on his expression of shock and disgust.

"Yeah, I screwed up, all right?" Fin flicked a hand at the television. "I should've been sincere."

"Have you talked to her?" Callie asked.

He shook his head. He'd never expected the attention to go on so long. *Three weeks.*

And just when it had started to die down, Traci had jumped on the media circuit to fan it back to life. He hadn't wanted to bother her in the hospital, but she was obviously doing okay now. He whipped out his phone and searched for her number.

"Who're you calling?" Callie stepped closer.

"Traci." He stepped out onto the porch, so he wouldn't wake Theo. *Just in case I lose my shit.*

"Hey." Traci sounded wary.

"It's Fin."

"Yeah, I know." A gust of breath blew static in his ear. "You're watching it."

"Trace, what're you doing?" He cupped the back of his head. "You had a chance to clean things up. Why'd you lie?"

"I didn't. I haven't lied once. If you pay attention, you'll see I haven't actually said anything bad about you. The *reporter* made it sound like you did those things."

"You didn't correct him."

She was quiet for a moment. "No, I didn't." She actually sounded *defiant.*

"I'm not that guy, Traci. We've known each other for years. Have you ever seen me treat anyone like shit?"

"No."

He wanted to put the call on speaker so Callie could

hear. He didn't want even a shadow of doubt in her mind. "Then why? Why are you doing this?"

"Because, honestly, Fin? It's not that big a deal to you." She grew agitated. "You get some attention for a few days, so what? It'll pass, and nothing in your life changes."

"*Weeks*. This has gone on for weeks. You've turned me into a meme. I'm an athlete, not some bad boyfriend."

"Hey. *I* didn't do anything. I didn't start this, and I have no control over where it went."

"Yeah, Traci, you did. You could've jumped on your Instagram page and told the truth, but you didn't. It's not too late, though. You can end it right now."

"That's so easy for you to say. You're a *billionaire*."

Of course. It always comes down to money. "I live off my own earnings. I've never touched my dad's money."

"Oh, please. You live on a compound with servants."

Servants? Jesus, the ideas people had about his family. But he wasn't about to correct her. His financial situation wasn't the point.

"And don't pretend you can't dip into that honey pot any time you feel like it. My parents are teachers, and the only money I've ever made has come from winnings and endorsements. Which I won't be getting anymore. So, I'm sorry that your reputation has taken a hit, but my career's probably over, and if I can get a few bucks out of you trending, I'm going to take it."

"You'll still make money if you tell the truth. In fact, the story'll get a new boost if it turns out your fans made it up."

"It's too late for that. Besides, this thing's going to run

out of steam in a few more days. And, while you'll get back to boarding with your boys in Japan or Alaska or wherever the cool kids play, I'll be in rehab for the next *year*. Look, I honestly didn't think you'd care, so...I mean, I'm sorry if you do. I really am, but I've got my own shit to deal with." She sounded despondent. "I gotta go. Bye, Fin."

Well, shit. He stood on Ryder's porch, looking out into the darkness.

The screen door creaked. "What'd she say?"

He didn't even turn around. "It's about money." Traci thought his pride had taken a hit, but what mattered was the blow to his professional reputation.

Sure, he could've told her the meme had cost him the *National Adventurer* nomination. Since she was facing the end of her career, she might've understood that getting the cover *this year* meant something. That it might never come around again. But his concerns were hypothetical. Hers were real.

"Yeah, I figured." Callie came up beside him. "She's probably thinking you could've done the same thing. Someone else in your situation might have ridden the wave and gone on talk shows, too. There's no such thing as bad publicity, right?" Her hand settled gently on his back. "She doesn't know what it means to you. How important it is for you to be known for your achievements. She doesn't know about your relationship with your brothers."

"It's nothing compared to what she's going through."

"No, it's not. But, Fin, you're the *youngest*. You could be the *eight*-time winner of the Games...you could make the *Guinness Book of World Records* for most gold medals in a lifetime, and your brothers will still make fun of you. That's never going to change."

He straightened, turning towards her. *She's right.* And it made him wonder, if he made the cover, would they respect him? Or would his one and only achievement for his dad's trophy room—the framed cover from *National Adventurer*—wind up with a Sharpie mustache on it?

"And, you know, at some point...you have to stop caring."

"I don't care that they mess around with me." Except that wasn't entirely true. He'd hated the sign they'd put at the end of the driveway. Sure, he'd laughed, and he'd retaliated by making them run to the summit, where Brodie had satisfyingly puked. But it'd still pissed him off.

And the way he'd bristled just then, imagining the mustache—yeah, he did care. Callie was right.

"They love you, Fin. And they obviously respect you since you're the one they go to for training."

"Yeah, cool, but I'm not an athlete to them. I'm just a reckless kid with a wild hair up his ass." He looked at her, deciding whether or not to tell the whole truth. Frankly, if he was going to talk about this shit, he'd only do it with her. "They think I'm doing it because I'm messed up over losing you."

Her eyes flared with surprise. "Is that true?"

He thought of Will flagging him down on his dirt bike, that crazy feeling he'd tried to outrun after Man-Bracelet's proposal, and he couldn't deny the compulsion for speed, the thrill of danger, was associated with Callie. "To some degree, yeah. Whenever I think about what I did to us, what it cost me, it stirs up all this crazy energy. And there's no outlet for it."

He dropped to a crouch, covering his face with both hands. "Hell." He couldn't escape the feelings. No matter what he did, they remained trapped inside his body. "It never goes away. I'll be in the shower or just drifting off to sleep, and it hits me. I see your expression when I told you I wasn't going to NYU with you. I destroyed you with that one stupid decision that I can't take back." He stood back up. "There's no peace for me. So, yeah, the adrenaline pushes it out."

"If we got back together—"

His heart flipped over.

But she held up a hand. "That's not going to happen but hear me out. If we did get back together, would you enter a competition? Would you train for an event?"

"Hell, no. Practicing the same trick over and over till I master it? That would bore the crap out of me. Groomed courses? I'd rather stay in bed. There's nothing like the thrill of riding a spine no one even knew existed. It's exhilarating."

She placed her hand on his arm. "Then it doesn't matter what they think because you love your work, and you have no interest in doing what they do. Do you know what I'm saying? You're not doing it because we broke up. You're doing it because it's who you are."

"Yeah, but I still want them to think I'm a badass."

"Believe me, they do. Everyone knows you're a badass. But they're your brothers, and they're scared you're not going to come home."

Like my dad.

"You have to get it through your head that you're on equal footing with them now."

Talking to her like this...his heart felt so full it ached. He'd missed being close to her. Only with her could he be his whole self. But it wasn't easy not being able to touch her, put his hands all over her. "Did you miss me at all?"

Callie always told the truth. And he saw in her reluctance to answer what it cost her this time. "Every minute of every day."

Adrenaline punched through his system. *Fuck.*

"I can't tell you how many times something would happen...I'd get an internship or some guy would take his pants off on the subway...and I'd reach for my phone to tell you first. Or I'd wake up in the morning"—she looked away, pain etched on her features—"and want to curl up with you, only to remember all over again what happened. So many times during class I'd check the time on my phone, counting how many minutes until I got to see you again. I missed our adventures—I've never had more fun with anybody than I had with you. I missed the way you held onto me all night long, like I was your place in the world."

"You were. You *are*. Jesus, Callie..." Hope flapped heavy wings inside his chest, and he cupped her cheeks, searching her warm hazel eyes for the truth. "Don't you feel this? Now that we're talking again? Doesn't it feel like you can finally take a full breath? Like the missing puzzle piece is back in place?"

"Honestly, yes. But..." Her fingers closed around his wrists.

In her eyes he saw an eagerness—a willingness—to throw herself all-in with him—he *saw* it—but he also saw Calliope, counting off all the reasons they couldn't be together—and he had this one shot to knock her over onto the side that had them naked under the covers and losing themselves in each other, and he'd be damned if he wouldn't take it.

"Fuck, Callie." As he brushed his lips over hers, he watched the way her eyelids fluttered closed. Her mouth opened to him, and he licked into that soft, wet heat—

The screen door creaked. They both turned to see Theo stepping out in his Superman pajamas, the elastic waistline hanging low, his hair sticking up on one side of his head.

His body still vibrating with need, Fin turned toward him. "Hey, little man. What's up?"

Keeping his gaze on Callie, Theo made his way over to him. Fin grabbed him under his arms and hoisted him up, holding him snugly to his chest. The boy's legs hitched up, hugging Fin's ribcage, and not for a minute did Fin take for granted the way Theo trusted him.

"You okay?" He said it quietly.

Theo nodded, a fist perched on Fin's shoulder.

"Can't sleep?"

Theo tilted his head toward Fin's neck, like he wanted to tuck in but still keep Callie in his sights.

She smiled warmly. "You want to read another story?"

He shook his head and whispered, "No."

Fin liked her ability to read her nephew. Most people turned it on, performing for the shy kid, but Callie gave him lots of space. He put his palm on the boy's back. "You know your mom and dad's plane landed, right?"

Theo nodded, but he seemed distracted.

"They're on their way from the airport right now. You remember what your dad promised when you wake up? Pancakes. Buttermilk flippin' pancakes." He held out a fist, and Theo bumped it, but it didn't seem like he had his parents on his mind.

Theo gave his aunt the side-eye, and then he reached out to her. "I made this for you." Slowly, he unfurled his fist to reveal a stone he'd sloppily painted red and black. That had been her art project with him tonight, painting rocks.

Callie's eyes went wide. "You made a ladybug? For me?" She came closer. "It's beautiful."

A blush spread across Theo's plump cheeks.

"Oh, I love it." Gently, she picked it up and examined it from all angles. "I love it so much."

Theo turned his face away, his breath warm on Fin's chest.

"Thank you, sweetheart." She pressed it to her heart. "This means so much to me."

When Theo's body relaxed into him, Fin got that he was ready for bed. He headed for the house. "Sooner you fall asleep, sooner you get to stuff your face with those pancakes. I'm gonna put that can of whipped cream we bought right on the middle shelf so your parents can see it the second they open the fridge. Hint, hint, amiright?"

He'd just reached for the screen door when Callie called to him. "Fin."

He glanced back, shifting Theo to his other hip.

"I thought I'd come home all grown up with my fancy boyfriend, and that you'd be...I don't know, jealous? I didn't do it consciously, but I knew by your reaction that I *had* wanted you to see me with a guy like that."

That got his interest. "What was my reaction?"

"You weren't jealous at all. You just looked confused. Like you knew he wasn't the right guy for me." She paused. "And, of course, you were right."

With a happy heart, Callie spread out the quilted blanket so the delivery men could set the rusted and dented Chevy door on it. "This is amazing." Since her article had gone out two weeks ago, she'd received lots of smaller items—as she'd requested—but nothing as big and interesting as this multi-colored door.

She peeled off the scrap of paper taped to it and read the note.

Fin couldn't keep a damn job. I was always the breadwinner. When I came back from yet another business trip, I put my key in the lock and it didn't turn. I looked through the living room window to find Fin on the couch with his pregnant girlfriend. Yeah, you read that right. Pregnant. He'd kicked me out—not just of my house, but of the life we'd built together. He had my car in the garage, my clothes, my furniture. And you know what? I let him have it. Didn't want a single damn thing that reminded me of that five-year waste of a marriage.

About a month later I saw my car parked outside my Ob/GYN's office. I got my brother to come over in his tow truck and take off the door. It's been in my garage for eight months, which means I have to look at it every damn day. So, I'm giving it to you. Now I've got nothing that reminds me. I'm free.

Callie smiled with a shake of her head. *I'm free.* She was glad for that woman. After signing for the donation, she reached into her pocket and pulled out a bill, handing them their tip. "Thanks, guys."

Fin strode in, commanding attention in his worn black jeans, motorcycle boots, and a white T-shirt that stretched across his broad shoulders. "When you heading out to see your Dad's booth?"

She tipped her head toward the seniors busy bringing her exhibition to life. "Soon as they're done."

"I got someone I want you to meet. Let's go now."

"I can't just leave. They're working their butts off to help me."

"Judy." Fin's voice boomed over the hum of conversation, the scrape of a ladder across the floor, and the clack of two-by-fours smacking into each other.

Judy looked down at him from a catwalk her team had built to install lighting around the perimeter of the ceiling. "Yes, your highness?"

Fin burst into a smile. It lit up his whole face and made her knees weak. "I'm gonna steal the boss lady for an hour or so. You good?"

"She's more organized than an air traffic controller," Judy said. "Go. Get her out of my hair."

"You tell him our plan?" Stan called from his huddle with some workers.

Oh, man. He's not going to like this. "Not yet."

"I need his okay," Stan said.

Fin's brow creased in concern. "Tell me about what?"

With a hand on his arm, she turned him away from the others. "Poplar Media's going to do a segment on the exhibition."

"Callie—"

"Wait. Just hear me out."

"No. Sending tear sheets to the board of directors from the local paper's one thing, but national exposure?" Fin's features hardened. "I don't want that."

"I knew that would be your reaction, but Stan and I talked about it. Right now, Traci's managing the conversation, right? She's all over the press and media, making you look bad. So, we brainstormed how you could take the control back."

"I want it to go away."

"I know, but that's not going to happen while Traci's on her press tour. So, let's get Poplar Media out here to cover the exhibition and your involvement in it. Let people see that you don't take it personally because it *isn't* personal. And then, when they interview you, you can tell the truth. You won't badmouth Traci. In fact, you'll only mention her in the context of your trip and her injury, but you'll be able to tell your side and let the world see you for who you are."

Crinkles appeared at the corners of his gorgeous blue eyes. "You trying to save me, wild thing?"

"You say that like it's a bad thing." She gave a smile that quickly faded. "I hate the idea that my exhibition will make things worse for you, and I think there's a way for it to maybe help. You game?"

"No. I appreciate you looking out for me, but..." He shook his head. "You go ahead and get the media out here. Just leave me out of it. Now, come on. Let's get out of here."

She hesitated, not wanting to leave all these people while they worked on her exhibition.

"Got a donor lined up for you." He pulled her closer. "She's at the fairgrounds right now."

His nearness made her heart beat thick and fast. If she turned—just slightly—their mouths would be a breath apart. She could cup the back of his neck and kiss him. Liquid heat gushed through her, making her body tingle all the way to the soles of her feet.

Gah. Shake it off. "A donor? Why would I take money for something so temporary?"

His muscular arm wrapped around her waist. "Wild thing, you just catapulted this thing to the national level. All your New York people are gonna see it. You want them to see a crude, homemade exhibit?"

The very idea sent fear like a slingshot right into her gut.

"You want to knock it out of the park, you need green. Besides, you think I didn't see how excited you got over that Chevy door? Wait'll you see what you get when we talk to some of my dad's old friends."

He was right. Without money, she had an interesting idea. With funding, she could turn it into something sensational. "I want that. You know I do. But..."

"You're a balls-out kind of woman, Callie. Why the hesitation?"

She gestured to the amazing space coming to life. "We've set the opening for this Friday night. That means it'll only be open for a month. It just doesn't seem right to take money."

"Why shut it down? You've obviously got something here. The donations keep coming in. The comment section on the website Barbara made is out of control. Day one, you got ten thousand hits. And the Cooters are into it. Look at them."

Overseen by Judy and Stan, at least a dozen seniors worked on various projects.

"Once it's set up, it'll run itself," Fin said. "With them as docents, they'll keep it going for you."

The slow bubble of excitement in her belly turned into a full boil. "I would *love* that. Even if I get the fellowship, it won't guarantee me a job. I'll probably be doing research for ten years before something opens up in the city."

"And if you keep this running, change it up every now and then, you get to keep the museum on your resume."

"It's an exhibition." She brushed off the irritation because she loved the idea so much. "Okay. Let's do this." Since the Cooters didn't mind anyway, she led the way out of the building.

Once they hit the sunshine, Fin said, "This lady we're going to see? One day I'll take you to see her art collection."

His boots pounded on the boardwalk. "You ever get sick of living in the city and want to come home to the wide-open Wyoming sky, you can make a serious living as an art consultant to her and her friends."

Oh. She'd never thought of that. With funding cutbacks in the arts, most of the work of a curator would be getting donations from people like Julian's parents. And it would take decades before she had any control over the installations. But as an art consultant, she'd focus on discovering art, presenting it to her clients, helping them decide which piece worked best in their spaces.

She would love that. Of course, no one would hire her until she had true experience. Until she'd developed a reputation in the field. So, the fellowship, a job, and then... she could consider coming home. She'd never really allowed for that possibility, but it made her heart expand with so much hope it almost hurt. "It's something to think about ten years from now when I have a track record."

He didn't break his stride, but she caught his expression, that flinch of his muscles. She knew he wanted to say something, to convince her that his dad's connections would help bypass whatever experience she thought she needed. The Bowies were tenacious. They wouldn't be champions if they gave up easily. She loved that about them.

If she came home, would that mean she and Fin could be together? The unguarded part of her heart hadn't learned anything because the effervescence of being with him infused her whole body.

But then, of course, reality smacked her in the face like

a cold, wet fish. Their single biggest issue hadn't changed. She could just see walking down the aisle, blinking away tears of joy to find the groom missing. Having her dad whisper in her ear, "Fin's got to help Will train for the Olympics, but he'll be back as soon as he can. He promised."

Nope. Never again. They didn't have a future.

Glancing up and down the street, she didn't see Fin's truck. "Where're you parked?"

He gestured in the direction of Megan's studio, to what used to be the Round Up Motel and had now become a collection of funky buildings. The original office had rockers on the boardwalk and wind chimes hanging off the eaves. Next to it stood a quirky little house covered in street and animal crossing signs, graffiti, snowboards and ski poles. Callie stopped to take it all in. "What is all this?"

"It's the Hartley's place." His tone indicated she should know that.

"Yeah. I know." In the fifties and sixties, the motel—owned by Megan's family—was the only lodging in their little town, but the boom hit in the eighties and tourists flooded into the area. In the nineties, the billionaires came. Construction went wild, including a private airport for their jets, ski lodges, fancy hotels, and big box stores.

Thanks to its kitsch, the Round Up Motel had lasted all the way through to when Callie had gone off to college. "But what is it now?"

"Megan turned the office into a yoga studio. And that building?" He indicated the one covered in signs and ski poles. "That's the Reliquary Museum. You remember Roxie Fitzsimmons? She runs it."

"What did they do with the motel rooms?"

A car door slammed, and she turned to see Megan drop her keys into a canvas tote and head toward them.

Fin gave her a chin nod.

"Hey." Walking right past them, Megan gave Callie a bland smile.

I hurt her so badly she treats me like a stranger. Fix it. "Megan, I'm in town for the summer, and I'd really like to grab a coffee and catch up with you."

Before Megan could respond, Fin jumped in. "You ought to give her a tour of the building. Show her what you've done with the place."

Megan raised an eyebrow. "Sure." She kept on walking. "Got some office work to get done before class." She unlocked the door and slipped inside.

Fin stopped in front of a motorcycle, dug his keys out of his pocket, and handed her a helmet.

She just stared at it. "I'm not getting on that."

"My Harley?" He looked at her in surprise. "You love riding with me."

She gestured to her linen dress and sandals. "I can't ride dressed like this." And wasn't he taking her to meet an art patron? She could hardly arrive with windblown hair and road dust.

Even if she couldn't see his eyes behind the black-out aviators, she knew that look of impatience. He reached for her hand and pulled her toward the studio. "Megan'll have something for you."

She jerked out of his hold. "Forget it. I was going to take my dad's truck anyway."

"We're taking the bike."

"Not a chance." With a ridiculously tight budget and countless elegant events to attend, Callie had become a pro at shopping designer sales. Over the last few years, she'd accumulated a lean but nice wardrobe. And she took immaculate care of every piece. Which meant she would absolutely not get on a motorcycle and risk tearing the seams.

He leaned into her, so close she could feel the heat of his skin. His delectable mouth curled into a smile. Which made her remember the way he'd kissed her. Which made her very, very uncomfortable because Fin's kisses were as dangerous as a riptide—beneath the basic mechanics of mouths joining and tongues tangling swirled a powerful current of hot lust that always yanked her under, swept her away, and made her lose all sense of time and place. She'd lost her head many, many times around this man.

"What do you do for fun in New York City? Fancy dinners? Walking around museums and art galleries?"

That's exactly what I do with Julian and his family. "There's nothing wrong with that."

"You're in Calamity now. Those fancy dresses are gonna get real dirty around here." He turned back toward the studio. "Come on."

"I'm not borrowing Megan's clothes." But, of course, he ignored her. She followed him up the stairs and across the boardwalk to the studio. "Did you hear me?"

He stepped inside. "Megan?"

"What's up?" She came out of a small office, with a pen in one hand and a cell phone in the other.

"You got something my girl can wear on my bike?"

My girl. He pulled each word from his quiver and shot them straight into her heart.

Meagan nodded. "After you mentioned my studio in that article for *Sports Illustrated*, my business tripled. You can borrow my firstborn child if you want. Hang on a sec." She slipped down a long hallway lined with hooks and cubbies.

"There's no way I'm going to fit into Megan's clothes. I'm twice her size."

Lifting the sunglasses, he gave a slow perusal from her breasts to her hips to her thighs, all the way down to the hot pink toenails peeking out of the cut-out in her wedges. On the way back up his lips curved into a wicked smile. "You're one hell of a beautiful woman, Callie-bell."

Heat burst in her core, the flames licking to the lobes of her ears.

"I want to see the wind mess up your hair." He stepped closer. "Want to hear you shout when I take a turn too fast." He lowered his face to her neck and inhaled before bringing his mouth right to her ear. "And I'm pretty sure you do, too."

Damn him for being right.

"Here you go." Megan came out with a pair of jeans and a purple T-shirt that said *I Yoga to Burn Off the Crazy.*

"You got any shoes?" Fin called.

"I've got some Keds." Megan turned to her. "You still a size seven?"

She nodded, but her friend had already turned back down the hallway. "Fin, I can't meet an art patron wearing a T-shirt." But she knew she couldn't hide anything from him, so he probably saw the gleam in her eyes.

Because no matter how wrong it would be to show up in jeans and a T-shirt when asking for donations, her body remembered the thrill of riding a motorcycle. Of the times she'd ridden on the back of Fin's, her hands on his stomach, her chest molded to his back. The way, on the long, straight stretches of highway, he'd hold her hand on top of his hard thigh.

It didn't take her long to change out of her designer dress.

And when she came out of the Ladies Room wearing the borrowed clothes and Megan's clean, white sneakers, Fin reached for her hand and slid his glasses back down. "Let's ride."

11

Arms fastened around Fin's waist, Callie tipped her head back and let the warm wind undo all the taming she'd done to her hair that morning. With the blur of the Tetons to her left and ranch land to her right, she took in the bright blue sky.

Everything she'd had on lockdown in her adult life unraveled like a spool of ribbon in the warm wind.

Funny how she'd thought that wild, uninhibited girl had been crushed under the heel of Fin's boot, when she'd been here all along.

Oh, cut it out. You crushed your own spirit. She could've responded any number of ways—railed at him, gone wild with her independence in the city—but she'd chosen to neatly pack away everything she'd once been to reinvent herself into this...refined woman. She'd quit making art to curate it. She'd let her hair grow out to its natural color, tossed out her hot pink patent leather boots, and sworn off wild love.

That was all on her.

But even as she cleared the path of lies, a bigger truth came rushing in. With every minute she spent in this town, her heart opened wider to Fin. Nobody—*nobody*—cared about her the way he did. He looked at her like she was his birthday cake ablaze with candles, his Christmas stocking stuffed with foil-wrapped presents. Like she was the light of his life.

And that was a heady feeling.

When Fin's big hand covered hers, a shock of awareness hit. She almost felt embarrassed, as if she'd voiced her feelings right in his ear. But, of course, she hadn't. He'd always had that sixth sense with her, probably because he paid such close attention. He picked up on her cues—when her body heated up or her expression changed or her fingers curled into fists.

She just...she felt too much for him. Unconsciously, her thighs pressed into him, and she tightened her hold. The smell of him—his shampoo, his clean shirt, his rugged, masculine essence—unearthed all the longing she kept at bay. That desperate ache to hold him. *Yes, God.* She'd give anything to be swallowed up in his big, powerful arms. His bear hugs kept everything bad in the world at bay.

He was right. His love had given her wings. The profound sense of acceptance had enabled the watchful, quiet girl to stand on the edge of a cliff and leap, knowing she could power herself to safety.

What a bitch she'd been to reduce their relationship to a high school romance in front of Julian. How petty of her to try to make Fin feel bad—to get back at him for hurting her. She wished she could go back and change the way she'd handled everything.

Fin held out his hand to indicate he was making a right turn. She looked up to see they'd entered the parking lot of the fairgrounds. Slowing, he angled into a spot in a row of motorcycles. The packed lot gave way to ticket booths and then acres of tents, white fences, and carnival rides.

It looked like any other fairground across America, except that this one was laid out in the lap of the Tetons, and there was no bolder, more dramatic sight than those rocks that shot seven thousand feet straight out of the valley floor.

He squeezed her thigh, reminding her to get off the bike. Holding onto his shoulders, she swung a leg off, her knees wobbly, the roar of the engine still humming in her bones.

Setting the helmet on the seat, she followed him to the ticket booth. After pulling two bills out of his wallet and paying, Fin led the way.

Growing up, she'd come every year. First, with her parents. Then, later, she and Megan would tag along with Ryder and his friends. She'd find every excuse to be near Fin, to position herself so she'd be the one sitting beside him on rides. For years, she'd watched couples and ached to be just like them. Holding Fin's hand, nuzzling into his neck. God, the yearning for his attention, his touch...

And then it had happened. At fifteen, they'd become a couple. So, to be there with him right then? It brought up *all* the feels. Especially when he automatically reached for her hand.

The path split in three directions: the rides to the left, the 4-H exhibits straight ahead, and food to the right. "Hang on," she said. "Let's grab something to eat. I haven't had anything since breakfast."

"You want barbecue or churros?"

A childlike happiness burst out in a smile. "Do you even have to ask?"

He went straight for the trailer that reeked of sugar-cinnamon and fried dough. Handing her the paper-wrapped treat, he grabbed her hand again.

"Let's go see my dad." They headed toward a tent set up like a bar. Her dad stood behind a table, arms folded across his stomach as he chatted with a group. Her mom tapped a keg that poured beer into a red Solo cup.

The banner stretched across the top read: Bell's Fine Ale.

Callie stopped walking to just take it in. A flap at the back lifted, and Ryder backed in, wheeling a dolly. "This is so cool." She couldn't deny the pang, though, of seeing her whole family working together. Without her.

Fin reached for her wrist and pulled her hand closer to his mouth, biting off a piece of Churro. "You okay?"

She shook her head with a smile. "You read me so well."

He tucked a lock of hair behind her ear, the tip of his finger lingering on the shell. "You feel left out?"

"Not left out." She leaned closer to him. "Well, maybe a little." Her brother leaned over their mom's shoulder and said something that made her laugh. "Yeah, I guess I do."

"Then let's do something about it." With a tug, he drew her closer to the booth.

Entering on the far side, Callie caught a whiff of must from the tent. When her mom glanced up from a row of bottles, her features bloomed in surprise—and so much happiness.

The mom she'd grown up with had practically lived at the diner; Callie had rarely seen her parents doing anything but work. But debuting their homemade beer made her mom look radiant and her dad truly engaged.

It meant the world to see her parents so happy.

In a quick scan of the area, she couldn't see an obvious way to get behind the table, so she dropped to a crouch and passed under it. Popping up, she pulled her mom into a hug. "This is amazing. I can't believe you guys are doing this."

"It's your dad. And he deserves this, right? Something that's just his?"

Her dad came over and cupped the back of her head so he could press a kiss to her forehead. "Thanks for coming, Callie-bear."

"I'm so proud of you, Dad." She'd missed out on so much. "I'm just..." She swallowed over the painful knot in her throat. "I really love you guys."

Her mom grabbed her first, but then her dad came up from behind and caged her in with his sturdy arms, and they rocked like that for a good, long moment. Until one of the workers drew him back to the customers.

Her mom smoothed the hair off Callie's forehead. "I love you, too, sweetheart. We're so glad you're home this summer."

"Callie." Ryder pulled off his work gloves and joined them. "You come here with Fin?"

"I did." She looked for him and found him listening intently to her dad's discussion. As always, he sensed her attention and gave her a smile meant only for her.

"Glad to see you can stand to be in the same room with him again." Ryder gave her a teasing smile.

"Barely." She reached out to rub his arm. "Hey, you've got an amazing little boy. I'm having the best time with him." *And can't believe I waited four years to get to know him.*

Ryder smiled at her. "He likes you, too. Especially that art stuff you're doing with him."

"Did you see the mosaic he made for me?" her mom said. "A *four*-year-old." She shook her head like her grandson was the next da Vinci.

An arm wrapped around her waist, and she breathed in the subtle scent of sage and fresh mountain air and everything Fin that made her pulse quicken.

"Marley's here." His deep voice rumbled in her ear. "You got a second to talk to her?"

She smiled up at him. "Sure."

He reached for Ryder's hand. "Hey, man. Knew if there was free beer, I'd find you here."

Ryder laughed and gave him the finger.

"I'm going to steal Callie for a bit," Fin said. "Hooking her up with one of my dad's old friends. We're gonna kick her museum into gear."

"I'm going to pretend you said exhibition, since you've

been working with me for two weeks, but let's go so I can tell her what I'm doing."

"Come on." Fin led her out the back of the tent.

She smoothed her hair and pulled down her T-shirt.

"Leave it," he said. "You look perfect."

"I'm asking for a donation. She wants to see a competent, sophisticated museum curator."

"She wants to see your heart and passion. She knows all about your degrees."

"You told her about me?"

"I tell everyone about you." His tone held so much pride.

"Yeah, but it's *what* you tell them that scares me."

She'd only meant to tease him, but he stopped and reached for her hair, twirling a lock around his finger. "I tell them the truth. I always tell the truth, Callie."

Her emotions rode high and strong. "I know that." Fierce affection grabbed hold of her body. *I wish so badly things could be different.*

One corner of his mouth tipped up, and he leaned in so close she could feel his scruff brushing her cheek. "You smell good."

Her breathing went shallow, and her skin tingled. She wanted to be in high school again, when she'd been free to touch him, because the impulse was strong to jump into his arms, throw her arms around his neck, and kiss him with abandon.

It never went away, that need to get closer, deeper. God, she wanted him so much.

But she wasn't in high school anymore, and the only thing she needed right now was distance.

She tried to step away, but he gripped her arm and held her in place. "It's all still there, isn't it? Between you and me." He gave her a wicked smile, before kissing the corner of her mouth. "And now that you've let me in just a little, all bets are off."

"Yeah, unfortunately, nothing's—" she began.

"Fin," a woman called.

He turned to an elegant woman in gray pants and a cream silk blouse. He swallowed her slight frame up in his arms. "Marla. Good to see you." He pulled back and gestured to Callie. "This is Callie Bell. The curator of the Exhibition of Broken Hearts."

She'd known he was messing with her every time he referred to it as a museum, so it meant a lot that he'd present it correctly in front of a donor. "It's so nice to meet you. You didn't come to the fair just to meet us, did you?"

"Oh, no. I'm with the Artists of Calamity Cooperative. We've got a booth over there." She motioned to another section of white tents.

Callie noticed the art on a flyer in the woman's hands. "Is that Alexa Rojas?"

"It is. I just picked this up from the Castro Fine Arts booth. They've got some wonderful pieces. If you haven't wandered through the gallery, you're in for a real treat. It's right off Main Street on Sundance Road." She turned the flyer to her. "You're familiar with her work?"

"I told you she just got her graduate degree from NYU," Fin said. "She knows her shit."

Callie elbowed him.

But the woman laughed. "Believe me, we're used to the Bowies. They're exceptional men who just need a woman's touch to balance out all that testosterone." She held out a hand glittering with jewels. "I'm Marla Gentry, and it's lovely to meet you. Fin's told me about your project, and I have to tell you I think it's wonderful. Heartache, betrayal, they're just so stubborn, aren't they? No matter how many years pass or new loves since, these are the kinds of emotions that linger. I believe you're onto something here, and I'd love to help in any way I can." She handed over a bright yellow shopping bag. "This is my anonymous donation. I have to get back to the booth, but if there's anything I can do, please let me know."

"Thank you so much."

The woman gave Fin a hug. "You have to come for dinner soon. Bring Callie, so we can talk shop."

As soon as she took off, Fin tugged on the handle of the bag. "What's in it?"

Callie peered inside and found an envelope she assumed held the check, but also a notecard. With the midday sun heating the crown of her head, fair goers moving in both directions around her, she read it.

My family summered in the Hamptons. Fin and I went from building sand castles together to sneaking around to applying to colleges in the same city.

"*Fin.*" He read over her shoulder. "Jesus Christ."

Intrigued, she ignored him.

I chose Tufts because he wanted Harvard. We stayed in love, or so I thought. I waited for him, dreamed of him, planned my life around him, all while he grew more distant. His excuses made sense, so I didn't push. School work, his fraternity, his extracurriculars...I understood. And then one summer he chose an internship in New York City over summering in the Hamptons with me. He fell in love with a girl who worked at the same firm. He said he didn't want to hurt me. He wanted us to stay friends. He'd always love me...just not like that. I never forgave him for falling out of love with me and, worse, I've kept a candle lit in the corner of my heart in case he came back to me. He hasn't.

Callie looked up but, of course, Marla Gentry had long since disappeared into the crowd.

"You know she's happily married, right?" Fin asked.

He always looked out for her. It had been six years, and she still felt so much for this man. Would it ever fade?

The moment she leaned her head back against his chest, his arm wrapped around her, pulling her tightly against him. Why did this one man feel so right and everyone else so wrong?

But then, Fin Bowie was a force of nature. Ruggedly masculine, he hurled himself into life, snatching every bit of joy he could grab with both hands. When he unleashed his energy on her, made her the object of his attention and affection, of course she got swept under.

And if she wasn't careful, she'd go right back into the life she'd once had. The one where they'd love each other with every fiber of their beings—and he'd bail on her every time his brothers needed him.

Yes, he was a great guy, and their connection was powerful. But she'd come too far to ever put her life on hold for him or anyone else.

Callie grabbed the tote filled with the laundered jeans and T-shirt she'd borrowed yesterday and headed for the door. A shout of laughter had her glancing back to find Stan leading Barbara around the room in a very sexy Bossa Nova. They were adorable.

Near the top of a ladder, Fin secured the tree to the ceiling with a thick hook and wire. Judy and her team had made it out of real wood. It stood squat with low hanging branches, easily accessible to visitors hanging their own stories.

Overcome with gratitude, she watched them for a moment. She'd started the project alone, and now she had this amazing team. After that first morning when Fin had shown up late and sweaty, he'd become dedicated to helping her. He'd brought her the Cooters, who'd been invaluable. Between their help and Mr. Martin, they'd turned her idea into something interactive and flashy.

In three days, the media would be in town for the July fifteenth opening, and she felt confident she'd created something worthy of the attention.

Stepping outside to the overcast, July morning, she crossed the damp boardwalk to Megan's yoga studio. The door was ajar, and she pushed it open. A shaft of early morning sunshine cut across the room, dust motes dancing and swirling. It smelled of lavender and vanilla.

"Megan?" The dark-paneled wood glowed in the soft light spilling in through windows.

Bare feet padded on the wood floor, and Megan appeared in leggings and a tank top. "Hey."

Her friend's flat expression made her uncomfortable. She thrust the tote out. "I washed everything, including the shoes. They got dusty from the fairgrounds."

Megan set it on a woven bench. "Thanks."

She had a shot; she had to take it. "You got a second? Maybe we could get a coffee or something. I really do want to talk to you."

"That's okay." Her lips pressed together, and her eyebrows lifted. *We done?*

Up until third grade, Callie had kept to herself. She'd bring a notebook and colored pencils in her backpack and sit alone during lunch, desperate for the time to pass so she could go back to class and not be an outcast.

But one day, while sitting on her usual bench in the corner of the playground, Megan had come up to her, hair windblown, eyes wild, and said, "Why do you sit by yourself?" Callie hadn't answered, and Megan had dramatically rolled her eyes, grabbed Callie's wrist, and hauled her over to the vault bar. She'd hopped up, slung a leg over it, and hurled herself forward. She'd spun around and around, a blur of pink and purple leggings and long blonde hair, until she'd stopped and hung there like a bat. "You try," Megan had said. And from that moment on, they'd been inseparable.

Until Callie had gone off to college.

"I'm a terrible friend."

Megan's body went on alert. "You're not a friend. Friends don't leave for college and never look back. Acquaintances do that."

"You're right. But it's not because—"

"Save it. Honestly? I don't care about your excuses. I mean, I moved away, too. I had my own drama, but apparently our friendship wasn't important enough for you to ask how *I* was doing. So, I've moved on, and I really don't have anything to say to you anymore."

"Hey." A woman hustled into the studio. "Sorry I'm late. I'll just grab my mat." She looked between Megan and Callie. "We still have a private session at nine?"

"Absolutely." Megan smiled. "Go on and get set up, and I'll be right with you." When she started to turn away, Callie panicked. She couldn't let her go. Not like this.

"*Wait.*" She had no rehearsed speech. She just had to wing it. "Every single memory I have from here has you and Fin in it. And when we broke up, the only way I could survive was to shut it out. All of it. And I'm sorry, Megan. I shut you out, too. I regret it with everything in me. I regret that I wasn't there for you when you left home, and I regret that I didn't let you or my brother or my parents or anybody be there for me. I can't change what I've done, but I hope one day you can forgive me."

Evening sunlight glanced off the lake, making it look like a sheet of molten silver. Turning away from the light to cut the glare on the camera, Fin reviewed the footage of Will's last attempt at a Rodeo 540. "You're not holding it long enough."

Brodie stood next to him on the platform with his arms crossed. "Probably shouldn't do ramps at the end of the day."

"He does look pretty tired." Fin watched his oldest brother bristle. "Maybe you should take a nap after lunch."

"That's a great idea, Fin." Brodie's exaggeratedly upbeat tone made Will's expression darken. "You should put that into training programs for the older guys."

"Fuck off." Will barely spared them a glance. "I'm not tired." He shot down the ramp and popped the lip.

As they watched him go airborne, Fin and Brodie bumped fists, appreciating how easy it was to push Will's buttons.

Will thrust his right shoulder up, pulled his legs in, and grabbed his skis. After rotating three hundred and sixty degrees, he landed in the lake. Water arced out from the impact.

"His landing's off." Turning off the camera, Fin climbed down the ladder and headed to the edge of the lake. Pine needles crunched under his boots, and a soft breeze sifted through his hair. When Will came into sight, Fin said, "You need a snack? Maybe a juice box?"

With a twist of his neck, Will flipped the hair off his face, droplets glittering as they took flight. "What the fuck does that mean?"

Fin shrugged. "You wobbled."

Brodie laughed.

"You're an asshole." They'd built a ramp with traction to make it easier to walk out of the lake with their skis. Will emerged from the water and dropped onto a log, swiping a hand across his eyes. He motioned with his fingers. "Let me see."

As Fin handed over Brodie's phone, his own cell phone vibrated in his back pocket. He pulled it out. *Wild Thing.* "Hey. What's up?"

"Fin. I...God."

He paced a few feet away from his brothers. "What's going on?"

"I just...*dammit.*"

"Callie." Both his brothers turned at his sharp tone. "Stop what you're doing and talk to me."

"Hang on. I should get a bucket." She must've set the phone down, because the sound of her shoes slapping on the wood floor faded into the distance.

Should he head into town? He shot a look to his brothers. No, he'd wait and see what was going on first.

"Okay." She blew out a breath. "I found some buckets in the utility closet."

"Talk to me."

"The ceiling's bubbling, so I guess there's a leak upstairs. I wanted to get a hold of you before it broke through, but it's already happening. It's about to rain in the left corner. Oh, dammit. There's—"

"Shut off the water valve."

"Upstairs or in the basement?" she asked.

"I don't know yet. But at least get to the one in the upstairs bathroom. If that stops it, I won't have to call the town manager."

"I have to protect the art first."

"You won't have any art left if you don't get a handle on the leak. Turn off the toilet and sink valve. Do it now."

"Yeah, okay. I'll call you—"

"I'm right here. Take me with you."

"Oh, good. Okay." A rush of breath sounded in his ear.

"I'm sagging." Will sounded like he couldn't believe his body had failed him. "Is it my speed? Am I not getting enough air?"

Fin held up a finger. *Hang on.*

Will shoved the phone at Fin. "I'm going again." Fin turned away, forcing Brodie to grab it instead.

"Callie?" He needed to hear from her. "Where are you?"

"Upstairs. I'm heading down the hall. Can you come over? No matter where the leak's coming from, I have to get the art pulled away from that section. I can't believe this is happening."

Fin glanced to Will, heading back to the ramp. He knew that look of determination. They wouldn't finish here until the last ray of sunlight dipped beneath the horizon. "Listen, call Mark Gorski, okay? He'll come right over."

"Who?"

"The plumber. Just ask your mom. She'll have him on speed dial."

"Oh, dammit. I have to go. Can you call him?"

"Yeah, sure."

"But you'll come, right? You'll come and help me?"

Fin watched his brothers climb the stairs to the platform. Brodie said something that made Will tip his head back with a loud bark of laughter. Will shoved him, but Brodie, the brick shithouse, didn't budge.

"Yeah. I can be there in an hour." *Don't let her down.* "Hour and a half at the most."

"What're you doing that you can't come right now? I mean, if you're eating dinner—"

"I'm not *eating.*" Food, he could reheat. "I'm training with Will."

"Oh." Resignation made the word sag. "Forget it. I'll figure it out." She disconnected the call.

She didn't even give him a chance to explain that Will couldn't compete until he worked out this one kink...but even as he thought it, the familiarity of his thoughts made him uncomfortable.

He was doing it again. It wasn't about putting his family before her. It was about not being dependable. Callie needed him right now, and he was telling her she couldn't count on him.

He called Marcella.

"What's up, Fin?"

"Hey, can you do me a favor?"

"I already washed your sweaty work-out clothes. If that isn't enough for one day, I don't know what is."

Fin smiled. "You could've left them on the floor. I'd have tossed 'em in the washing machine tonight."

"My eyes were watering. Anyhow, favor?"

"Can you please make two calls for me? One to Brad

Solheim, the Town Manager. Let him know there's a leak in the old Town Hall. He's got to get someone out there to shut off the main water valve. And Mark Gorski. Let him know there's an event the day after tomorrow. The art's getting damaged, so we need him there ASAP."

"Got it."

"Thanks. You're the best." And he meant that sincerely. He pocketed his phone, just as Will popped the lip of the ramp. Standing at the side of the lake gave Fin a different view of his brother's launch.

When Brodie reached him, Fin grabbed the phone. "Let me see." He reviewed it and caught the exact moment where Will was screwing up.

"Everything okay?" Will dropped onto the log.

"Leak at the old Town Hall," Fin said. "Marcella's going to get the plumber out there."

Will nodded. "So, how'd I look?"

"You gotta pick up some speed, man," Brodie said.

"No." Fin handed the phone over. "It's your thrust."

Will looked between them, but when he saw they weren't screwing around this time he reached for it and replayed his run in slow motion. "Holy shit. What's with my shoulder?"

Fin rewound and, when the moment came, he pointed to the screen. "See that?"

"Yeah, man, I do."

"Easy to correct." Fin handed him the phone. "Look, I gotta go. But I think you're overdoing it. You don't need to train this hard." The season had ended two months ago. Will should be working out and eating well but not training. Not yet. Not when competitions didn't start for another few months.

But there was something in his brother's eyes that held him in place. A starkness—a fear—Fin had never seen before.

But, of course, he knew. His brother would be twenty-eight at the next Olympics. Likely his last chance at the gold. He had to be in peak condition or forget about it.

Will stood and headed back to the ramp. "I'm going again. Get it right this time." At the foot of the platform, he turned back and gave Fin a quizzical expression. "Come on." He gestured impatiently at the phone.

"Brodie can record it. I'll look at it later." His brother would get in another dozen runs until it was too dark to do more. Meanwhile Callie was alone, trying to save her exhibition. He made his way to the path.

"You said Marcella was calling the plumber," Will said. "So just watch me one more time. See if I get it right."

"Brodie'll watch you." He headed up the trail.

"One more run. You're the one who caught the problem." His brother gave him as close to a pleading look as Will could give.

Heat rushed him, giving him a prickly sensation all over. He didn't want to let his brother down.

But he had to get over that shit, so he kept walking.

"Fin." When he didn't answer, Will said, "You're not a plumber."

"Doesn't she have the Cooters?" Brodie called.

Fin didn't even turn around. "She has me."

12

Fɪɴ ʟᴇᴀᴘᴛ ᴜᴘ ᴛʜᴇ ʙᴏᴀʀᴅᴡᴀʟᴋ sᴛᴀɪʀs ᴛᴏ ꜰɪɴᴅ ᴛʜᴇ doors held wide open with metal folding chairs.

Inside, Callie leaned into a huge squeegee and shoved a shallow pool of water out the door. He had to jump aside so it didn't wash over his boots.

"Nice reflexes." She thrust the water out, and it darkened the wood before cascading down the stairs.

"Thanks. I work out."

Unsmiling, she lifted the squeegee and went back inside.

He followed her, making a quick assessment of the damage. The ceiling had buckled, but the water hadn't broken through the plasterboard. She'd caught it just in time. "Where's the water coming from?"

"The utility room flooded." She spoke in a monotone.

"Marcella called the plumber. You hear from him yet?"

"Not yet, but I found the shut-off valve in the basement. Judy's sending some people out in the morning to take care of everything. She says we'll still be able to open on Friday."

"Hey." He stepped in front of her. "I came."

"I see that." She wouldn't look him in the eye. "Thank you."

"Then why're you pissed at me?"

She yanked out of his hold. "I'm angry at *me*." She tossed the squeegee, the handle landing with a smack on the floor. "I hate that I got all worked up over you not coming here to help me."

"I did come. I came as soon as we got off the phone—"

She held her palm out, eyes closing in frustration. "I know. That's not...Look, I never want to have this conversation again. It's like *Groundhog Day*. I shouldn't have called you. This project is your court-ordered assignment." She shook her head. "I know it sounds like I've always made you choose between me and your brothers, but that's never what I meant to do."

"I know that. You never had a problem with my family or their call on my time. What you couldn't handle—and shouldn't have had to—was the fact that you couldn't count on me. I haven't been dependable. My brothers and I...we think nothing's more important than what we're doing. I didn't see it before because it's just how we roll, but I see it now. It took losing you, but I get it."

"Well, that's...good." She stepped away from him. "But my point is that a month from now I'll be back in New York, so the only thing I should be focusing on is my work. I don't want to go back to all that drama we used to have. It's not you. You're not doing anything. It's me. It's my automatic reaction. I shouldn't have called you in the first place." She did that weird thing where she drew in a breath and composed herself, slipping into the role of Calliope again. "So, thank you for coming. I appreciate it, but I've taken care of the problem, and I won't reach out to you like that again."

"Like hell you won't. I'm not invested in your museum because of some judge, and you damn well know it. I'm here because it matters to you. And, yeah, you get all wrapped up in us because it's in your DNA to be with me."

She flinched, but he kept going. "Which means that's never gonna change. And believe me, I know you're leaving. But while you're here, I want to be with you. In any way I can, even if it's to help with a plumbing problem. I can't change what I did six years ago, but I'll never make a decision like that again." He stepped closer to her, tipped her chin. He didn't like her troubled expression. Something else was going on. "What's really going on with you?"

She tried to pull away. "Let's just get back to work."

"Not until you talk to me."

Defiance sparked in her eyes, but the longer he held her gaze, the more it fizzled out. She wrapped her hands around his wrists and pried him off her. "I'm just frustrated with myself."

Pushing her wouldn't help, so he waited for more.

"Look at me. I come home and fall right back into my old ways. Calling you when something goes wrong?" She raised her hands in frustration. "You're not a damn plumber." She forced a bitter smile. "You wouldn't believe how competent I am in New York."

It took everything he had not to reach for her, but he knew that wasn't what she wanted. "I want to be the one you call."

That sent a shimmer of tears to her eyes. "More than anything I don't want to fall back into bad patterns with you. I don't want..." She looked resigned. "When you said you were training with Will, it set off the same tirade I used to go through when you'd blow me off for something like the prom." She gave him a look that said, *Can you believe it?* "I'm an adult. I can call a plumber." She shook her head in obvious disgust. "But there I go testing you."

"Testing me?"

"To see if this time you'll love me enough to choose me." Her features turned pink. "I'm just so angry with myself."

She was breaking his heart, and he was done with the distance. Reaching out, he brought her palm to his mouth and kissed it. "Wild thing, you and me, we go deep. Too deep for us to have a fresh start. That means whatever bad patterns we have, we've gotta break them together."

"How?"

"Through honesty. Talking to each other. You tell me when I piss you off, and I'll tell you. And then *together* we'll find a new way to be."

She was too still, too quiet. When she gazed up at him, her eyes glistened. "You have no idea how much I'd like that."

To his utter shock, she raised a hand and scraped the hair off his forehead. And it felt so fucking good he wanted to toss her over his shoulder and drag her back to his bedroom. Lose himself in all the deliciousness that was Callie Bell.

"But it scares me." She drew in a shaky breath. "I think the reason I didn't come home much, the reason I stayed away from you, is because of this. These feelings. There's just something about you, *us*, that feels so right. And yet I know how wrong we are for each other." A tear spilled down her cheek. "It's just...when I'm with you, I forget."

He kissed it away, and then another one fell. He kissed it, too, but pretty soon he couldn't keep up with the tears cascading down her cheeks. "What we have? It's rare, wild thing. Are we perfect? Nah. No one is. But together, we're magic, and that means it's worth figuring out how to be right for each other."

When she gazed up at him, eyes filled with awe and vulnerability, he kissed her. That sweet, hot mouth opened up to him, and he dove right in, seeking the honey he'd missed for so damn long. She got up on her toes, pressing that lush body right up against his.

Mine. Every cell in his body acknowledged the truth: *this woman is mine.* He tilted his head, deepening the kiss, and she clutched his T-shirt. He felt her relax against him, and he snugged an arm around her waist.

Not letting her go. Not ever.

Their tongues tangled and swirled, and it felt new. Their bodies, their touch, their connection, it meant something new.

It meant forgiveness.

He tore his mouth away and whispered in her ear, "Together, wild thing. Swear to God, we can do anything, as long as we're together." He placed open-mouthed kisses down her neck, all the way to her collarbone. Her fingers fisted in his hair, and when he bit into the plump flesh of her breast, she yanked a handful.

Oh, fuck yes. Gripping her ass, he lifted her and carried her over to the wall. Rocking his hips forward to hold her in place, he worshipped that hungry, demanding mouth. The only mouth he'd ever kissed. Her legs wrapped around his waist, locking just over his ass.

When his hand shoved under her blouse and palmed her smooth, warm skin, his pulse thundered. She arched into his touch and, with a sharp exhalation, kissed the ever-loving fuck out of him.

Dammit, he was so hard for her, so desperate to drive it home, that he lowered her at the same moment his hips punched up, notching him right where he needed to be, the closest connection his body could get to her.

When she moaned, his need for her pounded in his blood.

But a signal in his brain reminded him that she still doubted him. *Them.* Which meant she wasn't ready. He backed away, even though she was gravity and he felt the pull of their separation deep inside. Yeah, he wanted her, but giving into his selfish needs might cost whatever ground they'd gained, so he reluctantly, gently, set her on the floor. She gazed up at him, cheeks flaming with confusion and embarrassment.

"I want you enough that I'm going to step away. Let you figure out what you want."

Anger flashed in her eyes. "My tongue in your mouth didn't clue you in to what I want?"

"You're lost right now. And there's not a chance in hell I'm gonna take my shot with you and have you regret it right after."

"You don't have a shot with me!" Callie's voice carried so far the tourists leaving Sweet Baby Jane's Tavern two blocks away turned to look at her.

Of course, *Fin* couldn't hear her because his bike shot off like a meteor into the night.

She felt eyes on her, and she turned to find a woman peering at her from the door of the yoga studio. Her hand flew to her mouth, and she closed her eyes. *Oh, my God.* All the hard work she'd done to become a better, more mature, person, and there she was shrieking like a harridan on the streets of Calamity.

If Julian's mother could see me now. She hurried back into the building.

But why had he gotten her all worked up like that just to shut her down? *Isn't that what he's wanted all along? To be with me?* The man frustrated her beyond reason. She grabbed her tote off the library table, dug around for her keys, and took off for the back exit.

Lost? What was he talking about? Next month she had an interview for her dream fellowship, which would lead to her dream job in her dream city. She was the opposite of lost.

She was a freaking warrior.

And why did he get to tell her what she'd regret?

Flipping off the lights, she pulled the door tightly behind her. Images chased her as she hurried to her dad's truck.

The silky strands of Fin's hair in her fingers, brushing over her cheeks.

His lips parting, closing over hers, so hot and firm and *determined*.

Her legs banded around his waist, grinding against his hard erection.

Awareness burst in her chest, sending a shower of sparks into her limbs.

It hit her with a wallop: she'd almost had sex with Fin against the wall in her exhibition space.

Of course, she wouldn't have gone through with it. She'd have come to her senses.

Except…when his hand had slipped under her shirt and skimmed her bare skin, need had ripped her wide open. The way he'd clutched her and squeezed so lustfully.

Okay, yes. Obviously, she would have. Well, who wouldn't want him? The way he looked at her? Like she was smart and funny and sexy. Like even at her worst, she still intrigued and delighted him. Like everything that came out of her mouth impressed the hell out of him.

Yanking the door open, she hiked up onto the seat, tossed her bag onto the passenger side, and jabbed the key into the ignition. What really pissed her off was that he'd acted like she didn't know her own mind. Like he was doing her some kind of favor by stopping. *Jerk.*

Buckling in, she tore out of the parking lot. A flash of his big hand cupping her chin, angling her for a kiss, sent another jolt of desire through her.

Come on, that wasn't a kiss. That was a claiming. It was more than mouths and tongues exploring. It was...God, it was two souls clawing to get closer...to join.

And he'd killed it. What, did he think he was the Overlord of All the Things?

It's my body. I get to decide what I do with it.

Her headlights lit up Main Street, a block ahead. Flashes of bright orange flames from the bonfire on the town green appeared between the bodies moving along the sidewalk. A band played in the gazebo, and barbecue from Skeeter's Bar and Grill scented the night air.

Hitting the turn signal, she bypassed the crowds and cut through the back streets. She was done thinking about Fin-freaking-Bowie. As soon as she got home, she'd make a spreadsheet for the donations that had been coming in, figure out how best to use them. If she kept this exhibition going after she moved back to the city, she'd need to pay someone to run it. Would Barbara want to be the director? Recently widowed, she seemed the most interested in finding a new direction for her life. Might be just the right timing and fit.

The back road to Fin's ranch loomed on her right. Her fingers flexed on the wheel, and she pressed the accelerator to avoid temptation. As much as she'd like to ask what the hell he'd been thinking—he'd finally gotten what he wanted from her and then he'd just tossed her aside—she was absolutely not going there.

Just ignore him. She'd pretend like he hadn't just kissed her like a demon determined to suck her soul right out of her body.

The sounds he'd made—the desperation. Desire sizzled down her spine.

Yeah, definitely not a good idea to see him right now.

Thank God she hadn't gotten naked. Imagine if she'd...*no.* Not imagining sex with Fin.

Especially since it'd been so easy for him to stop. Like it'd just been another kiss out of the millions he'd had over his lifetime.

Well, sure. He's a passionate guy. He goes hard into everything—including kissing.

She couldn't even imagine the trail of broken hearts he'd left over the past six years.

Whizzing right past the Bowie property, she noticed someone had left the gate open. She'd text him about that when she got home. No, she'd text Marcella. She didn't want to talk to Fin right now.

Damn him. How could he have been so blasé about that kiss?

And why did he get to be the decider anyway?

Does he actually think he knows me better than I know myself?

Callie slammed on the brakes. *No, he does not.* Executing a three-point turn in the middle of the road, she turned back around. She'd tell him just what he could do with his arrogance.

The truck bounced onto the rutted dirt road, and the moment she cleared the gate, she jerked the gearshift into

Park. Once she dragged it closed, she jogged back to the truck and hit the gas pedal. Her headlights lit up dual movie screens of dust and debris kicked up by the tires. Gravel pinged against the undercarriage.

If they were going to work together, they needed to set some boundaries. "Like no kissing." Her voice sounded loud in the small cab, making her a little self-conscious. She was getting way too worked up over the fact that Fin had... well, he'd rejected her.

She couldn't believe she'd gotten so carried away—she'd made *porn star* noises—when the kiss obviously hadn't meant anything to him. Mr. Badass, with his aviators and stupid motorcycle. Mr. Hot Stuff, with the hard body and tight, bubble ass. Mr. Women-Just-Fall-At-My-Feet-Because-I'm-So-Confident-and-Sexy.

A hot rush of desire had her squirming in her seat, and it was mortifying to be getting all worked up when she was trying to ridicule him.

When the dirt road met asphalt, the truck lurched onto the driveway. Tires squealed when she took the ninety-degree turn too sharply. A minute later she slammed on the brakes, shut off the engine, and hopped out of the truck.

She'd just been whining about falling back into old patterns, so...had it been a *pity* kiss?

She didn't need his pity. She didn't need anything from him.

But she couldn't stop remembering the way he'd pulled away from her—it had been like tearing off a layer of skin. Her legs had actually tightened around him. She'd come this close to begging him. And then he'd acted like he didn't want to take advantage of her, like she didn't know what she wanted.

I know my own damn mind.

I mean, maybe I'm a little confused, but if I've got my tongue in a guy's mouth, my intentions are pretty damn clear.

She climbed the porch stairs, and by the time she pressed the glowing light of the doorbell, she was so frustrated she wanted to spit.

The door swung open, and a towering wall of muscle smiled at her.

"Hey, Callie." Brodie, with his neatly trimmed hair and strikingly handsome features, lifted an arm against the door jam and leaned into it. "S'up?"

All that outrage flash froze and crashed to the ground, leaving her with nothing more than flaming mortification. But, then again, did she really care what these guys thought of her? *Not really.* They might put their bodies on the line, but they'd never risked their hearts. They could go suck it. "Is he home?"

Brodie stepped back to let her in. "Should be in his room."

Across the wide living room, Will leaned against the arched doorway to the kitchen. He wore athletic shorts and no shirt and looked like a cover model for *Men's Fitness* magazine. "Callie." He gave her a chin nod.

One lamp and a few recessed lights lit the cavernous interior of the overtly masculine home. Wrought iron and leather furniture made up clusters of sitting spaces around the gleaming dark-stained wood floors. The mantle and bookcases held no knickknacks and only a few framed photographs. In spite of the lack of feminine touches, the wide windows that let in the outside world, and the massive square footage, it still felt like a warm, comfortable cave.

Knowing the formidable block of support they made behind Fin punctured her purpose, starting a slow leak. "Excuse me for dropping by so late."

Brodie's eyebrows lifted in a look that made her realize she was doing it again, channeling Mrs. Reyes. *But you know what?* Screw them. Her tone might not fit how they remembered her, but it fit just fine in the world she was going back to. "Is he asleep?"

"No idea." Brodie gave a nonchalant shrug.

Soldiering on, she breezed past him and headed toward the grand oak staircase. As she started up, she heard their conversation—mostly because they didn't bother lowering their voices.

"What got up her ass?"

"No idea. Glad I'm not going to be the one to find out."

As soon as she moved out of hearing, she shook it off. She was here so she and Fin could get some things straight. With the opening the day after tomorrow, her focus needed to be on the exhibition and nothing else. Certainly not on *kissing*.

She headed down a long hallway lined with black-framed family photographs. No way did she need a trip down memory lane, so she kept her sights on the patch of yellow light spilling onto the hallway from the last bedroom on the left.

As intimidating as Mack Bowie had been, he'd also had

a surprisingly gooey center. When the boys had come back from their stint in New York with their mom, their dad had bent over backwards to make it up to them, starting by giving them free rein to design their own bedrooms.

Sports-themed, Will's had a basketball arcade game, a mini batting cage, and a zip line that went from his window to Ballard's pond. Brodie, always the most innovative, had a vending machine, an old school film projector, and a wall with a movie screen. True to Gray's easy-going nature, his room was like an opium lounge, designed for chilling. It had all kinds of gaming devices, a refrigerator, an air hockey table, and a mini bar.

Thinking about those rooms didn't prepare her for the hit when she barged into Fin's bedroom. She got slammed back in time. Hard. Nothing had changed. Unlike his brothers, Fin didn't have a theme or toys. He had an observatory. Basically, the bottom floor was a master bedroom suite furnished with a bed, a nightstand, and a couch, but a winding staircase led to the second floor loft with panoramic windows that let in the Tetons, the conifer forest, and miles of sage meadow. The mood of the circular room always reflected the weather.

A press of a button opened the blackout shade of the skylight ceiling. She and Fin had hauled a futon mattress up there so they could "camp out" under the stars. Her heart squeezed at the rush of memories. So much passion, intimacy, *love* contained within those glass walls.

She scanned the unmade bed where they'd spent countless nights talking under that navy blue comforter. By senior year their parents had stopped fighting them—why bother when no punishment had kept them apart?—so they'd spent most nights in each other's beds. How many times had they awakened each other, hungry for more?

That hunger—it had never gone away.

She remembered chasing him up that staircase, grabbing the back of his shirt, because he'd nabbed her pint of cookies 'n cream ice cream. They'd been laughing so hard he'd tripped, and she'd landed on top of him. They'd sat right there on the middle step, sharing the ice cream, bodies pressed together, as close as two people could get.

She missed that connection, that intense intimacy. Missed it with a constant, unbearable ache. She'd done a great job burying it under her focus on work, but Fin's kisses had reawakened it.

The glow of his laptop got her attention. Curious to see what he'd been looking at, she headed toward the bed, tripping on his sneaker. She caught herself on the edge of the mattress.

His room was the same disaster it had been six years ago. Their dad hadn't allowed Marcella to make the boys' beds or do their laundry. The older two, more competitive and disciplined, had clean, organized rooms, while the younger two, Gray and Fin, had pigsties. Still, they all knew how to cook, clean, and make repairs.

The room smelled of Fin's shower gel and...flowers? She noticed a vase of wildflowers on his nightstand. *What's that about?* He used to pick them for her. In spring and summer, wildflowers filled the meadows of Jackson Hole, so every time he'd gone out he'd grab a few for her. Automatically her hand went to her wrist, where she used to wear the flower chains he'd make. Instead, she felt the cool, hard gold of Julian's gift.

Had Marcella put them in his room? No, she wouldn't come in here. Then why did he have them?

And why did it make her so emotional to see them? They had nothing to do with her.

Oh, for crying out loud. What was she doing in Fin's bedroom? She'd lost her mind. She had to get out before he found her. Whirling around, she took one step and then faltered at the sight of him standing in the doorway of the bathroom.

"Wild thing." That deep, gravelly voice reached in and gave her bones a shake. Just out of a shower, Fin stood with his muscled arms over his head holding onto a pull-up bar. Broad shoulders, sculpted torso, and a light smattering of dark chest hair gave way to a plush white towel tied carelessly around his hips.

All her outrage turned to smoke and drifted away. Whatever she'd come to say flew right out of her head. "I..."

One half of his mouth cocked up in a smile. He knew his effect on her. "What can I do for you?"

"You can put a shirt on."

"Nah. I'm going to bed." He brought out the full smile, blasting her with its devastating mix of charm and carnality. "You know I sleep nekkid."

Well, she wasn't that seventeen-year-old girl ruled by hormones anymore. "I'd appreciate if you'd cover yourself up."

A dark cloud passed over him. "Well, *Calliope*. I'll point out that you're in my bedroom. So, if you want to have a formal conversation, I can put on some pants and meet you downstairs." He lowered his arms and crossed them over his taut stomach. Damn, those thick biceps did a nice job of framing his well-defined chest.

She forced herself to look away. "I'm not going to be here long. I just want to get a few things straight." Dammit, she did sound ridiculous. All prissy and uptight. But she'd lost her groove. There was the Calliope of New York and the seventeen-year-old Callie of Calamity, and she didn't feel like either of them.

He leaned down and swiped his boxers and T-shirt off the floor. Wadding them up, he tossed them into the closet. The flex of his muscles, the sheen on his smooth, tan skin in the soft light, got her blood humming. "Why don't you just spit it out? Whatever you want to say, talk like Callie. That's the language I understand. I'm not that fluent in Calliope yet."

"Would you stop making fun of me? I'm getting sick of it."

"Not making fun of you. I just don't like it when you talk like a fifty-year-old hostess at a Park Avenue dinner party."

Like his mom, that's what he means. Callie had passed Mrs. Bowie's building countless times on the Upper East Side but had never seen her. She'd only met the woman a few times in the early years, before his mom had stopped visiting.

"You don't get to tell me how to talk." *But thank you for reminding me why I came over here.* "Look, we have a lot of history, but it's just that. History. I'm focused on the future." Well, actually, at the moment she was distracted by the slight bulge under his towel. Had it been there all along? No, she would've noticed *that*. "My point is that, yes, I still have feelings for you. Of course I do. But I'm not going to act on them."

"So?"

"So, we can't fool around anymore."

"No fooling around. Got it. We done?"

"No, we're not done. I didn't come here to..." She turned away from the bulge—towel, whatever. "My point is that we have to work together, so whatever happened tonight, that can't happen again."

"Okay, I'll try real hard not to kiss you. I can't guarantee anything, though. That was a pretty hot kiss."

His flippant tone pissed her off enough to shake loose what she'd come to talk to him about. She charged forward. "And furthermore I'm not 'lost.'" *Oh, God*. She'd just made air quotes. "I hate when people tell me what I am."

He lifted his hands to his wet hair, scraping it off his face. The motion made his biceps bunch and flex, and it was just really, really...distracting. "Callie, maybe your friends in New York blow smoke up your ass, but I think you know I'm not gonna do that. I think you're lost, plain and simple."

"Okay, I don't even know what 'blowing smoke up my ass' means, but if it means they humor me or keep the truth from me, you're wrong." *Actually... he might be right*. Come to think about it, if she was always on her best behavior, what did they have to shoot straight about?

What about Julian? Given how polite they were with

each other, she couldn't imagine him bluntly telling her a truth she didn't want to hear. *This is not the point of why I'm here.* "The point is that I'm extremely focused and driven. Not many people can say they pulled together a pop-up exhibition in a matter of weeks. I know exactly who I am and where I'm going."

With a big gust of breath, his gaze dropped to the floor. "Yeah, okay." When it swung back up, he just looked sad for her. "We done now?"

And there he goes dismissing me again. "Oh, okay, awesome." She held his gaze for a long moment. *Did that kiss really mean nothing to you?* She should never have come here. Time to go, but her feet wouldn't budge.

"Come on, Callie. Did you really want me to fuck you up against the wall like some dirty hookup? Because that's never going to happen with us."

"Right. Because somehow you know what's best for me. I'm 'lost.'"

"I think we're both lost. Half of me's caught in what we used to be, and the other's excited about we're going to be."

"We're not growing—" His bulge had grown into a semi and, sorry, but given the tenting going on under that towel, it was impossible to ignore. "*Going* to be anything. We might've gotten a little confused for a minute there, but that's a good thing. We got the closure we never had. But I would..."

His hard-on pushed the towel out where the ends overlapped so that if she moved just to the left, she'd be able to see inside. Not that she would, of course. No, she'd stay right here.

"You would...?"

"I would appreciate—Jesus Christ, Fin. Put that thing away." How could a human penis grow to be that size?

But Fin, that gorgeous, rugged, sexy man, just tilted his head back and burst out laughing.

"Oh, my God, stop it. It's not funny. It's rude to sport a hard-on while I'm having a conversation with you." And it wasn't like she was standing there being all sexy. She was *yelling* at him.

But he only looked at her with total adoration. "What can I say? I'm a rude motherfucker."

"And horny, so I'll leave you to it."

"Oh, I'm not horny, wild thing. Already rubbed one out in the shower."

"*Fin.*"

But he ignored her. "After you got me all worked up with that kiss?" He gripped his erection through the towel, gave it a squeeze. "This is all your doing." He walked right past her, so close they brushed shoulders, and sat on the edge of his unmade bed.

"All right, this conversation is over." She started for the door. "And I'm hardly sexy right now, so let's not pretend there's something more going on here."

"But you are sexy." He leaned back, elongating that incredibly taut stomach and accentuating the brawn of his biceps. "Nothing turns me on more than when you get all fierce and wild."

"Okay, well, I'm telling you we're not going to finish what we started earlier. That's my whole point. We're not doing...that." She pointed to the towel that barely covered his erection.

"Nothing's gonna change my reaction to you. It's physiological. You talk, I get hard. You smile, I get hard. You get pissed at me and let me have it, I get hard." He shrugged. "Out of my control."

She should not be so thrilled by his words. "You know what? I shouldn't have come."

"Not unless you want to finish what we started."

"Which I obviously don't." Beneath the towel, his thick, hard length rose like a steel bar. She couldn't decide if he'd gotten bigger or—

"Obviously." He chuckled.

Caught staring at his package, heat swept up her neck and flooded her cheeks. "Oh, get over yourself. Goodnight, Fin." Just as she reached for the door, she realized she couldn't leave flustered and speechless. She had to pull herself together. Prove she was in no way lost. "Look, let's just focus on the exhibition and forget tonight happened. Starting tomorrow morning we'll just be cordial to each other."

"Cordial's not really in the Bowie playbook, but I gotcha. No more kissing."

"Exactly."

"I'll get my community service changed."

A slow roil in her stomach churned out sickening heat. The idea of losing him—not seeing him every day—sent her into a panic. She would miss his laughter, so infectious he made everyone around him break out in a grin. Those strong, capable hands that could fix anything. The brothers had grown up relying on their bodies, wits, and instincts to get them out of scrapes. There wasn't anything they couldn't fix. *That's hot.*

She cut a wary look to him. "You don't want to work with me anymore?"

"I think it's pretty clear I can't be around you and not touch you."

She understood that. It was exhausting to fight against her natural impulses around him, but they couldn't go there again. Not when she was leaving town so soon.

"You know that big bang theory Mrs. Summerville taught us in Astronomy?" he asked.

The fluttery feeling in her heart made it hard to respond. She barely nodded.

"You and me." His casual slouch belied the intensity of his tone. "We're two particles that got split in half. And no matter how far away you are, I feel you." He tapped his heart. "In here. You're my sun. And you could be in New York or on Jupiter, and I'm still going to feel the pull. The closer you are, the stronger the pull." He shrugged. "It is what it is."

Her heart punched the lights out of its jailor and broke free. "Fin." Emotion saturated her voice.

"Yeah, wild thing. I'm right here."

When he pushed himself up to a sitting position, she took off, skin tingling from the rush of affection for this man.

He had just enough time to get to his feet when her body hit his. He grunted with the impact, but those strong arms came around and enveloped her.

"Callie." He breathed her name, just as he dropped back onto the mattress, taking her with him. Nothing —*nothing*—on this earth felt as good as being in his strong, powerful arms. As his warmth seeped into her cold and lonely bones, he pressed kisses to her temple, her forehead, her cheek, everywhere his mouth could reach.

Yes, she was lost. And she only knew that because of this connection. No matter how she tried to cover it with a busy schedule and never-ending goals—to get straight As, to graduate, to get into a master's program, to get the fellowship—no matter how fast a pace she set, she couldn't outrun her feelings for him. *We're two particles that got split in half.*

She'd thought her inability to let him go meant she was weak, but it had never been as simple as missing him—missing the habit of him. No, he was embedded in her. And she knew that because being in his arms felt exactly like coming home after living out of a suitcase and sleeping on strange, uncomfortable mattresses for too long.

A strong hand cupped her chin, aligning their mouths. That first hit of contact—the heat and indescribable softness of his tongue—made her blood sizzle. His hands swept down her back, cupping her ass, and pressing her hard against him.

He kissed her deeply, lavishly, like he thought she might leave, and he had to get in as much of her as he could. And that drove her wild. His possessive grip told her he wanted her with every fiber of his being. The same way she wanted him.

Her heart pounded so furiously it hurt, and she needed

to feel him everywhere. She ran her fingers through his scruff, cupped the back of his neck, and rocked her hips against him. Desperation clawed at her, the need to get closer, deeper, be swallowed up so they could finally join with their whole bodies and souls.

His hand pushed under the elastic waistband of her leggings and gripped her bare ass.

"You better want this, wild thing." The growl in his voice set her on fire. "Tell me right the fuck now."

Her blood raced so fast she could hardly find the breath to speak, but he wouldn't touch her until she answered, so she pushed out a, *Yes*.

Rolling her onto her back, he pushed off the bed and yanked the towel off.

Dear God, that magnificent body was all hers. She took him in, from his muscled thighs to his thick, hard erection, all the way up that powerful torso. When she reached his handsome face, he cracked a cocky smile.

"Oh, get over yourself." Laughing, she reached for the waistband of her leggings, but he grabbed her ankles and dragged her toward the edge of the mattress.

"Can't help it if I like the way you look at me." Yanking down her leggings and panties, he tossed them aside. "Top off. I get all of you. Every single inch is mine."

With shaky fingers, she unbuttoned her blouse and shrugged out of it. Next went the tank top underneath, but when she reached behind her for the bra clasp, he lunged. Straddling her waist, he sat on his heels and skimmed his hands across her ribs and under her back. With one flick, he watched greedily as the bra loosened, and he flung it aside it. His big, warm hands cupped her breasts, and his features melted into pure, raw relief. Thumbs flicking her nipples, his gaze lifted to hers. "You feel this?"

She nodded, bones melting, toes curling with the sensations his touch stirred up.

He leaned over until his mouth was at her ear. "There've been days when I couldn't stand being so far from you. Thought I'd lose my mind. But right now?" He drew her breasts together, licking first one nipple and then the other, and then lazily, sensuously caressing the sensitive tip with his tongue. "I'm full. This is all I need. *Us*."

Desire roared through her body, making her jittery. But he didn't give her a moment to get her bearings. With firm pressure—as if he didn't want to miss a single curve or valley—his hand glided down her body until he found her wet, aching center. She arched into his touch, a flash fire racing across her skin.

His thumb rubbed a steady, maddening circle on her clit, while his fingers stroked her inner walls, making her cry out. He sucked on her nipple, tongue flicking the tip, sending a blaze of electric heat along on her limbs. "*Fin*."

She wanted his slick, hot mouth between her legs, his tongue swirling all over her sensitive nub, so she nudged the top of his head, her hips shifting restlessly. He responded instantly, pressing kisses down her stomach and along her inner thigh. Pushing her legs apart, he licked into her wet heat before taking the time to discover all the hidden places that made her hips rise and her fingers grip the sheet.

Erotic sensation spread, swirled, in a rising tension that

had her desperate for release. It felt so good, so delicious, and it was *Fin*. She thrilled at the sight of his dark hair gleaming in the soft light, his powerful shoulders spreading her legs wide. His big hands pushed under her ass, lifting her to his hungry mouth. It was all so unbearably exciting that desire whipped into a frenzy until she burst wide open. Freefalling through a space filled with light, heat, and sparkling color, she chanted, "Oh, God, oh, my God. *Fin*."

One last lick, and he rose above her like a predator. "I want you bare."

A shock of lust spiked through her at his gravelly voice, that fierce look in his eyes. "You can have me any way you want." She was on the pill, and she knew Fin would never compromise her safety.

"Fuck, wild thing. *Fuck*." Lowering himself, he took possession of her mouth, his kiss urgent, wild, like he was mad with lust.

She tore her mouth away. "Fin." It was just so intense.

His head lifted. "What?"

"Nothing. It's just...the way you kiss me. No one's ever wanted me the way you do."

"That's right. Because it's fucking *us*." He sat back on his heels, gripping her thighs and pulling her onto his lap. Grasping his cock, he gave himself a few hard tugs. "I want to watch." Planting a hand by her ear, he leaned forward and pressed at her opening. Slowly, gently, he eased inside. Color bloomed on his cheeks.

Every inch of her lit up as he pressed inside, sparks flaring. "You feel so good," she said.

From the sound deep in his throat, she knew he agreed.

He watched himself slide out and back in a few times, excruciatingly slowly, the strain building in his biceps, his jaw, and his neck.

The want became unbearable. "Now, Fin."

His gaze flicked up to her.

"I want to feel how much you want me."

His expression said, *You don't know?*

"No one touches me the way you do, and I miss it. I miss *you*. You fill me up. And I just...I need it. I need you."

His thighs pulled out from under her, and her bottom hit the mattress. Palms braced at either side of her head, he gave her a look filled with want and lust and so much love, and she reached up to run her fingers through his silky hair. "My Fin."

For a moment, his gaze caressed her features, and then he closed his eyes and snapped his hips. Sensation exploded, and her back arched off the mattress, as he powered into her. A sheen of perspiration broke across his skin, and his eyelids fluttered as if he were forcing them to stay open so he could watch her as he unleashed all his pent-up desire.

He slid a hand under her ass, tilting her hips, and her body burned as the friction drove her wild.

When he tucked his face into her neck, his skin turned hot and damp, and his powerful thrusts reawakened her craving for him. That frantic need for more, harder, deeper. She wrapped herself tightly around him, never wanting to lose this connection, this intensity.

His breathing grew ragged, and every time he drove home, he let out a grunt. With perspiration trickling down the side of his face, he shifted so he could watch her and, instead of the confident daredevil, she saw a vulnerable, wary man.

And that knocked her right out of the moment.

He'd told her he didn't want this kind of intimacy until she was ready. He'd worried it would scare her off.

"Wild thing?" His thrusts slowed, but she could feel the tremble in his arms. "You with me?"

Fear slid into her bloodstream. She'd gotten carried away, because yes, she was in it with him *right now*, but it wasn't like it could lead anywhere, right? She was going back to New York. She'd be stupid to give up everything she worked for to stay with him.

And as much as her heart screamed, *God, yes, I'm with you all the way*, she couldn't ignore the warning flares shooting out from the rational part of her brain.

This isn't going to end well.

13

"May I come in?"

Callie turned to see a petite, elderly woman in high-waisted khakis and a pale blue Polo shirt standing in the entryway. "Of course, but we don't open to the public until tomorrow." She climbed down the ladder and headed over, reaching for a postcard on her way. "Is there anything I can help you with?"

Her wrinkled hands tightened on her purse, as if she didn't want Callie to see inside. "I read in the paper there's a wall." She took a slow scan of the room.

She seemed an odd mix of confused and determined, so Callie figured she should explain the exhibition. "This is the Exhibition of Broken Hearts. It—"

"Yes, I know what is. I read there's a wall where we can connect with people."

"Hm. I don't know what you mean by *connecting* with people, but we do have one called 'Show Me Your Heart.' It's a curated selection of stories people sent in, along with a symbol of the broken relationship." She reached for the empty branch above her head. "This tree is for visitors to hang their own stories. Is that what you meant?"

The woman barely spared it a glance, so Callie kept talking. "The wall back there is where people can post a question to the ex who hurt them."

The woman lifted her purse. "A question? Okay, I'd like to do that." She looked at once hopeful and anxious.

"Good. I'm Calliope Bell, by the way."

The woman tore her gaze away from the back wall. "Helen."

"Let's head back there, Helen." She started off. "You see that basket?" She'd set up a long console table in front of the wall. On one end she had a basket full of numbered papers. "You write your question and pin it to the wall. That basket"—she pointed to the opposite end of the table —"has papers with correlating numbers. If the person who broke your heart happens to show up here, he can pin his answer next to yours."

"Oh?" Helen perked up.

"We don't expect to get answers, of course. It's more about voicing that one question we keep asking ourselves since the break-up. We all want to know why they did what they did, but most of the time we never get the chance. And I think if we ever want to heal, we need to finally say it out loud, you know? Even if the person never hears it, it helps to just say it in this public forum, this...*community* we're creating."

But she wondered if anyone could really answer such a complex question. *Why did you fall out of love? When?*

Why did you open the door to someone else—instead of ending our relationship first? Thankfully, that hadn't been her issue with Fin.

Fin. The thought of him hit like a shock of cold lake water. In a million years, she'd never imagined doing the walk of shame away from his house. She'd crept out the door before anyone had awakened, and then, instead of dealing with the fact that they'd *slept* together, she'd kept him busy all morning with a list of errands.

Coward.

"I don't have a question." Helen's firm tone drew her back to the moment. "I just want to leave a note for someone. Can I do that?"

Well, this woman had certainly aroused her curiosity. "A note?"

"Yes. I'd like to leave a note in case he stops by."

"We don't have a place like that."

The woman looked crestfallen.

"Maybe if I understood a little better. What kind of message are we talking about?"

"I want to explain why I didn't choose him." Anguish seemed to live in this woman's joints. She dug into the purse and pulled out an envelope. It shook with the force of her determination. "I want him to read this."

"Oh." Callie had designed everything for the people who'd been wronged. She'd never considered hearing an apology or explanation from the person who'd done the hurting. "That's...that would be incredibly powerful. I like that idea a lot." She looked around the room. "I don't know where we'd put it." They'd taken such care in arranging the exhibition to leave empty spaces. She took a moment to scan the room, and a rush of pride hit her. It looked good. Really good. She could never repay the Cooters, Mr. Martin, the donors, and Fin for all their help in putting this amazing show together in just two weeks.

She turned back to the woman. "What if we set up an easel with a corkboard on it? You could tack your note to it. We'll call it Connections. Does that sound good?"

Helen's chest rose as she drew in a breath. "Regret. Can we call it that?"

"Yes." *God, this woman.* "That's even better." This petite woman packed so much raw emotion, such determination, that Callie knew she'd do anything to help her find the person she'd hurt.

"Will it be up by the time you open tomorrow morning?"

"Actually, the preview for donors and press is tonight, so you can leave it with me. At lunchtime, I'll stop by the store and pick up an easel. I'll have it up by the time we open our doors." She reached for the letter.

But Helen quickly stuffed it back into her bag. "No, thank you. He wouldn't come for that." Busy with snapping her purse closed, she said, "He might not come at all." She started for the door but hesitated. "His wife passed a few years back, and I hear he's retiring. I think he'll leave town. There's nothing for him here anymore." She looked up at Callie. "I want him to know that I'm here. That I made a foolish, stupid choice."

Every hair on Callie's body shot upright, as she waited for more. *Tell me.*

"He had to stay here. His mother, his siblings, they needed him. And I had to go." She took in a sharp breath, the fingertips on her purse yellow with the pressure of her grip. "I should've stayed." Her shoulders pushed back, as she cleared her face of regret. "Will it be crowded on Saturday?"

"I believe so." Beyond the announcements in newspapers and social media, she knew word-of-mouth from Marla and her art-loving friends would have an enormous impact.

"I'll be here when you first open." Helen finally met her eyes, hers drenched with sadness, and she said a quiet, "Thank you."

"You're welcome." She watched the woman pull open the door and leave the building. She couldn't stand it. Couldn't stand that woman's pain and regret. Wanting to do something—anything—to ease it in some way, Callie grabbed her phone off the library table. Forget lunch hour, she'd ask Fin to pick up an easel right now.

Really? You're giving him one more errand?

But as soon as she swiped the screen, she noticed a pile of messages. When she saw Julian's name, she got a surprising zing of fear. Because what did they have left to talk about? If he'd forgotten to send her something, he could just mail it. Or, better yet, hold onto it until she got back in a few weeks.

Just read it. She opened the text.

Julian: Please return my grandmother's bracelet at your earliest convenience.

Her hand went immediately to her wrist, but of course

she'd taken it off that morning before her shower. She'd been in such a rush to get to work—*after sleeping with Fin last night*—that she'd forgotten to put it back on.

At your earliest convenience?

Talk about a stick up your ass. Is that what I sound like? Yeah, she guessed she did.

But...*wow*. Return the bracelet he'd given her as a gift. Who did that?

Honestly, she'd never seen this side of him. He'd always been charming. Of course, he'd been wooing her. But even when he was angry...*Oh, please*. Like she'd ever made him angry. She'd always been her best around him. Placid, tame.

Because you didn't want to be wild and passionate anymore, remember? Like you are around Fin.

She never got furious with Julian. She got frustrated or impatient, but nothing that would cause the kind of shouting matches she and Fin used to have. She could just imagine seventeen-year-old Callie reaming out Julian. With her platinum hair and leather bracelets, arms gesticulating like a windsock in a strong breeze, and Julian just standing there, all sealed up like someone had squirted lemon juice in his eyes.

And that's why Fin says you're lost. Because you're not that girl anymore, but you're not placid and tame, either. Frankly, it was exhausting trying to be on her best behavior all the time.

She didn't blame Julian—that was all on her. But she sure as hell blamed him for leaving her homeless. She tapped out a response.

How small is your dick if you can cut me out of your life just because I didn't share my past with you? Yeah, maybe not the best way to stay on good terms with him and his family. And not just for the interview, but for any hope of a job in the arts in New York City. She drew in a deep breath, calling up her composure, and tried again.

You want me to return your gift?

No, that was stupid. Obviously, he wanted her to return it.

Do you hate me that much?

Delete, delete, delete. She had no idea what to say when he'd just asked for his gift back. She'd just channel his mom.

I'm sorry I didn't tell you about my past, but why are acting like an asshole? I'm the woman you're supposedly in love with. It's not like I'm living some secret life. It's my past.

"Dammit." Her finger stabbed the backspace button.

You know what? You're giving him all the control. That's why you're freaking out right how.

Well, step one in taking it back was to not conduct her relationship via text. She dialed his number. It rang four times before going to voicemail. Seconds later, her phone chimed with a text message from him.

Julian: Can't talk. At the Met with my parents. Symposium on Peder Balke.

She reeled back, as shocked as if he'd just dropped out of the sky and landed in front of her. She'd reserved tickets for that event on the landscape and marine painter. In fact, she was the one who'd mentioned it to his parents.

She typed out a text. **I'm pretty bummed to be missing it**.

There. That was nice and would give him a reason to soften towards her.

But he didn't respond. And it was freaking her out. What did it mean that he would throw that symposium in her face? He hadn't had to mention it, so he'd done it to send a message.

And he certainly hadn't needed to text her about the bracelet while at the symposium.

Except...he's with his parents. Which meant his *mother* had told him to get it back.

Does she hate me?

That's not fair. Mrs. Reyes didn't know her side of the story.

She tapped out a response. **Don't want to trust the mail with a family heirloom. I'll just wait until I see you at the interview.**

That was good. If she remained calm and elegant, maybe he'd stop being such a dick. Her phone pinged with his response.

Julian: Best send it now. Thx.

Thx? They'd always made fun of people who couldn't spell out words in texts, and he'd *Thx'd* her?

She tossed the phone on the table and turned away, anxiety plucking at her nerves.

This is bad. This is so bad. She'd never seen him so cold. Not to anyone.

It made her sick to think he'd badmouthed her to his parents.

A spike of fear lanced through her. What if he'd asked them to remove her from the list of applicants for the fellowship? His parents held two of the eight board seats.

Did they have the power to cut her?

Slow down. You're totally overreacting.

But she wasn't because they did have that kind of power.

For two years, Julian had been nothing but charming and devoted to her. He'd been the best boyfriend, planning extravagant dates and bringing her flowers. He'd showered her in gifts and always asked about her feelings. He wasn't the deepest guy, but he took the time to listen and offer a solution before steering the subject in a new direction.

So, this complete switch to cold and businesslike signaled something. He was planning something.

You're doing it again. Giving him all the power.

Take it back. His parents only got to hear his side, so once she explained hers, they'd understand. She had a good relationship with his mom, so she could call her up— No, actually, that wouldn't work. A mother wouldn't believe an ex over her own son. *And it's not like I know what he told her.*

She'd send a card. *Yes.* Energy started pouring in. She'd tell her—no, she'd *thank* her for all she'd done to introduce Callie to her friends, loan her clutches and gowns for big events, and advise her. She'd end with how excited she was about the fellowship. Mrs. Reyes had pretty much *groomed* her for it. She'd remind her of that in a subtle way.

She thought of the notes she'd received from Mrs. Reyes, always on personalized stationery. Callie could easily get some made. She'd establish a relationship with his mom outside of the one she had with Julian.

Maybe she should invite her to the exhibition? Or mention her in one of the interviews Poplar Media had arranged. *Oh, this is good.* She'd actually thank her for all her help. Mrs. Reyes would love that kind of attention associated with an art event as hip and happening as the Exhibition of Broken Hearts.

Yes. Julian could tell his parents whatever he wanted, but the exhibition would show them why she deserved that damn fellowship.

Her dad's truck rumbled up the long driveway toward the Bowie house. Callie shifted the vent away from her face so the air conditioning wouldn't ruin the hair she'd spent an hour blowing out to glossy perfection. She could hardly believe the opening was tonight.

Prairie grass and wildflowers rippled in the meadows on either side, and the Tetons stood stark and imposing. As she approached the house, she checked for Fin's truck or Harley. If he'd come home for lunch he'd be parked there.

And if you hadn't snuck out of his bed in the middle of the night, you wouldn't be so anxious about showing up at his house right now. And, really, she didn't know what she'd do if he answered the door—throw herself into his arms or scurry past him and hide in the kitchen with Marcella.

How 'bout we don't deal with Fin right this minute? She'd talk to him later. First, she had to get through the opening.

The early July heat slammed her, as she got out of the truck and headed up the walkway. She didn't know why she'd let Fin talk her into letting Marcella take care of the hors d'oeuvres when Callie could have easily prepared them herself. Of course, he'd sworn that Marcella wanted to do it. With the guys constantly in training, their housekeeper rarely got to make desserts and carb-rich food. Still, the woman shouldn't have to do it by herself.

As she started up the porch steps, she heard male laughter. The garage door rumbled up, revealing three incredibly hot, brawny men in the shadowed interior. When they wheeled dirt bikes into the sunlight, she could almost hear the cheesy music from a porn movie. The scene would play in slow motion, the director firing a hose at them so their T-shirts and athletic shorts clung to their muscular physiques. Maybe Fin could shake the hair out of his eyes, winging water droplets—

"Wild thing?" Fin toed the kickstand and headed over to her. "What're you doing here?"

It took everything she had not to walk right into his arms. All the feelings last night had stirred up pulsed right beneath the surface. And the way he looked at her? His eyes, filled with relief, said, *You're here.*

I missed you.

God, she was happy to see him. *I missed you, too.* She'd

fought thinking about him all day. If she closed her eyes, she could smell the wildflowers in the jar next to his bed and the mix of his sage and fresh soap scent in his sheets. Every time she remembered the hard grip of his fingers on her ass, it sent a shock through her body.

"You need a minute, Fin?" Will asked.

"Yeah." When he reached her, he leaned in to kiss her cheek, and all her senses narrowed to him.

"Let's grab some water bottles," Brodie said, and the brothers headed into the house through the garage.

She brought her fingertips to her cheek, still tingling at the point of contact. "I thought I'd see if Marcella needs some help. She shouldn't have to do my work for me."

"This is the happiest I've seen her since..." His Adam's apple jumped as he swallowed. "Since my dad died, and her dinner party days ended."

She touched his biceps, warm and hard, and gave it a gentle caress. They held each other's gaze, so many unspoken words passing between them. She never should have snuck out last night; she'd hurt him.

But she'd have that conversation later, when his brothers weren't around. "Did you get the easel?" He couldn't have gone to Irving and back already.

"Yup. Got everything on your list."

"You took the chopper to Irving?"

He grinned at her sarcasm. "Got one out of your basement."

Electricity arced between them, and she couldn't deny the force of that charge. In the deepest part of her soul she knew she'd never feel this way for another man.

The intensity, their connection...it was unique. It was *them*.

She just didn't know what that meant.

And now was not the time to try and figure it out. "That was clever."

"Seemed the simplest solution."

It was. And if she hadn't been so intent on keeping him away, she probably would have thought of it herself.

"Things all set at the museum?"

She gave him her best scowl. One day, she'd get him to use the right word. "Things are perfect with the *exhibition*. This lady came in, though. She asked me to start a new section where people could leave messages for each other."

"What kind of messages? 'Single male seeking double-jointed swimsuit model who drinks beer and grows her own pot?'"

She smiled. "No, weirdo. *She* actually understands what I'm doing."

"I get what you're doing, wild thing."

Holding his gaze, her body filled with heat and desire. *Nope, not going there.*

"So that's what the easel's for? The messages?"

"Yes. This lady, she's the one who hurt someone, and you can see how much she regrets it. I've been so focused on people with broken hearts that I hadn't thought of showing the other side. And I can't imagine anything more healing than hearing from someone who's done it. It means so much to her, you know? She said..." Her heart squeezed at the memory. "She said she made the wrong choice. That her boyfriend needed to stay in town because of his family, and she needed to leave. But she wishes she'd stayed with him, and it's killing her."

"Fifty years is a long time to go without your heart."

She knew that because she'd lived without hers for six years.

And I'm going back to New York without it all over again.

Fear ripped down her spine. *I don't want to be Helen.* "She, um, she wants to get a message to her ex."

"So that means the guy's local. Why doesn't she just go and talk to him?"

"I don't know, but I hope he stops by. I really, really want him to read that letter." She needed them to find their way back to each other.

I'm ridiculously invested in this story.

Yeah, because I'm so close to making the same mistake. Now that she knew what it was like to be with him as an adult, why would she keep fighting these feelings?

"Fin." She reached for his hand, when all she wanted to do was hug him. *Just tell him the truth.* "Last night...it scared the crap out of me."

"Yeah, I know." He cupped her cheek. "You don't want to get back together. I get that. And if you don't want us to get nekkid, then we won't. But you're in my life no matter what, and we're gonna figure out a new way to be together."

She clasped his fingers. "You know I wanted last night as much as you did." *Needed.* "But I'm leaving, Fin."

"You carry that excuse around like a security blanket. Makes me think there's something more going on."

"My life isn't here."

"Yeah, sorry, but that one's made of the same cloth." He scraped his fingers through her hair. "What's got you running scared, wild thing? Tell me."

"I just did."

"Listen, if we've got any chance at all, we've got to talk to each other. So, let's do this. Let's pull it out by the roots. Because I'm telling you right now, I'm not going back to a world where you're not in it. It's not gonna happen. I get that you're not there with me yet, but we *are* going to find our way back to each other. And to do that you gotta talk to me. Come on. What's got you so scared?"

"I just..." Her heart raced, and her skin went clammy. "I don't want to be that girl again, okay?" She hadn't even known her fear until he'd pushed it out of her. "The one who lives for you. I have a life now, and I can't get lost in you all over again."

"So, don't. You're not seventeen anymore."

"You don't understand how...susceptible I am to you. Your voice, your touch...just talking to you makes me happier than anything else. I *like* you so much."

"I like you, too, wild thing."

"And I don't want to be...obsessed with you again."

"What if I stop wearing deodorant? Maybe fart under the covers every now and then? Would that help?"

Laughter bubbled out of her, breaking the tension. "There's nothing you could do to make me not attracted to you. That's the problem."

"That's a damn good problem to have, Callie-bell. And we're not gonna settle for less, right? Not when we've got *this*. That would be dumb. So, I've got a feeling you're stuck with me."

She threw her arms around his neck. He was right. Of course, he was. She didn't know how it could work—they lived in different worlds—but she let it all go when he gripped a handful of hair at the back of her head and tugged so he could take her mouth in a deliciously sexy kiss.

She had no answers, but she had right now. And this man...she couldn't deny what her mind, body, and soul recognized as *hers*.

His hands swooped down her back, cupping her ass, and hauled her up hard against him. He kissed her, the wet heat of his mouth so soft and sensuous.

"Whoa, dude." Will's deep voice tore them apart.

Dazed, she turned to find the brothers heading toward them.

"Give me a minute," Fin said.

"Already did that." Will tipped his head back and squirted water into his mouth. "And look how that turned out. How 'bout we hit the trails?" He tilted the bottle toward Callie. "And you come with us."

After all the time she'd spent on her hair? "I can't. Not today."

Fin stroked a hand across Callie's cheek. "Everything's all set for the opening, right?"

"Other than the hors d'oeuvres, yes."

"Come on, Callie, we haven't hung out with you in years." Brodie sounded earnest.

"And the preview's not till six," Will said. "It's only noon."

She appreciated that he knew the timing, but she wasn't about to tell them that she'd spent forty minutes blowing her hair out and applying make-up in a way that would only need a slight touch-up. She'd made sure all she needed to do was slip on her dress and heels. "Thanks for asking, but you guys go. Have fun." She headed toward the house to check in with Marcella.

"So that's how it's gonna be? You're just gonna walk away from us?" Brodie shot her his winning smile. "Come on, Callie. It'll be fun."

Damn, these men were gorgeous, sexy beasts. But between the heat and the exercise, she'd get all sweaty. "Sorry."

She made it to the front door, when Brodie said, "Since you've been home, how many times have you hiked?" He gestured to the Tetons in their backyard. "Jumped in the lake? You're in *Wyoming*." Reverence saturated his tone.

Her skin started to tingle—her body's memory of how much fun she'd had growing up here. How she'd taken advantage of everything Calamity had to offer. The mountains, lakes, ghost towns. The bison preserve she and Fin had broken into in an attempt to set the animals free.

She thought about Helen, and a fierce energy surged through her. "Yeah, sure. I'm in."

Fin gave her a wickedly irresistible smile. "No regrets. Right, wild thing?"

"No regrets."

14

Hot sun burned the top of Callie's scalp, and perspiration dotted her forehead.

As she pedaled along the flat trail leading to the mountain, she ran through her to-do list for the opening. Fortunately, most everything was done. She still had to get the food and drink tables set up, but that just meant spreading a tablecloth and setting out platters. Her parents would bring the ice just before the doors opened at six.

Her tire dipped into a rut, jarring her. *For goodness' sake, girl, you're in Wyoming.*

Pay attention.

Tightening her grip on the handlebars, she maneuvered onto the shadowed path at the base of Buck Mountain. Up ahead, the guys shouted to each other, pulling wheelies and abandoning the trail to race around a tree and then crash back onto the path. Their laughter made her smile.

Not that long ago, she'd kept up with them. She

remembered the burn in her muscles when she'd push harder to overtake them. The freedom in sailing over a creek, and the adrenaline rush of the landing.

When had she stopped taking chances? The forest passed by in a blur as her world went quiet and the truth rose tall and clear inside her. It hadn't been just about Fin hurting her. It had been about moving away from home for the first time. Going from the safety of her small town to the big, overwhelming city. She'd expected to do it with Fin. It wouldn't have been so scary if he'd made the transition with her.

And it would've been supremely selfish. He would have hated every minute there.

She knew exactly why she'd stopped taking chances. *Because the stakes went up.* If she didn't have great grades, she wouldn't get the top internships. If her bosses didn't like her, she wouldn't get optimal shifts. The risk of failure, poverty, suspension from school—real world stakes—had grown too high. So she'd chosen a lane—art history, on the track to become a curator—and once she had, she'd gripped the steering wheel and floored it.

She'd chosen Julian because he'd been in her lane.

Up ahead the guys had stopped, their feet on the ground, as they waited for her to catch up. Shafts of golden light splintered the shadows of the lodgepole pine forest. She breathed in the fresh mountain air, let it fill her lungs.

She slowed as she reached them, too aware of the way Fin watched her. Because it struck her that Julian's gaze expressed his pleasure with her. In it, she saw his approval of what she was wearing or his pride in the way she'd behaved in front of his parents or friends.

But Fin just saw *her*. She didn't have to talk a certain way or bring a perfect cheesecake to a dinner party to win his sexy smile. She just...she made him happy.

That was a heady feeling.

When she caught up with them, she braked and dropped her foot to the ground. She couldn't keep the grin off her face. He made *her* happy. And she knew he felt it, too, because color flooded his features.

"Ah, Christ," Brodie said.

"What is it with you two?" Will said.

She laughed because this was how it had always been between them. This intense affection for each other.

"Which way?" Brodie gestured first to the trail that wound up the mountain at a steep incline, and then to the flat path that led to the lake and circled around it.

"Up." Her response was automatic. Because she felt giddy and free.

"Hell, yeah." The guys shot up the trail.

She pedaled all of a few yards before the burn in her legs reminded her she was completely out of shape. *Not gonna happen*. For a moment she watched them, their hard, round asses bobbing in the air, their powerful thighs pedaling. They needed to train, and she wouldn't slow them down.

She turned her bike around.

"Hey." Fin held up a hand and his brothers came to a stop. All three turned to her.

She waved them on. "Go. Have fun."

Their resolved expressions reminded her of another of Mack Bowie's rules: leave no one behind. *Uh oh.*

Will gave a chin nod to his brothers. "Lake?"

And with that the guys came hurtling back down, kicking up dirt on the path around her.

"Guys, you don't have to do this."

But they didn't listen. They took off toward the lake, happy to just be together, out in the sunshine, and using their bodies.

Their enthusiasm was contagious. With the wind in her hair, Callie pedaled as fast as her legs could go. She hadn't felt this free in ages.

The forest gave way abruptly to the valley, all bright sunshine and soft green sage. Up ahead, on this perfect July day, sun lovers dotted the shores of the dark green lake with their beach chairs and umbrellas, and the water rippled with swimmers. The beach season was so short in Calamity that the residents and tourists took full advantage of—

Her wheel hit a root and sent her airborne. Adrenaline shocked her system, as the world spun like a kaleidoscope of bright blue sky, the brown and green of towering trees, and the spots of colorful umbrellas and swimsuits around the lake. And then her back slammed down on the hard dirt.

"*Callie.*" Fin was at her side.

Three large bodies blocked the sunlight, Fin crouching beside her. No one said anything, as they gave her lungs a moment to resume pumping oxygen.

When she drew a breath, Fin squeezed her hand. "You okay?"

She took stock of her body, her back, arms, and legs. "Yep." Planting a hand in the dirt, she pushed herself up. A breeze blew the hair off her face, and the lake smelled as clean as the snow it'd been only weeks ago. She smiled. "I'm good."

Fin held her gaze like he was giving his heart a minute to settle back in his chest. He brushed the hair out of her eyes and ran the back of his hand down her cheek, softly, slowly, looking at her like she was the most precious thing he'd ever seen.

Her heart pounded, the floodgates opening, letting in all the desire, want, and affection she'd held for this man since she was a girl. "I want to get nekkid."

His features hardened; his body tensed. "What're you saying?"

She understood right then that she'd never had a choice. Fin was right.

They were two halves of the same whole.

"Say it," he said. "Say it out loud."

"I want to be with you, Fin Bowie. I want everything."

———

Fin barely paid attention to the laughter in the garage or the clatter of bikes as his brothers lifted them onto the wall racks. All he could think about was Callie. Getting her alone.

Now.

"All right, I'm out of here." She pointed a finger at Fin.

"Get those platters to me in two hours." Her smile faded when she caught the look in his eyes.

Yeah, that's right. I'm coming for you. He stalked across the garage, grabbed her hand, and towed her around the side of the house. Pressing her back against the wood-shingled wall, he cupped one ass cheek and let her know with his mouth how fucking happy he was that she'd come back to him.

Without hesitation, she wrapped her arms around his neck and tilted her hips, capturing his cock between their bodies. *Oh, hell, yeah.* He caught her up in a full-body embrace and licked into her mouth, wanting every single thing she had to give. Wanting it right the fuck now.

His hands slid under the elastic waistband of the leggings, but she laughed and smacked his hand away.

"I didn't mean now. Five feet from your brothers." She cupped his cheeks. "But we're definitely doing it after the opening."

She's back. My Callie's back. He kissed her, hands gripping her hips. "I want you."

"I want you more." Her fingers sifted through his hair, tugging when they got to his scalp. "But right now, I have to go."

Reluctantly, he stepped back and watched her leave. Right before turning the corner and moving out of his sight, she paused to give him the hottest smile he'd ever seen. A mix of shyness, hopefulness, and a heaping promise of naughty.

Once she was gone, he pulled his phone out of his pocket. It had been vibrating for the past several hours. He needed to get his ass showered and dressed so he could help her set up the food tables, so he read his messages while climbing the porch stairs. When he saw several missed calls from his manager, he hit Aaron's speed dial.

He answered on the second ring. "Fin. Finally. Got some good news."

"Yeah? What's up?" He headed inside, the cool of the air conditioning a welcome relief.

"I heard from my contact at the magazine. He said when he came back from lunch he heard shouting in the conference room, and he opened the door to find them on your website. They were going nuts over the footage from Austria. He said, and I quote, 'That was some seriously crazy shit he pulled.'"

"Yeah, we had a good time."

"Sure, sure. It's just another day at the office for you, right? Jetting down a spine you've never been on, flipping off the edge of a boulder and spinning...what was that? Three full rotations? Yeah, no big deal." He chuckled.

Marcella called to him from the foot of the stairs and mouthed, *Everything's all set*. She pointed to the kitchen.

He gave her a thumbs-up and a silent, *Thank you*.

"Anyhow, the guy thinks you might be back in the running for the cover."

"Cool." Anticipation had him racing down the hall. He wanted to shout out to his brothers, but he'd learned his lesson. He wouldn't say a word until it was a sure thing. Except for Callie. He'd tell her.

"So, as long as you don't get into any more trouble between now and September, I think this might happen."

"Not even possible, man. I'm trouble-free. Listen, I've got to go."

"Training?"

"No, tonight's the opening." The sooner he got to Callie, the better. "Gotta get ready."

"The *opening*? I just told you to lay low."

"And I will." He stepped out of his athletic shorts. Setting the phone on his bed, he yanked off his T-shirt. When he picked it up, his manager was still talking.

"—where the central installation is your *meme*."

He slowed on his way into the bathroom. Aaron made a good point.

"Not to mention the fact that you only work there because a judge *ordered* you to. Can you imagine the headlines on that one? Judge orders Fin Bowie to make a museum about the World's Worst Boyfriend. In his *hometown*."

He laughed. "That would suck." He'd looked forward to seeing Callie in her element, leading art patrons around her exhibition. The project had lit her up, and he'd liked helping her realize all her ideas. "Yeah, okay. You're right. I'll skip it." He'd have her to himself the rest of the night.

And the rest of his fucking life. *Amen.*

Right after he disconnected the call, he texted Callie.

Can't come tonight. Mgr doesn't want me stirring up the meme.

His finger froze before hitting send. That made it sound like he wasn't dependable. *Reword it.*

Can't come tonight. Aaron thinks press would have a field day with me assigned by court to help set up the WWBF installation.

He hit send, not knowing how she'd react. What if the only thing she got out of that was that he wasn't showing up *again* for something that mattered to her? He sent another text.

Let me know when press leaves, and I'll come over and help clean up.

Better. At least she'd know he'd be there. He wasn't bailing on her. He was about to toss the phone on the chair when it vibrated.

Callie: Does that mean the cover's back on?

She got it. She totally got it. **Yup**. And she trusted him. Damn, that meant a lot.

Callie:

He smiled at her emojis. Mostly relieved he hadn't let her down.

He texted again. **Let me know when the coast is clear. I'll come after it ends and help clean up.**

Callie: You sure you want to come into town?

Fin: I want to be where you are.

When he came downstairs, he found Marcella on the house phone in the kitchen.

"I don't mind at all." The phone rested between her

shoulder and ear. "I live with a pack of wolves. Let me see how fancy people live for a minute."

"Is that Callie?"

Marcella nodded and got off the phone. "She asked me to bring the platters over, since you're banned from the premises."

"Hey, man. Go big or go home. Wasn't that my dad's motto?"

"Oh, yes, World's Worst Boyfriend. You're a real legacy to your father's teachings." Her eyebrows shot up in a comical expression of, *Yeah, I went there*.

He burst out laughing. Keeping his eye on her, he stealthily reached for one of the perfectly aligned cannolis.

She smacked his hand away but, fortunately, his reflexes were quicker, and he shoved it into his mouth, leaving a glaring space in the center of her design.

"Oh, heavens." She feigned alarm. "You ingested sugar. Should I call nine-one-one?"

He smiled. "I'll survive it this one time."

"Just curious...if you defile the temple, does it mean you lose your superpowers?" Lifting a tray, she tipped her chin toward Fin. "Help me get these in the van."

"I'll do one better than that." If he left now, he'd get there a full hour and a half before the opening. "I'll take it there myself."

"Callie said you're supposed to stay away."

"Yeah, at six. It's only four-thirty."

No one would be around.

. . .

Fin texted before he got out of the van. **Here. Open the back door**.

Shoving the phone in his pocket, he pulled out a platter. Just as he turned around, he saw Callie striding toward him.

Holy fuck. A silky white dress cinched at her waist and flared around her hips. The full skirt fluttered around her legs in a sage-scented breeze, and her long dark hair looked like something out of a shampoo commercial.

"I thought you didn't want to be here." The moment she reached him she took the tray.

Before grabbing another one, he leaned in to brush a quick kiss to her cheek so he wouldn't mess up the pale pink lipstick, but he caught a whiff of her expensive perfume and a hint of herbal shampoo and couldn't resist cupping the back of her head and kissing that delectable mouth.

She could always reapply lipstick, but he'd never again miss a chance to let his woman know what she meant to him. She stepped closer, her whole body softening, and it made him want to knock the platter to the ground and sweep her into his arms. Every kiss—*Jesus*—it set his pulse pounding.

But this was her night, so he reluctantly pulled away. "What time do the Cooters get here?"

"Everyone went home to shower and get dressed." With finger and thumb, she wiped the corners of her mouth. "They'll be back at five-thirty, and my parents will bring the ice at six."

"I've got plenty of time. Let's get these in there."

"Okay, but then you'd better skedaddle."

He smiled at her word choice. "I'm gonna skedaddle all over your ass as soon as this event's over."

"Keep it in your pants, champion. I have enough people helping me clean up. You just stay away. I'll come straight to your house when it's over." With a platter in her hands, she headed for the building.

The breeze lifted her hair, fanning it over her shoulders, and the silky fabric of the dress clung to her ass just like his hands wanted to do. She was the most beautiful woman he'd ever seen. Vibrant, elegant, and insanely sexy.

A wave of emotion rose up and crashed over him. "Callie."

She glanced back. When she saw his expression, her brow furrowed, and she turned fully.

"I've loved you as far back as my memory goes. My wild thing, she was my best friend, my heart, my everything." He shrugged. "But the woman you've become?" He cast his gaze down to the ground and cleared his throat before swinging it back up. "I didn't think it was possible to love you more, but I do." He swallowed past the painful knot. "You impress the hell out of me."

Her features tightened, and tears glistened. "Don't make me cry."

That was the last thing he wanted to do. "I never want to make you cry again, but you need to know...I love you, Callie. I fucking love you."

She blinked a few times, pulling in a sharp breath, before opening her mouth to say words that never came.

She hurried back to him, grasped his shoulder, and got up on her toes. With her face buried in his neck, she exhaled. "I have missed every single thing about you, Fin Bowie, but knowing you still love me like this? It's *everything*."

Oh, fuck, he loved this woman. Wanted her so badly. His hand caressed down her back till it reached her ass. He couldn't resist grabbing a handful and squeezing.

Laughing, she swatted him away. "You're not copping a feel in the parking lot. Come on." She turned back around and headed into the building.

Grabbing a pewter tray, he followed her inside. Stacks of boxes filled the hallway. "What's all this?"

"More donations."

"Holy shit."

"There're a lot of broken-hearted people out there."

He kicked the door closed behind him and made his way down the narrow hallway. Just before they entered the exhibition room, Fin said, "You sure no one's around?"

"Positive. It's just us, and the doors are locked."

Surveying the room as he entered, he watched her set the platter on a folding table set up for food and drinks. "Looks great."

"I love it. I love it more than anything I've ever done."

"Including your own art?"

"Believe it or not, yes. Art was how I expressed all the crazy emotions I didn't know what to do with. This..." She made a sweeping motion across the space. "I feel like it makes a difference. Every time I mention this place to someone, they either have a story of their own to share or ask if they can get involved. And the donations keep pouring in. What we're doing here matters." She smiled—a mix of his mischievous Callie and the accomplished Calliope—and she'd never looked more fully herself. "And it's *fun*. Everything I've done in the art world so far—interning at galleries and museums—has been so pretentious. So cutthroat and competitive. But this...I love the concept, brainstorming ideas for it...and I love all the people I've worked with." She slid both hands up his chest, resting them over his heart. "And best of all has been doing it with you. I feel like my best self is right here."

"Then stay. Stay here where you're happy." *Stay with me.*

Her smile flagged, and then happiness turned to worry. "I can't. This is a pop-up exhibition."

"Make more of them."

"I can't have a career based on hit-or-miss temporary exhibitions. I have to use my degree, build my reputation."

"And what about us? You got room for me on that career track of yours?"

"Yes." She said it firmly. "I don't know how we'll do it, but I do know that I was born to love you. That you're the *rest* of me. I don't know how to explain it. It's like, no matter what good stuff I'm doing, what great people I'm hanging out with, there's always something missing. It's only when I'm with you that I feel whole. Complete. Does that make sense?" She looked a little helpless. "I love you, Fin."

Love. He swooped down and kissed that word right out of her mouth. *She loves me.* And when she clasped a hand around his neck and angled him right where she wanted him, he lost it. Scooping her into his arms, he carried her over to the library table in the middle of the room and perched her right on the edge.

Breathing in her scent awakened every cell in his body. He tumbled into the soft, wet heat of her mouth. And, damn, it felt so good. His heart swelled with desire and hope, rousing a want so deep and intense he could barely contain it.

"Fuck, wild thing." He nuzzled her ear, licked the shell. "I need you."

"I need you, too." Her hands gripped his biceps. "So much."

His hands caressed down her slender back, pausing at the swell of her ass, and when her fingernails scraped across his scalp, he shoved up the skirt of her dress and palmed her smooth thighs.

Her legs banded around his hips, pulling him tightly up against him.

"Dammit, Callie." He slid a hand into the V of her dress and cupped the plump swell of her breast. "So fucking hot."

She moaned. "Fin." Her hand pushed between them, grasping his erection through his jeans.

His breath hitched, as desire streamed like liquid fire through his veins. His hips rocked into her touch, and she tightened her grip.

A shock of light behind his eyelids had him jerking away. Someone rapped on the door. He heard voices outside.

"Oh, no." Callie dropped off the table and shoved him. "Go."

But it was too late. At the window a television camera was aimed right at them. Anger cracked through him. "Who the hell is that?"

"Callie?" Stan called. "You want to let us in?"

"I'm sorry. He said he was coming at five-thirty. Is this... what does this mean for your cover?"

"Don't worry about that right now. It's show-time." He tipped his chin. *Go*. When she hesitated, he forced a smile. "They don't know it's me. Go on and let them in." He pressed a kiss to her mouth and took off for the back exit.

Voices flooded the room, and he heard Stan say, "Thought I'd let them in before the crowds come. Give you a chance to give them a private tour."

"That sounds great." Calliope was back, but this time it made Fin smile because she was so damn good at what she did. "Come on in."

"Where'd Fin go? We ought to interview him, too. Pretty funny, right? Fin Bowie, the World's Worst Boyfriend, helping set up the exhibition?"

Laughter filled the room.

At the back door, Fin closed his eyes.

He'd just lost the cover. For good this time.

Fin's headlight illuminated the bright yellow post reflectors on the old bunk house. A mix of elk and bear crossings and stolen street signs glowed in the darkness. He cut the engine and waited for Callie to get off his bike.

What's done is done. Besides, he wouldn't know the fall-out—if it came—until morning. Maybe he'd get lucky and *National Adventurer* wouldn't give a rat's ass about the meme anymore.

The important thing was that Callie's opening had gone well. And they were together.

He'd waited a long damn time to be with her again.

She propped her chin on his shoulder. "You brought me to your lair?"

It hadn't occurred to him she'd want to celebrate. "You want to do something? Get a drink at the Tavern?" He'd just wanted to be alone with her. Didn't want to go near social media or get calls from his manager.

"Oh, God, no. All that socializing sucked the energy out of me." With her hands on his waist, she slid off and set the helmet on the seat. "This is perfect. I have you all to myself."

Fuck, yeah.

Taking her hand, he led her to the door, sucking in the fresh pine-scented mountain air. The porch had a row of rocking chairs. Usually when he hid out here, he sat outside, listening to the coyotes howl and the owls hoot. But not tonight. Tonight, he wanted to be alone with his woman. He pushed the door open and stepped inside.

Flicking the light switch, he went straight for the kitchen. At the refrigerator, he said, "Water? OJ? Lemonade?"

"Lemonade, please." She stood in the entryway, taking in the foosball, ping pong, and air hockey tables that took up one side of the long rectangular building and the large, modern kitchen and custom-made dining table on the other. Couches, lounge chairs, and a few scattered tables filled out the room. "Nothing's changed."

"You were just here for the wedding."

"Yeah, but it obviously didn't look like this." She smiled. "Like a giant man-cave." Her smile faded. "It has so many memories."

It struck him—*that's why I brought her here tonight.* Here, they'd been their best selves. Away from family, friends, all the outside bullshit. Just *them*, real, whole, and true. "Good ones?"

"The best." She let out a wistful sigh. "It's just confusing. Two hours ago, I was wearing a designer dress and acting like a museum curator. Now I'm in jeans and back in the place I lost my virginity."

"You weren't acting. You single-handedly curated that exhibition."

A smile lit her features.

"What?"

"You called it an exhibition."

He smiled. He'd just been giving her a hard time.

She headed into the kitchen. "I love that it went so well, but what will it cost you?"

"Don't know, but I'm not going to waste time guessing. It'll be what it'll be." He reached into the fridge and pulled out a lemonade.

"What if you lose the cover?" On her way, she picked up a basket of napkins that had been knocked over. "Stan made a big deal out of the fact that the actual World's Worst Boyfriend helped put the exhibition together. At least he didn't mention the community service part."

"I'm not gonna make myself crazy over something that's beyond my control." He handed her the cold bottle and then headed for the air hockey table. He hit the switch, and the motor started humming. He raised his brow in challenge.

"Are you sure?" She gave a fake look of concern. "I don't want to make your night any worse by kicking your ass."

"Been playing a lot of air hockey in New York City?"

"I might not have had much playtime over the years..." Setting her bottle down, she rolled her shoulders, laced her fingers together, and cracked her knuckles. "But I'm pretty sure this country girl hasn't lost her touch." She dug a plastic disc out of the goal box and dropped it onto the table. Grabbing her striker, she cocked her elbow and took her first shot.

Within seconds, the sounds of clacking filled the room. They played fast and furiously, neither willing to accept defeat. Only when she unzipped her sweatshirt to reveal the plump cleavage bursting out of a low-cut black tank top did her puck slip past him and land in the box. Sirens went off in celebration.

He cut her happy dance short by immediately retrieving the puck and shooting it across the table. Even with her quick reflexes, it slid right in.

"It's air hockey." She straightened. "Not a blood sport."

"I think you know I play to win."

"It's *me*."

"Fuck, yeah, it's you. And since you're gonna resort to showing me your tits to win, then it's game on."

She burst out laughing. Damn, he felt good. Footage of him getting busy with Callie on a table might be going viral right then, blowing his shot at the cover, but he was back with his wild thing. So, when the puck came winging across the table, Fin lunged to block it. *Crack*. It soared back to her side, and she threw her body into the save, making her breasts jiggle. As soon as he whacked it, his gaze slid to the feminine slope of her shoulders and those hands that had always given him so much pleasure. He heard the smack about a second before the puck slid cleanly into the goal.

Callie pumped her arms and jumped up and down.

A love so strong it didn't fit inside his body had him setting down the striker and stalking toward her. He tucked a lock of hair behind her ear. "I love every fucking thing about you."

Excitement glittered in her eyes, and he cupped the back of her neck and drew her to him. His mouth sealed over hers, hot and wet, his tongue stroking inside and taking what he needed.

Leaning against the table, he pushed the hair off her face. He let her know with his kiss that she was essential to him. That, over a lifetime of knowing each other, his passion for her had never waned. Never would. Her palms pressed on his back, and her leg hitched, mashing their bodies tightly together.

His heart thundered when her hands pushed under the waistband of his jeans and squeezed his bare ass. "Fuck, Callie." His voice was more a growl.

"You make me crazy." Her breath whispered over his

skin. "When we're not together, God, I just feel like I'm missing something."

"Something?"

"My heart."

He could see what it cost her to say it, and it made him smile. "Yeah, wild thing. That's right. I'm your heart." He lifted her off the ground. Her legs banded around his hips, and he carried her to the couch. "And you're mine." He didn't give her a moment to think before he gently set her down, his hands sliding under her back. He lowered his mouth until it hovered over hers. "Guess that means we're stuck with each other."

He got lost inside that kiss, just dove under, right into the wet heat, the restlessness of her hands and rocking of her hips. Her scent called to him at the most primal level. He slid a hand underneath her tank top, and his body went up in flames at the feel of her warm, smooth skin.

Her legs cinched around him, her hands skimming up his back under his T-shirt. Her touch—so possessive, so hungry—made him wild. *Goddammit, I love this woman.*

He grabbed a handful of fabric at the back of his neck and yanked his T-shirt over his head, giving her the space to peel off her jeans. Her pale skin against the coffee-colored leather cushion made her seem vulnerable, soft, and unbearably feminine.

Overwhelmed, he buried his face in her neck. "Callie." Tugging up her tank top, he rocked against her. "Get this off."

She rose to pull it over her head and then reached for the bra clasp behind her back. When the straps slackened, she reached between them and rubbed him through his jeans.

And then her gaze flicked up, a mischievous grin spreading across her features. Her tongue peeked out, making a slow slide across her lips, as she popped the top button, then the second. Blood surged into his cock. He sucked in a sharp breath, hips straining. He wanted the slick heat of her mouth on him more than he wanted to breathe.

Tossing the bra aside, she placed a hand on his chest and pushed him back hard enough to topple him on his ass. Her fingers went back to his jeans and, as she hovered over him, those beautiful breasts bounced with each flick of her wrist. Once she got that last button undone, she grasped him. Her warm, sure fingers slid up his length. Lust swept through him so fast, he squeezed his eyes closed and thrust into her grip.

She gave him a firm squeeze, before flattening her hand and stroking his cock with the heel of her palm. Ass hiked in the air, her mouth closed over the tip and she sucked him in.

His hips shot off the cushion, and he palmed the back of her head, keeping her right there while that slick, hot tongue leisurely licked the sensitive head. "Fuck, wild thing." His legs jerked, but the jeans restricted him.

Pushing her back, he jerked them down and kicked them off his feet. "Need to be inside you." But as he loomed over her, gripping her thighs to spread her wide for him, she stretched out beneath him on the couch and grabbed his ass. A hiss of breath left his lips, as she brought his cock back to her mouth. He had to grab the armrest to keep from collapsing on top of her when she sucked him to the back of her throat.

Oh, fuck. "Yes."

Her tongue zigzagged along his length, her hands holding him to her face. Glancing down, he got a glimpse of her hips shifting impatiently, her tits bouncing and swaying, and the beast in him roared. "Jesus, Callie." *So fucking good.*

She gazed up, her slick, hot mouth full of his cock, as she licked lusty circles around the head and then lapped at the sensitive spot just under the ridge.

Electric heat burned and pulsed along his nerves. He rocked his hips, harder, faster, the quickening tension coiling so hard he knew he couldn't last much longer. When she moaned, the vibration coursed up his cock, making his spine tingle. He pulled out. "Gotta have you."

But just as he leaned back, his gaze snagged on her. He'd never seen anything sexier in his life than Callie's mouth swollen and wet, her expression filled with raw, carnal need.

He pushed off the armrest and straddled her, reaching for her breasts. Cupping them, he plumped them together and dropped his face into her cleavage. When she slid a hand between them and grasped his hot, hard, erection, sensation burst across his skin.

He thrust into her hand—once, twice, a third time—the pleasure so fierce he had to shut his eyes to hold it all in— before turning his attention to her. He licked her nipple, then sucked it into his mouth. She arched into him, her other hand going to the back of his head to keep him right where she wanted him. The sounds she made as he caressed one breast and flicked his tongue on the other nipple only made him grow harder, heavier. He had to have her now.

Sitting back on his heels, he tore her panties off her hips. Just before diving in, he noticed her hesitation. "What?"

"Nothing." She swallowed, looking at his collarbone.

"Callie...what..." Fuck, he was so hard he hurt. "What's going on?"

Her gaze flicked up, a hint of vulnerability. "Do I look... different to you?"

"I don't know." But he could see his answer mattered, so he took in the body that turned him on like no other. "I guess a little. Rounder, fuller." *Lush.* And then reality tore through the fog of lust. "You think you're *fat*?"

"Not fat, but my body's changed. I just...I don't know what you see."

Tamping down his body's demands, he took her in and saw nothing but his beautiful, sexy woman. "When I look at you my heart beats so fast I think I'm having a heart attack. I see the woman who doesn't take anyone's shit, and the woman who turned a crappy breakup into one hell of a great life for herself. I see the woman who looks at me like she wants to ride my cock one minute and wring my neck the next. I see *you*, Callie. I see us. And there's nothing I want more in this life. Now, can I fucking have you?" He knew he sounded desperate, almost angry. But he didn't want her to waste one more second being self-conscious around him.

With a sexy smile, she shifted her thighs to welcome him. "Well, when you put it that way…"

He appreciated her teasing smile, but he was too far gone. "Let it all go, Callie. Just let everything go so we can put ourselves back together again."

Passion softened her features. "I want that so much."

He lowered his face between her legs, kissing her inner thighs, and then licking a path to her center. Joy flooded him, as her thighs opened for him. She let him into her heart *and* body. Both hands clamped on her hips to hold her in place, he licked inside of her.

"God, Fin." Her knees lifted, the soles of her feet planted on either side of his head, and she grabbed his hair. Her hips rocked against his face. "I'm not…I'm gonna…*Oh*."

Her ass lifted off the couch, and she kept herself pressed to his mouth.

"Don't stop. Don't…*Fin*." She cried out as she shattered beneath him.

When her body crashed back down and her hands fell from his hair, he loomed over her and kissed her mouth with everything he had. Gripping his painfully hard shaft, he guided himself inside her.

But before he could sink in, she pushed him back. "Should we use condoms?"

"You said you were on the pill." He dropped his head to her shoulder.

"I am. It's not about me. Julian and I—"

"I don't want to hear about you and Man-Bracelet."

"I'm just saying I've always used a condom. And I haven't been all that...active."

Jesus, his cock ached for release. "Then we're good?"

She pushed him off her. "It's not about *me*. It's you. Your sex life."

He took himself in hand and squeezed against the pressure. "Wild thing, I don't *have* a sex life."

"Cut it out. It's not like I haven't seen you with other women." She made a sound very close to a snort. "You're a very sexual man."

"Yeah, I've been with other women." He couldn't hold back the smile. "I've traveled with women, eaten dinner with women, boarded with women, hiked with women, gone shopping with women...but I haven't had sex with any of them."

She eyed him warily. "A blow job is still sex."

"Callie. I haven't been with anyone since you."

"Oh, shut up. You've had sex." But it sounded more like a question.

"I haven't even kissed another woman."

"In six years?"

"Since the night before you left for New York." They'd had crazy sex on a mattress in his bedroom, under the skylight that August night. He'd been half out of his mind with love for her, fearful about what moving to New York would mean for his place within his family—meaning, would they stop needing him as a coach?—and dreading either decision he made, because both would have equally catastrophic consequences.

He smoothed the hair off her beautiful face. "Why

would I settle for anything else when I know what it's like with you?"

"Oh, Fin." His name came out a whisper, as she drew him to her.

And then he slid home, and nothing had ever felt so good.

15

CALLIE'S BODY HADN'T EVEN COOLED DOWN BEFORE Fin's breathing evened out. As soon as he'd collapsed on top of her, he'd rolled to the side. He had his back against the couch cushion, face burrowed in her neck, and arm slung across her stomach, holding on like she might slip away in the dead of night.

Sex got her riled up, so she had no idea how he could fall asleep immediately after. Easing out from under him, her body hummed and vibrated like a tuning fork. Swiping his T-shirt off the coffee table, she pulled it on. She hadn't eaten tonight, too busy leading tours around the exhibition and explaining the concept to reporters, donors, and patrons. So, she headed into the kitchen.

Frustration edged under her skin. All this time she'd imagined Fin going wild, having sex with random women on his travels around the world. But he hadn't. He hadn't *wanted* to. He only wanted her.

And that killed her because she'd lived with the

devastating pain of a betrayal that just hadn't happened. She'd moved on with Julian—a relationship so watered down, so...bland—all while Fin had been holding out for the real thing. For her.

His love is so pure. And she'd kicked it—him—to the curb.

All those lost years, all that heartache.

Except...had anything really changed? They still lived in two separate worlds. And this time, she'd learned her lesson—she would never ask him to give up his life and live in New York City with her. And she couldn't move home—not yet. She needed the fellowship and a few years as a curator to have any kind of legitimacy in the art world.

Why would I settle for anyone else when I know what it's like with you?

A shiver of delight ran through her at the memory of his words. She didn't have a lot of answers, but one thing she knew down to her bones. She loved him. Deeply, purely, and with everything she had.

She *couldn't* walk away.

Which meant, what? They'd carry on a long distance relationship for five, maybe even ten years?

Opening the refrigerator, she smiled at the contents. The main house had organic meat and vegetables, some fruit, nuts, and sweet potatoes. Fin and Marcella could do things with sweet potatoes that boggled the mind.

But in the bunkhouse, where they came to party with their friends, they had all the good stuff. She grabbed some cheese—a Bowie would never soil his body with cheese—

and found crackers in a cabinet. Hoisting herself onto the counter, she turned on the TV mounted under a cabinet.

When audience laughter blasted from the speaker, she found the remote and lowered the volume. It was *The Jimmy Dunlap Hour*, the top-rated late-night TV talk show.

"I mean, I want to be this guy, right? I can't see her face, but did you get a look at his latest girlfriend?" An image of Fin kissing her filled the screen.

A shot of adrenaline enervated her. She'd hooked her ankles over Fin's ass, one hand fisting his hair, the other clutching his back. He gripped her bare thigh, the folds of her white silk dress spilling off the table. They looked hot. Passionate. He kissed like he was drowning in her.

"Like, I'm straight," Jimmy said. "But if making out with the World's Worst Boyfriend is wrong, I don't want to be right." The audience burst out laughing.

Bare feet shuffled into the gleaming kitchen. "So, it's out." Wearing only black boxer briefs, Fin's sculpted chest, round biceps, and thickly muscled thighs were on full display.

Callie pointed the remote at the screen and turned it off. "Yeah, it is." She read defeat on his features. "What does this mean for you?"

He grabbed a glass from the cabinet and filled it with cold tap water. "Got a text from Aaron. It's over. No cover."

"I'm so sorry, Fin." There was nothing she could say to make it better.

He drank half the glass and then wiped his mouth. "I don't want to talk about it."

By his troubled expression, she suspected he did want to talk, but she let him take the lead.

He leaned back against the counter, crossing his powerful arms over his taut, tan belly. "I don't give a shit about being on the cover of a magazine."

"I know."

His facial muscles relaxed. "I just want one damn thing of mine in that trophy room. Just one thing."

Kicking out her legs, she wrapped them around his hips and drew him over to her. She scraped her hands through his long hair, pushing it off his face. "Do you remember what you used to say? We used to stand in that stupid room, and you'd look at all those ribbons and trophies and tell me a trained monkey could earn those."

"I still think that. I don't want to do what they do."

"You don't want the cover, and you don't want a trophy. So, what *do* you want?"

He clamped his big hands on her thighs and squeezed. "You know what I want. I want their acceptance. Their respect."

"Perfect, because you've got it."

He started to pull away when she tightened her hold. "Listen to me. Why did you bail on our prom?"

"Will needed me."

"You were seven years old when your dad hired a coach to live on the property with you guys. Will has a coach. He's always had a coach."

"Yeah, *one* coach for the four of us. And he was with Gray that week. You know that."

She cupped his chin so he'd hear her. "Your dad could

have hired ten coaches, but Will needed *you* to help him. That guy who keeps texting you, Nolan? He's got a coach, too, but he's begging *you* to look at his film. Coaches send you clips of their athletes all the time so you can help them figure out what they're doing wrong. Fin, you have their respect. You have the respect of everyone in your business."

"Yeah, okay, but I don't want to just be the pit crew guy with a wrench. I want one thing I can hold up that says, *See? I'm as good as you guys.*"

Pulling away from her, he dug into the box of crackers and shoved one in his mouth. His features screwed up and he spit it out in the sink. "How can you eat that shit? It tastes like a salt lick."

She draped her arms around his neck. "Can I tell you a secret?"

"You can tell me anything."

She leaned in until her mouth was at his ear. His silky hair brushed across her cheek, and she breathed in his masculine scent. "I can't believe you've only been with me."

His hand came up to her side, just under her breast. "I don't want to be with anyone else, Callie. I just don't."

She leaned back a little. "And that's the thing about you. You know your own mind. Your brothers want the shiny thing. They don't care how they get there; they just want the result. But you want the journey. You want to figure out what you're doing wrong so you can correct it—that's more important to you than winning an award. Do you see? You want different things, so you get different results. They follow your training schedule and eat what you tell them to eat because you've proven to them it will result in a trophy. *You* do all that because you're interested in seeing how it will impact your performance. Your brothers get respect for training their bodies to perform. You get respect for your knowledge, your insights, and your instincts. So, let the trained monkeys get their trophies. You get something else."

"Yeah? What's that?"

She pulled off his T-shirt and let it drop to the floor.

Color flooded his cheeks, and his nostrils flared. "I win."

Fin thumbed the button, killing the call. He stood immobile, staring out the window over the kitchen sink. But he barely saw the Tetons. Barely registered the blue sky and tufts of fat white clouds. "Holy shit."

Bottles rattled, as the refrigerator door opened. "That bear back in our yard?"

Fin waited for Will to close it and pop the top of his unsweetened ice tea. "Braverman just called." Two weeks after losing the cover, the brass ring had dropped into his lap.

Bottle aimed at his mouth, Will's chin lowered as he swung a look at Fin. "What?"

He couldn't believe it. *Holy shit. This is happening.* "Braverman. He offered me a contract."

And that was it—right there. The look of pride he'd

waited a lifetime to see bloomed across his brother's features. "You're shitting me."

Fin's brows lifted, and his expression said, *Did this just happen?*

"Bells and whistles?"

"Offroad RV, his best crew of photographers, videographer. All expenses paid."

"Total control in planning the trips?"

Fin nodded. "He's been following my page for a while and says he's never seen a better, more intuitive rider."

"He's damn right about that."

"What're we talking about?" Brodie tramped in, sweaty and muddy.

Before Fin could answer, Will said, "Braverman offered Fin a contract."

The pride in his brother's voice touched a nerve deep inside him.

"For real?" Brodie stood stock still.

"For fucking real."

Brodie threw himself at him, his hands clapping Fin's back. "That's amazing, man."

"Thanks."

His brother pulled away. "What's the commitment?"

"Two-year contract, four movies a year."

"Damn, man. That's..." Brodie shook his head.

Will reached into the refrigerator for another bottle of unsweetened tea and tossed it to Brodie. "Proud of you, man. Real proud."

Now that it had fully registered, he had only one place he needed to be. He blew past his brothers.

"Hey," Brodie called.

"Where you going?" Will shouted.

"Gotta tell my girl."

"Well, wait up."

A woman faced the wall, a hand over her heart as she read the mounted label under the PopTart display.

"Those her PopTarts?" Will watched with a confused expression.

Fin smacked his brother's arm. "What don't you get about a museum?"

"You said it's an exhibition," Brodie said.

"Yeah, not like *our* exhibitions." Top snowboarders held events to drum up interest in their sport. They performed tricks amidst live music and entertainment. "I thought your boss said you had to get back to the office or he was going to have to let you go?"

"I'm the best he's got," Brodie said. "So, he doesn't really mean it."

"You really want to test it when you're this close to getting on the dream design team?" Will said.

"I've got to get a few more things in motion with my project, and then I'll go." Brodie smiled. "Gonna do it in phases."

"Yeah?" Will seemed much more interested in Brodie's development plans than the Exhibition of Broken Hearts. "After you renovate the buildings, what else is there to do?"

Brodie grinned. "We're gonna have a train that'll take people all around our property and drop them off in the ghost town. Already had engineers out to the property. This thing is *on*."

"Excuse me." Strong perfume hit his nostrils as a woman in a pale blue blazer and white pants approached them. "I'm Amanda Baker from *Entertainment Update*. You're the Bowie brothers, right?"

Will nodded warily. He didn't care for the attention while competing, but in his off-season? In his hometown? Forget about making nice for the press.

"I'd love to interview you guys." She smiled broadly, her gaze fixed on Brodie.

"That's not possible right now," Will said.

"Uh, okay." The woman laughed. "I wasn't expecting that." She turned to Fin. "Well, how about just you? It'll be quick. I'd like a shot of you standing in front of the table." She gestured to the central installation where *#WorldsWorstBoyfriend* scrolled across the LDC screen.

Right at that moment, Callie joined them. "Hello, I'm Callie Bell. Welcome to the Exhibition of Broken Hearts."

"Amanda Baker, from *Entertainment Update*." They shook hands, but Amanda's focus was on her colleague who immediately hefted his video-camera onto his shoulder. "What you're doing here is incredible. When you think of the Bowies, you think of testosterone. You think of champions. You don't think of a man evolved enough to set up a museum as penance for wronging his girlfriend."

Oh, hell, no. But before he could defend himself, Callie smiled at the woman with all her polished grace. "Actually, Amanda, that's one of the things we're exploring in this exhibition. The genesis of the meme. If you'll come with me, you'll see we're working on a display showing exactly how it started."

Amanda and her film crew didn't budge from him and his brothers, but Callie remained unfazed, pointing to a corner of the room where Mr. Martin and his crew were working. "Mr. Martin, can you turn that on for me?"

"Sure thing." With a flick of his wrist, a television screen lit up. The exhibition had only been open for two weeks, and Callie was already expanding it.

"That's the original Instagram message. You'll notice Traci's handle only appears once in the comments, and that's just to say she's in the hospital and that Fin Bowie sent a text message. Nothing else." Comments scrolled across the screen. "The highlighted comments show how her followers made up the entire story."

Fin shot his brothers a smile. They looked impressed with her.

"Traci confirmed the story on our show," Amanda said.

"Did she?" Callie's head tipped, as though she was giving it some thought. "Mr. Martin?"

The teacher bit back a smile as he turned on the next screen. Traci appeared in an interview.

"We've printed out the transcripts, so you can follow the conversations. There isn't a single interview where Traci comes out and says she and Fin were romantically involved." She smiled at Amanda. "We've also got interviews from the other members of Fin's team where they stated that five men and a woman sharing two tents on a camping trip meant zero privacy, and no one saw any signs of a romantic or sexual relationship between the two."

Amanda turned toward Fin. "Is this true?"

"What's true..." Callie said, swinging the attention back to her. "Is that fans made assumptions about what the text meant until they'd built a narrative, which then snowballed into an international meme. And what developed out of that is this community of broken-hearted people healing themselves through sharing their personal stories. It's fascinating, isn't it?" She gestured around the room. "The donations you see here are only a fifth of what's come in. The whole second floor of this building is filled with them."

Will leaned in. "She's got this. Let's go."

Fin agreed, and the three of them quickly headed for the exit.

Just before he left, he turned back to watch Callie in action. Damn that woman, her fierce spirit and endless loyalty. He'd worried about her reaction to the Braverman contract. Worried she'd use it as an excuse to keep them apart, but in that moment he knew the solution to their problem.

And she was going to love it.

Callie's blood chilled. The words on the screen drifted like bubbles, so she'd only skimmed the surface of the message. She just couldn't concentrate.

"Look." Theo said.

Read it again. Maybe she'd misunderstood.

Dear Ms. Bell,

Thank you for your interest in the Hilda Morrison Curatorial Fellowship. We've received an unprecedented number of applications this year and are sorry to say that yours did not pass our initial screening.

We wish you the very best in future pursuits.

"Look, Aunt Callie. Look."

Through the shock, Theo's voice registered. Setting aside her laptop, she slid off the couch and crouched beside him on the floor. With a hole-punch and squares of felt, she'd made hundreds of dots in different colors. Using glue and framed canvases, they'd created pointillism designs.

"Look." Theo pointed to his canvas, filled with colorful dots and globs of wet glue.

Greens, blues, and a big yellow circle. She couldn't quite figure out what he'd made. "It's beautiful, sweetheart. It's really, really beautiful." The longer she looked at it, the more she started to see an actual design. "Is this the river?"

He nodded, and she could see his pride—that his fingers had been able to translate the image in his mind to the canvas.

"I love it." She started to get up. "We should hang this."

Like a little bird, he cocked his head, looking like he wasn't sure he understood what she meant.

"If we hang it on the wall in your room, you can see it all the time. Or maybe in here? That way everyone can see it. Uncle Fin, Gramma and Grampa, Mommy and Daddy?"

He got up, moved around the coffee table, and pointed

to the space behind his dad's desk. "You put my picture here?"

"I think your dad would love that. He'd get to see it every day."

His beautiful smile plumped his cheeks and made his eyes glitter. Rooting through the box of supplies she kept in the coat closet, she found a big, fat push pin. She showed it to him. "Come on. Let's put it in the wall."

Together they crossed the room. Lifting him easily off the floor, she breathed in the mix of his scents—baby shampoo, laundry detergent, and apple juice—and handed him the push pin.

Twisting his body toward the wall, he tried to press it in, but it wobbled. So, she closed her hand over his, and together they drove it into the wallboard.

With his tongue sticking out, he hung the frame—a little crookedly—off the knob.

She stepped back to take it in. "I love it."

He gave her a proud grin.

"Looks good, right?"

Just as she started to put him down, his legs tightened at her sides. For a moment he held her gaze, and then he put his arms around her shoulders. He held her tentatively at first, but then he cuddled up to her.

Tears burned as she held him to her chest. She'd loved every minute she'd spent with her nephew this summer, loved how close they'd become.

Right in time for her to leave.

But wait. She cast a glance to the glowing screen of her

laptop. She wasn't leaving, was she? Fear ripped through her.

She wasn't getting the fellowship.

Dammit. Is Julian behind this? Or had she legitimately been knocked out of the running? She had nothing left to lose so, as soon as she set Theo down, she grabbed her phone and shot him a text. **I can't help but think our breakup is the reason I got this letter today from the MoCA**.

His answer came right away. **You didn't seriously think we could work together?**

A volatile brew of fear and anger swept through her, making her sick to her stomach.

Bastard.

Wind chimes tinkled as she opened the door, and a soft breeze fluttered the hem of her dress. Callie entered the studio quietly, hoping she wasn't interrupting a private yoga session. In the foyer, she breathed in lavender and vanilla-scented candles.

She could hear Megan's voice—a one-sided conversation filled with pauses—and the pang of loss hit Callie hard. Megan's parents had been as busy with the motel as Callie's were with the diner, so they'd both been kids with too much time on their hands. But they'd bonded because they'd both preferred hanging out with each other to partying. She'd loved their friendship because they could tell each other anything and neither one had judged.

Megan came out of her office, obviously surprised to see Callie standing in her foyer. "Hey, what's up?"

"I have an idea." Just so she didn't sound selfish, she quickly added, "For both of us."

"Okay."

Callie didn't like her snippy tone, but she didn't care about that right now. She'd apologized. What else could she do? "I'd like to expand the exhibition."

"Aren't you leaving?"

"I just found out I'm not getting the fellowship." It made her sick to say the words out loud.

Megan lowered her cell phone. "Fellowship?"

"I got my master's degree in Museum Studies in May, and instead of getting an entry-level job in my field I wanted to fast-track my career with a fellowship. But I didn't get it." She exhaled. "My ex-boyfriend—"

"The douche who proposed at Ryder's rehearsal dinner?"

"Yeah. That guy. I'm pretty sure he saw the picture of me and Fin kissing—"

"The one that made the cover of the *New York Daily Times*?"

"Yes, Megan. That one." She cracked a smile. "Anyhow, his parents are on the board of the MoCA, and I'm—"

"Sure they saw their son's skanky girlfriend going at it in the museum that was supposed to get her the fellowship? Yeah, I get it. So?"

She didn't miss the curl of Megan's lips—she was messing with her—and that encouraged her. "So, I'm

317

screwed." But she also knew she wasn't the only one with problems, and she wanted to know her friend again. "Why are you living in Calamity?"

"It's a long story, but basically my college graduation present was the motel." Megan shrugged. "I didn't want to run it, but my parents owned the property, so I realized I could do whatever I wanted with it, and I wanted to have a yoga studio."

"Are you happy here?"

"I love it."

"A yoga studio in Calamity is enough for you?"

Megan looked at her for a moment, as though weighing how real she wanted to get. Callie waited, wanting more than anything for her friend to give her a chance.

Even though you're leaving? Yeah, even so. Because she was going to do so much better at keeping in touch this time.

But then Megan smiled. "Come here."

Callie followed her out the back door and into the bright sunshine of the courtyard. The U-shaped motel rooms faced the pool.

"Do you remember Muriel and Colleen Bronstein?" Megan asked.

The elderly twins had not only dressed identically, but they'd lived together, too. Neither had married, and their parents had left them a fortune so, as far as Callie knew, they'd never worked a day in their lives.

"They teach ballroom dancing." Megan pointed to the building on the left. "We knocked down walls for their dance studio, and they rent out half the bottom floor.

Upstairs is the Artists Collaborative. Each artist has her own space, and twice a year they hold an open house, where you can go into the studios and see what they're working on." She gestured to the right side. "Mike Marshall has a dojo, and Donna Teller teaches ballet."

"Megan. This is amazing."

"Yeah. It's pretty cool." Her pride and enthusiasm came through.

"You could do an acting studio. Or even a small theater." What had happened to Megan's dreams?

"Honestly, I didn't love theater. I liked being part of that world, but I didn't want to be an actor. I don't slip into someone else's skin very well. Or at all, actually. But I realized that even if I didn't have the talent, I could still be part of the arts community." Megan gestured to the buildings. "I get to teach yoga, while being part of this artist's collective. And I love it."

"I can see that." A frustrating restlessness stirred in her chest. "Looks like you've found your bliss."

"You haven't found yours?" Megan seemed surprised.

"I'm trying." *Too hard?*

"So, what do you need from me?"

"Well, I need that fellowship, and I'll be damned if my ex is going to keep it from me just because he saw me kiss Fin like that." She hadn't really put the pieces together until just then. But that had to have been what set Julian off. She'd certainly never kissed *him* like that. "I'm going to send the board of directors a video of my exhibition."

"Does Julian have that kind of power?"

"His parents do."

"But they saw the sex tape, too, and they know about the exhibition, right?" Megan asked.

"They've known about it for a while. I sent tear sheets to his mom." She couldn't believe she'd wasted money on personalized stationery. As if it would've had more impact than her son's side of the story.

"So then what will a video do?"

"Well, that's why I'm here. I'm adding classes to the exhibition. I thought I'd record them to show the board members a different aspect of it."

"Classes?" She sounded skeptical.

"This exhibition's about healing. So I'm going to offer classes...like bread making. You know, working your angst out through kneading dough." She thought of Theo. "Art therapy." *Ooh, that's a winner.*

"And you want me to teach yoga?"

"I don't know anything about it, but is there a style that lets the participants release their pent-up anger and hostility?"

"Purging yoga?"

"Is that a thing?"

"It is now."

"So, you'll do it?"

"Sure, I'll do it." She sounded hesitant. "But if they've already rejected you, I'm not sure adding classes will change their minds."

The high tide of hope that had carried her over to Megan's studio sputtered out. "I just...I'm so angry. I'm a straight-A student, I've done an internship every semester, I've got amazing references....I mean, come on. So what if I kissed a guy and Julian pitched a fit? They should evaluate me based on my resume, and I'm pretty sure no other candidate pulled off her own pop-up exhibition."

"Look, I get that you're fighting for the job. I do, but I just don't think going to the same people again will make a difference. Is there anyone else—maybe someone higher up?"

"There's no one higher than the board." *Wait a minute.* "Actually, it's the Hilda Morrison Curatorial Fellowship. I just assumed it's named after a patron who died and bequeathed the scholarship to the museum. But I don't actually know that. She could be alive."

"If she's alive, tell her about your exhibition. Better yet, show her. Send her the video. It's way better to see it than read about it."

Oh, I like that. "I'm not sure the board members would appreciate me going around them."

"But what if it gets you the fellowship?"

She thought about Julian's text. *You didn't seriously think we could work together?* And determination set in.

Megan started for her office. "Let's look up old Hilda and see if she's still breathing."

It took no more than a few clicks to discover that Hilda Morrison was alive and kicking on the Upper East Side. Living in a storied penthouse, her wild and colorful past included six husbands, a life of philanthropy, travel, and countless acts of outrageous behavior.

"Looks like Hilda's hitched her skirt up for plenty of guys. She shouldn't have a problem with your sex tape." Megan glanced up from her laptop. "Go get her."

Affection surged through her. "Thank you." She leaned down to give her a hug. The position was awkward, but Callie forced it. "Thank you so much."

"You got it. Now, go. I've got a class to teach."

As Callie left the office, ideas popped up on how to expand the exhibition. Her dad could do a bread baking class—Pounding Out Your Anger. Megan could do Purging Yoga, her mom could do gardening—Yanking Your Pain Out by the Roots. And what about getting a therapist to run a weekly counseling group?

Forget therapy. Make it a support group. Just give people a chance to talk to others who're broken-hearted.

Yes. This is so good.

As she stepped out onto the boardwalk, she realized she could only do the classes if the Cooters wanted to run the programs after she left. She'd talk to them before she did anything else. And then she'd find a way to get a hold of Hilda and convince her to give Callie a shot.

No way would the Reyes' win.

16

With Stan teaching a clunky and awkward Judy how to waltz and Barbara replenishing the sharpened pencils in a basket, Callie turned off the television screens. They'd already locked the doors for the day, and she couldn't wait to talk to Fin. Not only were the Cooters interested in running the programs, but they had great ideas for other classes.

When the music shut off abruptly, everyone turned to see Fin striding toward them from the back hallway. His athletic grace and masculine swagger, those lips curled into a delectable smile, made her blood fizzy.

"Well, I should get home." With eyebrows raised, Barbara tipped her head to the door.

Stan nodded. "Yep. Grandkids are coming for dinner tonight."

It took all of three minutes for everyone to leave.

With just the two of them alone, Callie shook her head. "Way to clear a room."

When he reached her, he caught her around the waist and kissed her soundly. "Got some great news." He set her down. "I got a call this morning. From Walter Braverman."

"Are you talking about Braverman Productions?"

His smile grew wider.

"He called you?"

With a nod, he said, "He offered me a contract."

"Oh, my God, Fin. That's amazing." Over the years, she'd heard the brothers talk about a contract with Braverman Productions. It was a big deal.

"He said he hasn't offered it before because I'm a Bowie and can fund my own trips. But he hasn't signed anyone in a few years, and there's no one he wants more than me, so he figured he'd take a shot and ask."

"He doesn't know you guys don't touch your Dad's money."

"No, he doesn't know."

She forced her smile to stay in place. *This is good for him. Really good.* "Fin...I'm really happy for you." But her heart hurt like hell. She wouldn't show him that, though. He'd earned this great honor. "I'm proud of you."

He cupped her chin. "Why so sad?"

"I'm not sad. I'm genuinely happy for you."

He lifted her onto the nearest library table and boxed her in with both arms. "Last time we messed up because we didn't talk to each other. You were so afraid I'd choose MSU that you didn't come right out and ask me if that was what I wanted. *I* was so intent on not screwing up your dream, that I didn't tell you about the pressure from my dad and brothers. But we should've talked about it. Because the foundation for everything going forward? Is that we're in this together. That's our base camp. From there, we figure out our plans, even if it means we ride different spines for a while." He leaned back, examining her expression. "What're you thinking?"

"You said we're in this together."

"That's right."

"I want that, Fin. More than anything, but—"

"There are no buts. The sentence 'more than anything' ends right there. There's nothing we want more than being together. That's our starting point. The rest we figure out together."

"It's not that simple. I've been cut from the fellowship."

He pushed back. "What's that mean?"

"It means there's no interview. I got a letter saying they have better candidates."

"Bullshit. Man-Bracelet saw the video and whined like a bitch to his mommy."

"Probably." She rubbed the developing ache over her left eye. "But Megan gave me a great idea to go to the source, so I looked up the woman who sponsors the fellowship and found her alive and well in New York. I asked one of my graduate professors if she has a way to get to her. Luckily, she does. So, I've sent her my resume and links to the exhibition, and I've asked if I can meet with her."

"This all happened since I saw you this morning?"

She nodded.

With a slow shake of his head, he said, "You're

something else, wild thing." With a determined gleam in his eyes, he caged her in again. "You want New York?"

"Yes." She had to get that fellowship. And Fin had to sign that contract. "And you're going off on your grand adventure." Mixed in with the dread of fearing their relationship couldn't work was hope. *Was* there some way to make it work? But he just stood there with that smirk on his face. "How is this funny?" She shoved at him, but he was a chunk of granite.

"What did I just say to you?"

"That you're signing a contract with Braverman, and I'm moving back to New York."

"You're not a very good listener." Still, with that stupid smirk.

"I'm a great listener." She shifted to slide under his arms, but his big body held her in place. "A world-class listener."

"How do you still not get it? *You* are my grand adventure. Some people want to climb Everest, some want to have a big family, some want to be world leaders. But I just want you. That's all I've ever wanted."

"I live in New York." Hope drummed a steady beat in her blood. "You're going to be in the mountains."

"Four trips a year. And the rest of the time I'm going to be with you."

Her body clamped down on a burst of excitement. "The fellowship pays twenty-four grand a year. I won't be able to come home that often." *Home.* She would miss her parents and Theo. God, that little boy had just begun to trust her. By the time she came back for a visit, would he have forgotten her?

She loved Theo. She didn't want to miss out on his life.

"We're the base camp, remember?" The look in his eyes —steely determination mixed with utter adoration—it was *everything*. "That means home is where you are."

Excitement fluttered in her belly. "What're you saying?"

"You got a new roommate yet?"

"No." She scooted closer to the edge of the table. "You're going to live with me?"

He smiled. "Of course."

"In New York?"

"If that's where you are, then that's where I'll be."

"How will this work?"

"We'll get a place big enough so my team can crash there when we're planning. I'll take my trips and come home to you."

"You'll hate New York."

"I'll get my fill of the mountains four months out of the year. The rest of the time, I'll be with you. Sounds damn good to me." He pulled away, worry darkening his gaze. "Is that not enough? Because I can tell him I'll only do three trips a year. Or even two—"

She put her fingers over his mouth. "No. You take as many trips as you want. I'd never hold you back from doing what you love." She threw her arms around his neck. "I love you, Fin, and I'm all in."

"Good, then let's get out of here."

They headed toward the back. Just as she reached for

the light switch, she heard a knock at the door. "Let me see who it is. One of the Cooters might've forgotten something." She hurried back to see.

An elderly gentleman in a Stetson rapped his knuckles against the window. When he saw her, he waved.

She unlocked and opened the door. "Hey, there. Can I help you?"

With his baggy jeans and worn cowboy boots, he looked like a rancher. "Evening." He pulled off his hat and held it against his chest. "I'm told there's a message for me here." His voice sounded as wrecked as his tanned skin.

Fin came up beside her. "Are you looking for Town Hall? Because it moved about two years ago. This is a museum now."

Callie elbowed him. *Exhibition.*

"No, sir. I'm told you've got a message board and that there's an envelope with my name on it."

Callie jerked like he'd just pinched her, and two pairs of eyes slid over to her. "Yes. There is." She stepped aside, ushering him in. "Please, come in." Excitement hurried her pace. "Right over here."

OhmyGodohmyGodohmyGod. She wanted to call Helen and shout, *He's here! He came!* But, of course, she had no way to contact the older woman who came in dutifully every day to check the corkboard to see if the man she hadn't chosen had come to claim his note.

Callie couldn't believe he actually *had*. At least she hoped it was the right man. She unpinned the envelope and handed it to him. "Are you Desi?"

For a long moment he didn't answer, just stared at the

handwriting. If the muscles around his eyes hadn't flinched, she wouldn't have detected an ounce of emotion in him.

The hand he lifted to take the envelope trembled. "Yes, ma'am."

When Fin grabbed her wrist and tugged her away, she gave him a foul look. *I was doing something.*

"Leave him alone." He said it in a low, gruff voice.

He was right, of course, but come on. This was Helen's man. But, fine, she'd busy herself with neatening the colored papers in one of the baskets, while keeping an eye on him.

Slowly, Desi pulled out the letter. The paper shook as he unfolded it.

She didn't see all that many words on the page, so it didn't surprise her when he quickly stopped reading. What did surprise her was the way he closed his eyes and just seemed to...*savor* whatever Helen had written.

After a moment, he slid the letter back into the envelope. "Did she leave a phone number?"

Oh, come on, Helen. You didn't leave a way for him to contact you? "No, she didn't." Thinking quickly, she snatched a pen out of the basket and a bright yellow piece of paper. "But you can leave her a note with your number." She reached for the envelope to exchange it for the pen, but he didn't let go. Finally, after a moment, he folded it and shoved it in his back pocket.

Callie shifted her gaze to Fin. *He wants to keep it. He loves her. He totally and completely loves her.*

Fin gave her an indulgent smile.

Without looking at her, Desi took the pen and wrote

something on the paper. Then, he folded it neatly and stuck it to the corkboard with a pushpin. When he turned to her, emotion clouded his eyes. He busied himself with setting the pen down and putting his hat back on.

With a nod, he headed for the door. "Thank you kindly. I hope I didn't keep you."

And then he was gone.

In that moment, Callie felt like she'd done something important. Something so much bigger than herself.

And she had to wonder what she was giving up by going back to New York.

17

THE BRACKETS FROM HER JEANS CLATTERED IN THE dryer drum, as Callie watched her going-away party from the laundry room window.

It was hard to believe that just eight weeks ago her life had been on an entirely different track. She'd lived a good but narrow life with Julian, one with little wiggle room. She hadn't noticed because she'd been so busy—*no, that's not true.* She had noticed, but the straitjacket had made her feel safe. Living within the lines had given her the false sense that nothing could go wrong.

But it had. It had gone spectacularly wrong.

Thank God. Thanks to Fin's speech and Julian's correct belief that she'd never really commit to him, she'd busted out of it.

Her gaze landed on Fin's brothers. They surrounded him, and he laughed like the wild, free soul he'd always been.

She should feel that same way. After a phone call with

Hilda Morrison, Callie had scored an interview in the woman's penthouse for the day after tomorrow. Not only had the patron loved the exhibition, she'd gotten a huge kick out of the footage of her and Fin going at it on the library table.

Callie was going back to New York. She'd get to live with Fin. And, if she got the fellowship, her career would be back on track.

Her heart squeezed, though, because she knew Fin would hate living in New York. It would kill him to live so far from his brothers. To not be able to train with them, advise them on what to eat, critique their torque on the trampolines. But, as far as compromises went, it worked, and it wasn't forever.

If she didn't get the fellowship and had to start as an archivist, it could take as many as ten years.

That's a long time.

But she loved him. Heart and soul, this man owned her. She'd have to stop looking so far into the future and live for right now. Embrace their life together.

"Look who's been asking for you."

Callie turned to find her mom coming into the laundry room with Theo in her arms. He twisted around to see his aunt, then shimmied free and came right up to her.

Pure love flooded her for this boy, as she knelt in front of him. "Hi, sweetheart."

Opening his fist, he showed her a palm full of crushed flowers. Oh, it was a daisy chain bracelet. Crushed, but still beautiful. "I made this for you."

"How did you know I love flower bracelets?"

Color rose high on his cheeks. "Uncle Fin told me."

"They explored the meadow while his parents got ready for the party," her mom said.

"Thank you, Theo." She carefully slid her fingers through the delicate chain. "It's beautiful. I love it." In her dress and wedge sandals, she sat on the floor. "I've had the best time with you this summer. I'm going to miss hanging out with you."

His brow creased. And, of course, she realized he didn't understand that she and his uncle would be leaving. They wouldn't be back at least until Thanksgiving, three months away.

Too long for a little boy. "Mom, can you please get your phone?"

"Sure thing." In a swish of fabric, her mom left the room.

Callie got up on her knees and felt around for her phone on top of the washing machine. "I live in New York City."

He shook his head. "No, you live here. With me. And Mommy and Daddy and Uncle Fin and Gramma and Grampa." He looked so earnest, so...adamant.

"I don't live here, Theo." She reached for him, holding his little hand. "But we're going to talk all the time." She opened her social media account and connected with her mom through Messenger.

Her mom came back into the room, answering the trill. She smiled when she saw her daughter's image on the screen. Crouching, her mom handed the phone to Theo.

Callie waved. "Hi, Theo."

He looked between her and the screen but didn't say anything.

Her mom got into the frame with Theo and waved back. "Hi, Aunt Callie."

The little boy looked like he wanted to leave, so she needed to find a way to make this interesting for him. "Do you want to do art with me?"

He nodded warily.

"We could do art every Sunday afternoon. Would you like that?"

"At my house?"

"Yes, you'll be in your house. And I'll be here. On this phone."

"Why are you going away?"

Her heart squeezed, and she blinked back tears. "Because I live in New York. But we'll talk every Sunday and do art together."

Eyes filled with disappointment, he looked away from her. "I go find my daddy now."

Frustration slammed her hard. She watched his little fist close around the handle on the door. Sunlight flooded the laundry room as he opened it and took off across the lawn.

Callie got up. "I'm going to stay in his life. I am."

"I know you will. And you'll be back for Thanksgiving and Christmas. It'll be fine. You'll see."

She had no option but to trust that it would all work out.

. . .

For their last night in Calamity, they'd opened the skylight's screen to let in the cloudless August sky. Moonlight poured like cream over their naked bodies, and stars blazed in a midnight panorama.

Callie had one leg hitched across Fin's thighs, an arm wrapped around his torso, and her head nestled into the crux of his arm.

She would get to do this for the rest of her life. She'd never have to feel the stark loneliness of living without half her heart. It felt almost too good to be true. Like she was waiting for the other shoe to drop. Because, really, who got this much happiness?

In a few hours, she and Fin would catch a flight to New York together. She'd booked them a great long-stay hotel near the museum and, better, she'd found an amazing apartment through her closest friend Delilah. A rent-controlled sublet in midtown that was unusually large for Manhattan standards, it had a master suite on a different floor to give them privacy when his team stayed with them. The owner needed to meet them first, but she couldn't think of a single reason to turn away a stable, employed couple.

She'd mostly packed her bags, printed out their boarding passes...everything was set for the next phase of their lives. She'd start her fellowship, and he'd plan his next trip.

Well, she hoped she'd get it. Hilda had seemed to be on her side.

Those damn fools have their heads up their asses. I might pull my fellowship, offer it to the Guggenheim.

She still had to get through the interview tomorrow, but even if she didn't get it, she'd find a job in her field and make her way to her dream job.

Callie snuggled closer to the love of her life. "I can't believe this is happening."

His fingertips stroked her bare shoulder. "I can."

They'd agreed to be honest, so she needed to get it off her mind. "I'm scared that you're going to hate New York. I'm scared you're going to miss your brothers."

"Do I get to wake up with you every morning?"

She smiled. "Yes."

"Then it's all good."

"And after a few years, I'd be open to coming back to Calamity."

His muscles tightened. "Yeah?"

"I want to raise our family here. I want our kids to grow up with my parents and your brothers. With Ryder and Theo."

"I like that, wild thing."

"So, we're good, right?" *You're not going to bail on me, right?*

"We're perfect.

She knew that. Of course she knew that. After everything they'd gone through? He'd never risk losing her again.

Fin jerked awake. It took a moment to figure out where he was and what he needed to be doing. What had awakened him? He didn't hear an alarm.

And then he remembered. He was leaving today. Moving to New York.

He glanced down to see Callie's hair spilled across his chest. By her steady breathing, he knew she slept soundly. She had an arm slung across his stomach, and her cheek on his right pec. His heart swelled so big it hurt.

He loved this woman.

Just the sight of her, the smell of her shampoo and the press of her body, got him hard. He brushed strands of her hair away from his mouth before reaching down to give his thickening cock a squeeze. *No more of that.* She needed her rest. They had a big travel day ahead.

Besides, he'd have her just like this every day for the rest of his life. *Thank Christ.*

A muffled bark of laughter and male voices jolted him. His brothers. *That's what woke me.* What the hell were they doing up this late—or was it early? He couldn't tell.

He should go back to sleep, but he got that familiar punch of anxiety from knowing they were hanging out without him. Carefully, he eased out from under her and slid his legs off the mattress. At the bottom of the stairs, he yanked on his jeans and T-shirt and headed out of the room.

"I'll take a leave of absence," he heard Brodie say.

"You can't come with me." *Will.* "You skipped out on your job all summer. I'll be gone two weeks."

Two weeks? Where was he going? In his bare feet, Fin hurried down the carpeted hallway.

"I did more work this summer than anyone else on my team," Brodie said. "And I can do modeling on my computer from anywhere."

"You don't get special privileges." Will sounded annoyed. "Everyone else has to show up for work. You don't get to spend the summer working remotely."

"Guys." *Gray.*

His brother was home? And they hadn't told him?

"Quit arguing about it," Gray said. "*I'll* go with you."

"Yeah?" Will said. "That'd be great."

The three of them making plans without him had him pounding down the stairs.

"I've got to find a new trainer," Will said. "With Coach retiring and Fin out of the picture, I have to find someone else."

Out of the picture. That shouldn't have gutted him.

But it did.

Crossing the living room to find his brothers in the kitchen, Fin squinted against the bright lights. "Hey, asshole." He caught Gray up in a big hug. "Thanks for telling me you were coming home."

"Got in a few hours ago." His brother's hair had grown to his shoulders, and his tan stood out against his white T-shirt. Funny how Gray came across as a total surfer dude, when he was actually a hardcore champion.

Fin pulled away. "Why didn't you guys wake me up?"

"You and Callie hit the sack early." Will bit back a smile, and they all shared a look.

"What's that mean?" He hated being left out of their inside jokes.

Gray smiled. "It means we're glad you and your wildcat are back together."

"Wild *thing*," Fin said.

"That's not what it sounded like." Gray cocked a half-smile.

"Fuck off." Fin turned to Will. "What's going on? Where you going?"

"I signed up for FreeFest."

"What the hell?" Since when did Will do FreeFest?

Snowboarders and skiers got medals and endorsements from the Games, but they got status from the annual post-season freestyle event, where the top athletes in each of the disciplines judged each other. The athletes considered it the purest acknowledgement of their talent when judged by their peers.

"I thought you didn't want to risk it?" With his eye on Olympic gold, Will hadn't wanted to screw around with ungroomed courses on remote mountains. *Look what happened to Traci.*

"Gray's home five minutes, and he already talked him into it," Brodie said with a laugh. "Told him to quit playing it so safe."

"But what about the Games?" Underneath the confusion and frustration, it all boiled down to *hurt*. Will had always consulted him on big decisions. They'd agreed that, with the highest scores consistently in the rankings, his brother didn't need to prove anything to anybody. The judges had done that for him. Will was in a class of his own.

Shake it off. This doesn't affect me. Fin had a full plate—moving with Callie and planning his trip for Braverman. *I'm good. It's all good*

It just sucked that they'd made a decision like this without him. Of course, since Fin was *out of the picture* and Will needed to replace him with a new coach, why would they need to involve him in their plans?

"So, cool." Will clapped a hand on Gray's shoulder. "You're coming with me."

"No, we're both going." Brodie's tone put settled on the discussion.

Fin turned on his brother. "You want to be on the Olympic design team or not?"

"You know I do," Brodie said.

"Then get back to work." *I'll go with Will.* His blood started pumping at the thought.

"This is *Freefest*, and he doesn't have a coach. We should both be there." Brodie motioned between him and Gray. "Besides, I want to. It'll be fun."

It *would* be fun. All of his brothers, along with their snowboarder and skier friends? At Freefest? *Hell, yeah.* "Where is it this year?" he asked.

"Chile," Will said.

"When?" They could have at least asked him if he wanted to go. He didn't have anything important going on in New York for the first few weeks. Callie had an appointment to see an apartment and an interview with the scholarship donor. He didn't need to be there for either of those things.

"We head out tomorrow for two weeks." Will turned to the kitchen table, scattered with photographs. "Before Callie gets up, you think you could look at these?"

"Yeah, of course." *Before Callie gets up?* What did that mean? "You're competing in FreeFest, of course I'll look at them. What does Callie have to do with anything?"

"You're leaving today. I don't want to stir shit up with her."

"She doesn't have a problem with me helping you."

Turning to the table, he sorted through the pictures, but he couldn't see the images. His heart beat too fast. Behind him, his brothers laughed, talking about their plans in Santiago, the house they'd already rented on the mountain, and the other athletes who'd signed up.

While Fin moved across the country, they'd go on hanging out like this, traveling together, eating dinner, training. What separated Fin from them was that he had Callie. His brothers might never fall in love, which meant they'd never have to choose.

It wasn't a choice, of course. He was Callie's, heart and soul. No question. He *was* moving to New York. He just didn't want to lose his connection with his brothers.

He didn't have to. He spun around. "I need to get a look at the mountain. When you first check in, there's a heli ride for all the competitors. I need to go on that."

"Wait, what're you saying?" Will asked.

Excitement barreled through him. "I'll go with you." Would Callie see that as letting her down? Other than the appointment with the landlord and her interview, they didn't have anything else going on. So, no. He wasn't bailing on her. He could go.

He could fucking go.

The smile left Will's face, and it looked like he was keeping his emotions in check. "You serious?"

"Yeah. If you need me, I want to be there."

"Of course I need you. But what about Callie?"

"It's two weeks, right? We don't have anything going on in the next two weeks. It's fine."

"We don't have anything going on?" Callie stood in the entryway, arms folded across her stomach.

Anxiety hit his bloodstream like cold fluid. "Oh, hey." He cut over to her, leaning in to kiss her cheek. She ducked and swerved. *Shit*. She was pissed. "Did we wake you?"

"No, I have to get up because I'm moving to New York today." Her tone said, *Remember?* "What's going on?"

"Will signed up for FreeFest."

"And you're going with him."

"I'd like to. It's just two weeks."

"And since we don't have anything going on in New York, it works out perfectly." She looked down at her white sneakers. "Okay." She turned and headed for the door.

Yeah, she was pissed, but he'd talk to her. If she really wanted him to go with her, he absolutely would. But first, he'd try to explain where he was coming from. "Hang on. I'll drive you." They'd talk on the way.

"No need. I have to get my dad's truck back to him."

He caught up with her. "Hold up. Listen to me. I'm moving to New York. I'm signing with Braverman. Our plans haven't changed. This is just two weeks, nothing else."

"I heard you loud and clear." She snatched the tote she'd left by the front door.

"Wait a second. This isn't like me bailing on the prom. All you have is the interview and apartment hunting." When she eyed him stonily, he said, "Do you want me there to see the apartment?" Because he could do that. Fly out of New York. No big deal.

Though he might miss the heli ride up the mountain.

"She's expecting to see a couple." She dug her keys out of the side pocket of the tote. "That's the whole point of the meeting. We're twenty-three, and she wants mature tenants."

"Okay, so I'll go to New York with you, and then the day after tomorrow I'll catch up with my brothers."

She did that thing again, where she drew in a breath and became weirdly composed. She even put a hand on his arm, like he was some old geezer she'd shown around the museum. "That's not necessary. Delilah will come with me."

"Just talk to me, okay? I don't know where your head is right now." He looked back to his brothers, watching from the kitchen. "If you don't want me to go... I just figured you didn't need me to choose an apartment. You have to know, I don't care where we live as long as I get to be with you."

"I know that." She gave him a smile. "Let me go. My mom's making a big breakfast for the whole family, and I don't want to miss it."

She acted like everything was cool, but Fin knew

something was off. He shot a look to Will. "I only have to go for one week. He really only needs my help choosing a spine."

Will gave a terse nod.

"Yeah, so, I'll just go for a week." Perfect solution. What was a week in the scheme of things?

"Great." She waved to his brothers. "Good luck out there, Will. Nice to see you, Gray."

Fin grabbed her arm before she walked out the door. "We're good, right? Nothing's changed?"

She gazed up at him, an unmistakable hint of sorrow in her eyes. "Nothing's changed at all."

18

In the Admiral's Club at Denver International airport, Fin stood staring out the plate glass window onto the tarmac. Instead of seeing airplanes, he saw the spine Will would ride in five days.

They'd gotten to the airport early enough that they'd rented a conference room. With photographs of the mountain spread across the table, his brothers studied the images, but for Fin it wasn't that literal. He took in all the available information and then processed it subconsciously.

But it was hard to concentrate when he hadn't heard from Callie since she'd left his house yesterday. Not once. Sure, she'd traveled all day, checked into their hotel, and probably crashed right away. Today, in about an hour, she'd meet with Hilda. And tomorrow she'd look at the apartment she really wanted.

She's pissed. Otherwise, he'd have heard from her. But he didn't get why. He didn't care where they lived. He could live in a yurt on the side of a mountain and be happy as long as he got to wake up to her. *This isn't like the prom.* If she'd had some event, he wouldn't have gone with Will.

The tightness in his chest made it hard to take a full breath. He didn't want her pissed at him. So, what could he do? *Cut the trip even shorter.* From the moment he'd agreed to go, he'd been examining photographs of the mountain face. That, plus the heli ride, would give him all the information he needed to work out Will's run.

He could fly to New York right after that. He'd be gone even less than a week.

"That'll only give you two jumps," he heard Gray say.

Where the other brothers lived their sport like a religion, Gray rolled with the weather, his posse, and his whims. He was so damn good at boarding and surfing that he could enter competitions when the mood struck him. And win. Since he wasn't part of a team or tour, he didn't have nearly as many trophies and medals as the other brothers, but Gray didn't give two shits.

"Better to have two fluid jumps then risk zigzagging for that third," Will said. Always the technician.

"You don't have to zigzag," Brodie said. "Fin measured it. It's a good enough distance to give you time to even out before hitting the next jump."

"Can't risk it."

And that was when Fin saw it. Crystal clear. He turned away from the window and reached for the photos on the table, shuffling through them until he pulled out the one with the best overview. "Here." His finger traced the line that would give Will the best flow and three solid but risky jumps. "That's it. Right there."

"I can't make that one." Will's finger stabbed a cliff.

"Sure, you can. Carve the edge and drop down over here. That'll take you—"

"Oh, shit," Will said. "I see it. That's fucking great."

"That's sick, man." Gray laughed. "How do you *do* that?"

"Jesus, Fin, I don't know what the hell I'd do without you," Will said.

But Callie knew, didn't she? She knew really well, since she was in New York City without him right then. Because he'd done it again.

Like blinking to clear his vision after popping out of a murky lake, he suddenly saw the world clearly and cleanly. "I'm done."

He finally got where he kept screwing up.

"With what?" Will glanced up from the photograph.

"I'm not going to Chile with you." It was the right decision...but the cost...the fucking cost. He didn't want to lose his relationship with his brothers, but he was twenty-three years old. Time to man up.

Will reared back. "What're you talking about? Our flight takes off in an hour."

"It's like Callie said. It's so ingrained in me that I don't even know I'm doing it. But I did it again. I dropped everything for you."

"You didn't drop anything," Will said. "There's nothing going on in New York right now."

"My life with Callie is going on. Or it should be." His spirits soared—for the first time in his life, he was free of this lifelong need to be included—but fear had a

347

grip on his ankles, holding him down. "I'm not your coach."

"I know that."

"No, you don't. And it's not your fault. It's *mine*." His brothers couldn't even talk about their dad. They sure as hell wouldn't want to hear his revelations.

But he needed to say it out loud. "I'm just so damned relieved when you include me that I throw aside whatever I'm doing. And that's the thing. Every time I do that, I'm telling you what *I* do doesn't matter." He looked at his brothers, gauging their reactions. Mostly, they just looked stunned. "I make my living freeriding, and the only reason you guys don't see it as a legitimate career is because I drop everything when you call. And Callie? I know you don't get it, but she's..." *Everything to me.* "I'm not even going to bother explaining. I'm going to show you what matters to me by making it my priority." His backpack leaned against the wall, but he couldn't get his feet to move.

He needed to get to the ticket desk and reroute his flight plan, but...he just had to say it, right? Even if they made fun of him. It was just so hard to think clearly when emotions kept rolling in.

"You all right, man?" Gray asked.

His brothers watched him with concern, as he drew in a shaky breath. He wanted—needed—them to understand. "My earliest memory...I was maybe four. Five. I woke up really fucking happy."

"You were a happy kid." Will's tone said, *Where you going with this?*

He nodded. "I got out of bed. Got my snowsuit on, put

on that stupid hat Mom got me, and these thick, wool socks."

Brodie's brow creased, and Will cocked his head. Yeah, he wasn't making a whole lot of sense.

Say it. "The night before, you guys thought I was asleep, but I was sitting on the stairs listening while you raided the pantry. You talked about hiding the skis behind the fence, bringing the brownies Uncle Lachlan had brought home from the bakery. You had this great day planned, and I couldn't wait. The four of us skiing? Eating brownies together?" He smiled at how much that had meant to him. "But when I came downstairs..."

Gray winced, and Will looked down at his black boots.

"You guys were gone. You'd...ditched me." It had hurt. So fucking badly. He'd gone wild. His mom hadn't known what to do with him. His dad had taken him to the cabin for the weekend—just the two of them.

But it hadn't mattered. Because his brothers had left him behind.

"We were just stupid kids," Gray said.

"You're *one year* older than me," Fin said. "It wasn't like you were so much more advanced than I was. But *I* was the one left behind."

"Okay, but we're all equals now." Will still didn't get it.

"That's bullshit, and you know it." Resolve pushed out fear. "You don't respect what I do. You think I'm just some reckless adrenaline junkie, while the rest of you are real athletes. And the truth is, if I didn't train you, I'd hardly see you. We don't live in the same worlds. The only thing that ties us together is me training you." He didn't even care if they made fun of him or used these words against him later because it felt fucking great to say them. "When I coach you…I'm indispensable. And if I stop training you, I'm invisible."

"What're you talking about?" Angry energy rolled off his oldest brother. "You're indispensable because you're my *brother*." He shoved the photographs. "Not because of this." He stood there looking pissed and confused. "Jesus, Fin, you're the best fucking part of us." Will's expression said, *How do you not know this?* "You're the *heart*."

Stunned, Fin blinked back the sting in his eyes.

"It's not like Brodie competes anymore," Gray said. "We're all doing our own things."

But that only highlighted the issue. "Brodie was a champion, too. The three of you…you're champions. I'm the outsider."

"There is no outsider." Will exploded with more emotion than Fin had ever heard. "We're brothers, and that's fucking *sacred*. It's unbreakable." He shook his head. "You came at me with a lot at once here. The idea that you think I don't respect you." He glanced out the window unseeingly before swinging his gaze back to Fin. "I examine the mountain from every angle. I plan out my every move. I practice my tricks until I could be braindead and my muscles would still remember what to do. But you, you're out there improvising on untouched terrain. You see things the rest of us can't because you've lived it. You understand nutrition and training better than anybody I know. No one has your vision, your knowledge, your intuitive understanding of our sport."

It was the first time Fin had ever heard these words, and he was floored.

"I respect the hell out of you and, yeah, I want you to coach me. I want to be the best, so I need the best coach. And, honestly, I take what you give me. But I never meant to hold you back. Jesus, I..." He scraped his hands through his short hair. "Fin, I'm sorry. I'm sorry if I made you feel like you have to *coach* me in order for me to spend time with you. That's not..."

"You're looking at it from the wrong angle, dude." Gray clapped him on the shoulder. "If any of us wants to spend time with Will, we have to be doing what he's doing. Training and competing is all he does." He smiled. "You're hanging out with the wrong brother."

Fin reached for his backpack. "I'm hanging out with the wrong gender."

"You gonna change your flight?" Brodie said.

"Hell, yeah." Fin hugged him and then turned to Will. "Good luck out there, man."

Still looking shaken, Will grabbed Fin and pulled him into a bear hug. When Fin started to pull away, his brother tightened his hold.

And when Will finally pulled back, he said, "Go get your girl."

From her seat across the table, Callie watched Mrs. Reyes hold court with a few of the ladies who lunch.

"So lovely to see you again, Jacqueline," one of them gushed.

"If you're looking for board members for the polo event this year," another one said. "I'd love to help."

Julian, sitting next to her, leaned closer. "I'm hoping you remembered to bring my grandmother's bracelet."

Callie jerked her attention away from the fawning display to focus on her ex. His cologne sent her back to the bathroom in his loft, where she'd always wiped down the counter with a hand towel and stored her toiletries in a bag under the sink so she wouldn't get in his way. "Of course."

"You're looking...relaxed."

Wonderful. A jab about her tank-style cotton dress and wavy hair. "It's a hundred degrees today, and ninety percent humidity. This is me." The moment Hilda awarded the fellowship to Callie, Mrs. Reyes had called to set up a meeting. Callie had only accepted because she had to work with these people and needed to be on good terms with them.

But she wasn't stupid. She knew exactly why Mrs. Reyes had invited her to lunch.

He picked up a lock of hair that looked like she'd dipped it in lightning. "Back to dying your hair, I see."

Instead of smacking his hand away, she reached into her tote and dug around for her wallet. Unzipping the coin section, she pulled out the bracelet he'd given her. "Here you go."

Just for one moment, his cold demeanor melted and hurt flashed in his eyes, but he quickly shut it down.

"Thank you." He reached across the table to hand it to his mother.

Mrs. Reyes waved goodbye to her friends with one hand and took the bracelet with the other. Discreetly, she pulled out a rectangular velvet case from her Chanel bag and draped it inside before snapping it closed. With her regal posture, she took Callie in. "The humidity's unbearable, isn't it?"

Automatically, she smoothed her naturally wavy hair, too aware of the frizz. But she crushed the anxiety. She didn't need glossy hair to have this conversation. *They're not my friends.* "So, I'm sure you want to talk about the fellowship."

She didn't miss the brief connection between mother and son, a look that said, *Gauche.*

But she was done playing games. "I know you can't be happy that I went around you to get it, but I earned it. Kissing my boyfriend in the privacy of my exhibition space doesn't trump graduating from NYU summa cum laude, a master's degree, all the internships I've done, or the fact that I created a very successful pop-exhibition on my own." She turned to her ex. "I'm sorry I couldn't love you the way you'd hoped, but you can't punish me for it."

She didn't miss the slight curl of his upper lip.

"Calliope, dear, you must know that Hilda Morrison doesn't choose the recipients." Mrs. Reyes gave her a pitying look. "Our sponsors sign contracts giving us the authority to screen and choose the candidates. There is so much more involved in the selection process than appealing to the sponsor."

"Considering that you cut me out of the process because your son and I are no longer dating, I'm not sure how relevant the process actually is."

"Many factors go into such a decision," Mrs. Reyes said. "And we had outstanding applicants this year."

Julian shook his head. "You can't think the MoCA would choose you after that sex tape went viral."

Megan had nailed it, hadn't she? "It wasn't a sex tape, Julian. It was a kiss."

"And how many guys would you kiss on tables in the MoCA?" he said in a harsh whisper.

"Grab me a place setting, would you, darling?" A big white leather bag landed on the table next to Mrs. Reyes, rattling the silverware. Hilda Morrison, in a hot pink suit, plopped into the last available chair and grabbed the napkin folded into the shape of a swan. Snapping it open, she patted the perspiration off her forehead. "It's hotter 'n a firecracker lit at both ends."

Callie smiled because the old woman didn't actually talk like that, but the way Julian and his mother stiffened had the desired effect.

Hilda pulled off her hot pink straw hat and fanned herself with it, the large red flower fluttering in the breeze. She lifted a finger to a passing waiter. Before he even arrived at the table, Hilda said, "You wanna grab me a martini? Bombay Sapphire, and make it real dirty." She added a little growl to the *real*.

The waiter bit back a smile, nodded, and headed for the bar. Hilda frequented the Four Seasons, so everyone knew her.

"So." Hilda set her arms on the table. "Did I just hear you tell my protégée I don't have a say in choosing the candidate for the fellowship I sponsor?"

"While we are deeply appreciative of your generosity," Mrs. Reyes said in a patronizing tone. "I'm afraid that, no, you don't have a say in the selection process."

Hilda tugged on the cuff of her sleeve until it peeked out of the blazer. "I had a nice chat with the secretary when I stopped by the office yesterday. She says Callie's application was pulled before anyone on the board reviewed it. That true? Or is she giving me a load of bullshit?"

Mrs. Reyes tilted her chin. "We had an unusual number of highly qualified applicants, forcing us to screen some of the candidates. Unfortunately, Calliope didn't make it to the next level. Going around our selection process is not going to give her the result she's looking for."

"Well, *Jackie*." And just like that, the grand dame of New York society dropped the persona and unleashed a cold smile. "Let's get something clear. You're trying to subvert a process designed to bring the best and brightest into the arts for a personal vendetta. So, regardless of formal agreements, Calliope will get the fellowship, or I'll cease sponsoring it."

In two years of knowing the woman, Callie had never seen Mrs. Reyes unnerved. But the woman took a sip of ice water before returning both hands under the table. "I'm simply a board member. One of eight. And after a lengthy meeting we concluded that while it would be unfortunate to lose this long-term fellowship, the process must be respected. Imagine if all our sponsors stepped in and undermined the process. Nothing would get done."

"You're a little slow on the uptake, Jackie, so I'll put it to you in a way you'll understand. If you fuck with me on this, I'll have you removed from the board of trustees of the MoCA, the New York City Ballet, the Requiem Dance Troupe, and the New York City Opera." Hilda twisted around towards the bar. "Now, where's my damn martini?"

New York at the end of August was hot as a bonfire. The cab didn't have air conditioning, so warm, humid air blasted in through the open windows. Cars honked, the radio played news in Spanish, but all Fin could think about was Callie.

He reread her email.

Dear Fin,

I love you. I do. I will always love you. I didn't handle our breakup well last time, but I'm determined to do it right this time.

A fresh batch of chills skittered across his skin. He reread the last line, looking for a different interpretation. But, no. She'd broken up with him. He drew in a shaky breath.

Look, we tried as kids and failed. We tried again as adults and…failed. Let's just call it, okay? We need to move on, or we'll be stuck in this pattern forever. And neither of us wants that.

Sign your contract. Make your films. You're the best in the world at what you do, so do it. I'm going to do my fellowship and see where it leads.

I'm writing this because I need you to let me go. If you come to New York and fight for me, you're only going to cause me more pain. We've had more than enough of that.

I love you enough to let you go. Do the same for me.

Bullshit. He logged out of his email account and checked to see how far they'd gotten up Park Avenue. 55th. Two more blocks to go. He'd do better on foot. "This is great, right here."

In the rearview mirror, the driver's eyebrows rose questioningly.

"Yes. Let me out here, please."

At the next traffic light, Fin checked the meter and handed the man a twenty. "Keep the change." And then he took off, weaving through heavy pedestrian traffic.

Love you enough to let you go? She was out of her mind if she thought for one second he'd let her go. She didn't know he'd finally figured his shit out, which meant he'd never mess up again. He needed to tell her. Right now.

When Fin reached the hotel, he went straight for the reception desk, but goosebumps sprung out on his arms and the back of his neck tingled. He turned to see Callie laughing as she came out of the restaurant with an older woman wearing a bright pink hat.

Her laughter faded as she turned sharply, her gaze landing unerringly on him.

Elation at seeing her flatlined when she looked anything but happy to see him. She held up a finger to the woman he assumed was Hilda and strode briskly across the lobby.

"What are you doing here?" Callie said.

Calliope. That uptight tone twisted through his guts like a corkscrew. "You look beautiful." He lifted a lock of her dark hair. She'd bleached the ends white. "Wild thing."

"Fin, I asked you not to come here."

"Yeah, I know what you said. I read every word, and it's all bullshit. We're not done. We're never going to be done." He stepped closer. "I figured it out, everything you've been trying to tell me. And I'm never going to let you down again."

"I'm with Hilda right now, and I will absolutely not have this conversation with you."

"I know. I'll just head to up our room till you're done. Take your time. I'm good. I'll just—"

"No." Her features hardened. "I meant everything I said in that email. You need to go home. You don't belong in New York, and we both know that. I never should have gone along with this stupid plan." And then she drew in a deep breath and softened. "Please, Fin, don't make this harder for us than it has to be. Sign the contract. Get on with your life."

"Not until you hear me out. That's why I didn't go to Chile, because I finally got it. They'll never respect what I do until *I* respect it. I show them my priorities every time I choose helping them over what's happening in my own life."

She sucked in a breath, pressing her lips together. "I did it again. I found the hotel. I got the apartment." She closed her eyes. "I even printed out your boarding pass. Talk about déjà vu." When she opened them, she had a look of steely resolve. "We did have something important going on, Fin. It's just that it wasn't important to you." She glanced back at her companion. "Now, listen, Hilda Morrison rarely asserts her authority in this city, but she did it for me. So, thanks to her, I get to live my dream, and I'm not going to let her down by being distracted by our drama. Let me focus on building this life I've worked so hard for. And, honestly, Fin? You should be doing the same thing." She stepped closer to him. "You say you get it, but you don't. Not really. I don't play second fiddle to your *career*. To something that matters deeply to you. I play second fiddle to your *brothers*. Where are *you* in all that?"

She spun around, the white tips of her hair arcing out as she headed back to Hilda, leaving him awash in her sweet, distinctive scent.

19

Pen in hand, Fin stared at the contract. He should sign it, but...he liked his own crew. Bram knew him, could anticipate his moves, so he didn't really want a new production team.

Maybe he'd check with him, see if he wanted to work for Braverman.

His phone buzzed, and he picked it up so fast it flew out of his hands. *Callie?*

But, no, it was Nolan. "What's up, man?"

"You were right." His friend sounded like a skeptical kid who'd just tugged Santa's beard and found it was real.

"Yeah? About what?"

Marcella bustled into the kitchen, grabbing a pot holder ·d opening the oven door. The smell of roasted sweet ato filled the air.

"I thought for sure you were just wasting my time. But I ·. I kept the log, and it's like you said. I didn't even · the shit I was doing."

"Like what?"

"I thought I was just having an occasional beer, but we've had people out to the house all summer. Romer and Gwen spent a long weekend, and Janey's folks came out for a week. So, between the food and parties, I've been drinking a lot more than I thought."

"Yeah, that's how it goes," Fin said.

"Janey's been cooking for everybody, so I've snuck a few pancakes, pasta, cookies and shit. It adds up. So, yeah, man, you're right."

"Good. That means it's an easy fix."

"You gonna look at my film now?"

"In a month. Lay off the shit, keep training, and then send me your footage."

"Damn. Wish I'd listened to you months ago."

"You've got plenty of time before the season starts. You're good." After he disconnected the call, he shook his head. Now Nolan got why he and his brothers were so disciplined.

Marcella pulled the sweet potatoes out of the oven. "How is your skin not orange?"

He stared at his phone, willing it to buzz. If Callie wanted to do a better job breaking up with him this time, then she'd won the gold. He hadn't heard from her since she'd left the hotel with Hilda yesterday.

How did he prove to her that he was done putting his brothers first? That he didn't need to go chasing their respect because he already had it?

What really struck him was that if his brothers hadn't been so influenced by their ambitious dad, they'd all be backcountry boarders just like Fin. It was in their blood to ride free. But that damn trophy room. He ought to just go in there and rip everything off the shelves. Turn it into a weight room.

A hand waved in front of his face. "Hello?" Fingers snapped.

He focused on Marcella. "What?"

"I asked you if I can at least make a sweet potato pie. You look like you could use the sugar rush right now."

"I don't care."

Her hip popped, and she gave him a questioning look. "Fin Bowie doesn't care if I serve pie for dinner?" She smacked the side of his head. "What's the matter with you?"

He'd just gotten in a few hours ago. No one knew what had happened. "Callie broke up with me."

"What happened?"

"I..." He didn't want to rehash it. "Whatever. It's done. I've lost her."

She flicked her kitchen towel at this chest. "Okay, drama queen. Skip the theatrics and spit it out. Tell me what happened."

"When I changed my ticket at the last minute to go with Will to Chile, she dumped me. I didn't think she'd care, since she didn't have anything important going on."

Marcella cringed.

"No, I mean like an event."

Marcella held his gaze, telepathing her message that he was too stupid for words.

"Yeah, I know. I get it. They need my help, and I drop

everything. I get it now. And I get that Callie thinks she can't count on me."

"She *thinks* she can't count on you, huh?"

He straightened. "No, you're right. She can't count on me. But I'm not going to do it again, and I don't know how to prove that to her if she's not talking to me."

"She doesn't want to hear your words."

"Yeah, I know that."

"She wants action."

Fin set the pen down, all his senses narrowing to the answers he saw in her eyes.

She picked up his contract. "How do you feel when you look at this?"

"It's cool. Braverman only offers contracts to the best."

"Uh huh. So, you feel proud that he chose you?"

"Yeah."

"You're going to sign this contract because it makes you feel like a badass? Like it legitimizes what you do?"

An uneasy feeling came over him. "I guess so." But the urgency to get Callie back—be the man she needed him to be—pressed him to think harder, go deeper. "Yes. That's why."

"Because your brothers will finally approve of what you do? Be a little envious?"

His muscles clenched, releasing a torrent of fear. Was he *still* not getting it?

What could Marcella and Callie see about him that he couldn't? "Yes."

"Son..."

Emotion slammed him, like a punch to the chest, and

he had to look away. His mom had left when he was six, so he didn't have a lot of memories of her. She'd shouted at them a lot, railed to their dad about them, but mostly she'd been gone. Either out of town because she hated the "whole cowboy scene" or out with her friends. Her attempt to "civilize" them in New York had ended disastrously when they'd crashed through the ice in Central Park's pond. They'd learned the hard way that it didn't get quite as cold in New York as in Wyoming.

When they'd come home, Marcella had been waiting for them. From day one, she'd asserted herself in their lives, never hanging in the background. She'd been hired to cook and clean, but she'd been so much more.

Fin loved her. But in all seventeen years of knowing her, she'd never called him her son.

She brushed the hair out of his eyes. "Sweetheart, you know what makes you special? What makes you stand out from your brothers?"

He waited, because other than the fact he was a freerider and loved Callie, he didn't have a clue.

"Your bravery."

Fin barked out laugh. "Have you seen the monsters Gray rides?" His brother didn't just surf—he was a *big wave* surfer.

She gently tapped his chest. "I'm talking about here. Your brothers have never risked their hearts, but you? As you boys like to say, you go balls-out. And that makes you the bravest of them all."

He'd never thought of it that way, but before he could let the words sink in, connect them to winning Callie back,

Marcella continued. "You're a special man, Fin, and Callie knows that. I have no doubt she wants you as much as you want her, but she's out there making her dreams come true. She knows what she wants and she's going to get it. So, if you want her, then you come to her as a man. Not the boy who's driving himself nuts trying to be what everyone else needs him to be."

"That's what I'm doing. That's why I didn't go with Will."

"No, you didn't go with Will because you're done fighting to be included." She drew in a breath. "What do you want to do with your life?"

"What I'm doing now. Freeriding."

"Yes, that's something you enjoy. But what do you do? Every day? What's your life's work?"

Something tugged inside his mind—like a song he wanted desperately to recall or a smell he couldn't quite place but that connected with a powerful memory.

"What articles do you read?" she continued. "What thoughts go through your head as you're brushing your teeth or running the trails? What *consumes* you?"

He read articles on nutrition. He reviewed footage coaches and friends sent him. He looked at training equipment, evaluating its merits.

He thought of Nolan. Of Will.

I rely on you because no one else has your vision, your knowledge, your intuitive understanding of our sport.

"I train." And the idea that he'd become a trainer was an insult. "You want me to work at some gym? Be a trainer?"

Snatching the towel off the counter, she actually rolled her eyes. "I'll give you ten seconds to Bowie-size that idea."

Warmth spread across his body, and a deep sense of satisfaction filled him.

If he took that damn trophy room out of the picture, eliminated his need to impress his brothers, he knew exactly what he wanted to do with his life. What he should be doing.

And while it didn't involve Callie right now, it would definitely make him the man he was meant to be. He'd already waited six years for her; if he needed to wait ten more, he'd do it. As long as it took, because there would never be anyone else for him.

Only her.

———

Amidst the hum of conversation and the wait staff delivering canapés and champagne on silver trays, Callie stood in the lobby of the MoCA for the welcome party for this year's fellows.

Her phone pinged again, and she discreetly checked the message.

Stan: What do you want me to do with it?

He'd accepted delivery of one half of a brown corduroy couch, and since they weren't expanding the museum, he wasn't sure if they should still take donations.

Her heart gave a fierce tug. She'd been gone three weeks, and her exhibition hadn't slowed down one bit. In fact, donations kept pouring in, and they had a wait list for their classes. She typed back a response.

Why don't we open the—

She stopped herself. Deleted the last three words. *It's not mine anymore.*

She tried again. **Do you want to rent a storage facility and turn the second floor into a display room?**

Stan responded immediately. **We're happy to keep the lights on, but we wouldn't know where to begin setting up a room.**

Callie thought about the next holiday, Thanksgiving. She worked all day Wednesday, and it took a full day of travel to get to Calamity since there were no direct flights. So maybe over Christmas?

Realistically, though, she had no business considering an expansion.

Expansion? What was she thinking? It was a pop-up exhibition, not a museum.

Her phone pinged with another text from.

Stan: **We'll put out the word that we're no longer taking donations.**

She responded immediately. **Keep taking them**.

Oh, hell. Why had she written that? Because she couldn't quiet the ideas that kept popping up. More classes, new displays. She wanted one called Hope, where people could share their journey to healing. What worked; what didn't. It would give encouragement and direction.

What do I know about healing? Since leaving Fin in the

lobby of the hotel, she'd barely been able to eat. Restlessness kept her up most nights. When she'd left Calamity, she'd thought she had a choice to make between living with an unreliable man and half a heart.

She'd been wrong.

There was no choice. Living with half a heart was intolerable. And no amount of work or social life covered for the fact that life without Fin was just going through the motions.

You're in my DNA. Well, it was true. And she didn't know what the hell to do about it.

Focusing on Stan, she tapped out a text. **If interest doesn't die down by December, I'll see what I can do with the second floor next time I'm in town**.

That comment Fin had made in the hotel lobby? *I get it now*. It had roused the relentless beast called hope. The least she could've done was hear him out, because she really didn't think she could go another six years without him in her life.

Maybe she'd cut out early and give him a call. She needed to hear what he had to say.

Callie glanced up from her phone to watch Mrs. Reyes chatting with a group of fellowship recipients. The woman had made a point to talk to everyone but Callie.

She hadn't seen that kind of behavior since middle school.

Whatever. She'd gotten the fellowship because she'd earned it. And Mrs. Reyes had gotten her due when she'd tried to use the system to squeeze out her son's ex-girlfriend.

The lights in the room flicked on and off, and someone tapped Mrs. Reyes on the shoulder. She took two steps up the staircase and then lifted her champagne flute.

Conversation quieted down, as everyone turned to face her.

"Good evening. On behalf of the entire board, we'd like to welcome you to the fall program. As you know, the selection process is extremely competitive, which means everyone in this room is a shining star." She beamed an approving smile to someone in the crowd. "Dahlia, who comes to us from Lasalle in Barcelona." Her gaze sought someone else out. "Lyndon, from the Sorbonne." She called out several others, looking delighted and proud, until her gaze turned brittle when it landed on Callie "And, of course, Callie, dear, who showed us that old Wild West frontier spirit of manifest destiny in claiming *her* fellowship."

Her blood turned hot at the same time her skin went cold. Manifest destiny? What, somehow Callie thought she was so special she could snatch the job away from someone else? The shocked gazes trained on her lit her up like spotlights.

"I'm certain by now you've all seen the exhibition she created from my son's idea."

Heat shot up her neck, spreading like a fever throughout her body. Embarrassment ignited into outrage—Julian had never had an original thought in his life. Why would he when his parents orchestrated his every move?

Satisfaction gleamed in the old bat's eyes, and an odd sense of calm and clarity took possession of Callie.

She stepped forward, clearing the crowd in front of her. "For a moment there I was confused when you credited your son for the Exhibition of Broken Hearts but, come to think of it, if he hadn't dumped me the day after he proposed in the middle of my brother's rehearsal dinner, if he hadn't tossed me out of the apartment we'd shared, leaving me homeless, I would never have come up with the idea to start my own exhibition. So, in that respect, I guess I do have your son to thank for forcing me to think outside the box and come up with some way to salvage my future." She raised her glass. "So please thank him for that. Tell him he's responsible for the best thing that ever happened to me."

A tense and horrible silence filled the room, but Callie didn't give a damn.

Because she'd finally figured out her bliss.

With a two-hour layover at the Salt Lake City airport, Callie wandered into a bookstore, tote on her shoulder and phone tucked against her ear. "What's all that noise?" she asked her dad. She was used to the incessant buzz of conversation in her parents' diner, along with the periodic outbursts of singing, but it sounded like a convention was going on in the background.

"There's a lot of activity going on at the Bowie place," her dad said.

Fin. She hadn't called him after leaving the reception.

Once she'd made up her mind to go home, she knew she had to have the conversation in person. They *had* to resolve things one way or another. She'd thought a lot about what he'd said, about her shutting down instead of unleashing on him the way she used to. And he was right. Once he'd decided to go to Chile, she'd shut down. Slipped right back into Calliope when she should've let him know what she was thinking. How his decision had impacted her.

But what if they couldn't work things out? She'd have to live in Calamity with him right there. She'd have to see him with a woman. A girlfriend.

A wife.

Carting a kid around on his shoulders—a little boy with his messy dark hair and blue eyes. The pain had her closing her eyes and turning away from a wall of books.

No, that wouldn't happen. It couldn't. A world without Fin and Callie didn't make sense. "What does that have to do with the diner?"

"You didn't hear?"

"Fin and I broke up, Dad." Strange how saying the words out loud felt like lying. "We haven't talked." A sense of urgency hit. She needed to get home and talk to him. She needed to be with him. What if he left town? He could be gone for a *month*.

"I thought he'd tell you about his plans."

Her pulse quickened. "No." *Plans? What plans?* "What're you talking about?"

"Between him and Brodie, they ought to bring a lot of business to Calamity."

What could that mean? The Braverman contract would

have Fin on the road half the year. "How would Fin bring business?"

The PA system drowned out her dad's voice. She hurried out of the store. "I didn't hear you. Can you say that again?"

"I said he's building a state-of-the-art training facility. He's already got athletes signed on. Big names, too."

"How can he do that and make his films?"

"He tore up the contact. He's training instead."

But would that make him happy? "Really?"

Her dad chuckled. "Took him long enough to figure it out."

"Figure what out?" She had to practically shout over the next announcement.

"What he's meant to do."

"Do you know why?"

"Sure, I do. He stopped by a couple nights ago. Never seen him so sure of himself. Said he—"

Another garbled message came on. Jesus, was she standing under a speaker? "Wait one second, Dad. I can't hear you over these damn announcements. Just wait."

Only this time something caught her attention. "Calliope Bell, please meet your party at the information desk."

"Dad?"

"Yes, sweetheart?"

"They're calling my name. I hope nothing's wrong with my flight." She just wanted to get home.

"No, doll, nothing's wrong with it. Go on and take care of business. I'll see you in an hour and a half."

"If my flight's on time, I'll be home in three hours." But he'd already disconnected.

Callie hustled along the concourse until she found the information desk. A few people stood in line, but a woman dressed in black pants and a short-sleeved black shirt looked up from her cell phone. She smiled at Callie and tucked the phone into her back pocket.

"Callie?" As the woman reached out a hand, Callie read the patch on her shirt. *AirTrans Pilot.*

"Yes. Hello." They shook hands. "What's going on?"

"I'm your pilot. Joanne Riley. Why don't you come with me?"

"I don't understand. I have a flight. It leaves in less than two hours."

"I think you'll prefer my mode of transportation." She tipped her head. *Come on.*

Callie gestured behind her, at the gate. "But my luggage."

"Everything's taken care of." She laughed again. "Believe me."

Callie followed the pilot through a door for Airport Personnel Only.

"Can you tell me where we're going?"

But the woman kept up a brisk pace down a long hall, before punching in a code and then pushing the release-bar of a door that led to the tarmac. "Here we are." A blast of hot air and the roar of engines hit Callie as she stepped outside into the blinding sun. Joanne headed toward a sleek gray jet.

Her parents couldn't afford to charter a flight, so a Bowie had to be behind this.

And then black boots hit the steps. Callie shielded her eyes with a hand to take in the jeans-clad legs that followed. A navy blue T-shirt covered a muscular chest and biceps.

And then that smile. He'd come for her. She'd told him to stay away but, of course, he hadn't.

Because a world without Fin and Callie didn't make sense.

Callie took off at a run, her heart full to bursting. "Fin." She slammed against his hard chest, and her body thrilled at the feel of his strong arms wrapping around her. *Home.* She was finally home. And this time she'd never let go. "I'm moving back to Calamity."

"I know, wild thing." His arms banded around her and lifted her off the ground as he held her tightly to his chest.

When he started to pull away, she tightened her hold. "Don't let me go."

"Never gonna let you go again."

She tucked her face into his neck.

"We're gonna get it right this time," he said. "You believe me?"

She pulled back. "My dad said you're going to run a training facility."

He nodded. "I finally figured out how to be the man you deserve."

"I think I figured out how to be the woman you deserve, too."

"What about your dream of being in the New York art world?"

"My job at the fellowship was about raising money for an installation that I didn't care about. I mean, there I was at the reception, texting Stan and Barbara, coming up with new ideas for the exhibition, and it struck me. I'm *already* a museum curator. I *love* what I do."

"That all you love?"

Tears spilled down her cheeks. "I love you, Fin Bowie. With everything in me, I love you."

He smiled, pressing a kiss on her mouth. "You gonna be happy in Calamity?"

"There's nowhere else I'd rather be." She wanted her time with Theo and her parents. She wanted her friendship with Megan.

And most of all..."I want to wake up to you every day of my life."

20

FIN REACHED INTO HIS BACK POCKET AND PULLED OUT one last purple larkspur. After a decade of making flower-chain bracelets for his wild thing, he knew exactly how many fit her wrist.

A year ago, he'd come home for Ryder's wedding with nothing but a fistful of hope that he'd find a way to get his woman back. Now...he breathed in the sun-baked sage with a full heart...now, he had it all.

His phone vibrated in his pocket, but he ignored it. He was done for the day. In addition to training his five elite athletes, he'd broken ground on the lodge that would house them, which meant the only thing left on his agenda was to spend his birthday alone with Callie.

The trail ended in his backyard, so he unlatched the gate and made his way around the covered pool. He saw movement through the windows, shadows milling around.

She wanted to make a big event out of it, huh? Didn't she know that after a day around his athletes, the full-time nutritionist and personal trainer he'd hired, the yoga instructor, his brothers, and Uncle Lachlan, he only wanted to be with *her*?

He'd go along with her plans, obviously, but then he was hauling her off to his bedroom to get their own private party started.

The sliding glass door rumbled on its runner, and he heard whispers.

"Shh, you guys."

"He's here."

"Woman," Fin shouted. "I'm home. Fetch me a beer."

His brothers, Brodie and Gray, burst out laughing, and conversation kicked in.

Callie strode into the kitchen. "You're such a jerk." She walked right into his arms, wrapped her arms around his neck, and kissed him soundly. "Happy birthday."

Taking in her long, wavy hair, the pretty wrap-dress she'd worn for a day in her museum, he breathed in her wildflower scent, and all the stress of the day dropped away. "How long till everyone's gone?"

"Hey, little brother, no one's going anywhere." Gray tossed a bottle of beer at him.

Fin caught it in the air.

"Come on out and say hello to everyone." Callie reached for his hand, but Brodie cut them off.

"Hang on. Let's give him his present first. Before he starts moonwalking on the dining room table."

"I was *ten*." Why did they have to bring up the same old childhood stories? He followed Callie and his brothers up the back stairs and down the hall. "Where we going?"

Brodie led them to the trophy room, and they all gathered outside the door. "Within these walls lies twenty-eight years of accomplishments. From local to county to state to national and world competitions, our achievements are all on display. All of us...except for you." Brodie drew a breath. "Today, that's finally going to change."

"About damn time." Gray clapped a hand on his shoulder. "Proud of you, little brother."

Fin glanced to Callie. He had no idea what they were talking about. He hadn't earned a trophy in his life, but their seriousness got him excited.

Brodie opened the door, and they all followed him inside the dark, windowless room.

Impatience had him reaching for the light switch, but someone's hand covered his.

"Hang on," Brodie said. "I just..." He sucked in a breath. "I'm damn proud of you, Fin. All it took was word-of-mouth to launch this training facility, and you've already got three Olympic athletes and two World Games competitors."

"He's had to turn people away," Gray said.

"All right, cut the shit, and turn on the light." Half of him was sure they were messing with him, but the other half was about to explode with anticipation.

The lights went on, and he scanned the shelves and glass cases—until his gaze landed on the massive framed magazine cover that took up half the wall.

His image smiled back at him. *National Adventurer* had declared Fin Bowie the most sought-after coach in extreme sports. *That's so cool.* He reached for Callie's hand and gave it a squeeze, emotions running high.

He didn't even care about the moustache someone had drawn over his upper lip in black Sharpie. But, from the tension in the room, he knew his brothers were waiting for his reaction.

He gave them each a hard look. "I always wondered what I'd look like with a porn 'stache."

They all burst out laughing. Gray drew him in for a hug, and Brodie piled on.

Too bad Will's not here. He was in Whistler, at the last competition of the season.

"Will's right, you know," Gray said into his ear. "You're the best out of all of us."

"Come on." Brodie slapped both of them on their backs. "Let's get out there. Callie got the entire town to come over and kiss your ass."

"She even made you a cake," Gray said

"Wait." Brodie headed toward the door. "You can make a cake with sweet potatoes?"

The brothers filed out of the room, but just as Callie started to follow them, he grabbed her hand. "Hang on."

His woman, his heart, turned back to him with a curious expression.

He gently tugged the flower bracelet out of his pocket and reached for her hand.

She beamed that fresh, sexy smile. "Thank you. I love it."

As he gently slid the chain onto her wrist, an image struck him. Callie, with a wreath of wildflowers on the crown of her head, her wavy hair a crazy rumpus around her glowing face. In a white lace gown, her feminine hand outstretched, waiting for him to put a ring on her finger.

I need to make that happen.

He'd always known he and Callie were forever, so marriage didn't enter his mind. In all the ways that mattered, he'd been married to her since high school. Who needed a piece of paper when she was half his heart and most of his soul?

But, right then, the symbolism mattered. Mattered a lot, actually, if his thundering heart meant anything. "I want to marry you, wild thing."

Her hazel eyes went warm and soft, and a look of joyful serenity came over her. "I want that more than anything in the world."

Hell, yes. "We're going to get married." Why did that make him so damn happy?

"Now you can finally make a decent woman out of me."

"Nah, I want to keep you as indecent as I can."

Cupping the back of his neck, she got up on her toes and kissed him.

Every time—every single damn time. All she had to do was look at him, and he lit up. But her touch? This connection? Jesus, he got so hot for her. Pressing her to the wall, he grabbed the backs of her thighs and lifted her, holding her in place with his hips. Her fingers gripped his hair, her legs banded around his waist, and she rocked into him.

"Want you," he whispered in her ear.

"Want you more."

He squeezed her ass, fingers slipping under the elastic edge of her panties and seeking her hot, wet center. "You're going to be mine forever."

"I always was."

"Do I need to turn the hose on you two?" Marcella stood in the doorway. She shook her head. "You got a house full of people who want to wish you a happy birthday, Fin Bowie, so how 'bout you come downstairs so I can roll out the cake and let them sing the damn song?"

Callie tucked her face into his neck, her body shaking with laughter.

"You want to give me a minute here, Marcella?"

"No, but for the sake of polite company, I will. One minute, Fin." She left the door open behind her.

Callie lowered her legs but kept her arms around his neck. "You'll get to unwrap your present after they leave."

"Damn right I will."

As they came down the staircase, he found the living room filled with familiar faces from his past and present. His and Callie's families, old teachers, Coach, his staff, neighbors, and his Dad's friends. A warm feeling settled over him. He had a full and beautiful life. He couldn't ask for anything more.

The moment he hit the bottom of the stairs, arms reached to embrace him.

"Happy birthday, Fin."

"Hey, man, happy birthday."

And then the group launched into the birthday song. Marcella and a cake blazing with candles parted the crowd as she made her way to him. Golden candlelight lit her features as she watched him with pride. The chorus grew louder and stronger, until she stopped right in front of him. Callie's hand rested in the middle of his back.

Someone shouted, "Blow out the candles!"

Just as he drew in a breath and leaned forward, he heard a voice call, "Excuse me?"

Everyone turned to see a woman standing in the doorway. In her arms, she held a little girl with a tumble of auburn curls. Her face was turned into the woman's neck, hidden behind the stuffed chicken she clutched in one tiny arm.

"I'm looking for the Bowies?" the woman said.

And with that the little girl's head popped up, and she eyed the roomful of strangers with a mix of challenge and stubborn determination.

A wave of shock rippled across the room. Someone said, "Oh, my God."

Because there was no mistaking it. From the bright blue eyes to the shape of her face and that defiant expression, that girl was a Bowie.

The question was—

"Whose kid is she?"

Thank you for reading KEEP ON LOVING YOU! If you want to watch an adorable little girl claim the heart of the oldest Bowie brother, check out WE BELONG TOGETHER.

. . .

Do you subscribe to my newsletter? Get on that right now because I've got an EXCLUSIVE novella for my readers in 2022! You'll get 2 chapters a month of this super sexy, fun romance! #rockstarromance #whenyourcelebritycrushbecomesyourboyfriend #teenidol

Need more Calamity Falls, where the people are wild at heart?

KEEP ON LOVING YOU
WE BELONG TOGETHER
THE VERY THOUGHT OF YOU
JUST THE WAY YOU ARE
IT WAS ALWAYS YOU
CAN'T HELP FALLING IN LOVE
COME AWAY WITH ME
WHOLE LOTTA LOVE
YOU'RE STILL THE ONE
THE DEEPER I FALL
LOVE ME LIKE YOU DO

Have you read the Rock Star Romance series? Come meet the sexy rockers of Blue Fire:

YOU REALLY GOT ME
I WANT YOU TO WANT ME
TAKE ME HOME TONIGHT
MORE THAN A FEELING

Look for LOVE ME LIKE YOU DO in September 2022! Grab a FREE copy of PLANES, TRAINS, AND HEAD OVER HEELS. And come hang out with me on Facebook, Twitter, Instagram, Goodreads, and Pinterest or in my private reader group.

EXCERPT OF WE BELONG TOGETHER

Here's an excerpt of book 2 in Erika Kelly's Calamity Falls Series, WE BELONG TOGETHER

UNDER THE BRIGHT BLUE UMBRELLA ON THE PATIO table, the little girl bounced a huge stuffed chicken in her lap. Her tumble of brown curls fluttered in the soft June breeze. Beside her, Marcella, their long-time house manager, read something on the screen of her laptop while talking on her cell phone...

...ordering a *stroller*.

Will Bowie couldn't wrap his head around it. That kid? That two-year-old? She might be theirs.

She *was* theirs. *Look at her*. A shaft of sunlight gleamed on her hair, revealing bronze and gold strands tangled among the brown—exactly like Will and his brothers. And those blue eyes?

They're mine.

But she wasn't his. He knew that for sure. So, whose was she?

In a few minutes, their lawyer would walk in the door with the birth certificate they'd subpoenaed from the hospital. But it wouldn't matter what name was on that document—all their lives would change.

Because they'd handle it as a family. The four brothers would raise her together.

"It's not complicated." From her throne on the leather club chair, his mom sounded exasperated. "Which one of you slept with Christy Leigh?"

Their mother had flown out to Calamity for the opening of his brother's resort. As luck would have it, she'd also gotten hit with the whammy of finding out she was a grandmother. *Maybe.*

Probably.

Had it been a boy, she wouldn't have cared. She'd only kept popping out babies in the hopes of scoring a girl. She'd washed her hands of the whole mess after the fourth son.

She wouldn't stay involved, though. The type of mother who could walk out on her own children—ages six, seven, nine, and eleven—wouldn't hang around to raise this feisty little girl. He'd give his mom a week before she hightailed it back to Manhattan.

"Well, it obviously wasn't me." His youngest brother, Fin, had only ever been with one woman—his childhood sweetheart.

"Obviously." Brodie laughed.

"But, seriously, man," Gray said. "You've never been the least bit curious what it'd be like with someone else?"

"No." Fin's response was so immediate, so frank, that everyone stared at him.

Anyway, that left the three of them.

Two. Will had never slept with Christy Leigh.

"Well, I don't even know who she is," Gray said.

"You say that like it eliminates you." Brodie, the brother closest in age to Will, grinned.

Gray seemed the most likely to have fathered a kid he didn't know about. He led a nomadic life, chasing the biggest waves and fiercest snowstorms. With his easy-going nature, he found fun everywhere he landed.

"You make an excellent point." Gray gave him a lazy look. "Nevertheless, the kid's twenty-seven months, which means she was conceived exactly three years ago. I'm in Bali every June, big brother. I couldn't have knocked Christy up."

The attention turned to the last remaining brother.

"Don't look at me." Brodie raised both hands. "I live in Utah."

All three brothers gave him a look that said, *So?* Brodie spent more time at home in Wyoming than in his office. In fact, he'd spent the past year turning the ghost town on their property into a high-end resort that opened to the public next week. So, yeah, he'd spent a lot of time in Calamity.

"She doesn't have to be one of ours." Fin pointed out the obvious. "The baby book says she's a Bowie, but there are other Bowies out there."

"In Calamity, there's only us and Uncle Lachlan." Brodie shook his head. "And there's no way Ruby's mom slept with an old man rocking a pompadour."

Two days ago, right in the middle of Fin's twenty-fourth birthday party, a woman had shown up at the house with Ruby Leigh in tow. Apparently, the little girl's mom had left her with a babysitter for a long weekend in Big Sky and never come home.

Brutal car accident on the Gallatin Road. *Damn.*

Thanks to Wyoming's Kinship Placement program, they'd allowed Ruby to stay with the only babysitter she'd ever known until they found a forever home for her. But when the sitter had gone to Ruby's house to pick up some clothes and toys, she'd found a baby book.

So, they knew everything about her firsts—first smile, first time she'd rolled over, and the first time she'd walked—and they knew a Bowie had fathered her.

They just didn't know which one.

In a rustle of fabric, their mom shot off the chair. "Stop playing around." She looked like she was waiting for them to feel chastised. When it didn't happen, she clamped her lips together and tipped her head back. "This stupid sense of loyalty your father drummed into you." She let out a frustrated breath and said, "You know she's Will's." She flicked a hand in the vicinity of the backyard. "She's a carbon copy of him."

The way she looked at him—with such disdain—sliced the skin of an old scar. But trying to prove himself to her was a waste of time, so he focused on his brothers. "We're not going to know anything until we get the birth certificate." Which would happen any minute. "So, there's no point in speculating. The only thing we do know is, if she's one of ours, we're going to take care of her. As a family. So, the important conversation is *how* we're going to do it."

"Her *father* will be responsible for her." Her gaze bore into him.

Jesus, would she ever see him as anything other than the reckless kid she'd left behind? "I know that. My point is, whoever's her father, we're all going to help. We're her family."

"Dude." Gray held out his arm. All four brothers reached in and bumped fists.

"I think that's a lovely sentiment, and exactly what your father would expect of you, but someone's got to be the voice of reason here. And the fact is none of you has any idea what it's like to raise a child."

To his brothers' credit, no one said the obvious, *And you do?* Because she wasn't the point. "We'll learn."

"On the fly," Brodie said. "Like every other parent."

Their mom folded her arms across her stomach. "Most parents don't have your lifestyles, which in no way suit raising a child."

"Our lifestyles will change," Fin said.

"Don't get me wrong," their mom said. "I think it's lovely that you want to take care of her, but she's not even two and a half. She's young enough that she won't remember her mother. She can assimilate quite seamlessly into a new family. Maybe the best choice is to give her that. A mother, a father, siblings. She needs the kind of dedication and care that four single men simply can't give her."

His mom had never been good at reading body language, so she probably didn't notice how all the men's postures went rigid, their features hard. Will spoke for all of them. "I'm going to pretend you didn't suggest we give our niece up for adoption."

"I'm sorry." But, of course, she sounded more belligerent than apologetic. She pointed to Gray. "Aren't you heading off to Bali for a surfing competition that will lead you to God knows what adventure next? You probably won't even be home until September." She lifted a chin toward Brodie. "You're missing the opening of your own resort to spend the summer in Asia."

She made it sound like Brodie was screwing off, but he'd finally realized his dream of making the Olympic terrain park design team at his firm, and construction for next Winter Games began this summer. He couldn't miss that opportunity.

Her hand flicked toward Fin. "And he's heading off to Europe for the summer with his girlfriend."

"Fiancée," Fin said.

"And while *you* might be home this summer..."Will's mom looked at him like he was a registered sex offender. "You've just come back from six months of competitions all over the world. None of you is in any position to raise that little girl." Still not reading their body language, she said, "None of you is ready to be a *father*."

It struck him how different this conversation would be going if their dad had been alive.

Not a day went by—a little more than two years since his death—that something didn't trigger a memory, giving Will a slam of grief that buckled his knees and knocked the air out of his lungs.

And the idea that Mack Bowie wouldn't meet his granddaughter—*dammit*. He turned away, sorrow crashing over him. That little girl would miss out on getting to know her grandpa, and that was a damn shame. Their dad was the best man Will had ever known. He'd know just how to raise this kid.

If she's ours.

Is she?

But his dad *wasn't* here, so Will had to handle it. He turned back to his mom. "I'm going to say this one more time, and that'll be the last we ever speak of it. If the paternity test shows she's our blood, we're going to raise her. If you can't handle that, then you'll need to leave, because there will be no discussion whatsoever of adoption or sending her away."

Remembering the ultimatum she'd given his dad, *You either send Will to boarding school, or I'm leaving,* Will's determination doubled down. "That little girl will never be exposed to any idea other than the fact that she's one of us and we love her. You get me?"

"Oh, don't make me out to be the cold-blooded mother who left her family. You all could have stayed in the city with me—"

Except me. You didn't take me.

You took my brothers—but left me behind.

No, Will didn't value her opinion much at all. "I'm going to need an answer."

She held his gaze with a defiant expression, but she had to know he'd follow through. He wouldn't let his mom anywhere near this child if she held even a sliver of belief that Ruby belonged with another family.

"I get you." Each word had the texture of hard candy stuck in her teeth.

"The only thing that matters is finding out whether she's a Bowie." He glanced out the window again. The chicken's big yellow legs flopped every time Ruby lowered it to the table.

His mom let out a bitter laugh. "Oh, she's a Bowie all right." Her gaze held accusation.

Will led a simple life. Sure, from an outsider's perspective he lived on a three-hundred-thousand-acre legacy ranch in the Tetons. He'd won the World Games Freestyle Halfpipe a good number of times. But he lived a clean life. He didn't lie, steal, cheat. So, the idea that his mom would think he'd deny sleeping with Christy... knowing the paternity results would show up in the next day or so....

It tells me exactly what kind of man she thinks I am.

Her opinion doesn't matter. "The point is—"

"Hang on a sec," Gray said. "I want to make sure I've got this right. Basically, you're saying the kid's Will's, but he's such a hooligan you'd rather see his daughter—your *granddaughter*—put up for adoption? Do I have that right?"

His mom narrowed her eyes. "That fine sense of loyalty

your father instilled in you might just be blinding you to what's in her best interests."

"It didn't come from Dad." The words tumbled out of Will's mouth without forethought, but he didn't back down. "A mother walking out on her kids teaches a hard lesson on family loyalty."

"Excuse me?"

But Brodie rolled right over the flare-up. "You get that Will just won the World Games for the *seventh* time, right? That means for seven years in a row he's outperformed every other freestyle skier in the world. That's unprecedented."

He wouldn't let them defend him to her. "I've already got a list of nanny agencies—"

"No, hang on." Gray, normally unflappable, stepped closer to their mom. "What he's accomplished? Winning *seven* times? It comes from pure dedication, determination. It comes from—"

"Stop." Will couldn't take another second of it. "Any minute now we're going to find out who her father is and, as soon as we do, I'm getting on the phone and starting the interview process." Their house manager was taking care of the nursery, and Callie, Fin's fiancée, was at the grocery store getting kid food. "Fin, you go to Europe with Callie on her buying trip. You two..." He tipped his chin to Brodie and Gray. "Depending on the results, you can do your thing. I'm here this summer anyhow, so I'll get everything set up, hire the nanny—"

"It's not going to be easy to find someone who'll move out here," Brodie said.

"That's for sure." Their mom, who'd moved to New York City seventeen years ago and never looked back, gave a bitter laugh.

"Unless they're local," Fin said.

"We don't want seasonal help," Brodie said.

"We don't?" Gray said with a smile.

An historical western town at the foot of the Tetons, Calamity's population swelled during tourist seasons. The resorts and restaurants had their pick of ski lovers and hikers who wanted to live in a mountain paradise for a few months.

"We need someone who'll stay," Will said. "We're not having nannies in and out of her life."

The doorbell rang. Everyone jerked toward the sound.

For most of his life, he'd had his dad to count on. In all the worst situations, Mack Bowie had taken control. He was the kind of man who faced his fears—walked right through them.

So, that's what I'll do.

He broke away from the pack and headed to the door. Sensation ripped across his skin as he turned the handle. But, instead of seeing their lawyer, his dark hair, pressed khakis and button-down shirt, he found the babysitter—the same woman who'd delivered the kid to their house the day before yesterday.

"Hi." She gave him a tentative smile. "I hope it's okay if I stopped by."

"Of course." He stepped back to let her in.

"I found something when I went back to get the rest of

Ruby's things." She lifted a white plastic garbage bag, the contents weighing the bottom down.

That's all this kid has in the world, what's in that bag.

No matter what name they found on the birth certificate, he would make sure Ruby had everything she needed. He'd take her into town that afternoon, let her pick out some books, puzzles, blocks...whatever she wanted.

"This was in Christy's desk drawer." She held up a file folder, turning it around so it faced Will.

Death file.

"It's got all her bank account and insurance information, passwords, stuff like that." She pulled out a piece of plain white paper. "And a will. Not an official one, but she says what she wants in the event of her death. And she names the father."

His brothers crowded around, as Will took the sheet of paper.

The woman gave an apologetic smile. "At least we know for sure she's yours." And then she looked beyond him to their mother. "I'm sorry."

Why would she apologize to their mom?

"Well, come on. What's it say?" Brodie leaned over to read the paper. "Holy shit."

Will skimmed until he got to a name.

"Who's the father?" Fin asked.

It was the babysitter who answered. "Mack Bowie." She looked right into Will's eyes. "Your dad."

ABOUT THE AUTHOR

Award-winning author Erika Kelly writes sexy and emotional small town romance. Married to the love of her life and raising four children, she lives in the southwest, drinks a lot of tea, and is always waiting for her cats to get off her keyboard.

https://www.erikakellybooks.com/

facebook.com/erikakellybooks

twitter.com/ErikaKellyBooks

instagram.com/erikakellyauthor

goodreads.com/Erika_Kelly

pinterest.com/erikakellybooks

amazon.com/Erika-Kelly/e/B00L0MLWUY

bookbub.com/authors/erika-kelly

Printed in Great Britain
by Amazon

14675397R00236